FIXING JUSTICE

Justice Brothers

Book 1

Suzanne Halliday

FIXING JUSTICE

Edited by www.editing4indies.com
Book Cover Design by www.ashbeedesigns.com
Formatting By Self Publishing Editing Service

ISBN-13: 978-1499541885
ISBN-10: 1499541880

Dedication

This book is dedicated to my family
My fabulous and hilarious daughter
My grandchildren who give new meaning to the expression YOLO
And
Sara ~ So there!

THWACK. CLINK. THUD. "Aw, suck my balls, Cam!" Draegyn yelled while clutching his crotch with a wicked laugh as his last two horseshoes made contract with a metal stake in the ground about forty feet away in a sand pit that was all of Afghanistan.

"Fuck you Drae!" Cameron yelled back heartily. "You totally pussied out last week when the Frisbees were flying fast and furious with that weak ass excuse that your neck ached. I think you set me up with all your wah-wah crybaby shit so don't go thinking this means anything!"

The two men grinned and flashed each other the finger as they indulged in a little down time at their austere combat base camp deep in the mountains of Afghanistan. All around them sand bags stacked high as a shield against every imaginable type of attack while overhead an American flag hung limp from it's standard in the stagnant air of a blisteringly hot day.

Their special forces compound was a rag tag set-up of tents, combat housing units, tin siding, barriers, sand dusted tables, lopsided chairs and car backseats that had been thrown around an area where the men gathered to forget about where they were and what they were doing.

Dressed in backward baseball caps with sweaty bandanas around their necks and standard issue green military t-shirts that the sleeves had been ripped from, Drae and Cam were fending off the long stretches of isolated boredom that descended upon their team in between missions.

Dressed in a pair of khaki ACU pants covered in Velcro pouches with the legs tucked inside a pair of hi-tech boots covered in the desert sand that seemed to cling to everyone and everything, Drae had discarded his tactical vest on the ground nearby. Dark sunglasses shielded his eyes from the relentless sun that had done a number on his fair coloring making him look like a piece of burnt white bread.

In tip-top physical shape after years in the military, muscled arms sporting a deep tan presented a tattoo-wrapped bicep that matched the one Cam had. Together as brothers-in-arms for the last five years, they were men of the Justice Squad. A gruff, no-nonsense special ops team who had been sucking in the arid sands of the God-forsaken place they had been in for far too long.

Shuffling across the hard-packed sandy ground, they stooped to retrieve their horseshoes, and continued to rib each other relentlessly about all manner of things that brought their manhood into question. It was a lighthearted moment in an otherwise deadly serious existence.

The low *woof-woof* of an approaching K-9 grabbed their attention as one of their squad newbies, a soldier they nicknamed 'The Kid', approached with a serious looking German shepherd on the end of his tether.

Everyone liked The Kid, although at twenty-five and after several long tours in various hot spots around the region, he was hardly considered a greenhorn. A communications expert who spoke several native dialects and handled his K-9 with adroit skill, he'd impressed even the most battle hardened of their squad. He wasn't standard military. Not exactly. Most likely he was CIA or one of the elite, super secretive counter-terrorism operatives deployed throughout the region. One of the norms in this corner of the world was that these men didn't ask questions of each other and rarely, if ever, used their real names. It was as if the time out of place nature of what they were ordered to do required a completely different mind-set than the one they'd relied on in the real world.

"Hey Kid, what's up with McLain? He seems a bit tense this morning," Drae asked while he studied the dog on high-alert, pacing this way and that, at the end of the tether.

True to a soldiers' habit for creating nicknames and catchy terms for nearly everything, this particular shepherd had been named after the Bruce Willis character in *Die Hard* because he had a small bald spot on top of his head. Their special tactical squad was even called Justice after the Justice League, the Stan Lee created super-heroes operating out of a hidden cave with a top-secret mandate to take on all villains who threatened the American way. Seemed oddly fitting in some perverse way.

Tugging on the tether to bring the dog under heel, The Kid shrugged, directing his reply to both men. "I don't know, Sirs. He got all antsy earlier at the south checkpoint but none of the other canines reacted so maybe he's just having a bad day." When the animal finally settled at his feet, tongue lolling out of his mouth as he panted and, ever watchful in his capacity as a bomb-sniffing guard dog, all three men studied the brown and black shepherd with keen interest.

Never taking anything for granted or at face value, each mulled private thoughts as eyes, alert and ever-vigilant, surveyed the scene around them looking for anomalies that might explain the dog's tension. Improvised explosive devices and suicide bombers had become the enemies preferred *fuck you* method when striking the coalition forces. Attacks had been happening more and more frequently, and in unexpected places, coming closer and closer to their secured areas.

Turning his attention away from the dog he had at his side, The Kid held his M-16 rifle protectively across his chest. "Hey, did you hear about Team Matrix? They were doing an overnight near the border when one of those motherfuckers blew a device on the convoy. Killed six, including an imbed from the BBC."

Hearing that bit of news, Cam and Drae looked at each other behind the dark lenses of their sunglasses. *Fuck.* Talking about body counts was usually immediately followed up with a swift change of subject that Draegyn was quick to provide.

"Have you been over to HQ yet, Kid? The Major has been holed up there for way too long with a bunch of heavy-vested pussies. Oh, my bad - I mean *politicians* who were making his life hell, last we heard." The disdain Drae felt for those so-called public servants was dripping from every word with special emphasis on the *pussy*.

Alex, the third wheel and most senior member in their long association, was a brilliant tactician with the body and brawn of a battle-hardened warrior. He was spending way too much time these days holding the sweaty hands of the never-ending stream of nervous politicians and state department yahoos who flew in under cover of darkness. After a dog and pony show visit, they would high-tail it back to the safety found on U.S. soil so they could whip up their constituents and department heads with dramatic tales about the sights and sounds of life in a forward operating base in the middle of what had become a never-ending war. All that PR shit wasn't exactly what Alex thought he'd be taking on when he was promoted last year.

"I saw Badirya headed that way earlier with Asef in tow. He asked where you were, Lieutenant," The Kid said in Cam's direction.

Asef and his mother, the lovely Badirya, were fixtures in their compound. Asef was maybe nine or ten years old and accompanied his mother nearly everyday when she came to work as a translator and secretary in the HQ. The youngster was bright-eyed and extremely personable. He loved all things American with a special penchant for anything and everything connected to Batman.

Drae cast Cam one of those knowing looks that bordered on a leer before chiming in with, “You’ve been spending quite a bit of time with the lovely widow and her son, Cam. You find a way underneath that hijab yet, dude?”

“Shut the fuck up, Drae,” Cameron snapped. “You’re way more likely to go for a pair of brown doe eyes beneath a veil than either of us would,” he added while gesturing with the tilt of his head to where The Kid stood. “Asef is a good kid, and it doesn’t hurt to show the boy that not all Americans are bloodthirsty dickheads worthy of jihad.”

“Hey, leave me out of that argument, Sirs,” The Kid added with tongue-in-cheek humor. “My fiancée would seriously kick my ass if she thought for one minute that any of the female locals were fraternizing with the enemy.” Mention of the fiancée gave Cameron and Draegyn pause. They’d seen pictures of the couple during happier times and had listened to many heartsick stories from the lonely warrior during his time assigned to their squad.

Drae’s ruthless reputation for fucking any woman with a pulse along with Cam’s bitter mistrust of the fairer sex and Alex’s coldhearted rejection of anything remotely romantic made them quite a trio. Truth be told, each of them envied The Kid in his own way. The battlefield hadn’t robbed him of the ability to feel or diminished the desire to forge a future beyond the shit storm they lived in now.

Suddenly, McLain jumped up from his at ease position and lifted his snout in the air. All three men, ever vigilant to even the slightest signal of danger, stopped in mid-thought and actively scanned their immediate surroundings. Something was up, they could sense it. By reflex and from sheer habit, Cam and Drae immediately hoisted their ever-present M-16 rifles and began moving toward the other side of the well-protected compound.

Shit got real when the K-9 took off running at a fast clip around a mortar pit with The Kid right behind him. A commotion was building just beyond their view. They could hear angry shouts and commands to stand down being barked out in Arabic.

All hell broke loose in the next ten seconds as gunfire erupted followed by a small explosion and then a massive *BOOM* that knocked Cam and Drae off their feet. Smoke, dust, shrapnel, and debris clogged the air.

Drae was propelled backward, landing with a heavy thud thirty feet or so from where he'd been as the blast rocked the camp. Debris pinned him to the ground where he lay stunned from the violence of the explosion. As his senses cleared, he could hear Cameron shouting, "Draegyn! Drae! Are you alright? Where are you?"

Fuck, he couldn't move for long moments, barely able to spit the putrid sand and dust from the blast out of his mouth. All around him there was darkness, partially from the tin and wood piled on top of him and partly from being inside a debris cloud.

Anger and fear spiked an adrenalin rush in Drae as Cameron lifted the tremendous piece of tin attached to a wooden post pinning him to the ground and wildly tossed it aside. Sucking in a ragged lungful of oxygen, Drae slowly lifted to his knees and nodded as Cam helped him get to his feet.

A heartbeat later, their years of training took over, and after checking to see that their weapons were ready to go, they started forward again in a fast sprint toward the center of the explosion.

Upon reaching the area of the HQ, the men stopped and assessed the scene before them. Bodies and body parts were everywhere as shouts of "medic" and "Code Red" filled the air. Half the HQ building was gone, and a fire had broken out in another structure nearby.

"Holy fuck, Cam!" Drae shouted. "Goddamn, motherfuckers," he growled. "We've got to get to Alex."

Both men took off in the direction of the building where they hoped their friend would be found unhurt. Along the way they encountered McLain, who was untethered and clearly in distress, wandering in circles around a clump of brown camo on the ground. Cam's stomach dropped away as he realized that The Kid had taken the worst of the blast while the dog had somehow survived. Fear arced up his spine, propelling him forward in search of Alex.

Drae got there first, shouting, "Alex, Alex! Talk to me, man! Where the fuck are you?" All around them soldiers were frantically tossing debris aside in search of the injured and dead.

They found Alex, badly hurt, with blood pouring out of every inch of his body, and a leg wound that looked like ground meat. He was alive, barely. The instinct to survive, no matter what the situation, had been branded on their souls in such a way that a pulse meant victory in an otherwise horrendous scenario.

Luckily for Alex, it took only seconds for an entire team to descend on the area and take control of the situation. In the end, sixteen military personnel had been injured or killed along with seven civilians. Magically, the visiting politicos had escaped unscathed, having left for the airfield earlier that morning.

After seeing to Alex's care and satisfied that he was alive and on the way to the hospital at Ramstein, Drae and Cameron were left to deal with the aftermath of what turned out to be a suicide bomber. In the days and years to come, each battlefield brother would have wounds and emotional scars to contend with. Not only was Alex critically injured and The Kid going home to his fiancée in a body bag, the bomber turned out to be the doe-eyed widow Badirya who sacrificed her only child Asef in some deranged act meant to re-unite her with her dead Afghan husband.

On that fateful day, The Justice Bothers were born from the smoke, death, and despair of an Afghan battlefield. Things would never be the same for any of them and each would carry demons, ghosts, and nightmares from that time into the future. In the two years that followed, one by one, they would leave the desert hell-hole behind and seek a future together, far away from war, in the hot, dusty winds of southern Arizona.

WHAT A FUCKING MESS. Standing in the aftermath of a celebration that had been more than memorable, Draegyn St. John surveyed the carnage left behind. Everywhere he looked was evidence of the Valentine's Day nuptials that had taken place littered throughout the massive Spanish-styled courtyard at Villa Valleja-Marquez.

Taking a hearty slug from the champagne glass clutched in his hand, Drae contemplated the past few days while shaking his head in amazement. After jumping on a plane in Washington, D.C., he'd landed in the midst of an off the hook celebration. The compound where he lived, along with his two business partners and one-time military brothers, technically belonged to the oldest and most senior of their group, Alexander Marquez. They called it the Villa, a sprawling complex spread out among hundreds of acres of breathtaking Arizona scenery, dominated by an enormous Spanish influenced hacienda.

The glorious southwestern weather he loved was a welcome respite from the bitter cold and the never-ending snowfall he'd dealt with in D.C. Not one to usually gripe about anything remotely connected to being out-of-doors, he'd come to despise the winter weather back East. Having to clear off his car every morning, from either a coating of ice or inches of snow, had seriously pissed him off.

After leaving the nation's frigid capitol, he'd found himself immediately immersed in a thousand last-minute details for a wedding that had surprised them all. He still couldn't fathom how the dark and brooding mass of contradictions that was Cameron Justice had ended up married. *Married*! Jesus H. Christ. Just the word brought shudders of distaste racing through his mind. *Ugh, no thanks*.

Marriage and its false promise of commitment were a social convention that he'd vowed never to allow in his life. His parents had taught him the hard way what a charade all that was when he'd been shocked out of his perfect family bubble as a hormonal fourteen-year-old. Having fallen hook, line, and sinker for the faultless picture of social, marital, and domestic bliss that defined the St. John family, he'd been duly horrified after happening upon his, *Do as you're told!* Father, diddling the giggly twit who worked for the family as a quasi kid minder for him and his younger sister.

Dear old Dad had been dismissive of Drae's shock and cruelly arrogant when the time came to explain his actions to his only son. Hearing that his parents' marriage had been an arranged affair between two old-school, upper-class families had destroyed the image of who he'd thought they were. It had all been a lie.

His mother hadn't made it any better. Not only did she not care about her husband's wandering penis, she sarcastically informed him that 'this was how things were done' in their world. A cold, intolerant bitch on the best of days, Draegyn had tried more ways than his teenage brain could count to be the son she wanted, only to never feel any warmth or genuine approval from the woman. Now he knew why.

She'd married for social status and prestige and did what was expected of her in the deal, popping out the perfect set of perfect children for their perfect family. Even now, all these years later, the thought made him sick. She made it sound like she'd consented to be bred in order to live an affluent lifestyle. *Who fucking did that?* He never trusted any woman's motives from that moment on.

Wandering to a bench swing beneath strands of tiny white lights strung around the decorated courtyard, Drae flung his half-inebriated ass onto the seat and forced his thoughts back to the present. All around him was evidence of the romantic, country chic wedding that had joined Cam to the blond-haired lovely who had changed everything with her quiet smile. He liked his new sister-in-law very much. She was unique and absolutely perfect for his old friend; one of the few females Drae hadn't immediately mistrusted.

Lacey Morrow had been quite the surprise when she'd turned up last autumn in Cam's company. That the two ended up together hadn't shocked anyone in the least, except Cam himself. Drae couldn't help the half grin each time he thought about the unusual parade of events that brought his old friend to his knees where Lacey was concerned.

Miraculously surviving the minefield of bullshit surrounding their relationship, once they became an official couple, his friend had become an A-1 besotted, romantic fool. Drae supposed it was probably just an over-reaction to the years of emotional isolation that had defined Cam's life. Once the floodgates of hearts and flowers had been breached, though, the man had gone ape-shit with one over-the-top romantic gesture after another, culminating in the red and white wedding he insisted take place on the one day every year when true love was supposed to be celebrated.

Ha! True love. *What the fuck was that, anyway?* Even so, he was happy for Cam. Truly. Knowing that one of them hadn't been doomed to an eternity of solitude made the burdens each carried lighter. It sure as shit wasn't easy dealing with what they'd done and witnessed during their time together in the puke-fest that was Afghanistan.

Swinging absently, Drae tilted his head back and watched a million twinkling stars shining overhead. Stretching his arms wide on the back of the swing, he sat there in his perfectly tailored Tom Ford tuxedo and let his champagne-fueled mind wander.

He'd gotten into Special Forces as an extra special *fuck you* to his parents. He could still remember the way his mother, with her tight-assed need to control him and his little sister, had gone ballistic at his announcement. She'd been apoplectic learning that he'd already enlisted by the time they found out what he'd done. Hidden in the dark memories that haunted him, he remembered the woman freaking out on her husband. "Fix this!" she had screamed. "Arthur, you fix this right away. He's *your* son after all. Do something about his attitude before he ruins everything I've sacrificed for."

Ah. Yes. He'd been Arthur St. John's son. Not hers. She'd made that abundantly clear. Understanding that he and his sister held no emotional importance in her world-view, beyond the parts they were expected to play, had been the final straw. Of course her *fix him* attitude had landed on his psyche and stuck to him like fucking fly paper.

And his parents had tried to fix him to no avail. The military tried to fix his bad attitude too and while he'd certainly adjusted somewhat, he always managed to walk the fine line of insubordination. He didn't need fixing, *thank you very much*. He was just fine as he was, calling the shots, and answering only to himself.

He was also a card-carrying male chauvinist pig with a scornful arrogance about the travesty of marriage. Keeping clear of powerful women, because they all but ate their young and generally came with a shit-ton of issues, hadn't been that difficult. He wasn't the sort they'd be interested in anyway. That left the rest of the female population in the available category. Except for the innocent of course – they were out-of-bounds. He wanted no responsibility, *ever*, and virgins came with a truckload.

Admitting that Cam was an exception to the rule, Drae wished his old friend nothing but happiness. Lacey was one in a million, and if the emotional wedding they just pulled off was any indication, they'd be wallowing in contentment for all time. He'd been honored to serve as best man *and* maid of honor while Alex had done his Big Daddy duty by walking the beautiful bride down the flower-strewn aisle. Standing as a second to the bride and groom had touched Drae's heart; not that he was going to admit it anytime soon. He played his role as the sarcastic, conceited brother to perfection and kept the ribald comments flowing.

He'd gotten a good laugh at the devious way Lacey's mind worked when she chose an outrageous mermaid style gown that framed her ass because as she'd put it, 'Cameron was a dog for her backside'. Drae fell over laughing at her choice of words, and the two had giggled like conspiratorial girlfriends plotting his lovesick friend's downfall. *Serves Cam right*, he chuckled, because there was nothing guys enjoyed more than laughing at their buddies when a woman turned the tables.

Well, the deed was done, and the Justice Family now included a wife. Wonders never ceased. Now that the happy couple had flown off via private jet to an extended honeymoon in Hawaii, some semblance of order and calm would return to the Villa. He hoped.

During the month he'd been gone before the wedding, Alex had finally found an assistant to keep him organized, busy, and out of everyone else's hair. *Thank fucking God.* Drae had been ready to strangle the man, even from a distance, because Alex without a rudder was like a never-ending shit-storm of angst. He'd gone for months without someone to trot along after him, cleaning up the crap he always seemed to leave in his wake. Luckily, Betty had finally returned, so the office continued to run once Lacey relinquished her temp duties to focus on the wedding.

Making the decision to stay put in Arizona was easy once he started making secret plans to create an addition to the happy couple's cabin as a wedding present. Cam's passion for black and white movies and old-time Hollywood gave Drae the idea to create a home theater he knew the couple would enjoy. Starting the very next morning, once his hangover eased, work would begin straightaway as the clock was officially ticking.

Enjoying the post-reception solitude and what was left of his Cristal buzz, Draegyn was startled when movement along the periphery of his vision had him shifting to high-alert. He wasn't alone anymore although who or what was prowling in the shadows was a mystery since everyone else had long since staggered away to sleep off their over-partied aftermath of the day's events.

Tori had been quickly scurrying along the outskirts of the courtyard where a family wedding had taken place, on her way from seeing off the caterers to her tiny, functional studio apartment above an old barn that served as meeting space and offices for the Justice Agency.

She was exhausted after a long day of holding down the fort so the entire kit and caboodle of interesting people who made up the Justice family of partners, workers, and friends could join in the wedding festivities.

Having only been at the Villa for a few weeks, she'd been happy to pitch in wherever she could while also managing to stay invisible. She liked these folks, especially Alex, who she'd been hired to assist. With her personal life in shambles, she'd jumped at the job opportunity hidden away in the middle of a desert. Preferring to stay clear of social situations, she'd insisted on taking over on the day of the event so everyone else could enjoy it. Ever since the scandal that rocked her word exploded in the press, she'd been working overtime to stay off the radar.

She hated being the center of attention. There was a reason her dad had lovingly referred to her as his little mouse. Lighting up around his only child, the two had shared a special father - daughter bond. Being something of a tomboy with a serious streak a mile-wide, the times they spent holed up at the library or exploring museums had helped her forget that she was a simple girl. No great beauty like her glamorous mother, as a child Tori had been every inch the quiet, bookish mouse her childhood nickname implied.

When her father had passed away, she'd been too young to understand at the time what having cancer meant. After the shock of his death receded, her day-to-day reality became even more introverted. With a mop of bushy brown hair that never, *ever* did what she wanted it to and a slight frame with little in the way of feminine curves to grab a guy's interest, Tori was content to disappear behind ugly eyeglasses a shade too big for her face and basically hide from the world. That didn't however make her a pushover by any means. Schoolyard bullies had been the scourges of her childhood, and she'd learned early to stand up for herself. Along with a fierce determination to level the playing field by leaving her peers in the academic dust, she'd also mastered the art of the scathing verbal put down and never looked back.

Possessing an astute mind and a brilliant reputation for anything having to do with numbers meant she'd been labeled a financial genius while still in grad school and ended up at a world-class investment firm based out of London. Europe had been an eye-opening experience for the plain twenty-four-year-old that included hobnobbing with royalty and an inside view of sophistication and power fueled by the sort of wealth that boggled the mind. That new life had offered exciting challenges and the opportunity to shed some of her natural reserve.

When Tori and her remarkable skills had fallen under the attention of a senior partner who also happened to be an Earl, it seemed like angels had touched her as a fascinating new world opened up. Before too long, she was working side by side with the Earl, Wallace

Evingham and enjoying one bold success after another.

At his insistence she'd undergone a complete makeover at an exclusive Hyde Park spa and revamped her wardrobe. In the end she got what she deserved for being so naïve, she thought wryly. Wallace had been using her financial skills while distracting her with a rather public interest that led many, including herself, to believe he was grooming her to be his future Countess. God, she'd been such a twit.

It all blew apart in spectacular fashion. Just when speculation had peaked that an engagement was only days away, she'd stumbled upon evidence that Wallace was up to no good. He'd been raking in tons of cash in schemes that, while not necessarily illegal, were certainly unethical. And she'd been unwittingly helping him by being so trusting and free with her business acumen. Oh yeah, and he had a string of mistresses to boot. *Asshole.*

She hadn't hesitated to alert the authorities. The blowback had been dreadful, and a major scandal ensued. Wallace was detained and their relationship paraded through the nightmarish British tabloids with headlines like 'Billionaire Earl Tricks American Plain Jane'. A particularly vile tabloid reporter had referred to her as a spinster as if being twenty-six and unmarried qualified for such a loathed status. One minute she'd been the darling of the financial sector and the next a laughingstock.

To make matters worse, it came out that the mistresses knew about each other and were all too happy to join together and cry foul at her betrayal of poor Wallace. The whole thing was embarrassing, sordid, and ugly. She'd been the injured party yet, as the American outsider, she was shunned and ridiculed by everyone. Within weeks, the firm had paid her off handsomely to just simply go the hell away. That was three months ago.

And now here she was, tucked away in the Arizona desert with a bunch of ex-Special Forces men. Her mother had some connection to the Justice Agency and through that association had asked for a favor. Discovering that Alexander Marquez was in need of an assistant with experience in technology, it seemed a perfect fit. Tori needed to fly off the radar for a while and losing herself in the desert with some nerdy computer geek seemed like the perfect solution.

When her new boss turned out to be more of a handful than the dweeb she'd imagined, Tori had welcomed the intense, thrown-in-the-deep-end quality of work she was confronted with. Alex was a brilliant man but something of a mess when it came to practicalities. She spent just as much time trailing behind him, and the loveable dog that followed him everywhere, keeping things organized and running smoothly as she did working with the mind-boggling array of technology and cutting edge electronics that the agency had.

Right now, though, she was exhausted and feeling cranky. Knowing that Alex had been fully invested in making sure the intimate wedding event was something unique and special, she had been tap-dancing on the head of a pin all day, running from one challenge to the next. She was beyond tired but satisfied with how everything had turned out. Thank God she knew a bit of Spanish. Came in handy when she had to put out a particularly vexing fire between the obnoxious and uppity caterer and the troop of ladies from town who'd come out to work the reception.

There was an intense camaraderie amongst the people at the Villa that she privately envied. The radiant bride and handsome groom had smiled and kissed to the satisfaction of one and all before going on their merry way to a honeymoon that was so perfect it sounded like a movie producer had planned it. Their guests had been partying hard most of the evening. The place was a mess now that the festivities had wrapped up. Tomorrow would be soon enough to set about putting everything back in order.

She'd been stomping along, unconcerned that she looked like holy hell in a pair of sensible flats and a non-descript skirt outfit, when she came up short spying what had to be the most beautiful man she had ever laid eyes on. Holy shitballz, the guy looked like a movie star!

About forty feet away and sitting on a swinging bench, he was staring at the sky. An empty champagne flute was on the seat next to him. She actually put her hand on her chest in both surprise and instantaneous attraction as she took in the whole of him with hungry eyes that missed nothing.

Wearing the same style black tuxedo that Alex and the groom had worn, he had opened the collar button and left the formal bowtie hanging around his neck. Bright silver cuff links, sparkling at her under the twinkling lights, adorned the sleeves of his impossibly white shirt. From where she stood it was easy to see the exposed skin on his neck as his head lolled on the bench's high back. The chin angled up at the stars suggested a take no prisoner's attitude. Even without seeing his face, she knew he'd be gorgeous. And dangerous. Everything about him screamed of something wild and exciting.

She must have made a sound because quite suddenly his head lifted and searched the shadows. Not having more than a second or two to school her expression into passivity, she found herself trapped in the laser-like beam of his stare when ice-cold blue eyes zeroed in on her. *Uh oh.*

DRAEGYN HADN'T NEEDED NIGHT vision goggles to find the movement in the darkness that interrupted his solitude. He'd found his quarry in less than a heartbeat, instantly intrigued by what he saw.

It was a female. At least he thought it was. The small figure lurking along the pathway was covered up by a hideously bland outfit that was so awful it almost hurt his eyes, along with a pair of ugly shoes that were better suited for a nun. Hovering along a path lit by the moon and strands of twinkle lights, the creature locked in his stare had a fey quality that got his blood pumping.

"Who's there?" he barked in an authoritative tone he used to scare the shit out of the agency's recruits. When no sound came, he moved into the shadows with a cat-like swiftness honed during his decades of training in the martial arts. It was unlikely that an unauthorized person had found their way past the Villa's elaborate security system so Drae was more than curious as to who was prowling in the darkness.

"Show yourself."

When he came upon her, the first thing he noticed was an

enormous pair of oval shaped, chocolate brown eyes blinking up at him in the dim light. His initial reaction was that a man could easily become lost in their sweetness. *What the fuck*? When had he become a poet, waxing lyrically about some pretty brown eyes? Goddamn wedding must have addled his brain!

She wasn't very big at all – almost waif-like in stature. Her face had high cheekbones and a straight nose that drew his eyes to a mouth that could only be described as pouty. There was an ethereal quality about her made even more fascinating by the fact that she wasn't wearing a lick of makeup. Most of the women he knew preferred a somewhat lacquered appearance. The fresh face before him had a pale coolness that shone in the moonlight.

Even though he'd barked at her, she didn't look frightened at all. Mostly she seemed stunned. And intrigued. They were sharing the same reaction. She wasn't anyone he'd seen around the compound before. Drae was dying to know who she was.

Tori was tongue-tied and frozen in place the moment that icy blue stare locked on her presence. *Good grief!* The man rose from the swing and stalked into the darkness was even more gorgeous up close than she imagined. He should definitely be declared illegal, because nobody so devastatingly handsome could possibly be good for her health.

He wasn't huge in that steroid-crazed way so many men had these days, but he had a menacing air about him that did more than hint at his domineering nature. The tuxedo told her he was the missing Justice Brother who had flown in at the last moment for Cameron and Lacey's nuptials. So, this was the infamous Draegyn St. John. Didn't take but a second for her to understand why everyone joked that he was the agency's equivalent to James Bond's 007.

The man was exactly what you'd expect. *God*, she nearly laughed out loud at the notion that he was probably in his natural state, dressed in a designer tuxedo, sipping extremely expensive champagne. Tori had a hard time working up a vision of him in jeans and a t-shirt.

Unlike Cam who was built like a movie star superhero or big, burly Alex, the fair-haired god invading her body space was lean and graceful with an underlying air of menace that tingled along Tori's nerve-endings. Immaculately groomed hair the color of wheat framed a face showing the lines and crinkles of a very adult male. Besides the piercing blue-iced eyes, she saw a nose that had probably been broken once or twice and a short jagged scar barely visible between blond brows. With cheekbones that any male model worth his salt would die for, and a light smattering of pale body hair showing at the opening of his shirt, it was his mouth that had Tori's eyebrows reaching for her hairline. She'd never seen a mouth quite so uncompromising or blatantly sensual as his. He was just so damn perfect. Everything about him seemed hard and unyielding. Even before he'd spoken, she knew he'd be an arrogant devil.

Clearing her throat, hoping it would help get her wayward thoughts under heel, she tried to answer his question but found she forgot what he'd asked. Hot damn, the man actually scrambled her brain! She thought such things were the stuff of overactive imaginations. Apparently, she had a living, breathing fantasy right in front of her. Fan-fucking-tastic! Just what she didn't need.

"Um, hi, Mister St. John. I'm, uh - Alex's assistant?" *Ah, fuck my life*, she thought as her eyes momentarily squeezed shut at how absurdly lame she sounded.

Smirking, the blond Adonis asked, "Is that an answer or a question?"

Godammit. "Oh, um....sorry. Guess you took me by surprise. I hadn't expected anyone else to be out here." Extending her hand politely she tried for something sounding a bit less dumb. "Mister St. John, *hello*. My name is Victoria Bennett. We haven't been formally introduced yet, but I am Alex's new assistant. It's nice to finally meet you."

He took hold of the hand she offered and held fast, making her heart skip a beat and then speed up at an alarmingly quickened pace. *Wow*. This guy was good. One touch and she was almost drooling. She knew all about his sexual history. The women in the Villa were quick to point out his man-whore reputation. Apparently there wasn't a supermodel or actress he hadn't bedded. Her initial impression that he wasn't going to be good for her health lit up inside her head like a warning beacon.

His voice had a distinctive, upper class drawl that rumbled up from his chest, adding to the raw, masculine appeal he had in spades. "Ah, *Victoria*." The way he pronounced her formal name almost put her silly ass in a swoon. "Please call me Draegyn. I'll have none of that Mister St. John nonsense. I'd heard Alex found a lifesaver to keep him in line and stop all of us from wanting to murder him in his sleep. Despite the lack of a formal introduction, I am pleased to make your acquaintance."

Shit. He was still holding her hand. It felt a little like he was taking her temperature through his touch. She doubted her reaction to his oozing sex appeal was going unnoticed.

"Yes, well, uh, if you'll excuse me," she blathered while trying to extricate her trembling hand from his powerful grip. "I have a few loose ends to take care of. Nice meeting you, Mister…..um, I mean Draegyn." *Oh my God*, she was an idiot! Could this possibly get any worse?

With the precision and speed of a frightened mouse, which was just how she felt, Tori scurried away from the temptation that was Draegyn St. John and made a beeline for the safety of her apartment. He stayed put in the shadows as she ran away, but she felt his eyes on her the whole way. Just before she turned the corner, a quick glance over her shoulder revealed his startling blue-iced gaze following her every move. *Oh my, my.*

Well, that had certainly been interesting, Drae thought as he watched the intriguing female with the God-awful dress sense bolt for safety. Searching his champagne-fuzzed brain, he recalled Alex telling him about the lucky find he'd stumbled on in his search for a right-hand, but not much else. Truth was, he hadn't given a fuck about the details at the time. All he cared about was that things would return to normal now that their tech-guru had gotten some help. Alex might be brilliant, even scarily so, but without someone to keep him focused and on task, he had an easy time making a mess of things. *All of it intentional*, he admitted with a small grin.

Jamming his hands into the pockets of his pants, Drae wandered to the front of the Villa where he'd left one of the many expensive and indulgent cars at his disposal. It was well past time for him to face plant in his own bed, which was a quick, five-minute ride further into the compound. There were still a couple of vehicles scattered around the wide circular driveway, left by anyone too drunk to drive safely or from those staying over.

Folding his lean, muscular frame into the low, super charged beast that rumbled to life at the push of a button, Drae eased the red sports car onto the lane that wound behind the hacienda, past Cameron and Lacey's homey log cabin, and down onto a low-lying stretch of flatland where his house sat.

Each of their homes was unique. Alex, of course, lived in the main house. An enormous, sprawling Spanish hacienda that matched old-world elegance with modern style. From the wow factor standpoint, the Villa took the prize with its multiple courtyards, breathtaking interiors, and attention to classic Spanish architecture.

Cameron's impressive log homestead actually made light of the term *cabin*. Drae had been involved in the design and layout of Cam's home base. If it came from a tree and was carved or cut, Drae was the man to go to. The woodworking hobby he'd begun as a boy had developed over time into an all-consuming passion.

His own home was quite different. Unlike Cam's rustic log structure, he'd designed his home to be a statement in modern practicality with almost five thousand square feet of contemporary craftsmanship featuring a heavy-timbered soaring roof structure, and an open interior with stairways and a second floor overhang that resembled a wood bridge.

He enjoyed pulling into the stone drive and seeing the massive two-story home with its unusual angles and corners punctuated with enormous windows and clever glass walls that captured the beautiful vistas and the changing light throughout the desert day. Sometimes, it was good to be him.

Tomorrow would be here soon enough, he thought after closing the door behind him and taking a deep breath to clear some of the champagne buzz. For now, he needed to indulge in his high-tech wet room with its steam shower and multiple sprays. Maybe he'd follow-up with Alex in the morning and find out more about the odd creature he'd just met. She'd piqued his curiosity; that was for sure. If he were being honest, he'd have to admit that the way she had run off threw him just a bit. Usually, his well-practiced charm earned him more than a quick dismissal.

Thinking of being thrown to the curb made Drae remember how he'd rather ruthlessly done just that not all that long ago, when it was time to end his most recent sexual interlude. He couldn't help the sneer that lit up his brain or the nod that came along with acknowledging that he didn't do relationships. It was sex and nothing more. Before his latest assignment in Washington, he'd been babysitting a high profile teenage heartthrob during a world tour that had stretched on for months. Drae hated having to take that obnoxious little fucker on, but the kid actually did need a serious security arrangement, and his record label had been willing to pay through the nose for the agency's services.

Surrounded by bodyguards with their own headshots and Hollywood aspirations, plus the endless wave of hangers-on and an entourage of sycophants that stretched his nerves to their limit, the appearance one night of a certain actress with a set of expensive tits and the randiness of a sex-addict had helped ease his annoyance. Jessamyn What's-Her-Name had set her sights on Drae the moment she saw him. The kinky bitch got off on the fact that he wore a shoulder holster. *Women*, go figure.

He'd seduced the skinny actress out of her thong, after a bottle of Ciroc and rather straightforwardly telling her, *if you come any closer I'm going to have to fuck you.* Apparently America's latest manufactured sweetheart liked it nasty. She'd flitted in and out of his bed for months while the European leg of his assignment ground on.

Jessamyn – *who thought up these ridiculous names,* he wondered – had been an energetic lover willing to do just about anything and then some. He'd sometimes found her enthusiasm tedious and questioned how many of the dramatic screaming orgasms she had were actually real or just performances in her repertoire of acting credits.

Shedding his tuxedo, Draegyn stepped into the luxury en suite and headed for the shower. Catching sight of his naked body reflected in the glass enclosure, he paused and took stock. Except for a few new nicks and scars, he looked as he always did. Fit, lean, and rocking a seriously hard-core body. Years of martial arts and hand-to-hand defense training had given him a textbook perfect physique.

Thinking about the sex-obsessed Jessamyn and how they'd more or less fucked their way across Europe had unfortunately triggered the start of an erection that wasn't exactly welcome at this moment. Seeing his rising cock made him pause. He was too tired and, truth be told, disinterested in the idea of jerking off to take matters into his own hands.

Remembering how he'd firmly informed Jess that their fun times had to end only turned her into stage-four clinger. She'd cried and begged, told him how much she loved him. Who the fuck had brought love into the equation? He sure as hell hadn't. Drae was very good at spelling out the limits of being involved with him right from the beginning. Since she'd obviously disregarded his warnings and turned hysterical, he'd quite literally thrown her out. When it was time to move on, well - it was time to move on.

Setting the shower controls he flung himself into the steaming water and simply stood there letting the water pound away the champagne buzz and tension in his body. Hopefully, the hard-on would fade, and he could think about other things. Things like chocolate eyes and a pouty mouth.

Well shit. That thought came out of nowhere and certainly wasn't helping things. The minute he envisioned Victoria Bennett, and her irritating dismissal of him, his cock rapidly stood at attention in the hot shower. She wasn't his type, not by a long shot, so why she was appearing in his thoughts baffled him. Drae preferred his women sophisticated and experienced. He wasn't looking for any sort of relationship or happily ever after bullshit. The bodies underneath him in bed were interchangeable and forgettable as a whole. Some mousey computer nerd was in no way his style. So why then did his thoughts circle around to her?

Once he'd asked the question, his mind flooded with a montage of sex-fueled scenarios all featuring the plain little woman with the mouth of a goddess. He bet she gave a mean blowjob with those pouty lips of hers. It wasn't a stretch to imagine her down on her knees with his thick cock sliding in and out of her lush mouth. When his staff pulsed, Drae groaned aloud at the irony of his situation. He didn't want the anorexic actress with the insatiable sex drive. Instead he was fantasizing about some plain little nobody who in just a few short minutes had climbed inside his libido. So much for being disinterested in jerking off. His dick had other ideas as it throbbed and twitched in the pouring water.

Alright. *Fuck it*, he thought as he grabbed hold of himself and gave a good squeeze. Sometimes a guy had to do, what a guy had to do. Unable to dismiss the picture of Victoria's striking brown eyes from his mind, he thought about what having the small woman climbing all over his rock hard body would feel like and decided she'd be a definite turn-on in the sack. Hell, she was so petite, he could probably twirl her around on his dick without much effort.

His hand stroked while his mind conjured up one sexy visual after the next, all starring the strange fey woman. He was surprised at his reaction to these thoughts as his excitement ramped up higher and higher with each slow caress of his engorged flesh. Before too long, his heart was beating with the force of a bass drum while his balls filled and tightened.

Wondering what it would be like to sink into her body as those sinfully sweet eyes stared up at him had Drae moaning within seconds. *Christ*. He bet she'd be tight and wet. The idea of pounding away at her until she cried out while coming all over his dick made his impending orgasm build strength and speed. A few quick, efficient strokes of his big hand detonated an explosive climax that started in the bottoms of his feet and shot along his nervous system with astonishing force. Throwing back his head, his neck corded with tension from the release. He felt his cock jerk and pulse under his fingers. The sensation went on forever, something that didn't normally happen in these hands-on situations. When it was finally over, he was hanging onto the wall for dear life as deep, gasping breaths filled his lungs.

Holy mother of God. What the fuck just happened? Had he actually had one of the most intense orgasms of his life, alone in a shower, while fantasizing about a woman he'd spoken to for less than five minutes? To make matters worse, his dick wasn't exactly settling down either. *Goddammit.* This wasn't like him. Wasn't like him at all. It was going to be a hell of a night.

BREATHE. RUN. BREATHE. RUN. The sound made by Drae's feet, thundering along the hard packed dirt, echoed in unison with his breathing as he mentally chanted the running mantra through the last leg of an early morning power-jog. It felt good to push his body to go harder, faster, longer. He hoped the intensity would clear the cobwebs from his brain after a short, sleepless night.

The cadence of his pounding legs got inside his head, pushing him harder. Dressed in baggy sweats that had seen better days and a faded Corps t-shirt, he'd been running from the devil for the last hour. Up ahead his house came into view, where he stopped and grabbed some water before continuing up the lane. He kept running, only slowing for a cool down in the last stretch.

Arriving at Cameron's cabin just as the contractor began setting up a work zone with his crew, Drae channeled the restless energy he'd been trying to burn off into the building project. Looking around, he was satisfied that every attention was being paid to the details he specified, right down to the extensive desert landscaping that would be needed along the outside of the addition. A couple of minutes later, Alex rolled up in an ATV, waving to Drae.

As soon as Alex eased off the seat and started walking toward him, Drae was struck with concern for his friend. Obviously, being on his feet most of yesterday and then dancing and partying well into the night had taken a toll on the man's body. Reminders of the day when Alex had almost eaten it courtesy of a suicide bombing never really faded, not when old injuries reeled their ugly head. The dude was struggling to put one foot in front of the other.

"Hey man," Drae called out as Alex neared. "Some fucking party last night, huh?"

At Alex's snort of amused agreement, Drae eased off a bit. Thank God his friend wasn't snarling and acting like a king-sized control freak. "They're getting started early," Alex murmured, taking in the bustle of activity unfolding around Cameron's house. "Oh, by the way - there's a message for you in the office. The company doing the video install has some questions. Sounded important, too. Whatever you chose six weeks ago is apparently obsolete today!"

"Of course," Drae chuckled with a half smile. "Why the fuck not? Do you have any idea what they're talking about? All that technology shit is your area of expertise. I only picked the flashiest system with the most bells and whistles because it was top of the line. Beyond that, I have no goddamn idea!"

Alex laughed along with him. "If you want, I'll take a look at that end of things so you can concentrate on being the Wood Whisperer."

Booming with laughter, Drae asked, "Wood Whisperer? What the hell is that? Sounds kind of depraved!"

Alex grinned broadly. "Dude. Didn't you know? That's what some of the workers call you. Hilarious, really. I think Gus overheard one of your long-winded rants about a piece of lumber in the shop. He came up with the tag and it stuck. You really do sound like a chick picking out a prom dress sometimes, Drae."

"Suck my balls!" Drae laughed good-naturedly at the friendly taunt. Yeah, he did sometimes get *way* into his woodworking. It was, after all, its own form of meditation for him.

Turning to him with palms placed in blessing position at his chest, Alex bowed slightly in mocking supplication and said, "No thanks. Your balls are of no interest to me!"

Slapping his old commanding officer and good friend on the back, Drae gestured to the ATV and suggested they ride back to the main house for a swim. The idea of diving into the cool water, after the sweat he'd worked up on his run, sounded like heaven.

After they'd climbed into the double-seated vehicle and began the drive back to the main house, Drae suddenly blurted out the question he had about the mystery woman from last night before he realized he was doing it. "So, I ran into your new assistant last night, Victoria."

Alex flashed a quick smile. "You mean Tori? Yeah, she's great. Totally lucked out finding her. She tell you to call her Victoria? That's odd." The unspoken question and surprise in Alex's response didn't sail over his head.

He wanted to come back with a snappy retort. Maybe an off-hand slap on his own back about her having been addled by being in his presence, but he didn't. He wanted to find out exactly who the small, plain woman was without piquing too much of anyone else's interest to why he was so curious. "Yeah, yeah. She introduced her-self with her full name. NBD, man. Must have been the tuxedo and the way I barked at her." *Good way to cover*, he thought.

"Well, watch yourself around her. She's one smart cookie. Hav-ing her around is going to be great for everyone, not just me. Tori has an extraordinary ability to interpret complex systems and pat-terns….."

Drae chuckled at his friend's description. "Alex, I have no fuck-ing idea what that's supposed to mean! It's enough that you do, though. Where'd you find this brainiac treasure? I don't recall you actually doing a search. She turn up out of thin air?"

"Jesus, Drae. That's a bit cynical even for you. No, I didn't interview anyone else but yes, she's been carefully vetted so you can relax!"

They'd arrived at their destination behind the main house next to a short walkway that led to the pool and cabana area. Alex slightly struggled when getting out of the ATV. Drae had to pull back from offering assistance. He knew the help would not be appreciated. Alex hated feeling like he was debilitated in any way.

Covering for his wobbly posture, Alex suggested that Drae grab some swim trunks from the cabaña and join him in the pool. "I'll give you the four-one-one on Tori. That way you can save the trouble of an investigation. She's good people so ease up."

With Alex's words hanging in his thoughts, Drae slipped into one of the changing rooms, pulling on a pair of swim trunks in supersonic time. Finding Alex already in the pool, he dove into the deep end in a smooth arc. There really wasn't anything quite like being fully submerged as your body sliced through the clear, cool water. Dolphin kicking leisurely to the side of the pool, he came up for air and waited for Alex to fill in the blanks in Victoria's story.

"Okay. So where was I? Oh, right. You asked where Tori came from." Alex eased onto a step and flexed his leg while he gathered his thoughts. *Just like Alex*, Drae thought wryly. Pull together the basic information. Sift through it. Decide which points were worth sharing, and go from there. He hadn't been their commanding officer for no good reason. Even so, if he didn't get on with it, Drae was going to smack him.

After a minute, Alex scrubbed his hand through already mussed hair, making it even worse. He couldn't look any more like an absentminded professor if he tried.

"Around eighteen months ago, the agency sent some randos from the B team to do security for a beauty contest. It was good practice for our guys, herding a bunch of pageant models through a big media event. Anyway, our liaison from the pageant coordinators was a woman named Stephanie Bennett. Former beauty queen. Two months ago, she contacted us again for an upgrade consultation. I handled the technical stuff and during one of our conversations she mentioned a daughter. Do you remember that British financial scandal last year?"

Drae did remember. He'd been in Europe at the time with the heartthrob superstar kid. Staying on top of what was going on with the press had been part of his security headache. When the banks and brokerage houses scandal hit, the story had exploded in the tabloids. Those things always got ugly, and he pitied anyone who had gotten caught in the mess.

"Well, it seems that the whistleblower was none other than Tori Bennett."

Drae blew a dramatic whistle at the shocking reveal. Searching his memory, the basics of the scandal popped up. Some rich guy's financial house of cards had been toppled by a do-gooder, supposedly a girlfriend. Victoria was involved? That hardly seemed likely.

"I know! Right?" Alex chortled when he spied Drae's look of astonishment. "She doesn't seem the type but the way her mother told it, she was overwhelmed and duped by an older man who played the game very well. He was a Duke or an Earl or something. Earl of Bullshit if you ask me!"

Drae struggled to wrap his mind around what he was hearing. That diminutive lump of no-frills brown had taken down half of Europe's financial big-wigs? Oh man, this was getting good.

"The tabloids chewed her up and spit her out according to her mom. Judging by how Tori came off when she got here, I'd say the whole thing traumatized her pretty damn good. Y'know I hate that kind of shit. Why is it the people with a moral compass are so often the ones who get run over?"

He wasn't surprised when Alex started talking ethics and the principles of behavior. No one was more honorable or decent than Alexander Marquez. The man still carried the burdens of having been a wartime commander. People died on his watch and not just the bad guys.

"In the end, it was an enormous shit-storm. She bolted back to the states and went in to seclusion at her mother's. To be honest, I was curious by the story so I did some checking around."

The raised eyebrow of surprise Drae offered earned him a stern look in return. "Not the scandal, you dickhead. I was curious about the woman who single-handedly spanked so many rich and powerful people. Being an economic prodigy meant her services were in high demand. I discovered that she'd come to the attention of financial bigwigs from Wall Street to the London Stock Exchange. That's how she wound up overseas."

"So let me get this straight. Your new assistant is a financial Einstein who you rescued from tabloid infamy? Am I anywhere near the truth?"

"You hit it right on the mark, actually." Alex laughed. "But do *not* go comparing me to Cam! This rescue most definitely isn't going to lead to romance. I'm no knight in shining armor. She needed to start over and with her mad skills, I'd have been an idiot not to snap her up. Really, Drae. Once you get to know her you'll see she's fucking brilliant. She's got a head for details and doesn't ask stupid questions. I'd say that makes her a perfect fit for the agency."

Conversation essentially over, the two broke apart and swam several dozen laps, churning the pool with their workout. Drae considered everything he'd learned about the woman he couldn't dismiss from his thoughts as he pulled his body through the water. With each punch of his hands hitting the surface, his mind picked apart the information available. No matter how he tried, there was no way to realistically link the prim and proper creature he'd met last night with the very different picture Alex gave of Victoria Bennett.

Tori was in search of her boss. When Alex didn't turn up at his usual time or text her with a change of plans, she dutifully got down to business and awaited his arrival. She'd eaten up a big chunk of time doing random nothingness until her restless frustration turned to irritation. *Where the hell is he*?

Admitting that patience wasn't one of her best qualities, she tried to diffuse her annoyance with positive thoughts and failed miserably. She leaned down and scratched Alex's big Labrador behind her ears, mumbling to her about how irritating men could be.

Finally, she decided to find out what was going on. If Alex hadn't wanted to work today, he should have said so, dammit. She hated when things were disorganized, and she especially objected to wasted time. There were easily fifty things she could have focused on instead of where the hell her boss was.

Furiously pushing her glasses back on the bridge of her nose, Tori stood and grabbed for her cellphone while mumbling under her breath, "Heaven save me from all men! They are more damn trouble than they're worth. Even the brilliant ones …"

Shooing Zeus from the workspace and into the doggie bed Alex kept nearby, Tori clomped her way out of the building and started her search. It hadn't taken long to head in the right direction after she'd run in to Ben, the property manager, and he told her to check by the pool. The pool? Really? It was a workday, after all. Wasn't it a bit early to be lounging about? *Ugh!*

Continuing on, she searched for the swimming area, startled when she found a long, open cabaña that was more a luxurious outdoor living room than a place to put pool loungers. The pool itself was enormous. Easily forty or fifty meters in length with a second raised platform at the end complete with spa and waterfall. The overall affect was out of this world!

What was also bang-up fantastic was the scene she'd stumbled upon. While Alex pounded out steady laps in the pool, Mr. 007 himself was standing nearby, toweling off. With his back to her she had the perfect opportunity and vantage point to survey Draegyn St. John's, er….attributes and boy, she wasn't disappointed.

Not every guy looked good in swim trunks. That would *not* be true in this case. *Holy shit.* Tori watched, glued to the spot as he lifted a leg to dry it off, giving her an appetizing view of the way the dark blue suit with contrasting trim molded to his body. No one had the right to look that hot! Her brain was cataloging the moment. *L-A-S-C-I-V-I-O-U-S. Adjective, meaning feeling or revealing overt sexual interest.* That pretty much said it all.

Next thing she knew, he put his leg down and turned to look at her. No, he wasn't just looking. More like gaping. *Yep, yep.* He was gaping at her while she ate him alive with her eyes. Dammit all! She'd totally gotten caught ogling one of her bosses. Wasn't this when the earth was supposed to crack open and swallow her alive?

Well, there was nothing to do then but slap a business-like expression on her face and pretend that she had even a shred of dignity left. Pushing at her glasses in a purely reflexive move, she strode forward as confidently as her trembling legs would allow. Brushing past him with only a nod would be rude so she slowed her pace, while he stood there watching her, a towel clutched in his hand. She wished like bloody hell that the wet bathing suit did a better job of concealing what was going on in his trunks. The closer she got, the harder it was to keep her eyes from wandering south on his torso.

"Um, good morning Mister St. John. I was searching for Alex, and it seems that I found him," she indicated by nodding her head toward the pool. "If you'll excuse me," she mumbled trying to slide past him.

"I believe last night we agreed you would call me Draegyn, and good morning to you as well, Victoria." The way he said her name made warmth spread through her veins. She didn't welcome the feeling one bit.

Shrugging and pushing at her glasses, she took a step away, biting her lip until it hurt. "Okay, uh….you're right, *Draegyn*. Sorry.

Please don't let me keep you. I really should go speak to Alex."

The smile he shot her way held a trace of icy brutishness. "You didn't seem in that much of a hurry a moment ago." His smirk was meant to let her know she'd been caught at what men high-five each other for doing every damn day, checking out a gorgeous piece of ass. His arrogance made her furious. She'd had enough of smug, self-centered, conceited men to last a lifetime. *Screw him.*

"Yes, well," she sniped, pulling straight every inch of her five and a half foot frame. "I was blinded for a moment." His smug reaction to her words was so damn predictable. The disparaging smile she offered in return wiped the grin from his face. "The sun must have been in my eyes." *Snap*! He looked a little stunned at her obvious attempt at a putdown.

She managed to dash forward and slide past him before either of them could say anything else. It was a struggle not to look over her shoulder at his reaction. When his laughter split the air she didn't know whether to be relieved or mortified. That man was definitely going to be trouble. She had to steer clear of him at all costs. She knew she was being prickly, but honestly, what was she supposed to do? Hadn't the last few months been horrible enough? Some lessons were learned the hard way. This was her chance to start over. Entertaining dirty thoughts about someone she worked for was a stretch too far.

Some time later, long after the rest of the day had flown by, Drae was remembering the surprising encounter he'd had this morning with Victoria. He'd messed with her simply because he could and was shocked when she shut him down. When he discovered her lurking near the cabaña, it was as if by thinking about her that she had been conjured up out of thin air.

Of course if that *had* been the case, he would have materialized better clothes than what she'd been wearing. Her fashion sense was appalling. The way she dressed was like fingernails on a chalkboard for a man like Drae. Everything she wore was downright repulsive, from the god-awful clogs to the painfully dour-looking trousers that made her look like a blob.

Women were mysterious and sometimes complicated beings. Mostly, he appreciated the endless sizes, shapes, and colors that they came in. He hadn't earned the reputation he had without finding the opposite sex appealing and challenging. Victoria Bennett simply did not fit any type or sort of female he'd previously encountered. Was she trying to make herself downright fugly? He didn't get it. Not only that, everything about her conflicted with the image of a savvy, economic guru in the high-powered atmosphere of the financial world. Grabbing a beer from his fridge, he decided to take ride on the Internet and see for himself what he could find out about Miss Victoria Bennett. Occupational hazard? Perhaps. Being skeptical came naturally to him.

An hour and another beer later, Drae had more questions than answers, although a clearer picture was starting to form in his mind. Googling the scandal resulted in a flood of sensational tabloid reports. Typical crap, but it told him a lot. All of it amped up for maximum shock value.

She had indeed been recruited by one of the top financial firms in London. The reports made her sound like a female nerd. Head for numbers, plain Jane with a scary ability to decipher complex systems. No wonder Alex scooped her up. He couldn't help but wonder if she was prickly and stern with everyone or if it was just him that set her off. In his view, the lady was an enigma, but Alex seemed to be having an entirely different experience with her.

From the images and news clips came other evidence. The petite, smartly styled woman in the photos didn't much resemble the drab techie scurrying around the Justice compound. Some serious shit must have gone down. That was the only way to explain her transformation from quiet elegance to dowdy.

He tried not to be influenced by the snarky tone of the tabloid reports, preferring to come to his own conclusions, but the relentless insistence that she'd been a nobody who saw a chance to gain a title and an easy life had hit the mark. His deeply held belief that women were self-serving opportunists with an eye on the prize jaded his outlook. Was Victoria one of those types?

Slamming the empty beer bottle on the desk, Drae eased back in the suede desk chair, letting his head fall back on the rest. Why was he so damn curious about the little brown mouse? He must be bored or distracted by the lack of female companionship now that he was back in Arizona. He never brought women to his home, ever. Seducing everything that moved was one thing; doing it in his own bed was another.

The unexpected loss of control in the shower last night had more to do with a good case of sexual frustration than the woman invading his thoughts. He grinned knowing she'd probably be horrified to learn he'd been fantasizing about her as he came. Women generally didn't find that shit amusing. When his sex started coming alive at the mere thought, he groaned like a dying man. No way was tonight going to end like last night. Mind over matter, right? *Shit.*

Shutting down the computer was his final thought on the matter. Victoria Bennett wasn't the first stray soul to wind up at the Villa, nor would she be the last. The unique solitude that came from living and working in the bubble of a desert ranch had proved healing for so many. He, Alex, and Cam included. He wouldn't begrudge the little mouse her opportunity to do the same.

COFFEE. WHERE'S THE GODDAMN coffee? Tori was out of sorts and cranky as hell as she slammed around her tiny kitchen. Not even another glorious southwest day was making a bit of difference in her mood. She liked the constant sunshine, warm climate, and desert vistas she'd found in Arizona. Such a change from grey, damp England. But right now, she didn't give a good goddamn about the weather. All she could concentrate on was mainlining some caffeine, stat!

Frustrated, she pulled handfuls of unruly hair away from her face, yanking the mess into a sloppy bun on top of her head, securing it with a clip she'd found discarded on the counter. Padding in bare feet across the cool tiles of the eat-in kitchen, she thumped a cabinet door shut then stood there, hands on hips, looking as frustrated and ragged as she felt. There was nothing like an edgy sleepless night to bring out the foulest of her moods.

After the humiliating scene with Draegyn at the pool when he'd caught her checking him out, she'd focused like a laser for the rest of the day on anything and everything that could divert her thoughts. Distracting herself from mulling over every detail of the man's chiseled features. It hadn't been easy.

Emotionally exhausted by the end of the day, she'd been relieved to shut the door on the outside world and retreat to her mini-apartment. Mister Secret Agent had been wreaking havoc on her senses the whole damn day. She was keyed up, restless, and fighting a good case of sexual frustration brought on by her acute awareness of Draegyn St. John's masculine charms.

Nothing she did banished him from her mind. She tried doing mundane chores like laundry and tidying up her bathroom, but he was there with her the whole time. It had made her edgy and even more restless. In a final ditch attempt to rein in her careening senses, she'd curled up on the overstuffed sofa with a pile of books at her side. Reading was a favorite pastime. Her most secret guilty pleasure was an unabashed love for trashy romance novels. There was nothing like a good bodice-ripper.

Unfortunately, reading only made matters worse. During one particularly steamy scene from the book she'd chosen, the dashing hero had been swimming in his birthday suit when the startled heroine innocently stumbled upon the private moment. The description of Lady Abigail's eyes tracing the drops of water falling down a firmly muscled chest, and the way the sexy Duke was described in full, sensual detail, had been like adding jet fuel to the flames simmering in her insides.

She wasn't totally inexperienced when it came to the opposite sex. Okay, maybe more like *mostly* inexperienced, but still, that had to count for something. She'd been intimate before although looking back, *intimate* might be using the word in a stretch. Her college boyfriend had been an uncomplicated geek who challenged her mind way more than her senses. Keith was a nice guy who hadn't elicited much excitement between the sheets. He preferred a lights out, sex by the numbers approach that was as predictable as it was bland. She got to know his moves by heart. A little bit of awkward kissing followed by a boob grab that was more medical exam than sexy caress.

Eventually, he'd put a finger inside her. Just one. He didn't care for touchy feely stuff so touching him was a no. The actual act never lasted more than a few quick minutes and was more of the same follow-the-numbers stuff. Insert, pause, thrust, pause, and then pause some more usually followed by a minute of silent bucking before uninspiring Keith shot his load into the condom he insisted on. It was all so clinical and detached.

She had yearned for the sort of heart pounding lovemaking she'd read about in books, but alas, mild-mannered Keith wasn't going to rise to that standard. *Ever*. Tori wondered if men like the titillating alpha males she was drawn to in the literary realm actually existed in real life. Wallace certainly hadn't fit the bill either. Just thinking about him made her skin crawl and bile rise in her throat.

Where the hell was that package of coffee pods she'd just bought? Thinking of the smarmy, two-timing Earl made quickly downing a jolt of caffeine an absolute necessity. Even the slightest reminder of the way she'd been deluded by his suave, aristocratic approach got her anger up. Unfortunately, a cabinet door got the worst of it as she slammed it shut with a resounding smack.

Scuffling around the tiny kitchen, she finally located the coffee and made fast work of getting a steaming hot beverage in her hand. Would it help her think more clearly and be less of a grump? Probably not. Her sleepless night was the result of fantasizing about the yummy Draegyn St. John, not the unctuous Wallace Evingham. The two men could not have been more different.

She'd been surprised and swept off her feet when Wallace had taken an interest in her. During the year they were together, the Earl had been painstakingly sincere and respectful while insisting their relationship take a slow course. At the time, she'd thought it wonderfully romantic even though it meant the sum total of their physical relationship consisted of a few kisses and one, less than stellar, make-out session. Being wooed and fawned over by any man, aristocrat or not, was every girl's secret wish, wasn't it? Finding out it was all a ruse made her feel stupid and naïve.

She wanted what her parents had when it came to romance. Her mom and dad had been so in love; at least that was how everyone who knew the happy couple told the story. Her mother had been a twenty-one year old beauty queen when she met and fell hopelessly in love with a young lawyer from Atlanta. She and her lover eloped just months after they'd met with Victoria arriving a year later. They lived a charmed and perfect life for ten years until illness claimed her father's young life. Their love had been so powerful and infinite that all these years later, her beautiful, talented, successful mother had not only never remarried, she rarely if ever toyed with the dating scene.

Comparing her parents' love story with some conceited aristocratic jerk didn't come close to the image of the perfect mate she'd dreamed of since girlhood. And then there was Draegyn. The hard-bodied, sexy secret agent might be making her panties damp, but he was not to be taken seriously. There was no way to fix that kind of self-important belief system. He'd always be a dog, sniffing after every available female's skirt he could find.

Still, after lights out, her thoughts conjured up Draegyn sneaking into her bed. She imagined the blond Adonis teasing her with risqué suggestions. She'd fallen asleep while visions of hot and sweaty sex with the fair-haired super-hunk played out in her mind. She awoke feeling more exhausted and edgy than when she'd fallen into bed.

Letting loose with the mother of all heavy sighs, Tori glanced at the time and saw she needed to be getting ready for work. In the bathroom, she stared at herself in the mirror, taking detailed stock of her appearance. Wearing a threadbare concert t-shirt that had actually been her mother's, she couldn't help but scowl at her uninspiring reflection. Whipping the t-shirt over her head and tossing into a nearby hamper, the image staring back at her was of someone who had woken up on the wrong side of the bed. Without much in the way of boobage, and a figure that was plain-vanilla at best, the sloppy hair and wretched glower defined her way more than her body did. People rarely looked past what was visible on the outside. Maybe that was why her love life had been less than stellar. She was hardly the type to inspire great passion in a lover.

Oh, for heaven's sake, she thought. This was ridiculous. Why did everything always have to circle around to that? Couldn't she just focus on work and be content? Crying for something she'd never had, and probably didn't really exist anyway, was no way to live.

Besides, men like Draegyn were not boyfriend or husband material. He lived in a world occupied by polished, worldly-wise women. Supermodels and actresses. She'd checked him out online. If you believed everything written about him in the media, he had a sexual history as long as her arm, with a cast of glamorous, elegant females who knew how to satisfy a man like him. He was trouble with a capital T and way, way, way out of her league.

Switching on the shower and turning the temperature to sizzle, Tori stepped under the stinging spray and tried to erase these vexing thoughts from her mind. Best she remember the shit storm her life was recovering from before she did or said something stupid. Draegyn St. John might be the sexiest man alive but he was also technically her boss and a step too far down a road she best not travel. No, women like her were doomed to be sensible. Being practical and down-to-earth was her lot in life. Plain and simple.

After another busy day, Tori was home trying to relax but Jesus, her nerves were frayed. It didn't help any that she'd lost her appetite for anything except oceans of coffee and the occasional bowl of ice cream.

It had been two weeks of sheer hell at work as she tried to steer clear of Draegyn, which was no easy feat. No matter what else was going on around the compound, he found time daily to stop by and spend time with his brother. Avoiding him was impossible considering how closely she worked with Alex.

It didn't help that he was constantly goading her any time they were alone or near each other for longer than five seconds. He wanted her to lose control and throw a hissy fit. She could feel it. That was why he tried so hard to get under her skin. Unfortunately, it was working. Though she fought to remain impassive, his attitude was messing with her head. Two weeks of it had all but wiped her out.

Grabbing her cell phone, she flipped through a bunch of playlists until she found one that wouldn't make her weepy or get her all worked up. Snapping the phone into the music system dock, she adjusted the volume as a classic soft rock song came through the speakers. It was just what she needed to unwind and relax on a Friday night.

With a new group of visitors arriving on Monday for a series of training events, Family Justice was gathering for the evening in the big conference room for a movie night before things got hectic. Carmen said it was a chance for everyone to chill in advance of a busy week. She'd been invited, of course. Everyone was. But she was feeling fuzzy, tired, and vulnerable. Not a good time to be socializing.

Eyeing the stack of books on the side table, she decided against diving into one. A racy, erotic story wasn't what she needed right now. No, that wouldn't do at all. Her dreams starring the sexy secret agent were torment enough. Adding literary sexual frustration to that seemed sort of stupid.

Two glasses of wine later, she was camped out on the big comfy loveseat, long after the sunset had shifted to darkness. Tori loved the simple stillness of the desert nights. It was so quiet and calming. When one of her all-time favorite oldies started playing, she couldn't help but sing along. Maybe it was the wine, or maybe it was the long sleepless nights that filled her voice with emotion, all she knew was how the song made her feel. The emotions it was unleashing in her soul. And just like that, out of nowhere, she burst out crying. What started as a sniveling whimper quickly escalated to a full-on crying jag.

Okay. *This nonsense has gone on long enough*, Drae thought as he looked around the room filled with people and nodded his head for the hundredth time in realization that Victoria hadn't come out for the evening's get-together. He wasn't stupid. Ever since he caught her eating him alive with her eyes out by the pool, she'd been avoiding him. When it became apparent that she was going to be a no-show, his irritation level went up by degrees as the evening wore on.

He tried to ignore the heavy feeling invading his groin but the thought of Victoria and her ballsy attitude kept flitting in and out of his mind. Why his cock woke up and made an unwelcome guest appearance every damn time he thought about her, which was often, was a continuing puzzle. She just wasn't his type by any stretch of the imagination. His usual modus operandi with a beautiful woman was to imagine her naked in his bed. If his libido seemed interested, game on. With the little mouse though, picturing her naked wasn't so easy. He had no idea what kind of body lurked under the hideous clothes she wore. Confusing matters even more was her talent for making herself so bland and unremarkable as to be rendered nearly invisible.

Just about the time the group of super-heroes joined forces to defeat a movie-perfect villain, Drae threw in the towel and quietly slipped away from the group screening. He needed to find out what little miss do-gooder was up to.

There were a couple of studio-style apartments on the property where he learned Victoria had been staying. Living in town had been an option. Not everyone was a resident in the main compound, but according to Carmen, who seemed to know a little bit of everything, Victoria preferred some privacy, staying mostly to herself when not working. All signs pointed to someone who was running. Or hiding. Maybe a combination of both.

Climbing the stairs with a light tread, he arrived outside her door, tapping lightly to get her attention. When the sound of sobbing was the only indication that she was home, his gut tightened. What the hell, man? Was that her weeping for all she was worth? He tried knocking again, this time a bit harder. "Victoria. Open up."

Still nothing. *Shit*. Oh well. Resting one hand at his waist and raking the other across his head till he was gripping the back of his neck, he thought, *maybe it is best this way*. He shouldn't involve himself in whatever was fueling her tears. That was not the way he was built. When his feet started to move in retreat, he paused for half a second, long enough for her whimpering sobs to reach inside his chest and give a mighty squeeze. Reflexively, his hand tested the doorknob and finding it unlocked, gave a little shove, opening the door to the scene inside.

She was huddled in the corner of a small loveseat, arms crossed on the padded back while her head hung and shoulders visibly shook. Deep shuddering sobs wracked her body, giving the impression of a rag doll caught in the throes of overwhelming sorrow. It was too much for his brain to take in so his body took over, forcing him to move toward the despondent woman.

"Victoria?" Gulping at the ragged sound of his own voice, he had the distinct impression that the floor was falling away underneath him.

Her head jolted when he spoke. Red-rimmed eyes overflowing with tears pinned him to the spot. "Get out!" she screamed as a sob ripped from her throat.

"No," he gritted at her, surprising himself with uncharacteristic emotion clogging his voice. He gestured at her dishevelment and asked, "What's wrong?"

She scrambled off the loveseat, jumping to her feet in a tangle of shaking arms and legs. "You can't come in here!" she wailed.

While his mind analyzed her distress, taking note of every word and action, his libido fired up at the sight of her in a pair of baby-doll style pajamas that sent his pulses racing. He didn't need to wonder anymore what was under the ugly clothes.

At a little over six feet, Drae might be the smallest in stature compared to Cam's impressive height and Alex's solid build, but next to her he was a generous half-foot in height taller. The picture she presented was delightfully feminine with an added fragility from her crying jag which only added to her appeal. She had beautifully shaped legs with small feet and delicate looking ankles. Wondering what those legs would feel like wrapped around his hips and if she would dig her feet into his butt as he rode her into oblivion shouldn't have been a thought he entertained in this situation. But he did, dammit.

The cut and style of her pajama top wasn't revealing until she went to snatch a tissue from the coffee table. As she bent over, the top gaped enough for him to get a clear view of her perfect breasts. The way they swung and the modest handful in size told him they were all natural, topped with tantalizingly puckered nipples that made his mouth actually water. *Down boy, down*, he chanted silently as his cock woke up and stood at attention.

Blowing her nose with an unladylike honk and sniffling like crazy, she watched him warily while angrily scrubbing the tears from her eyes. "I said get out Draegyn. I don't want you here."

She was trying to conceal her distress with a flash of female bravado, but he wasn't fooled for a second. It wouldn't take much for the waterworks to start flowing again. "I get that Victoria, and I'll leave you to it once I know you're alright." His eyes narrowed when he spied the way her hands trembled as she twisted and crumpled the tissue she held.

Stomping her foot, she tried snarling at him, and he wondered if she realized just how adorable she looked. "I don't want any help. Leave me be," she hiccupped as fresh tears streamed down her blotchy face.

Not knowing exactly what to do, Drae's inner good-guy took control of the situation. Going to her, he grabbed hold in the same moment that he sank down onto the loveseat, effectively bringing her down onto his lap. When her perfect ass thumped against his hardness, he had to swallow quickly and shut his eyes for a second against the blazing desire that shot through him.

"Tell me what's wrong, honey," he murmured as his senses filled with an awareness of her that emptied his brain of coherent thought. She smelled like an apple orchard, and something else, a scent unique to her alone. A curtain opened inside his walled-off heart exposing a place waiting to be filled. He hadn't expected to feel the way he did with her body trembling in his arms. Holding her tight, he sat there for an eternity as she sobbed into his t-shirt. Liking the way she fit so perfectly on his lap wasn't helping any. In fact, it wasn't helping at all. He let her cry it out, running his hands up and down her back in slow strokes meant to soothe her anguish.

Speaking in a gentle voice he told her over and over that everything would be all right, although he had no idea what that meant. He just knew her tears were ripping him apart. As the crying slowed, he laid his chin against the top of her head. They fit together like puzzle pieces, and it felt oddly right. Eventually, she raised her head off his chest.

"Oh my God," she cried. "I've snotted all over your shirt!" Squirming like a fish tossed on dry land, she wiggled off his lap, diving for the box of tissues. He stood when she did, quickly adjusting his jeans when the bulge under his zipper pulsed uncomfortably.

This time when she bent over, he was treated to the sight of her bottom clad in a pair of skimpy pajama shorts, with the hint of her ass cheeks peeking out. Turning to him with a tissue to use on his shirt, an arc of electricity surged between them when her hand touched his chest. Her sweet brown eyes turned a deeper chocolate, flaring at the contact, but she didn't move away. They both stared where her small hand lay on him while his chest rose and fell with each deep breath he took. Her fingers pressed lightly on a spot just above his heart.

He growled her name in warning as the tether he kept himself on snapped. "Victoria."

She looked up at him, blinked once. And then again. When her eyes moved to his mouth and didn't look away, he felt like he was falling out a window. The final straw came when her tongue peeked out and swiped along her lips. At the delectable sight, his hardness throbbed and his heart all but thundered out of his chest. *Fuck.* He didn't hesitate, just gathered her into his arms and crashed his mouth onto hers. She opened under the onslaught, answering his desire with her own. Victoria Bennett tasted like heaven with sweet, hungry lips that eagerly devoured his. Kissing her was like nothing else he'd ever experienced.

He needed to be closer to her, wanted to feel her body arching and writhing beneath his. Putting his hands on the back of her thighs, he scooped her up into a more intimate fit while guiding her legs around his waist. Moving them to the nearest wall he slammed her against it, holding her in place, grinding his hips against her. She was like holding wildfire in his arms. Everything about their kiss was hot and over-the-fucking top in seconds. Dueling tongues invaded and swirled while sounds of their panting split the air. How long they stood there, devouring each other with a hunger that rocked his world, he couldn't tell and didn't care.

Spurred on by a fierce yearning for more, he rushed a shaking hand beneath her top to cup one of her perfect breasts. He swept his thumb repeatedly against a tight, little nipple and moaned like a dying man into her mouth. Her arms tightened around his neck and shoulders as her tongue slid against his own in slow, erotic swirls. It wasn't until the sultry scent of her arousal pierced the sex-fueled haze in his brain that he realized what they were doing. And where it was headed if he didn't put the brakes on. Fast. Wrenching his mouth from hers, he stared down at her, astonished at how quickly they'd gotten out of control.

It took a minute, with each of them sucking in oxygen, for sanity to return. She pushed against his chest, and he reluctantly eased her off his body. A deep blush accompanied the horrified look on her face. It was clear from her stunned expression that she hadn't expected something so incendiary to flare between them any more than he had. Drae reached out to swipe his thumb against her bottom lip where the telltale signs of saliva were all that remained of the deeply satisfying kiss they'd just shared. He didn't want her to put too much thought into what had exploded between them so he blurted out the first thing that came to his mind. Turned out it was the stupidest thing he could have said.

"It was just a kiss, Victoria. No big deal." Suddenly, the distinct flavor of foot-in-mouth invaded his senses. She looked at him like she'd been struck.

"Please let yourself out the same way you got in." And with that, she turned and fled to the safety of her bedroom where she slammed the door with a resounding thud. The sound of a lock turning was going to be her final statement of the night.

He stood stock still for long moments, head hanging with hands on his hips, while he struggled to find control. *No big deal? Really Drae?* He couldn't believe he'd been such an insensitive dick. Who was he trying to kid? What they just shared was wilder and hotter than any other kiss in the history of kissing. Even her tongue fit him with perfection, and what had he done? Told her it was nothing.

With retreat as his only option, Drae let himself out of her apartment, making sure to engage the lock on the door before pulling it shut behind him. A very cold shower was in his immediate future if the fire burning out of control in his pants was any indication.

TORI COULDN'T BELIEVE HOW fast she had come undone in Draegyn's arms. One second they were standing there, and the next, he had her anchored against the wall while his tongue invaded her mouth and his hips bucked against hers. She'd never, *ever* experienced anything like that before. When the insanely sexy lips she'd been staring at crashed on her own, she'd lit up like a Chinese firecracker. Feeling hot and cold at the same time, she wriggled against his solid frame trying to climb inside his skin in a need to get as close to him as humanly possible. Where had all that passion come from?

Touching swollen lips with fingers that still trembled; she tried to calm her careening emotions. No big deal indeed. Of course it was nothing to someone like him. There was enough proof to be found on the Internet of his sexual dalliances to make that statement hit home with cruelty. For a man like him, there was nothing special where her kisses were concerned. Unfortunately, the same could not be said for her. That was the very first time she'd experienced the mind-numbing desire she read about in books. Nothing she'd experienced in her pitiful, lackluster sexual history had even come close to what Draegyn St. John made her feel. She. Was. An *Idiot*. A desperate idiot if her response was any indication. He was probably laughing at her right this very minute.

Tori shuddered with embarrassment as vivid, colorful images of her climbing all over him dressed in a sleep outfit with tiny undershorts that barely covered her ass danced in her mind. Oh yeah, that and her snot and tear stained face greedily sucking on his mouth. What a splendid picture it all made. Groaning aloud, she knew the images would probably haunt her forever.

Peeking cautiously from behind the door she'd slammed in his face, Tori made sure he was gone before leaving the bedroom. The minute she stepped into the living room, her senses erupted with memories of what had taken place. He may have said it was no big deal, but even she knew a hard-on when she felt one. Especially when it had been grinding against her core while her thighs were open wide and gripping his waist. Remembering the way his warm hand had sought out her breasts and teased an aching nipple into taut attention made warmth flood between her legs. As if she weren't wet enough. He might have said it was nothing, but his body told a different story. Maybe if she had been more aggressive and taken what she'd been dreaming about they'd be in her bed right now doing a hell of a lot more than just making out.

Realizing that Draegyn must have come looking for her when she hadn't attended the movie night get-together, she wondered why he bothered. It wasn't like they'd been forming a friendship. On the contrary, she'd been avoiding him like the plague. It didn't make sense that he would even have noticed her absence. God. She really wished she had more confidence where men were concerned. Maybe she wouldn't be suffering from such a lack of experience if she'd ever managed to come out of her nerd-shell and find some hunka hunka burning love to do more than turn out the lights and see to his own gratification. She just wanted somebody to see her. She wondered if that sounded weird.

That was what all the boohooing had been about earlier. When feelings of being trapped by the past shook her, she wondered if she really was the scheming nobody the papers portrayed. Had she insinuated herself in the trappings of Wallace's lifestyle, only to turn on him when his flaws became apparent? It certainly didn't feel like the truth, but she knew that was what people thought. Hauling ass away from that life might have looked like she was running but fading into the background seemed somehow safer and easier. At least until a certain seriously hot secret agent appeared in her life.

Well, there was nothing she could do about it now. Making a total fool of herself in his arms certainly wasn't fading into the background behavior. Knowing she had to see him at work every day only made things worse. If she caught him laughing at her, why, she'd what? Smack him? Fall at his feet? Grovel for his attention? None of those scenarios held much appeal.

A symphony of sighs split the air as she climbed into her fluffy bed and flicked off the light as she tried to get comfortable. Unfortunately, her body wasn't ready to simmer down. Still keyed up, she shifted around under the sheets trying to find a cozy spot. When her mind clogged with thoughts about what it would be like to share a bed with Draegyn, she squeezed her eyes shut as lusty fantasies taunted her.

Shit and fuck. Twisting and turning she tried to settle down but all she could think about was the way her nipples still ached and stung as they rubbed against her nightclothes. What would it have been like if he'd taken one of the tender nubs into his mouth and sucked? Hard. Would he groan with delight? Would she cry out and beg for more?

"*Aaargh*," she moaned, lifting the sheet, exposing her body to the cool night air. Pounding her hands on the mattress in frustration she squinched her eyes shut even harder in a desperate attempt to banish the pulsing desire heating her body. *Please let me get some sleep.*

In the silence, Tori made out the faint snick of an old, wind-up travel clock on the bedside stand. Each tick seemed to match a rhythm in her body that was making it impossible to fall asleep. Tick. *Pulse*. Tick. *Throb*. Tick. *Surge*. Every time she shifted position, the fabric abrading her nipples was a torment. Recalling how perfectly her breast felt in Draegyn's warm hand drew an agonized croak of desire rumbling up from her melting core. The dampness between her legs was only making matters worse.

Snaking a hand across her stomach, she reached into her pajama briefs, aware all the while of the heat radiating in waves from her sex. She'd touched herself before. What woman hadn't? The thought of stopping to locate her trusty vibrator was quickly squashed. The mechanical device certainly did the job but she sometimes felt afterward as if she'd been hanging on to a belt sander. There really was such a thing as too much when it came to those battery-operated toys.

Would Draegyn be gentle or would he demand more from her than anything she'd experienced before? She shuddered at the thought. Biting her lip while exquisite tension raced through her body, she found the pulsing bundle of nerves and circled the swollen nub until her hips began moving against her fingers. Tori was crazy wet and practically at the brink. There was something decidedly wicked about how she must look. Sprawled on the bed, hand inside her pants. *Oooh*, how she wished Draegyn would reappear at this very moment and replace her trembling fingers with his. The visual of them, naked and sweaty on the bed, exploded in her brain. It wasn't more than a few seconds later when her insides tightened and clutched.

Digging her heels into the mattress, she felt the storm building. When she started to spasm, and an orgasm detonated in her body, Tori lost control, grinding her palm against her throbbing clit. She'd gone ballistic thinking about Draegyn but in the aftermath of her climax, she was left with a deep ache that a quick, self-induced orgasm wasn't going to fix. The man was like flypaper for her fantasies. *Shit.*

Drae didn't know what Victoria was up to in her small room across the compound. All he did know was that he wanted more than anything to go back and re-write the entire last scene of their kiss. Only this time he wouldn't be left standing alone while she slammed a door in his face. No, if Drae had his way, instead of once again finding himself in a hot shower with a raging hard-on, he'd be fucking the petite woman senseless. The desire to empty his balls inside her was working overtime on his composure.

He couldn't believe the way she responded. How quick she'd gone from crybaby to wanton seductress in his arms. Grinding against her open thighs had been torture and the sweetest form of arousal he could imagine. When she went wild in his embrace, he responded in likewise fashion. What was it about the woman that got him so worked up? Well, now that he'd seen her glorious body with those flawless tits and pebbled nipples, he at least had a partial answer. They fit together perfectly. She was utterly irresistible in ways he was only starting to recognize. Victoria Bennett was also big trouble.

He shouldn't have gone after her. It wasn't like him at all. Used to beautiful, savvy women who kept their emotional baggage to themselves, the deliberate emotional distance he kept meant that sex was all he had to offer. At no time could he ever recall getting involved in or giving half a shit about anyone else's personal issues. What the hell was happening to his ability to stay detached and indifferent?

His hard sex bouncing under the pounding stream of water

bewildered him. How many more times could he insist it wasn't like him at all with any kind of believability? Sighing, he realized all he had to do was conjure up the moment when he'd easily lifted her in his arms and felt those toned and fabulous legs of hers wrap tightly around his waist and he had his answer. None.

Turning under the steamy shower, he let the water cascade in endless streams while he tried to get his damn shit together. When he'd picked her up, a primitive satisfaction he'd never felt before ripped through him. Add another notation to the *not like him at all* column. Drae enjoyed all women whether one hundred and twenty pounds or two hundred and twenty. A sexy, confident woman was just that, no matter the size, but there was something about Victoria's waif-like body that turned up the heat in a big way. It hadn't been a stretch to imagine going from lifting her against his rock hard body and slamming her against a wall to having her writhing on top of him while he moved her around on his cock with his hands gripping her shaking hips. Fuck, fuck, *fuck*. These thoughts were not helping at all.

The water pouring from the showerhead turned icy when his hand shot out and turned the temperature to frigid. He'd be damned before he sank to jerking off in the fucking shower again. Goddammit! Enough was enough.

Things hadn't actually improved much by the next morning. How could they after the night he'd just had? When he awoke, his bed had been a mess after hours of tossing and turning due to the nocturnal images of wild sex scenes, all starring the delectable Victoria, which had haunted his dreams.

"Just fucking great," he grumbled out loud, tossing the

bedclothes aside while struggling to sit up, which wouldn't have been so difficult if his dick hadn't been particularly hard, and *not* in that morning wood kind of way. This was getting ridiculous. Really ridiculous. When his brain tried to slot *not like me at all* into his thoughts, he stood up bellowing at the frustration that had him in its grips, "Enough!"

He wasn't some pathetic, randy teenager who couldn't control his libido. Stomping naked from the bedroom in search of caffeine to take the edge off his pissy morning 'tude, he cataloged a dozen reasons why he shouldn't be so ruined by a spunky female who *really* wasn't his type. Slamming a mug onto the marble countertop a bit more forcefully than necessary, he reminded himself that not only had he been a hard-assed Special Forces operative with a slew of medals and commendations, but in the years since, he'd earned a solid reputation as a highly successful security professional with mad hand-to-hand skills who made the MMA dudes working the pro-circuit look like a bunch of amateurs. Truth be told, he could pretty much kick anyone's ass with one hand tied behind his back. The fucking secret service even sent recruits his way for personal, one-on-one training. Oh, that and the fact that he could shoot like nobody's business.

Doubling up on the coffee grounds he'd shoveled into the brewer, Drae kept up the personal inventory that should have made him immune to the greedy desire ripping him apart. After all, being a St. John also meant that he certainly never lacked or wanted for anything his entire life and that included eager bedmates. Money and power were powerful aphrodisiacs. Why then were his thoughts and dreams being overtaken by someone who had, until she'd lost all control in his arms, given off the distinct impression that he was about as interesting to her as the crap on the bottom of her shoes? He let his irritability have full reign as he sucked down the hot, black caffeine jolt. His thoughts turned sharply dismissive. *Fuck Victoria Bennett*, he thought. She might be hot as hell in his dreams, but she was also someone who had probably been shopping for an aristocratic lifestyle.

He was being a dick, he knew that, but if that was the shit he had to place on his emotions to keep whatever this was from continuing to chip away at his sense of control, so be it. Dumping the rest of his coffee down the sink, Drae made his way back to the bedroom so he could drag on sweats and running shoes. Time to remember who the hell he was.

Fifteen minutes later he stood at his back door, setting the timer on his watch before heading out for an uphill run that he hoped would wipe away the remnants of the previous night. Shutting the door after him with a forceful slam seemed apropos since that was exactly what he was trying to do with his wayward thoughts; slam a door on them for once and for all.

HUNCHED OVER A STACK of reports that Alex needed organized, Tori was already two hours into her workday before the boss man appeared at his regular time. He'd clearly been surprised when he found her hard at work. "Early start today, Tori?"

Shrugging, she answered with, "Yeah," sounding as tired as she felt. "These files weren't going to take care of themselves. Now seemed as good a time as any to clear some of this paperwork." Turning back to the task at hand, she ignored the quizzical look on Alex's face, and thought, *whatever*. Let him think what he wants. She had been hired to work, not to moon around, seething with desperation for an arrogant man who didn't have any emotions. Draegyn's off-handed, *no big deal*, continued to echo uncomfortably in her mind.

She'd kept her head down and nose to the proverbial grindstone all morning, an act of defiant denial that was apparent to no one but her. Alex had been off and on the phone troubleshooting some crisis while she shuffled through the endless mounds of paperwork. In this instance, she was glad her boss was a disorganized mess. Gave her something to do without having to interact with anyone. In her present frame of mind she would have struggled to be civil.

Sounds of his rising annoyance drifted in the background from time to time as the day sped by, but Tori stayed out of whatever was going on. Judging by Alex's flaring temper, something, somewhere, had gone terribly wrong. When he flung his cell away, it slid across the floor into her workspace and hit the leg of her desk with an ominous thud. *Oh shit*, she thought. Looks like I'll have to turn around and see what was going on.

Annoyed, she bent and picked up the abused phone, turning it over in her hand to see if it was broken or cracked. Only Alex would treat a piece of equipment like it was disposable. Of course, the several brand new phones she knew were in a cabinet in the office meant that this was his usual behavior. Spares were readily available for quick activation in case he snapped one in half or tossed it in the pool, as he'd done in the past. At least, that was the story Carmen told. Apparently, mild-mannered Alex could find his inner testiness fairly easy.

Warily approaching him like a caged beast, she eyed his body language for clues to what she was getting herself into. "Uh, I think you dropped something," she muttered in a barely audible voice. "Best be careful with that," she added, nodding at the phone as she dropped it onto his workbench.

When he didn't move a muscle or make a sound, retreat seemed like her best option. Before she could back away, the phone rang again. "Answer that!" he growled, shocking her into stillness. For a brief second she didn't know what to do until she saw him grip his thigh and rub. Looked like he also wasn't having the best day of his life.

Quickly pushing the call button, she answered with her very best, *'I'm the assistant, and you're not getting past me'* tone. When the call ended, she had a pretty good idea of what had caused his bad temper. A security system the agency installed in a luxe Vegas hotel casino had taken a shit overnight causing all sorts of mayhem. The hotel was gearing up for a high profile event. Having a misbehaving security set-up was creating chaos.

Quickly and efficiently sharing the details of the call with her boss, she had to choke back a hiccup of distress when he fixed her with a menacing look and barked, “Find Drae. Now!”

Oh shit. Whatever this was, it wasn’t good. Realizing she didn’t have the vaguest clue how to *find Drae* as he put it, she simply nodded at the order and hurried from the tech cave before he ate her for lunch.

Carmen or Ria would know how to locate him, she was sure of that. With the housekeeper being more of a major domo and the cook something of a gossip, both women had a finger on the pulse of everything that went on at the Villa. Finding them on the patio outside the kitchen had been the easy part. Must have been break time because they were sitting under the pergola talking quietly but stopped and looked her way as she quickly approached.

“Hi ladies,” she said with a half-smile on her face that felt forced and artificial. “Alex sent me to find Draegyn. How would I go about doing that?” They must have noticed the anxiety she hoped to conceal, giving each other a meaningful look before answering.

“Poor dear,” Ria offered. “Is he being impossible today? Don’t let it bother you. His bark is far worse than his bite.” They chuckled with clear affection for their boss.

“I think demanding is a better way of putting it, but in this case, with good reason. I really must find Draegyn. Um, Alex was most specific about locating him with emphasis on the *now*.” If the anxiety made her twist her hands together any more she was going to rub off the top layer of skin.

This time it was Carmen who answered in near-perfect English. “He’s at the newlywed’s cabin, checking on the addition. He was here less than half an hour ago. We gave him a basket of snacks for the workers.”

The cabin? Where the hell was that? She knew there were

homes further along the main drive where Draegyn and Cameron lived, but she'd never ventured that way on any of her walks. "Can you point me in the right direction?" She was starting to get frantic.

The two women both stood at the same time, waving her into the kitchen with them. "We can do better than that, honey," Ria said. Picking up a cordless phone she punched in a series of digits and handed it to Tori saying, "I dialed his cell phone. He never goes anywhere without it. If it rings through, leave a message because when he's working, his hands might not be free to answer. He'll call you right back." Reaching out, she squeezed Tori's arm and smiled, "Don't fret so! Alex can be a boob at times with that attitude of his!"

Tori nodded at the description with a weary smile as she lofted the phone next to her ear. "Thanks Ria. Carmen. I don't know what I'd do without you guys."

"What?" came a thundering bellow through the phone, shocking Tori back to the task at hand. *Oh great*, she thought. Two irritated men at the same time. Why the hell not?

Taking a deep breath for false courage she stiffened her spine and jumped in to the deep end. "Draegyn? This is Tor….uh, Victoria. Sorry to bother you, but…"

He cut off her off in mid-sentence with a brusque growl, "This better be good."

Really? That was how this was going to go? Well, someone had another thing coming if he thought she was going to cringe at his tone. Two could play that game. "I beg your pardon?" she snapped into the phone. When he paused at her incensed tone, she ran right over the hesitation with aplomb. "You will have to take up with Alex whether the interruption is worth your attention. He wants you. Now! As in right this second." She stopped long enough to take another deep breath.

"Oh, and Draegyn? This is a 'don't shoot the messenger' moment. I suggest you remember that the next time you try to bite my head off." And with that she pushed the disconnect button, quickly replacing the handset on the cradle. When she looked up there were two shocked faces looking at her. Damn. She forgot she had an audience.

Before she could make excuses for the way she'd just spoken to one of her employers, Carmen and Ria started laughing in big whoops of giggling delight. Apparently hearing her give the high and mighty Draegyn St. John his comeuppance cracked them up.

Looking around with uncertainty, Tori didn't know whether to go check if Alex had eased down off the ledge or to wait where she was for Draegyn to make an appearance. Neither option seemed all that appealing. The commonly held belief that women were the high maintenance sex was so off the mark as to be laughable! Between Alex the Bear and Draegyn the Cocky, she was pretty sure high maintenance was an understatement.

The housekeeper and cook must have sensed the way her thoughts were going, because they suggested she wander onto the patio and enjoy an ice-cold glass of lemonade while she waited.

Biding her time under the shade of the pergola as the mid-day heat gathered in intensity, she took a huge swallow of Carmen's amazing homemade lemonade, enjoying the cool liquid with a bit of tart and a jolt of smooth sweetness, as it slid down her parched throat. *Mmmmm.* Twirling the tall glass causing the ice to clink against the sides, she heard the approach of an ATV and knew the short wait for Draegyn's arrival was over.

She'd be dammed if she were going to jump up and stand at attention for the arrogant playboy just because he'd tried to intimidate her on the phone. He *seriously* had another thing coming if that was what he was assuming. She'd been browbeaten and harassed to within an inch of her sanity and come out the other end of that experience wiser and determined to never allow anyone to bully her ever again.

Projecting an air of cool civility wasn't easy, especially since her heart was beating out of her chest and a swarm of butterflies had descended into her stomach. Just as the man himself started around the corner on the far side of the patio, she quickly pushed her glasses up her nose. Looking up at his approach while jamming her unruly hair into a tight bun, she was stunned as always by his presence. He was so visually masculine, from the way he stood and held himself, to how he strode through whatever space he occupied, as if he owned it.

One of her first thoughts on meeting him had been that he looked completely normal dressed in a tuxedo. The formal attire and the mystery it evoked seemed a natural fit. Dressed like the jet-setting socialite she knew him to be, he radiated power with a touch of ruthless authority that made everyone, men and women, sit up and take notice. But today, in well-worn denims, dusty work boots, and sporting a very sexy tool belt, he was nothing short of magnificent. *Oh dear God*, she thought as a jolt of awareness followed by panic flooded her system. Why had she imagined a tuxedo would be his best look? Nothing could hold a candle to the sight of his hard-muscled body in a sweaty t-shirt stretched tight across his broad chest, tucked into a pair of jeans that somehow managed to perfectly frame what he was packing under the zipper. The tool belt only made it worse.

He looked - well, he looked smokin' hot. And she didn't just mean his temperature. This was a new side to Draegyn. One that she hadn't anticipated. He obviously was not adverse to hard, physical work and judging by the well-worn look to his boots, it was something he did a lot. He was stomping toward her, removing a pair of work gloves, with a rather stern look on a face streaked with sweat and grime.

She froze, swallowing hard, a hand tangled in her hair, while a flood of heat slammed into her. He looked a little dangerous and instead of taking his dour appearance as a warning, she felt a shocking desire to find out just how dangerous.

Draegyn was annoyed that one of Alex's temper tantrums was taking him away from the theater room project. Working with his hands was something he loved and was good at. From the first time he'd made something out of scraps of wood in a high school shop class, he'd been hooked. Designing, building, crafting – if it involved woodworking, he was the master.

When his phone rang he answered as he normally would, with an abrupt greeting that was actually a shout of annoyance. He hadn't expected to hear Victoria's voice on the other end. Barking at her came from the frustration of having to stop working at a moment when he was in the groove. He had just started to scold himself for his crappy behavior when her voice turned ice cold, and she tried handing him his rude ass on a platter. The lady had quite the mouth, and he definitely didn't want to come up against her in a verbal confrontation. She was that good.

Victoria's tone not only left him speechless it also allowed her to have the last word *and* the chance to hang up on him. He'd been churning on it the whole way here. A haughty manner was something he was familiar with and intensely disliked. Thinking she had sounded exactly like his cold-hearted mother had fueled his temper on the ride from the cabin. Typical. Just more proof that Victoria Bennett was like all the other women he'd known. Self-centered, manipulative, heartless.

When he rounded the corner from the driveway and saw her across the patio he detected a defiant bitchiness emanating from her that got his hackles up. She was pushing around that sloppy hair of hers while fearlessly staring him down. Everything about her attitude hit him like a challenge. His blood started to seethe as sparks of awareness fired off in his head. Narrowing his eyes as she turned her head to tuck the hair away, he caught a telltale flutter on her neck that let him know she wasn't as cold or bitchy as she was letting on.

Jesus. Had he actually just stumbled a bit? Already out of sorts, he continued thumping across the patio, smacking his work gloves against his thigh and quickly stuffing them in a back pocket. In just a few more steps he was standing right in front of her. Between the physical work he'd been doing all morning, the mid-day heat, and the way his temper had been boiling since she hung up on him, Drae was hot and perspiring like crazy. Without a second thought he yanked his drenched t-shirt from the damp waistband of his jeans, pulling it up his chest and over his head. Using the garment as a towel he rubbed his face against the soft cotton before using it to scrub at his neck and chest. Tossing the grimy shirt aside, he plucked his sunglasses from where they hung on his tool belt and pushed them on, all while continuing to glare at the woman who was messing with more than his schedule. Shoving his hands to his hips, he stood his ground, demanding her attention with a single word. "Well?"

His attitude suggested he not be screwed with, but the lady was trying awfully hard to appear unmoved by his king-of-the-world performance. Aside from the evidence of an accelerated heartbeat, she was cool as a cucumber and if his eyes weren't fooling him, she was also biting the inside of her mouth in what looked like an attempt not to laugh at him. He wanted to wipe that smile off her lips and kiss her into submission.

Just at that moment he felt a bead of sweat forming at the base of his throat and start to slowly move down the center of his chest. Before he could reach up and swipe it away, her eyes found the wet drop and all evidence of an impending giggle were wiped from her face. He watched her sinfully decadent brown eyes deepen in hue as they blinked a few times behind the hideous frames she wore while she studied that slow motion bead of sweat.

Two things happened simultaneously. First, he felt a slight shudder of super-focused awareness along the same path as the trickle of perspiration and second was the way his groin tightened at her gaze. It didn't escape his attention that with her sitting in one of the patio chairs and positioned as they were, his bulge was at her eye level. It was his turn to focus like a laser on her sexy mouth as his mind flooded with thoughts of how easy it would be to slide his zipper down and release his throbbing dick so she could wrap her luscious lips around his heated flesh. He was thankful to be wearing sunglasses that shielded his expression from view.

"Victoria!" he barked. "What's this all about? I really don't have time for any nonsense."

She jumped slightly at his severe tone and leapt out of her chair. Picking up a glass that looked to be full of nothing but melted ice, she quickly bit her lip and just like that, the tension between them eased off. She wasn't as sure of herself as she tried to let on and neither was he. Seems they were even on that score.

"C'mon inside and have some lemonade. You need to cool off before you talk to Alex."

"Victoria," he growled in warning.

"Oh, give it a rest," she snapped. "This is agency business and as I said before, don't shoot the messenger!" With that she turned and made for the house, managing to bump into almost every object that stood between them and the door. Watching her hasty retreat, Drae couldn't stop from noticing how her backside tightened when she was angry or the way her bland slacks didn't disguise the lean legs he knew were hidden underneath.

Since there was nothing to do but follow her inside, he was quickly on her heels before the patio door shut him out. The cool air-conditioned temperature inside the hacienda had him walking past Victoria into the mudroom behind the kitchen where he was sure to find a shirt or two hanging on the coat hooks. Tossing the sunglasses aside, he pulled an old t-shirt over his head and began making his way to Alex's tech-room.

She caught up with him and pushed an icy cold glass into his hand as she hurried along at his side. "There's a problem with one of your systems in Las Vegas. I think Alex tried to troubleshoot over the phone but got nowhere. I took a call from the security chief and gathered from what he said that the issue is critical."

Slugging back the entire glass of lemonade in one gulp and dropping the empty glass on a nearby table, he considered what she'd told him and knew right away this wasn't an ordinary temper tantrum. The Vegas casinos and hotels were some of their most fervid clients. Alex's techno-wizardry meant he could custom design systems to their exact specifications and could do so on an ever-evolving basis if necessary. The hackers trying to bypass casino security were legion. Keeping several steps ahead of them was a daunting challenge. If one of those systems was in crash and burn mode, some serious shit was probably going down.

"Um, there's something else."

He realized she'd stopped walking so he turned around. She looked all kinds of tentative as if she was unsure of herself. Normally, she was a spunky little thing so her sudden change in demeanor got his attention. It also irritated the hell out of him for no good reason. She got to him in more ways than he cared to admit.

"What? What else is there? Do me a damn favor and just tell me everything instead of…" He waved his hand at her and grimaced, searching for his next words. His annoyance couldn't overwrite the arc of sexual lightening that streaked through his system. So much for keeping his shit together. Around her it was impossible.

"Instead of what?" she snarled. "Instead of laying out the facts for you with a minimum of delay? For heaven's sake Draegyn, give me a break!" The mouth spitting furious words at him also promised erotic delight. Pouting for all she was worth, Victoria shot a dour glare his way. "Why do you have to be such a bully?"

In seconds, he'd flattened her against the nearest wall using his body to keep her in place. "You have a harsh tongue!" Lowering his head in slow motion he watched her eyes grow huge as she pressed back in withdrawal. "Perhaps, I should tame some of that sharpness."

He hovered as his words sank in. There was less than a sliver of space between them; they were close enough to feel each other's breath. She didn't move a muscle, just stood there with him looming over her. Silence reigned. After a moment he moved back but never released her eyes. She swallowed and drew a rasping breath.

After he stepped away she raised a shaking hand to push her glasses back and smooth her hair. "That wasn't necessary," she whispered.

"Oh, I think it was." A heated response to her nearness, even though she was being a wretched shrew this morning, had settled in his groin with alarming speed and strength. How he kept from tossing her over his shoulder like a caveman and dragging her off to his lair, where he could take her hard and fast, was a mystery.

Her confused, flustered expression had him shaking his head. Damn woman. She made him act in ways that surprised him. Had he tried to intimidate her physically? *Yeah*, he had. It was that smart-ass mouth of hers that pushed him to the edge. He didn't like being told off, even if there was a grain of truth to her words.

"I am *not* a bully." She raised an eyebrow at his grumpy declaration. "If I were, your panties would be down around your ankles, and I'd have you bent over the end of that bench behind us."

Victoria blanched at his words as she glanced at the bench he referred to. When she looked back his way, her cheeks were flushed pink and the chocolate eyes that had seemed so huge in her face just seconds ago, sparkled brightly. She got the message he was sending and the way she bit down on her lip told him he had rattled her cage with his frankness. Good. He was a lot of things goddammit, but a bully wasn't among them.

"Now tell what else is going on before I have to face Alex." She shook her head letting him know that yes, she would tell him everything, but it took her more than a minute to regain her composure. He had to hand it to her though, she knew when to back off and regroup.

Tori got it together and even managed to keep up with Draegyn when he continued in search of Alex. The man was just so damn frustrating! He was either needling her for no good reason or busy making her feel like a piece of furniture. Neither of those scenarios worked for her. With his bossy attitude, he'd get the facts and nothing else from her. "I believe Alex is having a bad day'" she informed him. "And before you snap at me, by bad day I mean, he's showing signs of discomfort." *Crap.* Why did she always sound so uptight when she talked to him?

His steps slowed and lines of tension formed around his mouth. There was no doubt he understood what she was trying to tell him and for just a moment she was full of concern for Alex. "He's been overdoing it," she added, looking up at him through her lashes.

It took him a few moments to meet her eyes, but he finally did when they arrived at the corridor to Alex's inner sanctum. She tried not to flinch at the stony bleakness she found in his expression. Draegyn St. John might be the most infuriatingly arrogant man to ever walk the planet, but he was also a fierce friend. His obvious concern for Alex was there for her to see. Clearly from his reaction, when Alex hurt, so did he.

His expression was open and unguarded as he bent to her saying, "Thanks for the heads up." He looked away, hesitated, and took a deep breath. "And, I apologize."

She met his steady blue-eyed gaze, crossing her arms defensively across her chest. "For?"

"I don't know what for!" he barked. "For whatever it is about me that pisses you off!"

Her chin went up. "Don't yell at me!" Damn the man.

"Woman, just take the damn apology and let it go! Not

everything needs to be picked apart and examined!"

His behavior was almost funny. It was patently clear to Tori that he wasn't the sort of man who found himself on the giving end of an apology very often. She sniffed, irritated. No doubt he was used to his every word being hung upon and never questioned. Sighing, she knew that since neither of them were naturally inclined to admit being wrong-footed, she had to be the one to break first.

"Truce?"

The gleam that suddenly appeared in his eyes matched the rush of excitement slithering along her nerve endings. When his gaze devoured her face, stopping for an eternity on her parted lips, and then continued down her throat, she inhaled raggedly. His nostrils flared as he stared at her chest as it rose and fell in short, choppy breaths.

She remembered another moment when his fingers had sought her naked flesh and how she moaned into his mouth when he touched her aching breast. The slash of color making its way across his cheekbones and his labored breathing told her he was remembering too. Surely, the world stopped spinning when his eyes returned to hers. It was the only explanation for the tilt-a-whirl her senses were experiencing.

His arrogant smile returned as a damning blush started in the soles of her feet and spread like wildfire until she was certain her face was bright red. Lifting an errant curl between his fingers he teasingly pulled on it before pushing it behind her ear. "Truce for this skirmish, Victoria." He chuckled. "The battle, however, rages on."

Whenever he was around, she felt his eyes on her. Watching, ever critical of her every word and move. Their verbal skirmishes happened by rote. He spoke, or smirked, or did something she perceived as arrogant or tyrannical, and bam, her mouth was off and running. Truth was, all he had to do was breathe, and she was a bitchy mess.

Making matters worse was the obvious physical tension

whenever they met. Just because she wasn't pretty or vivacious didn't mean she was dead inside. She'd have to be blind or insane not to be affected by those intense blue eyes, the superhero physique, or the way all the oxygen got sucked from a room when he entered. No, she was together enough to honestly admit he got her panties wet without even trying. She would have cringed at the thought if not for her sure knowledge that Mister Cool was just as affected as she was. Like all things having to do with Draegyn, even his bulge was impressive. That was no hypothetical she felt grinding against her spread legs the other night. Nope, that was one hundred percent pure, excited male.

Oh goody! She felt *soooooo* much better knowing that their tendency at every opportunity to verbally slash and burn each other was fueled by sexual awareness. That it erupted without warning was a sure-fire recipe for disaster. Just fantastic.

He stepped around her while she stood planted, immobile in the doorway to the tech room with her jaw hanging slack. Laughing was about the last thing she expected after that bold taunt, but dammit if he didn't do just that as he passed.

HUNCHED OVER A COMPUTER set-up, Alex had his back to the corner of the room where Tori lingered. Draegyn was leaning behind his friend, staring intently at whatever Alex had pulled up on the screen. She noticed his tool belt had been discarded and tossed on a countertop. Seeing him without it, from a rear vantage point, hit her like a knock-out punch. From behind, he was so mouth-wateringly sexy that it was all she could do not to walk right up and stroke her hand appreciatively along his perfect backside.

Recovering, she lifted a hand to her hair and smoothed it along the nape of her neck. Yanking down the front of her plain button-down shirt, Tori pushed the unkempt top into place and strode forward with an air of confidence that was more bravado than substance. She heard Alex muttering terse words that she hadn't been meant to hear.

"Fuck that guy, Drae. You get in there and straighten that dickhead out. Tony Barnes is seriously deluded if he thinks he can scare Justice with some lame lawyer talk. The system is fine. We have to do a reboot and a software update, maybe reconfigure the server, that kind of stuff. Your job is to get Barnes in line."

Alex noticed her presence and swiveled around in his seat fixing her with a serious stare. Tori squirmed awkwardly knowing that seconds ago she'd been smacking her lips over the ass of one Draegyn St. John, who now stood with his arms across his chest and hips resting against the console behind him. The lazy way he eyed her from the flat brown shoes peeking out from the legs of her wide trousers to the plain functional blouse up to the messy half-bun on top of her head made her skin prickle.

When he finally found her eyes, she fixed him with a look that suggested he bite her. His mouth, which had been set in a rather taut line, curled up at the corners in a mocking smirk. When she refused to back down from his ice blue glare, he flashed her a pointed look that made her think of naked bodies entwined on a large bed, sweating and slippery, sliding against each other.

Maybe wetting her lips at that moment hadn't been such a swell idea because the way his eyes narrowed as he zeroed in on the movement took away her breath. Smirk now gone, she found herself staring into the face of a hot, sexy male who was looking at her lips in a way that made her think of sliding them, slowly, along his shaft. When their eyes met she was certain he had been thinking the same thing.

"Is that okay with you, Tori? It really is the only way. I can't go and this isn't Drae's area of expertise. Besides, we need him to keep the owner calm and working with, instead of against us. We can manage any problems by video messenger."

Dammit, Alex had been talking but she wasn't listening. Wait! What did he just say? Was what okay with her? Something wasn't right. "I'm sorry. What did you say, Alex?" Tori asked. Tension filled the air as she gulped in a shaky breath while Draegyn's steely-eyed calm held her in place like a tractor beam.

She jumped when Alex slapped his hand on the console. "Are you two even listening? This is important people!" he griped.

Breathless, she tried to form a coherent reply, but Draegyn was making it difficult to concentrate. Removing her glasses with a sigh, Tori tried to play it cool. "I'll do whatever you ask, Alex. Just tell me what's needed," she declared, fixing her boss with a clear gaze and a tilted chin while ignoring the other man.

Rising from his seat Alex moved to the desk area to grab a folder. "Here. You'll need this. It's an overview of the whole system. I'll walk you through each phase."

She took the folder while confusion etched her brow. "What?"

An exasperated Alex looked like he was going to lose it. "You're going to Las Vegas, Tori. With Drae. *Tomorrow*."

As Alex's words registered, it was impossible for her to determine which of them was the most surprised or who bellowed the loudest as they shouted, "No!" in perfect unison. Drae jumped from where he'd been lounging seconds before as Tori waved her hands furiously in denial. As if on cue, they wheezed an emphatic, "No!" for a second time within a second of one another. Alex's eyebrow rose clear to his hairline at their odd behavior.

It was Draegyn who stepped into the breach, turning a stern and unwavering look at his friend. "Absolutely not, Alex."

"Stand down, man. This isn't a request, it's an order."

"You aren't the commanding officer now!" Draegyn growled, earning a surprised flinch from Victoria.

Alex nodded slightly, acknowledging the truth in his words. "You are correct. We are equals in all things Justice. But this is not negotiable. I can't go and you know why. You don't have the expertise for the hands-on part but Tori does. I don't see what the problem is." Narrowing his eyes, he looked sharply at each of them.

Drae shrugged. "I'm busy," was all he could think of to say. Victoria didn't help things when she blurted out almost the exact same words.

"Okay," Alex barked. "I don't know what the hell is going on with you two, but whatever it is, get the fuck over it!" From the corner of his eye, Drae saw Victoria swallow hard at the unexpected outburst.

This is ridiculous, he thought. Why would a Justice assignment with the little brown mouse make him react so harshly? Was it because he was careful to never mix business with pleasure and the distinction was gradually being obscured with Victoria?

At first, he hadn't thought of her as particularly sexy or even remotely attractive, certainly not in the mold of his usual type, but he had to admit that his growing reaction to her was throwing a monkey wrench into things. He shouldn't want her but he did.

Drae thought of himself as an intelligent, levelheaded guy. Drama was not in his wheelhouse. Pulling it together, he squared his shoulders. "Map this out for me, Alex. And speak English if you don't mind. None of that tech-talk shit." Moving closer to Victoria who stood frozen in place, he spared her tense face a fleeting glance. "No surprises, I'm not in the mood. Just give it to me straight."

Tori was silent as dread seeped into her nervous system one slow drip at a time. Alex and Draegyn arguing over her head made her feel like she was standing on the tracks as a freight train came barreling toward her at supersonic speed. No matter what the outcome, some sort of collision was about to happen. The suggestion that she and the bossy golden-haired Justice Brother head off together to fix an agency problem had come completely out of the blue.

Keeping her composure around Draegyn was hard enough as it was. Being thrown together with him on a twenty-four seven project was asking for trouble. The sexy arrogant man would try to dominate her every move. Why that thought had her feeling all tingly and breathless made her uncomfortable as hell. *Shit.* Focusing on the conversation he was having with Alex, she noticed the barely leashed power radiating off his hard male body. He was one notch under being openly aggressive and clearly unhappy.

Alex ran his hands back and forth across his already mussed hair and sighed. When he spoke, his tone had an edge of irritation that surprised Tori. "The man is a king-size dick, and he got what he deserved. He's using this crisis to try and stoke an old flame. Tori can do the update and reboot with her eyes closed. We both know you are the only one who can put that motherfucker in his place. You guys fly in tomorrow. I'll have Betty make all the arrangements. Two, maybe three, days tops." Turning a worried frown her way, Alex gazed at her for the longest time with an enigmatic void in his dark eyes. "I could use your help, Tori. Justice needs you."

Dammit. Her brain defaulted to idiot mode as she searched for something sensible to say. When her eyes lifted she saw Draegyn's mocking smirk and realized the jerk expected her to make a scene and bring the whole plan crashing to the ground. Something about the smug superiority on his face got to her. She might not be able to stop the train from plowing her down, but she was certainly going to derail some of his arrogance. "When do we leave?" she asked as she put her glasses back on with a butter-couldn't-melt-in-her-mouth sweetness that almost made her gag. Only the look of shocked disbelief on her nemesis' face kept her calm. *Oooh*, how she wanted to stick her tongue out at him!

With a cool expression, she turned away from both men, gathering a stack of magazines and papers to hide her trembling hands. "I'll leave you two to work out the details," she said and then fixed her boss with a perfectly blank expression. "You'll want to brief me on the system?" Acknowledging Alex's brief nod she simply melted into the shadows and made for her office.

It was there that Draegyn found her half an hour later. Time enough for her to have gotten her shaky senses locked down tight. She knew one or both of them would eventually seek her out, and no way was she going to show any weakness.

The minute the glass door swayed shut behind him, Tori felt the temperature in the confined space go up a dozen degrees. The skin on the back of her neck prickled as his icy blue gaze pinned her down. Was he mad? She couldn't tell. Reading him wasn't all that easy. While tension bracketed his mouth, he didn't seem to be directing any of it at her. And then he smiled. Sort of. Actually, it was more like a crooked grin that got her senses churning quicker than a bark of anger. *Oh dear.* Anger was one thing. That she could handle. But he seemed amused, and she sincerely hoped she wouldn't end up being the butt of the joke.

"Alex will be along in a moment. He seems to think I've been a bully toward you." Her eyes widened and mouth opened in shock. "I'm to make nice and promise to mind my manners so that's what I'm doing." Tori barely had time to recover from the *bully* word being thrown in her face when Draegyn offered up a completely disingenuous formal bow. "Miss Bennett, please accept my apology for any brutish behavior that may have offended you."

He was mocking her to her face she fumed as she opened and closed her mouth a dozen times as one pithy comeback after another threatened to roll off her tongue. "I didn't tell him, of course, being the gentleman that I am, about your predilection for shrewish comments," he murmured silkily, "or that we'd found a way to discipline that awful habit."

She stomped her foot and swung her hands onto her hips, snarling, "Oh, stuff it St. John. Someone needs to put your arrogant ass in its place."

"Oooh, such strong words from someone who was caught checking out said ass." His smug grin suggested he thought that comment would shut her up. *Hmmm*, how many ways could she prove him wrong?

Pretending to organize a stack of files, she shrugged and smiled sweetly. "Ah yes, well….who could blame me? After all, your ass is legendary. I'd have been remiss not to take advantage of the opportunity. Of course, not everything is as good in person as what one imagines."

Damn him but even that little put-down didn't so much as slow him down. "If you play nice Victoria, I'll let you get up close and personal with my legendary backside."

When she narrowed her eyes at him and blew the curl of hair hanging in front of her eyes with a heavy breath, he smiled even broader. "Men! Is that all you think about?"

Draegyn stepped quickly to her side and placed his hands on her as an arc of heat from his touch took her by surprise. "Easy," he murmured. "I didn't come in here to get you all riled up, but really woman, sometimes that attitude of yours makes it too easy."

She couldn't help herself from staring up into his face as they stood inches apart with his hands gently touching her shoulders. His thumbs were drawing lazy circles at the base of her neck causing all sorts of havoc inside her. They eyed each other for a long moment before she spoke. "Well, maybe if you didn't try to rile me up at every opportunity."

"Ah," he whispered, "but I like winding you up. Like the way your chocolate eyes shoot golden sparks when you're mad." One thumb moved from her neck to run absently along her bottom lip. An impulse as old as time made her touch the tip of her tongue to his finger. His glittering eyes turned suddenly smoky. "You will pay for that Victoria," Draegyn murmured darkly.

Deftly stepping back from the sexual heat and tension that pulsed between them, he offered a half smile that didn't quite reach his eyes. "Alex will be upon us in a few moments. He thought we needed some time to shake hands and sing a round of "Kumbaya" before finalizing the Vegas plans."

Oh crap. She'd almost forgotten what had started all this. Alex. Vegas. Draegyn and her traveling together. "I'll behave." She sighed. "If you promise to stop being such a …"

"I am not a damn bully!" he growled before she could finish. "Why does everyone want to paint me with the same brush?"

Wow. He really didn't like that expression. And especially wasn't happy that anyone saw him in that light. Apparently he had feelings just like everyone else. "Well, I was going to say stop being such a control freak." She paused for good measure. "And I'll amend what I said earlier about the bully thing. It isn't right for Alex to draw such a conclusion. I'll set him straight."

He chuckled and motioned with his head at Alex's approach. "No need to defend me, but I appreciate the sentiment. Let's just get this job done with a minimum of snark, okay?"

Tori's eyes noted Alex's slow approach, gauging how much time she had before he reached the door handle. Turning fully toward Draegyn who strategically placed himself on the other side of the cramped room, she pushed her glasses up the bridge of her nose, making specific use of her middle finger in the process. The icy sparkles in his eyes briefly exploded, letting her know he'd caught the insult. In the split seconds before Alex stepped through the door, she slapped a fake smile on her face. Through lips forming a friendly smile she growled, "Eat me, St. John."

She hadn't expected the intentionally snarky retort to bring him snapping upright and moving toward her so swiftly that she actually squealed in alarm. Panicked, she dropped onto a tall, high backed stool and tried to swing away from his approach. He didn't stop her, in fact, crowding her from behind was just as devastating to her senses as if they'd been face-to-face. She could feel his breath on her neck as the familiar whoosh that signaled the opening of the office door gave her some sense of relief.

"That's two, Victoria," he murmured deep and hushed so that no one else could hear. Her startled gasp let him know she remembered how he'd warned her after she licked his finger. That he'd make her pay. The fog of sexual awareness that surrounded and penetrated her made her heart feel like it was going to thump right out of her chest. Alex, who as usual had been talking out loud as he entered, was caught in muddled professor mode and thankfully didn't pick up on the tension in the room.

Tossing a mass of papers in front of Tori, Alex prattled on as if they'd all spent the last twenty minutes yakking it up. She knew that was his way. He had a way of spontaneous communication that felt like every conversation began and ended in the middle. Usually, she had to grasp at straws to figure out what the hell he was talking about until a focus became clear. Turning her full attention to her boss, she tried to disconnect from the confusing signals Draegyn was sending.

A good hour and a half later, the three of them had brainstormed a step-by-step plan to deal with the crisis in Vegas. At some point in the discussion, Ria had appeared, pushing a kitchen trolley loaded with snacks and a large carafe of steaming coffee. They worked well together, once they put their minds to it, even stretching out the kinks and reaching for something to munch on at the same time.

Tori pulled her knees up on the rungs of the tall stool and poured over a series of schematics with a mug clutched in both hands. At times, coffee was her salvation and not due to the energizing effect people craved it for. Truth was, most of her favorite java blends were decaf anyway. No, Tori liked the whole sensory experience from the pungent earthy aroma of the coffee grounds to the way a hot mug felt in her grasp. Those first sips of a fresh brew on her lips always brought a wonderful sense of satisfaction. A good cup of Joe was also a touchstone, something concrete that her analytical mind could attach to. She did some of her best thinking with a mug nearby. Right now, it was helping her stay focused on the task at hand and the incredible degree of trust that Alex was placing in her to save the agency's ass.

Mr. Double-O-Trouble had been surprisingly accepting of her role and even deferred to her once or twice when the subject was heavily technical. Perhaps Draegyn didn't actually dislike her as much as his arrogantly superior attitude suggested. He was talking quietly to Alex, both of them with smartphones in hand, tapping away. *I can do this*, Tori thought as her inner cheerleader made an appearance. She could step out of the shadows where she'd been hiding. There was no doubt in her mind that she could handle the technical aspect of the assignment. After all, with her background and experience, she might even be able to best Alex in a couple of years. She understood the way his systems were designed.

Alex was studying her intently. Suddenly looking as if he was seeing her for the first time, he said, "Wear something like that outfit you had on for our interview. You'll be representing the agency Tori. If you need or want anything, let us know, and we'll get you set up."

Drae picked up on a change in atmosphere the moment Alex mentioned Victoria's clothes. God, what she wore was so boring and predictable, as if they came from the, *Take Me Seriously I'm a Professional Catalog.* What could she possibly have that would make her seem even a tad less wonky? He didn't understand why women, especially the one perched on the stool with the chocolate eyes and sulky mouth, felt the need to dress like men in the business world.

Eyeing Victoria's reaction, he noted her quick nod followed by the way she bit her lip at Alex's declaration that he'd set her up with anything she needed. Maybe there was an opportunity to update the brown mouse's wardrobe. Well, the whole trip would be worth it to see her dressed like a damn female for a change.

"Betty already made the travel arrangements. You fly out tomorrow morning on the Gulfstream. Quick flight to Las Vegas. She got you situated in a two bedroom suite," Alex said pointedly while directing his comment to Victoria. "Things are crazy there right now with the awards event this weekend so that's the only option."

Drae chimed in. "It's fine, Alex." She watched him shrug off the glaring eyeball his friend shot his way. "Relax, man. Victoria and I have this. *Right*?" Lobbing the ball into her court, he waited for a response.

Sighing, Tori considered what strange creatures men were. On the one hand, there was Alex, her boss. He was obviously concerned about how she felt. The other one, not so much. It wasn't that she minded sharing a suite with him, but rather that his tone suggested he didn't care one way or the other. A moment of panic upset her equilibrium as she wondered if his reluctance was due to her presence cramping his style. Maybe the bonus for a trip to Sin City was a little showgirl action for the sexy Draegyn St. John. The thought made her stomach lurch. Just because he made her think deep, dark thoughts about things, *intimate things* that had nothing to do with business, it didn't mean she was going to play second fiddle to his overactive sex drive.

Maybe it was time to cast aside the dowdy costume she'd been clinging to and start living as a functioning female again. A plan was developing in her mind that would give Draegyn, and everyone else for the matter, something to think about.

Sliding from her stool, she smoothed the hair tumbling into her field of vision and began to wrap up their meeting. "It's all good gentlemen. Don't worry about me. I'll be ready on time," she mumbled in Draegyn's direction. "And Alex, if you would email me the last code sequence we went over, that would be helpful." Checking her watch she was shocked to see that it was well past dinnertime and probably already dark. She had to get moving if her plan was going to work out, so Tori gathered a pile of folders and print-outs and raced for the door. Turning for one last time she acknowledged both men with a curt nod, mumbled, "Night," and left before anyone could say anything else.

"Dude!" Alex barked, clearly not pleased. "What the fuck was that all about? God dammit Drae. I told you to watch yourself around Tori. Why do I get the impression you two are rock 'em sock 'em robots when nobody's watching?"

Drae eased against a table and crossed his arms across his chest as his gaze lingered on the spot Victoria had just vacated. He didn't want to get Alex's temper up and thought he'd done a pretty damn good show of acting like a perfectly reasonable guy around the man's assistant. Obviously, he'd underestimated Alex's powers of perception. The darkening cloud on his friend's face let him know that beating around the bush wasn't going to help.

With a crooked grin he rolled a shoulder and leaned back, fixing his stare on the ceiling. "She makes me crazy," was all he said. Looking back at Alex, he saw him weigh what he'd been told with a series of short, quick nods. "I know you seem to think she's god's gift to nerds but all I get from her is a smart-ass mouth and an attitude to go with it."

"Are you saying she doesn't like you? Shit! That has to be a first." Alex chuckled.

Drae couldn't help but share in the laugh. Everyone's belief that there wasn't a woman alive whose panties he couldn't steal made admitting that Victoria cast him with a jaded eye a huge admission. "If you ask Carmen or Ria I'm sure you'll learn that your spitfire assistant quite literally ignores me completely or tries to hand me my ass on a platter every damn time we meet. I've no doubt it's the talk of the Villa!"

Alex roared with laughter at that. Drae had to admit it really was kind of funny. He wasn't the sort of man that people crossed. Not if you had a brain. Hell, he couldn't recall anyone ever being foolish enough to spar with him for no good reason. Victoria Bennett, however, sailed right past his *don't fuck with me* attitude and needled him at every opportunity.

"Give her a chance, Drae. This isn't about you. Try and remember that when you're dealing with that asshole Barnes. Your job is to keep him away from her so she can focus on the job she's been sent to do." Eyeing Drae with a look he'd never seen before, Alex finished, "And maybe you should consider staying away from her as well. She's not built to handle your unique brand of bullshit."

"Understood," he replied with a frown. What else was there to say?

LETTING HER DAMP HAIR loose from the towel wrapped around her head, Tori chucked the wet flannel onto the floor and turned her attention to the reflection in the mirror. Checking the time, she noted the early hour and breathed a sigh of relief. It had been awhile since she'd tackled a dressed to shoes morning routine that involved anything more than a face wash and some hastily pulled on clothes.

A satchel of grooming tools and makeup pouches she'd pulled from the closet sat next to her on the bathroom floor. She'd gotten up super early to allow plenty of time for a long shower so she could shave her legs and do a quick facial. After that had come a necessary coffee jolt followed by the best mani-pedi she could manage by herself. Just because she wasn't classically beautiful like her gorgeous mother didn't mean that she didn't know all these beauty routines by rote. She was a woman after all.

Getting her sloppy head of hair under control was next up on the agenda so she grabbed a hair dryer, straightener, and a couple of spray bottles to help the transition from flyaway mess to perfectly groomed. It took a while and tested her calm as she painstakingly blew out each section of hair until her reflection showed the shoulder length mane tamed into submission with the extra assistance of the flat iron. After that it took a few tries before she managed a backswept chignon with just enough poof on top for wispy bangs that softened what would otherwise be a severe look.

Using an old trick she learned from her mother, Tori snapped a quick pic with her phone of the back and sides of her self-styled hairdo to make sure it looked good from every angle. Satisfied, she laid out the contents of the makeup pouches and considered the best way to proceed. Glancing in the mirror at the outfit hanging on the hook behind her, she was pleased with the daytime attire and accessories that she'd chosen. When Alex suggested she wear the ensemble he remembered from her interview, she knew he was telling her to drop the dull wardrobe she'd been wallowing in.

Relying on a minimum amount of makeup, it didn't take her long to apply to her face. After that came some seriously feminine lingerie. There was something about the sheer lace bra with the equally sheer thong that made her feel naughty even though the in-your-face appeal of the sexy lace was lost on her unremarkable figure. Ah well, there was no use in crying over something that couldn't be helped. Wishing for voluptuous breasts and a curvy ass wasn't going to change what nature had given her.

Dancing through a perfume cloud, Tori let the scent seep into her senses. It was light and airy, with an undertone of vanilla that suited her. She preferred something subtle to the harsh, cloying perfumes that lingered in the air way too long. By the time she'd pulled on the sleeveless dress and soft cashmere sweater, her nerves were starting to unravel. "Keep breathing. Just keep breathing," she muttered aloud. Coming out of her self-imposed brown shell was harder than she thought it would be. She felt awkward and exposed without the predictably bland head to toe uniform.

The beautiful dress she chose was a mid-tone fawn shade that suited her coloring and fit like a glove. Stopping well north of her knees, the simple sheath transformed once she donned the coordinating sage green cashmere sweater that cinched at her waist with a gold metal belt. Pushing the sleeves back she added a matching gold bangle bracelet and delicate hoops at her ears. Slipping into a pair of neutral colored platform pumps, Tori checked out her reflection from every possible angle. All in all, she liked the look. It was young, had a designer label, was the right color and silhouette, and most importantly, was the last thing anyone expected her to be wearing. Game on!

Toot, toot! The jarring beep from the horn of the ride sent to fetch her to the carport startled Tori as she rushed to gather some last second items that she feverishly shoved into her luggage. With one last look in the mirror, she swung a garment bag over her arm, yanked up the handle of her rolling bag, and headed down to meet her ride. Striding with determination, she pushed down the anxiety that popped up, pulling her suitcase with more force than necessary, and came to a stuttering halt at the colorful scene waiting at the end of the ramp that led from her apartment.

It was Betty behind the wheel of her kooky, golf-style cart with a neon-striped awning and fluffy pink seat covers waiting to give her a lift to the carport. The Justice Brothers had gifted their office manager with the elaborate cart when she returned from an extended leave. From the moment she'd been given the keys, Betty had taken enormous delight in zipping all around the compound at every opportunity. Tori smiled at the over-the-top ride.

The look of pure shock on the older woman's face when Tori marched down the ramp in her fashionable outfit with the platform pumps was almost worth the hours of preparation she'd gone through. "Cooey! Look at you little missy!" Betty cried out, clapping her hands in delight. "Oh my lord, Tori! Is that you?" she added with an amused smile that let Tori know her transformation would not go unnoticed. "Talk about hiding your lamp under a bushel! Honey, don't you ever go back to what you've been wearing. Seeing you like this, well - it's amazing!"

After helping Tori stow her bags in the back of the cart, Betty grabbed her by the hand and swung her around in a square dance move that made them both giggle. "Why sugar," she drawled in her perfect southern belle way, "I'd say there's a man about to eat his shirt if I'm not mistaken." The look of approval shining from the woman's eyes gave Tori's confidence an extra boost. It also gave her a second's pause.

"Alex asked me to dress the part. That's all."

Laughing as they settled into the cart for the short drive across the compound, Betty shot her a sardonic look. "Oh, don't play that with me Tori. I'm not blind, y'know. Poor Draegyn won't know what hit him!" the woman shrieked with unabashed glee. Tori squirmed knowing the office manager had seen the way she and that blond devil went at each other every chance they got. Wiping the cool, controlled smile off his handsome face had been the motivator behind todays' shock value makeover. Betty apparently put the pieces together in correct order.

Draegyn paced back and forth along the short drive as he waited for Victoria's arrival. They weren't on a rigid schedule since they were flying in the company plane but even so, he was anxious to get moving. Dammit. Why were women always late?

Ben was fussing in the trunk, making room for Victoria's bags, when the Betty Buggy came tearing up the drive, stopping on the far side of the car. The open trunk obscured his view, but he heard murmured greetings being exchanged followed by Betty's full-throated laughter. *Well, at least someone is in a good mood,* he groused.

Drae's impatience got the better of him as he skirted around the back end of the car, his forward movement stumbling to an awkward halt the moment he saw Victoria. Shock. Pure, libidinous amazement knocked him sideways at the sight of her dressed in a very smart outfit and wearing the sort of heels that drew a man's eyes. Jesus, she looked so perfectly *female*.

At first glance, with her back still to him, he was overwhelmed by her altered appearance and let his mouth drop and eyes widen from the surprise. Holy shit, talk about a complete transformation! She had gone for the gold and to say he was impressed with her efforts was a pathetic understatement. If anything, the way his balls tightened and his dick grew firm from a simple glance went way beyond just *impressed.*

He realized he must have stood there, staring like an idiot, for far too long when the trio went silent and turned his way. There was not a doubt in his mind that he'd been caught slack-jawed from the mocking expressions he noted coming his way from Ben and Betty. Judging from their smirks, they both were very much enjoying watching him flounder as he searched for his equilibrium.

Feeling her eyes on him, he nonetheless took his time about checking out every inch of this new Victoria, from her feet in the ridiculously high shoes upward. His throat turned raw and dry at the sight of her delicate ankles and toned legs with smooth calves and shapely thighs that melted his brain. Remembering how those beautiful legs felt wrapped around his middle made controlling his body's super-heated reaction unbelievably difficult.

She was standing holding her bag in one hand with the other propped on her hip. It was the way she stood with her legs on view in the short dress as she cocked one leg slightly inward in an innocently naughty way that rocked him hard. He sensed the challenge in her posture and felt a surge of good, old-fashioned lust. The lady wasn't going down without a fight, and he had to hand it to her, because she definitely scored big in round one. The thought turned up the heat in his response.

By the time his gaze lifted to her face, he had subjected her to a torturously slow appraisal that left a riot of pink on her cheeks. *Good. Serves her right*, he thought. She showed balls trying to flat-foot him in front of witnesses, although the mere fact that she tried excited him. Suddenly, his non-interest in the quirky Victoria Bennett flared into a full-fledged sexual bonfire.

He continued peering over the top of sunglasses that slid down to reveal his eyes, taking in every detail of the lady's appearance when Ben finally broke the silence. "She sure is a looker, isn't she, Mister Drae?" *Fuck my life,* he silently answered. Yes, she sure as hell was. Victoria shifted uneasily in a way that let him know she wasn't entirely sure of herself.

"Victoria," he murmured, moving forward on feet that had turned clumsy. "You look lovely." When a tiny smile lit up her face, his heart knocked forcefully against his ribcage. Swallowing the dryness in his throat, Drae reached for the hand she held at her waist, enclosing her cold fingers in his and gently squeezed. Luckily, his action brought her sexy brown eyes swinging to his. She was so damn pretty with her hair done in a perfect bun low on her neck. If they didn't have an audience he would have taken advantage of her sweet, kissable lips to let her know just how beautiful she was.

Tori's blush started in the fire raging between her legs, spreading upward across her belly, singeing her breasts, before blooming on her face. Feeling like a bug under a microscope with people watching the interplay between her and Draegyn, she found herself rethinking the wisdom of playing this moment out in public. She felt his shock – it slammed into her full force during the visual inspection he subjected her to. She'd expected him to be surprised, but she hadn't anticipated the heated silence, or the way she had to fight back the urge to giggle like a swooning schoolgirl at the approval glittering in his gaze.

When he enclosed her hand in his, she felt tiny and small in his overpowering presence, a thought that spread warmth deep into her bones. She was shocked at the realization that he saw her as a woman. Not just a brain on two legs. She bit down on her lower lip to keep the treacherous sigh she felt from escaping as he increased the pressure of his touch until she looked up at him. There was a roaring sound inside her head, like what she imagined an avalanche sounded like. Starting off a low rumble in the distance, building intensity and strength until the booming sound became a shockwave of sensory input. He was staring at her mouth, and this time she knew, without any doubt, that he wanted to kiss her. And heaven help her, she wanted him to. She was in trouble. Big time.

A warm smile softened Draegyn's face, probably because he could read her thoughts. Pulling on her hand slightly she had to step into him to keep her balance. Tori couldn't help the unladylike snort of startled laughter that split the air after he leaned close to deliver a taunt with heated breath close to her exposed ear and neck. "Truce derailed, Victoria," he murmured. God, she really liked the way her full name rolled off his tongue. "But you've won the first encounter, milady."

That was all they had time for as Ben cleared his throat to remind them that they had a schedule to keep. Tori felt like she was walking on air as she hurried to the car door that Betty was holding open for her. "Way to go, sugar," the woman teased quietly as she helped Tori settle into the back seat of the big car. All she could do was smile. Seconds later she felt the trunk shut with a determined thud before Draegyn eased into the seat next to her.

She inquired how long the trip to the airport would take and was impressed by how calm her voice sounded. Tori wanted to to settle back in her seat and just drink in the sight of him. He always looked magnificent and so totally male whether in a tuxedo or old, worn jeans. Today, in his grey business suit he looked, well - he looked yummy. Nothing could disguise the confident way he moved and commanded everything and everyone around him and in the confines of the car she was supremely aware of every damn breath he took and movement he made, no matter how small.

Hearing the question, he turned and looked at her. At least, she thought he looked at her but who could tell with those blasted dark shades? That was just one of the problems she had with being in close proximity with him. He was so guarded and closed off that she didn't have enough data to form a full picture of who she was dealing with. The dark glasses that kept his eyes closed to her viewing left her feeling unsteady. Since she couldn't read his eyes, Tori was left to contemplate the mouth beneath the glasses. The line of his humorless expression was unyielding but it was his full, wide bottom lip that occupied her thoughts. Perfect to the point of being indecent, she stared, remembering having nipped the lush flesh and sucking it into her mouth. The echo of his groaned response as it reverberated in her memory nearly drowned out Draegyn's answer to her question.

"It's early enough that there won't be much traffic. If that's the case, we should arrive at the hangar in thirty minutes." He leaned toward her as he looked out her window. After a moment he straightened in slow motion and Tori could swear she heard him inhale deeply. When he lingered she almost jumped in his lap.

"I expect we're looking at wheels up about fifteen minutes after boarding. The flight to Vegas only takes an hour. Are you okay flying, Victoria? I assure you the agency aircraft is quite comfortable, and our flight crews are top notch." Even with the dark glasses concealing his eyes she could feel genuine concern.

Turning to the desert landscape passing by because she just couldn't look at him anymore and keep her dignity intact, Tori smoothed down her dress where it stretched across her thighs trying to distract from the way her knees pressed together each time he spoke. Alone as they were and seated so close together, her body reacted to the deep timbre of his voice like a plant desperate for water. The low throb coming from her womb mirrored the rhythm of his speech as moisture drenched her tiny panties. *Concentrate!*

"Actually, I've had my own air mileage account since I was a college student so you don't have to worry about me white knuckling the takeoff. This will be my first time though."

She bit back a laugh when he pulled off the dark glasses to reveal eyebrows shot straight to his hairline. "We're in virgin territory?" he mocked with a lazy smile.

She reached out and impulsively smacked a palm against his thigh as she giggled and elbowed his big body playfully. "Behave Draegyn!" she laughed. "I meant my first time on a private plane, but I suppose that, yes. *Yes,* we're in virgin territory!"

He laughed along with her, rubbing his hands together with gleeful intent. Snapping his finger for emphasis he grinned like the devil he was, declaring, "Now that's what I'm talking about! *Finally!* A virgin to sacrifice."

"The only thing you're going to be sacrificing, mister, is your dignity if you keep this up, so yuk away while you can. I'll be over here plotting ways to get you back."

"Ah. Feel free to plot away woman. And for the record, you only get this one Miss Bennett," he teased. "I won't underestimate you again." She beamed at his admission. "But if I recall, the count is currently two to nothing on the payback list."

The lighthearted banter came so easily. Something significant had changed in their relationship, or maybe it had been shifting all along. She still wanted to smack the overconfident grin from the man's face but less and less was it about him and more about her. She had leveled the playing field by putting on her big girl panties and getting rid of her costume and mask.

"Hmmm," he murmured, narrowed eyes fixated on her face. "Something's different. Wait a minute," he growled. "Where are your glasses?" he demanded. "Oh my God, woman!" he barked. "You don't even need them, do you?"

Oh, come on, she thought. Was he reading my thoughts now? Had he somehow picked up on her silent admission that she didn't need the props anymore? Before she could come back with a reply that didn't make her sound like an idiot, he tapped her lightly on the bridge of her nose, the exact spot where her glasses usually sat. With a tone as serious as a heart attack he told her, "You are a fraud Victoria Bennett. "

She must have looked like a guppy as she sat there opening and closing her mouth over and over while no sound came out. Dammit. He was right. She *was* a fraud. Hiding away had been the coward's choice until a certain blond-haired devil appeared and reawakened her fighting spirit. It was no exaggeration to say she wouldn't be sitting there, dressed as she was, if he hadn't challenged her.

"I'm going to enjoy finding out who you really are, Victoria," he whispered. And just like that, her knees squeezed together again.

THEY WERE SET TO land at an airstrip catering to the private planes flying in and out of Las Vegas after just over an hour of flight time. For once, Drae regretted the short trip because nothing pleased him more than spending time with Victoria. He thought, quite impossibly, they might at the very least become friends.

This two-point-zero version of the mousey little woman, who'd been getting under his skin from their first words, was nothing short of charming. Hell, he thought, they could have flown through the eye of a hurricane, and he would barely have noticed. Drae nearly vapor-locked when he followed her into the plane, up a short flight of stairs that put him face to face with her tight little ass in the seriously short dress. He'd barely had time to recover. The picture she made, sitting opposite him, was female perfection. Crossing her legs pushed the skirt higher than she was comfortable with giving him a satisfying opportunity to sit back and watch her wiggle about, tugging down the dress's hem. Even their conversation had been like nothing he'd experienced before. Ordinarily, he didn't open up or explain anything to anybody. With Victoria, he found himself yammering on like a talk-show host.

Once they were in the air she took him by surprise blurting out, "Explain why Alex kept saying he couldn't go to Vegas. He put so much emphasis on the *couldn't* that it was kind of hard to ignore what was unspoken. You don't have to tell me," she quickly added. "I am the last person wanting to poke around in someone's private life," she assured him. "But I thought it might be helpful to understand the subtext."

When she asked, he took a minute to loosen his tie and unhook the top button of his dress shirt. The story was Alex's to tell but he supposed a Reader's Digest version couldn't hurt.

"No, you're right. There is a story, and believe me, Alex wishes there wasn't. He has a history with the casino owner we're going to meet. The guy's name is Anthony Barnes. He's a weasel, but that's beside the point. Couple of years ago, Alex was involved with a woman in Sedona. They'd been casually dating for several months when out of the blue an estranged husband appeared on the scene."

"Casually hanging out or casually hooking up?"

"Mmm, I really don't know. Maybe both." He shrugged. "It's hard to read him sometimes. In either case, it was uncomfortable so he tried to distance himself from the situation. After everything he's been through, Alex has a low tolerance for drama."

Victoria frowned at him. "That's what the messy hair is about, isn't it? I noticed he rubs at his head when people are being idiots."

Drae nodded. "That's very perceptive of you. It's his tell, if you know what I mean." Laughing he added, "We don't let him play poker anymore because of it! That's the reason behind Betty's crazy cart. She got him going over something dumb that his superior intellect just couldn't fathom. He lost a bet with her 'cause she could read him like a how-to manual. Next thing anyone knew, she was grinning like a Cheshire cat while zipping around the compound in that ridiculous buggy. Just to needle him over the lost bet she pressed for a classic surrey with the fringe on top model. When the cart was delivered, we all laughed so hard I thought he was going to blow a gasket!"

"He has a scary temper at times," she said with mock solemnity.

"Yes, he does," Drae agreed in the same tone. "And that's why the Tony Barnes drama got so messy. Even though Alex tried to stay out of whatever went down, Barnes went out of his way to insinuate that Alex had stolen his wife. How you steal something that you don't have to begin with is something of a mystery. Obviously the marriage had broken down or the woman wouldn't have been living on her own in Arizona. In the end, there was an ugly confrontation. Alex took as much as he could and then morphed into the incredible hulk. Some punches were thrown. A shit-ton of yelling and threats flew. Finally, Alex walloped Barnes and broke his jaw. From that moment on, the two have been at each other every time they meet."

"I'm surprised that Tony Barnes would let Justice anywhere near his security set-up. With that kind of animosity it can't be pleasant doing business with him."

Drae snorted. "Barnes may be a prick, but he isn't stupid. He wanted the best, and for that, there's only Justice."

"I see," she offered quietly. "Alex told you to keep him away from me. What did he mean by that? Is the guy still married? What became of the woman Alex was involved with?"

He almost laughed. She tossed out questions like a seasoned prosecutor. Direct and to the point.

"I don't know what became of the woman or if he's still married although somehow I doubt it. As for keeping him away from you, that's just Alex being big daddy. My job is to manage Tony Barnes. Part of that involves making sure he doesn't try to even the score. If he messes with you, just let me know, and I'll handle it."

She swung the foot crossed over her leg and fixed him with a stern look. "In case you hadn't noticed, I can take care of myself, thank you very much."

"That may be but know this," Drae growled. "I protect what's important, and right now, that would be you."

The foot stopped shaking at his declaration and the "Oh" that she muttered hung in the air for long moments.

As if the short flight into Vegas aboard the private jet wasn't eye-opening enough, the moment they arrived at their destination, Tori was treated to an up close view of what it was like to be treated like a VIP. It hadn't taken long to understand that Draegyn St. John didn't have to snap his fingers to get something done. No, the world he lived in revolved around seeing to his unspoken needs in an invisible but powerfully intoxicating way that had her sitting up and taking notice.

With Wallace, all that deference was the result of having been born to title in a culture that catered to its aristocracy whether they earned it or not. People had rushed to protect and vindicate his immoral behavior without conscience just because he was an Earl. His brand of conceit was the sort born of entitlement, of feeling that he was somehow better than the common man.

Draegyn on the other hand wielded an authority that emanated from his DNA. It was part of his emotional makeup and not because he was born to it. She wondered if it was the result of so many years in the military. There was a precision to everything he did, whether adjusting the cuffs of his shirt as he stood buttoning his suit jacket or his posture as he relaxed.

She was mostly silent, taking in the rush of activity that greeted them. Before the plane even came to a halt, someone from the flight crew had briefed Draegyn on the arrangements for their return. A personal assistant from the casino had been sent to see to their every need. Tori was impressed with how adroitly he managed the endless flow of information and people that came across his radar. Peering from the open door she spied a big black limousine waiting on the tarmac to whisk them off to their hotel.

He made sure to formally introduce her as his associate, ensuring that she would be treated accordingly. At every turn there were people taking care of the details meaning she didn't have to see to her carry-on or do anything more strenuous than carry her purse. The ballet of deference shown to him was eye opening and a little exciting. She'd been momentarily stunned when he offered her his arm after descending the steps of the plane, but she'd been quick to slide her hand where he indicated. She'd been even more surprised when he covered her small hand with his much bigger one in a way that seemed possessive. The quiet thrill twinkling along her nerve endings lasted until an employee from the hotel, who was waiting for them by the car, cast her a dismissive glare seconds before she rather pointedly checked out the man at her side in a head to toe inspection that was a bit too brazen for Tori's liking.

He didn't seem to notice, which was a good thing, because she was thrown off by the sudden flare of jealousy that stiffened her spine. Explaining her reaction would not have been easy especially since she couldn't defend it to herself. He was technically one of her employers. She worked for the man and had no business letting female inclinations cloud the air. She was on his arm because of business. Period.

That didn't stop Tori from fixing the unctuous woman ogling Draegyn with an incendiary glare that she noted with satisfaction hit dead-on when the woman found some sense and backed off with haste. It helped that he had been the picture of a gentleman, assisting her being seated in the car and seeing to her every comfort before taking the seat beside her. She was feeling rather smug and full of herself for so neatly having warned off the big-boobed female with just a look. Her days of being minimized and glossed over were through. For all that woman knew she and Draegyn were an item. They might just be business associates, but that didn't mean she was invisible.

Why the hell is my skirt so damn short, she wondered, irritated that she had to keep smoothing it over her thighs unless she wanted to show more leg than was prudent. As she wiggled trying to adjust her dress, she was aware that Draegyn's eyes were watching her every move.

"Enjoying the show?" she breathlessly bit out once her legs were adequately covered, and she'd settled back in the seat. His eyes glittered with what she hoped was appreciation, but it was so hard to tell with him. "I'm out of practice with all this girly stuff."

He smiled into her eyes and laughed. "You look lovely Victoria, as I've already said. Stop fishing for compliments."

Outraged, she gasped at his comment and spit out the first thing that came to mind. "I am *so* not fishing for compliments!"

That had him laughing even more. "You're so easy to wind up! That smart mouth is going to get you in trouble some day. Relax, I was *trying* to yank your chain woman!"

God, men were dense at times. "Oh. Well, you succeeded," she sniffed dismissively. "Maybe you could use a signal to let me know when you're being an ass so I don't have to play into your hand each time." The one finger salute he swiftly gave in response to her suggestion had her choking back a wicked snicker.

"Will that one do?" he asked with mock lechery that forced the laugh.

"Oh, shut up!" She grinned at him, biting the inside of her cheek to keep from dissolving in a fit of giggles.

"Thank you," he muttered softly into her smiling expression.

"For what?"

He propped his torso on the armrest separating their seats and leaned into her, wiping the smile from her lips, and making her eyes widen. "For saving me from being swallowed whole by that set of fake fun bags who met the plane."

"I don't know what you're talking about."

"Nice try. You know exactly what I'm talking about," he teased. "You stopped her dead with nothing more than a look. I'm impressed." When she didn't answer, he chuckled softly and made like he intended to tickle her. "Paybacks are a bitch!" he warned which triggered a blast of laughter from both of them as she playfully slapped his hands away and suggested he mind his damn manners.

Draegyn was enjoying himself. This gentler, less snarky person kept surprising him at every turn. The way she put the double D woman on blast with a dark look had intrigued him and re-ignited the heat growing in his groin. Maybe these couple of days working together wouldn't be such a hardship after all.

Their limousine bypassed the busy, brightly lit entrance to the hotel casino and pulled in to a secured area reserved for VIPs. As if on cue, just as the car stopped, both their cell phones went off. Drae's gaze dropped to the incoming info and muttered, "Barnes," as Victoria sighed, clicked the talk button, mouthing *Alex* a second before answering her call. He and Victoria exited their car and made their way inside the building to a bank of elevators, while each of them conducted phone business.

Once in the elevator he turned and told her they would stop briefly in their suite to make sure everything was in order and then immediately head off to the hotel's operations center. As he was speaking, Drae caught their reflection in the highly polished steel panels of the elevator's interior. She was looking up at him with her head tilted back, both hands resting in the small of her back. He watched as the purse she clutched by a golden chain, sway against the back of her legs.

His part of the reflection showed him leaning in close, almost looming over her, even though the added inches from her heels brought her closer to eye-level. He watched as her chest rose and fell quickly, bringing her breasts surging close to him with each rapid inhale. A few strands had escaped the hair gathered at the nape of her neck, making loose tendrils of brown mixed with muted gold highlights frame her face. His words halted and thoughts shut down on the vision forming in his mind of sliding his hands up her neck and into her hair, releasing the locks and spreading them over her shoulders. With his fingers planted firmly in her hair he could angle her head just so as his mouth leaned the rest of the way in to feast on her tempting lips.

A pithy swear word erupted in his overactive brain making him jerk suddenly upright, away from the insane temptation that was Victoria Bennett. Now that they weren't hissing and snarling at each other, their dynamic had turned blatantly sensual. Somehow the little brown mouse had become a desirable, although surprisingly innocent, temptress who no longer fit into the mold of avaricious female that was his default impression when it came to the fairer sex.

The elevator swooshed open to a sumptuously decorated foyer with ornate, doublewide carved wood doors for each of the three suites on their floor. A personal assistant, assigned by Tony Barnes himself, stood with a practiced smile by the entrance to their suite. "Mr. St. John, Ms. Bennett," she nodded to each of them. "I think you'll find everything in order." Opening the doors with a flourish she escorted them with businesslike efficiency around the suite pointing out amenities and comforts that were reserved for the hotel's elite guests. "The master en suite is equipped with a large spa tub and electronic shower while the second bedroom features a French boudoir design."

Drae was used to such luxury. Judging by Victoria's matter-of-fact demeanor, she was either used to traveling first class or a very good actress. Remembering her past association with European aristocracy, he was irritated when jealousy eked into his thoughts. He wanted to be the one to spoil her with indulgent luxury. The thought shocked him although he was careful not to let it show. Instead, he kept a hand low on Victoria's back, satisfied with that small contact for now although he was starting to suspect a lot more than casual touches were coming their way.

As soon as the assistant left them alone, she dropped her bag on a huge sofa that needed its own zip code and made a mad dash for the bathroom, breathlessly telling him, "Thank God that's over! Someone needs to tell Julie the Cruise Director that this isn't our first time in the big city. Sheesh!"

He was still smiling when she reappeared a few minutes later. "Sorry for the frantic exit," she told him. "But when a girl has to pee, well, a girl *has* to pee!" His mask of cool reserve fractured at her audacious declaration.

"What?" she mocked with a wry grin. "Too much information?" Grabbing for her bag she fished around inside it, pulling out a small container of hand lotion that she hurriedly squirted onto her palms. Rubbing the cream into her skin, she fixed him with an impatient look as the subtle scent invaded his senses. "Are you going to stand there all day and gape at me, or are we going to get this show on the road?"

Snapping his jaw shut, Drae considered that he had in fact been staring at her. "You are full of surprises today, Ms. Bennett. And for the record, there's no such thing as TMI between us, Victoria. Remember that, and if I seem, oh, I don't know - at a loss for words, it's because you are, as I told you earlier, a complete fraud." She grinned at his words. He added, "Bet you want to push those ugly glasses up your nose right about now, huh?"

Sashaying past him, she pursed her lips in dramatic fashion then smiled prettily toward his amused face saying, "Bite me, Mister Double-O-Trouble," as she made for the door.

Throwing back his head to let loose the bark of laughter rumbling in his chest, he reached out to guide her by the elbow while raking her with a deliberately provocative leer. "Double-O-Trouble? H*mmmm*. I like that almost as much as the idea of biting you."

THE REST OF THE day slogged by on an endless loop of highly detailed technical work, video chats with Alex who was following along step-by-excruciating-step from Arizona, and flying by the seat of her silk covered derrière the rest of the time. *This is no minor tech glitch*, she huffed restlessly as she visually prowled the pile of documents and schematics littered on the table at her side.

Her back was killing her from hours of hunching over a keyboard, plus she thought she might float away if she drank any more coffee. The only time she'd been able to get up and move around to burn off some energy was on her many trips to the restroom. Gallons of coffee has a way of doing that. And especially so when an absence of real food accompanied the hot beverage. Feeling grumpy and on the edge of bitchy, she started imagining a hundred colorful scenarios because the Justice Brothers were gonna owe her *big time* after this was over.

She hadn't seen Draegyn since he'd delivered her safely into the company of the hotel's security chief who practically fell at Draegyn's feet when they shook hands. Tori was seriously impressed. Clearly, his reputation preceded him.

Sighing as she stretched, feeling her spine unkink and shoulder tension ease, Tori had to admit he breathed power. The man was an alpha male who was just so damn sure of himself. She suspected he'd take charge in the bedroom and while the thought gave her a thrill, she wondered what it would be like to be the one commanding him. A very naked and very aroused Draegyn, under her control, was a swoon-worthy scenario, indeed.

Back to the matter at hand however was the fact that she was tired and hungry. There wasn't much more she could accomplish this evening. Alex was handling a critical piece of the programming by remote. There would be time tomorrow to finish up and tidy any loose ends. Right now she just wanted to find a change of scenery and a spot to unwind.

Shutting down the equipment she gathered her purse and a couple of files to look at later. Checking the time on her phone, Tori groaned when she saw it was after seven. Satisfied everything was in order until tomorrow, she flicked off the desk lights and turned to make for the door only to find her way blocked by the outline of a large, broad shouldered man. Her heart skipped a beat. Even in the dark, he was magnificent.

Hunger, different from the growling stomach, seized her senses. What would it be like to walk across the space between them and move into his embrace? Shaken by her response she reverted to habit, driven by too much caffeine and stress, letting a petulant whine escape before she could call it back, "It's been hours. I thought you'd forgotten about me."

He moved out of the shadows, stepping closer to her. "You've been the only thing on my mind, Victoria." Taking the stack of papers from her hands he put a hand to her elbow, guiding from the darkened office. "I told the security chief to keep an eye on you. I've been jerked around by Barnes most of the day and couldn't get back here to check on things. Why didn't you text or call?"

Tori knew she was being foolish so she kept silent as they

walked to the elevator bank and by the time the elevator doors closed, she felt reasonable enough to attempt conversation. Leaning her head back against the wall, she turned to look at Draegyn. "I'm sorry for whining." Heaving an enormous sigh she continued, "It's just that sometimes handling so much information makes me…."

He smiled down at her. "Full. It makes your brain full, I know. I see the same thing in Alex. We've been known to tell him when to *control, alt, delete* before he overloads. You have that look."

"Control- alt -delete. Cute." She nodded. "I'm gonna remember that for the next geek convention." Her stomach chose that moment to rumble loudly in the confined space of the elevator. Concern and something that looked like anger flashed across his face as she placed a hand over her growling tummy. Suddenly lightheaded from hunger and fatigue, she lifted the other hand to her forehead.

Putting an arm about her waist, he hauled her tight against his side. "When was the last time you ate?" His eyes narrowed as tension bracketed his mouth. Drae was suddenly furious. He'd left strict instructions that she was to be taken good care of. Hearing hunger gnawing at her insides sickened him. He was supposed to be watching over her but judging by the dark smudges growing under her eyes and the paleness of her complexion, she'd been worked too long and hard and was barely able to stay on her feet.

Stepping from the elevator he gently guided her to their suite. She stumbled in her sexy high heels going through the door so Drae simply swung her up in his arms and kicked the big wood door closed. "What are you doing?" she gasped.

"I don't know," Drae muttered, as confused as she was surprised. Stalking with purpose to the sofa, he gently lowered her onto the plush cushions. He laid aside the papers and her purse before taking a seat by her side. "You're white as a sheet. We need to get some food into you stat. Are you alright while I call room service?"

He was beyond relieved when she spared him a nod and quick smile. "I'm okay, really. But if it's alright, I'm just going to stay put and enjoy the view. Try to empty my brain." She turned and looked at the breathtakingly gorgeous sight of the legendary Vegas strip lit up at night. On an impulse he quickly made for the bar area and poured her a small brandy. If nothing else it would relax her and take some of the edge off while they waited for their meal.

As he returned to her side, he noted that she was less unsteady than a minute ago. Having kicked off her shoes she was seated with legs drawn under her backside revealing only a small strip of her dress. The randy fourteen-year-old hormonal teenager that never really left any guy wanted to slide his hand under that scant piece of fabric into the shadow between her thighs. Remembering that he was a grown man who knew how to control his impulses was harder than it should be.

"Here." He handed her the small snifter with two fingers of amber liquid sloshing in it. "Drink this. It will help while we wait." Sweeping her tongue along her mouth, she took the glass and lifted it slowly to her lips for a tiny sip. When she pulled the glass away, he could see remnants of the amber liquid clinging to her lips. The temptation to lick it off roared to life inside him.

Loosening his tie and top button, Drae slid off his suit jacket and rolled back the sleeves of his shirt, never letting his eyes wander from watching her. "Instead of just ordering up some munchies, how 'bout we stay in tonight and relax? I'll have the hotel send up dinner, and we can hang out here."

He saw signs of improvement, but she was still hanging by a thread. Expecting her to handle a restaurant outing was ridiculous. He'd make sure she didn't nearly pass out from hunger tomorrow, or the day after that or the day after that. He wasn't sure where this sudden protective impulse came from, but he was responsible for her well-being so he better get his shit together. No way was what happened earlier acceptable.

"Oh, I'd like that Draegyn," she murmured softly, rewarding him with a quiet smile. "I'm glad you understand. There is such a thing as too much input. I don't think I could stand any more stimulation right now."

Jesus Christ. Did she know how provocative that statement was? He wanted to show her that she could handle quite a bit more stimulation. A whole lot more, in fact. "Hold that thought, honey. I'm going to call and arrange for dinner. You relax."

"Mmmmm. I'm stuffed!" Tori giggled as she set down her fork, pushing away the half-eaten portion of creamy cheesecake. Grinning sheepishly at the sweet treat she admitted, "Desserts are a guilty pleasure!" in an adorably conspiratorial voice. "Well, desserts and coffee," she amended.

Throwing his napkin on the table, Drae sat back and patted his stomach. "Give me meat, anytime. Something I can sink my teeth into. There's nothing like gnawing on a succulent piece of flesh."

She flashed him a crooked smile that let him know she got the intended innuendo. "Really?"

His shoulders lifted in a half-assed shrug. "I'm a guy. What can I say? You set 'em up honey, and I hit 'em out of the park!"

"I like you when you're like this." The woman was direct and then some.

"I like you too, Victoria."

"Is our truce still in effect?" she teased with humor glinting in her chocolate eyes.

"For now," he growled. "Why? What's on your mind?"

"I have a question."

Well, *duh,* he thought. Curious about what was rattling around in her female brain, he nodded and gave the green light. "Ask away."

"I'm just curious, but do you see," she grappled with the words,

"I mean, are you aware of how people treat you? All that bowing and scraping and the way the women look at you like a gourmet delight. Does it bother you?"

Wow. Of all the questions she could have asked, the lady wanted to know what it was like to be him. To walk through life with more privilege and power than the average person even dreams of. "Ah, so you want to get serious, hmmm?" he teased earning a slight blush in response. "Let's get comfy on the couch and get to know each other better."

She nodded and rose to her feet as he added, "I told you I'd be eager to learn all your secrets, Victoria. This seems like the perfect time." He didn't miss the way she stumbled slightly as she padded barefoot to the sofa. Turn about after all, he thought, was fair play. She had questions? Well, so did he.

Reaching for the high-tech systems pad that controlled everything electronic in the suite, Drae lowered the lights, sparked a blaze in the fireplace, and found a quiet music channel on the satellite system for background ambiance. He watched from the corner of his eye as she undid the clasp on her belt and let it drop away, settling onto the sofa with her feet tucked neatly under her backside.

Pouring from the bottle of wine they'd been enjoying with their meal, he rounded the sofa and handed her a half-filled glass. Pulling up a plush ottoman, he dropped down next to her and swung his legs onto the stool. They sat for a few moments savoring their drinks, as the twinkling lights in the nighttime vista outside their wall of windows made the silence around them seem almost magical. Drae couldn't remember the last time he felt so content.

He enjoyed that she didn't prattle. Didn't feel the urge to hear her own voice or fill in every empty moment with inane chatter. She formulated her questions, shot them out like cannon fire, one after another, and then waited.

"To answer your very astute question," he finally said, noticing the way her eyes brightened at the compliment, "Yes, I do notice.

It's hard not to. I grew up with servants. My sister and I were very aware of the invisible line of demarcation between those of wealth and privilege and the people whose job it was to make our lives comfortable."

Drae stopped and thought about his younger sibling. Like him, she had taken drastic measures to escape the fake, vapid life of their parents' world. He wished he could spend more time with her now that they were both adults. Desirée had been conscientious throughout his time in the military about writing letters and sending packages to the big brother she adored. Now that she was married and raising a family far from the world of Fifth Avenue and Paris Fashion Week, they rarely saw each other. But that didn't stop him from being a doting and attentive uncle, from afar, for his young niece and nephew.

"We never tried to take advantage of the situation, unlike my parents who take great delight in playing the upper class hand at every turn. The military wasn't the wake-up call my folks imagined it would be. Mommy dearest thought I'd crash and burn in basic training without all the privileges I was used to but being able to turn my back on their empty existence was the greatest opportunity of my life."

"You don't get along with your parents." She made it a statement not a question.

Remembering that she had lost her father at an early age, it must seem strange to her that he didn't particularly care about his relationship with the 'rents. "Not all families are created equal."

"I know that," she said with a dismissive shrug. "It's just a shame that they're missing out on knowing their children as adults." The expression on her face led to a flush of warmth invading his chest.

"What you see now has little to do with being born to wealth and status. It's part psychology and part other people's perception. I admit that money has something to do with it. The Justice Brothers have done more than okay in the past few years. Wealth brings access to power, something we have in spades. There's something unique about getting a personal phone call from a head of state with a problem that only you can solve. Makes other people view you differently, hence the bowing and scraping, as you so aptly put it."

"I think I understand. Alex scared the stuffing out of me when we met in Phoenix. He had one of your operatives running interference for him and at the time it felt like he had a bodyguard although I don't doubt for a second that even with his limitations he could seriously kick some ass. My mother thinks quite highly of him, you know. It was sort of fascinating to watch while the hotel manager, the concierge, everyone really, stood on their heads for him." She paused to reflect on their conversation.

"Do you think it's different for you and Alex because of your family connections? Does Cameron also enjoy this VIP treatment?"

Drae laughed good-naturedly. "Fucking Cam. All that smoldering movie star heartthrob shit he's got going on gets him plenty of attention. Believe me! He got what he deserved though with Lacey. Knocked him down a few pegs." She smiled at his choice description of the newlywed groom.

It had always been Cam with his massive height and bad boy good looks that got the first glances whenever the three of them were together. Drae had benefitted plenty from the bevy of beauties eager to get close to Cam who ended up frozen out by his surly attitude and less-than-sparkling personality. The man was a serious pussy magnet who could not have cared less. Drae, and Alex to some degree, were happy to step in with the legion of disappointed females left in his wake. Of course all that was in the past now.

"Enough about me, lady. Tell me something I don't know about you." He refreshed their wine glasses while she considered his question.

"I would marry chocolate if it was legal." He tried not to laugh at her smart-ass answer and gave her one of those, *are you fucking kidding me* looks. Victoria chuckled and groaned, "Alright! Alright! Something you don't know. H*mmmm*,"

She took a sip of her wine and glanced around the room as though some sort of inspiration was going to appear out of nowhere. God, she was unique. It had been his experience that women couldn't wait to talk endlessly about themselves. Watching her struggle told him that she didn't see herself as particularly interesting. It must have been hard to be a girl who excelled in a predominantly male world. Not even nerds were immune to big tits and a botoxed smile.

A thought must have formed in her mind when her eyes sparkled with mischief and a huge smile lit up her face. Bringing her finger up to her mouth she said, "Shhhhh! Turns out I have a secret!" Setting her glass down, she sat up straight, placing both hands on her knees. She looked for all the world like a naughty child about to admit to having gotten caught in the cookie jar. "Next to coffee and desserts, I can not live without trashy romance books!" She said it quickly, like she was admitting to a serious crime.

"What?" He burst out laughing. "Are you joking?" When she turned solemn, truthful eyes on him, and nodded her head indicating that she wasn't kidding around, he was beyond charmed. "Are we talking mommy porn or Lord Higginbottom ravishes the maid?"

"Oh God, that mommy porn stuff isn't for me. My safeword would be a knee to the groin," she giggled. "And yes, Lord Higginbottom has probably figured in a story or twelve. Right now, cowboys are all the rage and billionaires of course!"

"You are full of surprises, honey." He chuckled with delight. A brilliant thought flashed in his mind as he asked, "Do you have one of these trashy books with you?" She looked slightly taken aback by his question. She was fucking adorable.

"Well,…uh," She coughed to clear her throat. "Actually, yes I do. I like to read before bed. Helps me get to sleep," she muttered as a deep shade of red crept up her neck and across her cheeks. Why, she was embarrassed!

"Let me check this trash out!" he snickered playfully pushing her from the sofa to go get the book. She resisted as best she could, even laughing at his efforts.

"No, Draegyn, stop! C'mon. You're embarrassing me."

"You brought it up!" he barked. Knowing how to get her running for the book, he made to tickle her into compliance, even getting in a few good groping touches, before she gave in with a shout of laughter.

"Enough! I surrender," she wheezed between giggles. Standing before him in her bare feet with the sweater hanging loosely around her, she impishly wagged her finger in his face threatening him with dire circumstances if he ended up laughing at her.

He couldn't help but swat her behind when she turned to walk away. "Hurry up!' he commanded as she stuck her tongue out at him in reply.

Returning less than a minute later, she had two small paperbacks clutched in her hand and a wicked look on her face. "You choose," she said. "Either the rugged, sexy cowboy or the handsome Viking with the big, uh….*sword*."

"Do you have a favorite?" he inquired silkily. "Which hero do you prefer?"

She thought about it for a minute then answered, "Mmmm. I think the cowboy."

Without another word, he reached up and pulled her onto his lap where she landed with a thud. She might be small but her body colliding with his when she wasn't expecting it meant she was mostly dead weight.

"Read to me."

***HOLY SHIT*, TORI THOUGHT** as she tried to retain some dignity and not squirm on his lap. The minute she fell onto him, her senses were assailed with the warmth coming off his body. She hadn't expected to find herself perched on his thighs and struggled to contain her wild excitement at the intimate closeness.

From their position, she was at eye-level with him, breathlessly aware of the arm stretched across her thighs holding her in place and the way his other arm curled around her waist. She couldn't help but stare at the undone button on his shirt or the skin of his neck. This close, she fell into the glittering blueness of his penetrating gaze. As usual, she lost all coherent thought when her eyes dropped to his mouth. *Damn*, he had tempting lips.

She felt his fingers brush against her hip then settle on an exposed patch of skin. When he stroked high up on her thigh, she nearly moaned out loud. *This is dangerous*, she thought. If she had a lick of common sense she would run from the room before their truce turned into something hot and naked. *Eh*, screw common sense.

"What would you like me to read?" she quizzed in a husky

voice.

"How about you just open the book to any page and go from there?" The hoarse sound of Draegyn's answer let her know she wasn't alone in the battle for good sense.

Not knowing how to get comfortable without grinding her bottom onto his groin, she tried to sit still and upright. *Good luck with that*, she thought wryly. Try as she might to appear blasé, the warmth gathering between her legs had to be making an impression on his senses. She might not have all that much experience but she knew a growing erection when she sat on one.

Fanning the pages of the paperback she made a production of randomly picking a page to begin reading. Just her luck that the scene she chose was full of sexual tension and building intimacy. Uh, maybe this *really* wasn't a good idea.

He kept his fingers stroking lightly along the skin of her thigh with one hand while the other played with her knees in a way that made it difficult to think. "Read, Victoria," he murmured.

She cleared her throat and prayed she wasn't about to make a huge fool of herself. Without thinking what her action would do to the body underneath her, she wiggled her bottom until she found an easy position and began reading quickly.

"Okay. Well, let's see. We're on page ninety-four. Jake, the rugged hero is about to seduce Wendy, our spirited heroine." She cleared her throat and started reading: "*Your shirt's all wet darlin'. Jake's voice had gone husky, his gaze fastened on her plump breasts clearly visible beneath the damp cotton. Wendy's heart thudded in her chest as she watched his tongue touch one of the pebbled nipples she couldn't disguise. Take it off, she demanded as he peeled the soggy material from her. She felt a slight shudder run through his body as he devoured her naked flesh with his hungry eyes. I'm not very good at this sort of thing, she blurted out. Turning eyes blazing with desire to her shocked ones, he murmured softly, My body thinks you're better than good at this. She slid her hand inside his open shirt with shy hesitancy and ran questing fingers over his chest, pausing to gently examine his male nipples. More, he groaned as his mouth latched onto her neck with a series of sharp, stinging nips that brought a burning need spreading through her heightened senses. She moaned in helpless delight, not caring if his teeth left marks on her flesh. His calloused cowboy hands cupped her tender, swelling breasts, squeezing the fleshy orbs, until she dug her nails into his skin. Tweaking her tightened nipples, she slid her hands into his hair and groaned. Please, Jake! What baby? He growled. What do you need? Please, she cried again. Take it into your mouth, hurry! She cried. When he did, she arched her back as wave after wave of sexual desire flooded her panties.*"

Tori stopped reading to catch her breath. *Dammit.* A couple of paragraphs about a sexy cowboy and a warm lap with a very big hard-on pressing into her sweet spot had raised her awareness level to near painful heights. She was frantically deciding what to do next, since continuing to read any more of the story was going to make matters worse, when Draegyn reached for the book and took it from her hands. He looked at the cover illustration for a moment and then at her. She found herself helplessly drowning in the smoky eyes of an aroused male. Tossing the book aside, she felt the hand curved around her waist, slowly rise up her back until he reached the hair secured at her nape.

In seconds he had the pins removed and was running his fingers through her locks in a way that got a husky purr from her. She loved the way he took control. It was just what he did. This was the thing about him that turned her on without any effort at all. He commanded every situation he was in and right now, he was most definitely the one in charge.

His fingers tangled in her hair, as Tori rubbed her scalp against his firm touch. It felt like she was free-falling and all he'd done was stroke her head. Needing an anchor in the sensory storm, she laid a hand upon his chest and snaked the other around his neck for good measure. When he pulled her mouth to his, she let him. Gladly.

This was nothing like the flash fire she remembered from their first kiss. No, this one was slower, wetter. He simply joined their mouths and went deep. All she could do was groan and clutch helplessly at his shirt. He accepted the parting of her lips with a slow slide of his tongue that grew steadily fiercer. A sensual shudder of desire ripped through Tori, making her hips roll on his hardness. She arched against his chest asking for a whole lot more. Taking a cue from the story that ignited this quickly escalating bonfire; she made short work of his tie and the buttons on his shirt so she could slide her hand inside the parted material.

Rubbing her fingers along his heated skin was a sensual delight. He was pumped up, hard to the touch yet soft at the same time. Skillfully devouring her mouth with an unhurried rhythm, his breathing turned ragged. With each tongue swipe, she swirled hers around his, eventually whimpering like a hungry child begging for more. While her touch on his chest had been gentle and shy at first, as he deepened the kiss her caresses grew desperate.

Her marauding fingers descended as far as they could as his big solid body shuddered when she traced the taut skin on his abdomen just above the waistband of his trousers. Wrenching their mouths apart, his head fell onto the sofa back as his chest heaved with the effort to bring oxygen into his lungs. Tori leapt on his exposed neck without hesitation, falling on him while her tongue and lips kissed, licked, and nipped every bare inch. He tasted like a man should. Warmth met her tongue as she slid it against his collarbone until the flames of desire reached into her core, making her clamp down hard on his sensitive skin. She moaned and sucked on his flesh, becoming even bolder when she felt his hand reach into her hair, encouraging the ravishing kisses.

They were both struggling to breathe as Tori squirmed on his lap until he let out a desperate groan. The sound accompanied his fingers sliding up her thigh, under the hem of her dress until he touched the lacey thong that wasn't doing much to contain the dampness spreading between her thighs. When he ran a single finger under the elastic she started to come undone in his arms.

They'd gone from zero to heart-stopping arousal in no time flat. There was no denying that she wanted him in the worst way. Apparently, not being each other's type hadn't stopped nature from staking its own claim on the situation. The intoxicating balls-out lust that drove them into each other's embrace was stronger than anything she'd ever felt before.

They were back to devouring each other's mouths when an odd sound made its way into the sex-drenched haze that surrounded them. At first, she only noted that there was a sound, not what it meant. Since their incendiary kiss hadn't lessened at all, she tried to ignore the interruption until finally, they drew apart as the sound became a persistent shrill. It was one of their damn cell phones.

Tori groaned in frustration and slapped her hand against the back of the sofa a second before she scrambled awkwardly off Draegyn's lap. She surprised them both when a hoarsely muttered, "Fuck," slid from her throat.

"I couldn't agree more," he grumbled, reaching for the offending object and snatching it up without humor. "What?" he barked into the phone as she sank to the cushions in a melted heap of overly sensitized flesh. "This isn't a good time, man." She heard him murmur. A few seconds later he said, "No. Victoria is right here. She's fine. We both are. Why the late call Alex?" He wasn't even trying to hide the impatience or irritation in his voice.

Pulling herself together so Draegyn could find out what was stuck in Alex's radar, she stood up and smoothed the material of her outfit over trembling thighs. Somewhere during their heated embrace, she had lost the sweater, leaving her in just the short dress. As she bent to retrieve their wine glasses she caught Draegyn looking at her with undisguised arousal shining in his eyes. She felt like strangling her interrupting boss right then.

Hurrying from the room with the empty glasses and wine bottle in her hands, she managed to stub her toe on an end table, muttering a dramatic, "Ouch!" that left her limping and annoyed as hell. Dropping the glasses and bottle on the counter of the luxurious wet bar, she caught her reflection in the mirrored backsplash and nearly died. She looked like a wild animal had mauled her. Peeking over her shoulder at said wild beast, she had to wonder how far their interlude might have gone if not for the damn inconvenient timing of Alex's call.

Draegyn stood and moved to the bank of windows that looked out over the city lights as he continued speaking quietly into the phone. She might appear a little worse for wear from their sensual activity but so did he, she thought, taking in the heart-stoppingly gorgeous picture he made standing in the dimly lit corner of the room.

Tori had done quite a number on his shirt, which hung open while one shirttail remained tucked into his pants. Her greedy eyes drank him in, unflinchingly satisfied at the prominent bulge that pressed against the front of his pants. Any lingering self-doubts she carried about not being pretty or sexy enough for a man like him evaporated at the sight of that undeniable proof that he had been as aroused and excited as she had been. Fuck Alex and his shitty timing. God dammit! What did a girl have to do to catch a break?

Mentally conceding the phone call was a surefire buzzkill, she tidied up the mess they made, even stacked the remnants of their meal on the room service trolley, and wheeled it to the door for housekeeping. Not sure what else to do, she lifted her gaze to Draegyn only to find him staring intently at her. She blushed and tried a weak smile.

Twin slashes of color highlighted his cheekbones, a testament to how seriously out-of-control they'd gotten with each other. He didn't look happy about the interruption, and the tiny shrug and brief grimace that crossed his features effectively brought their relaxed evening of getting to know each other to a screeching halt.

She felt stupid just standing there. It seemed a bit desperate in her mind. Like a puppy waiting for attention. Since it wasn't very likely that they were going to continue what they'd started, not tonight anyway, Tori decided it was best to retreat. Grasping hold of her confidence with determination, she ambled to where he stood with the phone pressed to his ear, enjoying the way his eyes darkened and mouth grew taut at her approach.

She stopped inches away from his body, reaching out to run her hand flat down the front of his chest. His nostrils flared at her brazen touch. Leaning in she breathed, "G'night," close to his mouth. He took the invitation and closed the distance between their lips for a swift, hard kiss filled with the frustration and regret they both were feeling. He mouthed *goodnight* and before she did something she shouldn't, like let her hand drift over the front of his pants, she spun and walked toward her bedroom. Turning to him one last time, she flashed him a sultry smile that left no doubt how disappointed she was. As she slowly swung the door closed, he met her look, expression for expression. She was sure her heavy sigh hung in the air long after the door clicked shut.

Well, this sucks, Drae groused silently. One minute he had a sexy and very turned on waif writhing in his arms while they engaged in the hottest, wettest kiss he'd ever experienced and the next, he was immersed in a cock-blocking phone call that doused their sensual fire quicker than a tsunami of cold water. If it weren't for the fact that something serious was being brought to his attention, he would have been sorely tempted not to strangle Alex.

Remembering the hot passage that Victoria read aloud from her romance paperback, Drae knew it was going to take a hell of a lot more than a phone call to ease the throbbing hard-on he was experiencing. It had been a day of surprises where that little lady was concerned. As if his reaction to her makeover hadn't been enough, discovering that she liked her reading materials spicy with a double dose of naughty had been a huge turn on. He had little doubt that if their interlude hadn't been so rudely interrupted, his questing fingers would have ended up delving deep into her damp folds instead of stopping at the skimpy silk panties.

Her passion hadn't surprised him, not after the way she had come alive in his arms that night at her apartment when she'd been crying. No, tonight's surprise had unfolded slowly, like their kiss. It was her untutored response to him that shook his world. There was absolutely nothing about Victoria that was fake or contrived. When she shook in his arms, it wasn't part of an act meant to enslave his senses. It was one hundred percent pure response and as a result, he'd never felt so primal or more male, in his entire life.

Maybe it was a good thing that they'd been interrupted. After all, he already admitted he really like her. Very much. If they'd gone on much longer, they would have indulged in a one-way journey to pound-town even though that wasn't what he wanted from her. No, a good fuck, no matter how erotically charged, was something he had little trouble finding. Victoria, however, wasn't in that category. When he did finally have a chance to take her to bed, it wasn't going to be a randy plowing for the sake of relieving a basic need.

Her hot kisses and the way she clung to him made him want to explore the unexpected and unfamiliar depth of feelings he was experiencing. He might very well be losing his fucking mind, but the way he felt when she wrapped her arms around him, or the little sounds she made while her tongue dueled so sweetly with his made Drae want to strip her naked, as slowly as possible and avail himself of every centimeter of her delicious body. He wanted to make love to her for hours, watch her writhe in his arms as he sank into her wet depths until they couldn't take it anymore. And he especially wanted to lose himself in her gorgeous brown eyes as she came around him while his cock was buried balls deep.

Just thinking about being inside her made his heart thump wildly. The only thing stopping him from kicking down her door so he could plunge into her silky wetness were the very thoughts he'd just had. He wanted more from her. Victoria Bennett wasn't anything like the jaundiced first impressions he had of her. There was something special, unique, and sweet about her that made him feel protective as well as aroused. She'd blown apart the lifetime of distrust he'd been nursing where women were concerned with her smart-ass mouth and adorably prickly assertiveness. He'd never wanted a woman the way he wanted her and especially had never craved a connection the way he did where she was concerned.

Aww shit. While he was lost in his private thoughts, Alex had been nattering on, and he hadn't caught but a word of what had been said. Eyeing Victoria's closed bedroom door with regret, he sighed and tried to concentrate on the situation at hand. Tomorrow would be soon enough to see where all this was heading. He owed it to everyone involved, and that included the agency, to keep his wits about him and not do anything that would cause problems down the road.

"Yeah, I'm still here, bro. Just thinking, that's all," he murmured into the phone. "Let's rework the problem and come up with an alternate plan, okay?" It would be almost an hour more before the call would wrap-up and by then he was more than ready to fall facedown onto a soft bed.

TORI WOKE TO A dream hangover. *Oh God.* There was nothing worse than rolling out of bed feeling foggy and disoriented. Crawling from the warm cocoon, she stumbled into the bathroom and flicked on the unforgiving lights. “Bad idea,” she muttered, quickly turning off the offensive lighting. She turned to the mirror above the sink and did a quick morning assessment.

Hair? An absolute mess. Huffing irritably, her fingers snagged through the tangles, sweeping the brown locks back from her face. It didn’t matter how carefully she styled her hair because after a night of tossing and turning, she managed to resemble a wind tunnel mannequin. She would never be one of those women who woke up looking perfect and flawless.

Making a quick ponytail, she went through the motions of a morning routine with a minimum of effort; brush teeth, cleanse face, and apply moisturizer. She didn’t like to waste time on anything more complicated. She was who and what she was and no amount of fussing was going to change that. The under eye shadows were a result of having her sex drive unleashed, by a master no less, only to end up without a way to manage the unfulfilled aftermath. She was still annoyed by Alex's untimely interruption.

In the dead of night, after she'd awoken from an erotically charged dream, Tori slipped quietly from her room to retrieve the paperback romance she'd lost track of after Draegyn had taken it from her hands. Maybe reading for a while would help her brain empty so she could get back to sleep. Although she looked everywhere, the book was nowhere to be found, forcing her to simply tough it out and pray for sleep to return.

And now here it was, way too early in the morning to be up and about. This seemed as good a time as any to hit the hotel fitness room before the regular morning rush. In her present frame of mind she didn't want to compete for time on the equipment. No, what she wanted was to be left alone to work up a serious sweat and clear away the hangover cobwebs.

Checking out her reflection one last time, she grabbed a pair of ear buds, her phone, and after hastily scribbling a short note to let Draegyn know where she was, headed off to the workout facility. Because it was so early, she had her pick of machines, settling on an elliptical she knew would give her a fierce workout. Scrolling through her playlists she found something that would definitively have her up and moving.

Three quarters of an hour later, with thighs on fire and her arms set to explode, she yanked the earphones out and eased into a cool down rhythm. It felt good to push her muscles and it really did go a long way to helping restore focus.

No urgent messages. *Good*, Drae though as he flung his phone aside and made for the suite's kitchenette. He'd found Victoria's note letting him know she'd gone to the fitness center the moment he'd stepped from his room in search of coffee. Knowing he was alone, he hadn't bothered to fully dress, preferring to suck back something dark and hot before jumping in the shower. The old sweats he'd pulled on hung low on his hips and actually did more to emphasize his manhood than conceal it. As usual, he was dealing with a morning hard-on that seemed to be mocking him.

Ah, let's see now. What've we got, he wondered while spinning the elaborate carousel crammed with every single cup brew imaginable. Absently rubbing his abdomen while he thought, Drae tried to concentrate on the task at hand and failed miserably. His night had sucked balls. Far from restful, he'd been plagued all through the long hours, when he should have been sleeping, with vivid images of Victoria writhing in his lap and the way the skin along her thigh had prickled at his soft touch.

He hadn't helped the situation any, he reflected grimly. No, fool that he was, he'd picked up Victoria's romance book and taken it with him when he finally got off the phone with Alex and retreated to his bedroom. He was curious, especially after the racy passage she'd read to him. In the end, he'd read the whole damn thing. Aside from the sometimes-mawkish story line and the you-had-to-have-seen-it-coming-ending, he enjoyed the tension between the two main characters and found the love scenes nothing short of hot.

Reading that book had given him a step-by-step blueprint of what an erotic seduction looked like in her head. Something he really didn't need to be thinking about. Leaning his hips against the counter while waiting for the coffee to brew, he sighed. Nothing he did seemed to take the edge off what was a growing need to take the woman invading his thoughts and dreams and make her his and his alone. The very idea fucked with his head in every way it could. He'd never, *ever* felt that way about a woman before and frankly until now thought such feelings were a load of crap. Romantic fodder for the foolish. How far the mighty have fallen, he thought.

A soft, female voice coming from the foyer, broke through his musings. “Hi. I’m back,” he heard Victoria say. Turning expectantly toward the sound, when she stepped around the wall blocking the door from his view he wondered if the gods were having a good laugh at his expense as, coffee forgotten, he experienced a free-falling sensation when all the blood in his body rushed into his cock. One look and he was a horny teenager with raging hormones that no amount of age and experience could control.

Even though he knew the answer, the very turned on voice in his brain hollered, *What the fuck is she wearing?* His head exploded at the sight she made. Dressed in a skintight pair of workout bottoms with the top rolled over exposing her entire abdomen, he found her belly button an outright provocation. Add to that the short crop top barely covering the perfect globes of her breasts and he was almost gasping for breath. As if on cue, his sex surged and grew tight.

Tori stopped dead in her tracks the moment she spied Draegyn standing across the big living area wearing nothing but an indecent pair of worn sweats that did absolutely nothing to conceal his swoon-worthy attributes. Muscular shoulders above a perfectly sculpted chest covered by a smattering of light body hair, made her mouth water. *For real.* If all she did was stare at his magnificent torso, that would probably be enough. Luckily, the entire delicious package was on view making it impossible to stop the downward trek of her gaze.

There was something about the way his brawny arms hung at his sides that sent a shiver skittering along her nerve endings. Every time she found herself in his embrace, she felt soft and feminine, a perfect counterpart to the powerful virility coming off him in waves. She watched, mesmerized as his hands clenched, a sure sign that he was following her thoughts as she greedily drank in the sight he made.

As if the bare chest wasn’t enough to strike her deaf and dumb, the tufts of blonde hair below his navel leading into sweats slung low on his slim hips made her mind go completely blank. The barely leashed power she'd come to associate with this man was on full display in the tense, controlled line of his body. She knew there was no way to ignore or look away from the clearly obvious erection bulging in the front of his sweats that grew larger with every second. She stared fascinated at the way the soft material clung to every inch of his swelling flesh. It was all so erotic making Tori painfully aware of her bra-less nipples peaking and throbbing inside her cotton top.

She heard him hiss making her gaze swing to his eyes at that critical moment. Her gasp of startled awareness split the air when she caught sight of the aroused flush on his chiseled features and the way his ice blue eyes had turned dark and stormy. Whatever was going on in his head either got decided or was pushed aside when he stalked across the space separating them, his eyes locked on hers, a look of carnal intent etched on his face. Automatically dropping what was in her hands, the sound of a water bottle and her phone smacking on the tile floor barely registered when he reached out and hauled her forcefully into his arms.

She had enough time to reassure herself that she wasn't dreaming before his mouth crashed down onto hers and all sensible thought flew out the window. *Oh dear lord*, she thought. His mouth was hot and demanding as he crushed her against him in a fevered kiss that stopped at nothing. When he licked along the seam of her lips, she whimpered softly, letting the tip of her tongue touch his a second before she surrendered to an open mouth ravishment that stole her sanity.

Wrapping her arms about his neck, she pressed against him as best she could until two strong hands cupped her bottom and lifted her into a mind-blowing embrace that reinforced with astonishing swiftness the appeal of the male body she'd just been scrutinizing. She could feel every ripple along his abdomen as she clung to his massive shoulders, sending a flood of aroused, wet warmth to her aching center.

There was nothing about what was happening that wasn't wild

and electric. Slamming her body against a wall as he ground against her spread thighs, Tori fed desperate moans into the mouth greedily feasting on her own as her hips bucked against him. Grasping and clutching his neck and shoulders in an ever mounting frenzy to get as close to him as possible, she was having a hard time keeping her shit together as he drove them both into a storm of powerful need.

Holding her in place, his hands slid under her short top to curve around her aching breasts as a deep groan rumbled out of his chest and into her mouth. Losing herself in a tidal wave of sensation, Tori sucked his tongue deeper as her fingers dug into the skin of his shoulders. A purely feminine, female grunt of satisfaction broke through the silence when he shuddered under her rough, demanding touch.

Time stopped the second she felt his thumbs sweep across her swollen nipples. Longing, deep and intense, gripped her senses as he kept up the sensual caress. Wrenching her lips from his, she burrowed into his neck, biting feverishly at his flesh, while he molded her breasts. Pushing her top up and ripping it over her head, Draegyn stared down at the naked flesh gripped in his strong hands and then into her eyes. The look he gave her left nothing to the imagination. When his mouth moved downward, she gasped and cried out as firm lips closed around an aching, pebbled nipple, sucking her deeply into his mouth. The sensation of his wet mouth on her aching flesh and the sounds they were both making, acted like a match held to a pile of kindling. She went up in flames and not even an interrupting phone call was going to stop the fire raging between them this time.

It wasn't until she felt herself being lowered to a mattress and registered the shaking hands removing her pants that Tori realized he'd been guiding them to the bedroom. They hadn't spoken a single word. None were necessary. It didn't matter who or what had started the raging inferno playing out, all she cared about was the way he made her feel as he devoured her mouth and massaged her flesh. My God. She wanted him inside her. Now. Wanted to know what it felt like to absorb this god of a man in her body.

When he stepped back to shed his sweats, she had a moment of doubt as the full measure of his size and girth was revealed to her hungry eyes. She knew he was big. There was no disguising that fact each time his arousal made contact with her body, but she was not prepared for the reality. She wasn't ignorant of the male physique. Not by a long shot. But the way his sex stood out from his taut abdomen and the sight of muscled thighs that did more than just suggest strength and power, made her quiver with uncertainty. She felt so small next to him.

She raised approving eyes that she knew were tinged with apprehension and his understanding smile was her undoing. Excitement, pure and carnal, raced along her spine. What she saw in his gaze suggested he was going to enjoy taking her. Moving purely on instinct her hips rolled in an invitation as old as time. She would think back later and know with certainty that was the moment when all control, hers and his, snapped.

DRAE HAD SEEN A lot of things in his life but absolutely nothing prepared him for the burst of red-hot lust that gripped him when Victoria walked into the room. The workout outfit that was little better than a second skin had taunted his control, but it was those big brown eyes devouring his body that turned what had been a manageable throbbing ache into something a lot more dangerous. He watched as her tongue flicked along the pouty lower lip of her mouth, as though she could taste him, and had all but leapt across the space between them to get to her. There wasn't a nerve in his body that hadn't tightened as she mapped every inch of his flesh. He couldn't wait to strip her naked and avail himself of her sweet little body.

He wasn't sure how long they stood there eyeing each other but when he noted her nipples, pebbling beneath the thin crop top, all sense took a hike. If he wasn't mistaken, she was trembling so badly, he could see her skin vibrating. The space between them melted away in the blink of an eye as he simply gathered her to him. Within seconds they were caught up in a head-on sensual collision that had him groaning into her mouth. He felt a wild, primitive beat pound in his head when he lifted her petite frame until her legs wrapped firmly around his hips. Drae loved how perfectly they fit together as he bucked against her to intensify the pleasure. By the time he got her top off and started suckling like a dying man at her breasts, he was well and truly lost. How he maneuvered them down the hallway and into his bedroom was a complete mystery. All he knew was a driving need and growing desire to get her naked and underneath him as quickly as possible.

It had never been like this before, not with any woman. Drae hardly knew what he was doing as the need to possess her took over. After he stripped off her clothes and saw her fully naked for the first time, any hope of taking things slowly vanished. When she rolled her hips at him, he knew he'd never keep himself in control. The way his sex exploded at the sight of the soft brown curls between her legs and the perfect handful of breasts with their deeply flushed nipples changed everything.

She'd stared unabashedly at his raging hard-on, and when eyes filled with desire lifted to his, he caught a brief moment of vulnerability in her gaze that brought the primal man inside him roaring to life. He knew what that look meant. Knew she was trembling because she wanted him so badly and knew his size had shocked her. He never gave much thought to his manhood, figuring it was what it was. But seeing it through her eyes only made his dick throb harder and grow impossibly firmer.

His hand came out to trace a single finger across her lush mouth, down her neck, and between quivering breasts begging for his attention. Drae hiked up onto the bed, coiling his hand around her ponytail and tugged so he could have access to the long column of her neck. She shuddered under his hands, groaning out his name in a voice choked with desire. "Draegyn, Draegyn."

He devoured her neck with long slow strokes of his tongue while she shook in his arms. Each time her back arched, he ground his hardness against her. It was like a magnificent symphony, the way she tasted, the small whimpering sounds coming from her throat, her small soft body moving against his much larger, harder one. It was - *perfection*. Every inch of his body was pumped up and throbbing with arousal. The sensation of her delicate fingers digging into his flesh brought a grunt of pleasure from deep inside him.

He was lost. Completely. Rolling her beneath him, he spread her legs with his powerful thighs as she latched onto his chest with her hungry mouth. Fireworks went off behind his eyes with each nip and bite as her tongue and lips drove him crazy. Groaning something that sounded like '*fuck*,' he reached between them and knew he was a goner the moment he found her hot wet center. Somewhere in the heated inferno engulfing them, Drae knew he should slow down, take his time, and make love to her the way she deserved. The way the hero in her romance book had done, taking here with patience and sensitivity. Neither of those two things was in the room with them right now though. A wild, primal compulsion had taken over, finesse be damned.

Putting both hands under her bottom, he pulled Victoria into position. The room spun as he opened her for his possession. His first thrust into her body was met with a sharp cry that quickly faded when he bit down hard on her neck. Groaning in an agony of pleasure, Drae tried to hold back while her body adjusted to his presence, but she was so incredibly tight and wet that he couldn't help himself. The way her passage fit around his twitching staff melted his brain. Nothing had ever felt so good, so right.

Slow and easy became nothing but empty words as he pulled back and slammed into her again and again with a ferocity that stunned him. With each stroke she whimpered and shook as her thighs moved restlessly against his. When he shifted his weight and brought her legs around his waist, he sank deeper into her hot, clutching body. The sensation of her inner muscles squeezing along his shaft as he pounded into her was beyond anything he'd ever imagined. Grunting with each forceful thrust, he set up a merciless rhythm highlighted by the sound of his sex being sucked into her dripping wetness.

The whole thing became a seething storm of desire that built sensation upon sensation, with Victoria grasping at the sheets while she writhed and bucked under his relentless thrusts. Bringing them both to the edge, Drae groaned deeply when, buried deep inside her, he felt the initial flutters of her orgasm start to pulse along his cock. "Oh God, Victoria", he cried as her sheath squeezed and tightened around him like a fist. With her heels dug forcefully into his haunches she went ballistic underneath him, grinding against his marauding body, screaming in helpless abandon as an explosion detonated deep inside her. He almost blacked out from the blinding pleasure she gave him as her orgasm lengthened and impossibly, deepened.

His eyes never left her face as he watched her come undone and luxuriated in the sensation of her fierce inner muscles contracting along the length of his pulsing cock. Unable to slow his own completion, Drae felt a thunderbolt of pleasure rocket from his feet, up his spine and into his groin as he drove into her with one mighty thrust after another. Pumping his hips, he convulsed as the whole experience coalesced into one long, shuddering orgasm when he emptied into her. Time stood still as he shook and bucked wildly, dimly aware of her soft cries of wonder.

The sensual storm that had overpowered them didn't lessen in intensity for a long time after that. Drae rolled onto his back, bringing Victoria with him, as she lay sprawled in a boneless heap upon him. He was aware of the warm, sticky wetness, where it clung to both their bodies. Something about that bold awareness struck him between the eyes with a powerful slap of reality. Not only had he taken her with an animalistic ferocity that made him cringe, he'd done so without any thought of protection. He was stunned by the realization of how he'd behaved. A tirade of self-loathing accusations attacked his consciousness. What the hell had he done? Jesus

Christ. She deserved better than to be fucked by an out-of-control madman.

"Are you alright?" he muttered cautiously when she began to stir. If she started to cry or turned away from him, he didn't know what he'd do. Pretty much the last thing he expected was for her to put her mouth on his chest and gift him with a sweet, moist kiss. "Is that a yes?" he asked hopefully.

"Shhhh," she replied. "Don't say anything, please." Her voice sounded small and hesitant.

"Victoria," he rasped, "I'm serious. Did I hurt you?"

The concern in his tone brought her head up from his chest to look him straight in the eye. He shouldn't have been so surprised. She may be small, but she was a feisty little spitfire. Not even an episode of rough, demanding sex was going to make her cower. She searched his face for a long time and then laid her chin on the hands she'd folded upon his chest.

"I'm fine," she murmured. "Maybe a bit sore, but ….."

When her silence led nowhere he was forced to consider every possibility of unspoken words imaginable and didn't like where his thoughts led. She said she was fine but sore. The part left hanging made him feel like a prick.

Laying her gently to his side, Drae sat up and smoothed his hands down her arms reassuringly. "Sit tight," he prompted as he climbed off the bed. "I'll be back in a minute."

Hurrying from the room, he made for the massive en suite, gathering an armload of towels along the way. It only took a few seconds to switch on the digital controls that operated the multi-head shower and then he was sprinting back to her side. She was lying curled on her side in a fetal position that struck at his conscience like a sledgehammer. "God dammit", he muttered quietly as he scooped her from the bed and stomped toward the shower.

"What are you doing now?" she shrieked in surprise.

He didn't answer. After all, what could he say? There weren't any words to cover the self- loathing he was heaping upon his head. The emotions racking his body and mind would have to wait for another time to be picked apart and considered. All that mattered at this precise moment was taking care of Victoria and making sure he hadn't been too damn rough with her.

Tori was in shock. Or something very close to shock. When she'd returned from her workout, the last thing she expected was wild, unrestrained monkey sex with Draegyn. Everything had happened so fast. And now, here he was, carrying her, god knows where, and all she could think of was how soon they could do it all again. He was freaking her out though with his somber demeanor. Instead of enjoying the afterglow, he was behaving as if he'd committed the ultimate sin. Had she missed something?

Realization of where they were struck as he lowered her gently to the tile floor of the massive shower. Steam had already gathered inside the glass enclosure, snaking warmth along her limbs as feeling and sensation returned to her sated body. He stayed close, keeping an arm around her while he played with the controls, giving her a chance to find her footing.

Confusion battered her sense of well-being at the solemn note to his voice. "A warm shower should help," he murmured. Help what exactly, she wondered? His hesitation baffled her. Standing naked, as they were, inches apart in a steaming shower, there wasn't any way she was going to miss the way his sex hung at half-staff. She wanted to reach out and coax his manhood back to throbbing life. The soreness she felt was nothing next to her desire to do it all again. And again.

He wasn't meeting her eyes, and Tori felt a rapid escalation of anxiety invade her senses. Had she done it wrong? Was he disappointed, or worse, turned off by the way she'd gone crazy in his arms? Oh God, she felt ill.

"Would you like me to help you, uh," he stuttered. "What I mean to say is, well…" He was all over the place and clearly struggling. "God dammit Victoria," Draegyn groaned like a man in the throes of agony. "I shouldn't have been so rough with you! What can I do?"

Ohhhhhh, she thought. I get it now. He thinks he manhandled me or some sort of ridiculous crap like that. Was he kidding? The look on his face suggested he wasn't. How could she let him know that what they'd done, while raw and uninhibited and yes, a bit demanding on his part, had been nothing short of amazing? Hell, amazing wasn't a good enough description. It had been transcendent. Opting for audaciously cheeky, she turned and bent forward to grab a poof from the shower bench knowing full well she was giving him a direct view of her bottom.

Turning back to Draegyn she quickly noted the way his lashes lowered in an attempt to shield his reaction but not before she caught the glint of awareness light up his eyes. Handing him the poof she gave a melodramatic sigh and asked, "Will you do my back, please?" She almost laughed when his hands shot out to grab a container of shower gel with all the awkward clumsiness one would have expected of a teenage boy experiencing his first co-ed shower.

Whirling away before he saw the laughter in her eyes, Tori leaned her hands onto the dark tile wall and let a stream of water slide down her back, over the swell of her backside. She sensed when he shifted closer to her. Even in the steamy waterfall, she could feel his heat. The scent of spicy citrus wafted in the humid air as he began swiping the length of her torso with foamy suds. It really did feel wonderful. The small sigh of contentment that rushed out was no lie.

Drae tried to concentrate on what he was doing but the sensation of his hands on her wet skin replaced his conflicted thoughts with ones of a more lascivious nature. When she winced as his fingers swept across her hips and thighs he zeroed in on her slight curves, making out faint outlines of bruised flesh. Releasing a self-castigating tirade, he spun her around so fast she wobbled in his arms. His attention was riveted on the physical proof that he'd behaved like an animal. The thought made him ill. He'd done a lot of things, the kind of things that smack of life or death, but he'd never raised a hand in anger to a woman and had never gotten so completely out-of-control that he'd been aggressive. Until twenty minutes ago.

Dropping to his knees, Drae grimaced as his mouth went dry at the sight before him. She was so damn slender that he could nearly span her waist with his hands. He remembered gripping her hips in desperation while thundering between her open thighs. A quick glance confirmed his worst fears. An imprint from his domination was evident on her smooth, creamy thighs and across the flesh of her ass and hips. Her hand touched the side of his face, making him look up into the mesmerizing depths of her beautiful eyes. "Draegyn," she whispered softly. Nobody ever called him by his full name. He liked hearing her say it. "I'm fine, really," she said emphatically.

"These bruises tell me otherwise, Victoria." He couldn't feel worse or sound more bummed if he tried. "I don't know what to say that will make this better," he groaned.

He was being his arrogant self again, as if he'd been the only one grunting and groaning in that bed. Even though she kinda liked the down on his knees thing, she was starting to feel weird about it. He didn't have a damn thing to apologize for. She'd been with him the whole way, clinging to his shoulders, devouring his mouth. It had all been so intense, so wild and hot, that all she could do was hang on. The way he'd cried her name when her orgasm exploded had excited her. She'd been exquisitely aware of his cock buried deep inside her and every pulse and throb when he came with shuddering groans. The knowledge that she could be so primitive was shocking enough. Having him apologize for it was not what she needed right now.

"How 'bout you don't say anything?" she bit out. "Really Draegyn, I'm fine. You going on like this is ruining everything!" Was that her wailing? Shit. It was. She hazarded a look at the man on his knees before her. He looked, well - he looked a bit stunned by her outburst. Thinking she could explain, Tori shook her head and frowned. "Look, what just happened? Well, it was amazing." She felt a blush coming on but plowed ahead anyway. Now was a moment for total honesty. "Don't apologize, please. That was a first for me." She quickly dispelled his look of confusion. "No, I wasn't a virgin but that was another kind of first." When his eyebrows quirked at her statement she rushed the rest before she chickened out. "Orgasm," she offered. "First." Now that really did get a raised eyebrow from him. "Clinically speaking, I've experienced a climax of course, but never during sex." She coughed to clear her throat.

He stood up in slow motion, never letting go of her eyes. When he loomed over her she felt consumed by his size and presence. "Let me get this straight." A muscle in his jaw flexed. "Just now, when you came," his expression suggested he was remembering in fine detail the moment when her body had clutched at his invading cock, "That was the only time you'd had an orgasm with a man?"

"Don't look so smug!" she cried. "It just happened that way, is all."

"Oh, no you don't!" Draegyn crowed. "Do not rob me of the satisfaction from knowing I not only made you come but got you to scream while doing so."

She thumped him in the middle of his chest. "Shut up!"

"Make me," he murmured silkily, leaning his hips against the shower wall.

She took a deep, calming breath that didn't do much to help her careening emotions. "I suppose we'll have to get into this at some point, but right now we both need to finish showering and get dressed. " She hoped the change of subject worked.

Draegyn smiled slowly but not before raking her body with a look that was hot enough to sear her skin off. "Yes, I suppose you're right. You win this one for now, little lady, but know this. At some point we *will* talk."

CHECKING HIS WATCH FOR the umpteenth time, Drae was relieved to find the workday coming swiftly to an end. He'd been hovering near Victoria all day, keeping his distance but having her in his line of sight at all times. If she moved to a different area, so did he. Not wanting a repeat of the previous day when he'd found her half-starved and cranky as shit after being left to her own devices for hours, he'd resolved to keep an eye on things but do it in a way that didn't totally piss her off. She liked thinking she was in charge. He snorted at the thought.

Scraping his chair back to stand, he looked around the command center for the hotel complex, which was laid out in a series of spaces separated by glass walls. Monitor lights and blinking screens were visible all around but nothing could obscure the sight she made, standing rooms away from him. He didn't think anything could top the astonishment he'd felt at the first sight he'd gotten of her yesterday morning in her smart designer outfit and high-heeled shoes. Just one more thing he'd been wrong about. She'd taken his breath away after their shower. He vaguely remembered mumbling something about how nice she looked when *nice* didn't even come close to the fantastic sight she made in an eggplant colored sweater dress with a wide leather belt that highlighted her trim waist and lean figure. A pair of sexy knee-high suede boots completed the mouth-watering picture. She'd blown her hair out so it tumbled in soft chestnut colored curls against her shoulders. How could this be the same woman who'd been scurrying around for weeks, hiding behind ugly glasses and bland, baggy clothes?

He watched as she rolled her shoulders and let her head loll back tilting her chin up, shaking her hair back and forth. God. Even when she didn't know he was watching her, everything she did seemed like a sexual provocation. He wanted her. Again. Just as hard and demanding as that first time until she begged for release. He'd never wanted anyone like this. Now that the genie was out of the bottle, he couldn't think of anything else.

Before stalking off in her direction, Drae tugged the cuffs of his shirt and adjusted his tie just as the security chief appeared with questions. It wasn't but a couple of minutes later when Drae saw Tony Barnes appear and make a beeline for Victoria. Fuck. Just what he didn't need.

Tension was rolling off of her in waves. Glad to have this assignment wrapping up, Tori had been trying to relieve some of the stiffness in her body when she heard a sound behind her. Expecting to turn around and find Draegyn stalking her as he'd done all day, she was startled to find a man she didn't know bearing down on her with a look that made her shiver in revulsion.

Dressed in a double-breasted suit, the stranger carried himself with a smug superiority that instantly rubbed her the wrong way. Beside the fact that the tailored suit made him look like an Italian waiter, he also had jet black wavy haired that was severely slicked back giving him a phony air, setting alarm bells clattering in her mind. When he reached her and offered an introduction, she was dismayed to see a garish twinkle on his extended hand. *Ewww.* She hated a pinkie ring on a man. Wallace had worn one. It was an ugly thing with a family crest that he toyed with incessantly. Of course this douchebag, whoever he was, would be wearing a ring. She knew before he even spoke that he was a poser, plain and simple.

"Miss Bennett, I believe?" he hissed in a smarmy tone. "I have been remiss. Please permit me to welcome you to my hotel. I am Anthony Barnes." His hand slid around hers, reminding her of a snake wrapping around its prey. She detested him on sight. *Be nice*, her inner voice coaxed. *Don't bite his obnoxious face off just yet.* Knowing what little she did of this man, Tori understood immediately why Draegyn thought he was an asshole.

Confirming the introduction with a slight nod, she quickly reclaimed her hand and went so far as to push it behind her back, far from his reach. "Good afternoon, Mr. Barnes," she said in a no-nonsense voice. Instinct told her the less said the better so she left it at that. Didn't take a rocket scientist to figure out he had an agenda; she'd been warned that may be the case. *God*, she thought. Men were so annoying at times.

True to form, he twirled that stupid ring on his short, stubby finger earning him a scowl of distaste. "I understand from my people that you've single-handedly saved the day. Or rather, saved the Justice Brothers' bacon," he added in an insincere way.

Mmm-hmmm. Quite an asshole, she thought. She turned cold, businesslike eyes on the man trying to goad a reaction from her for the sake of his enormous ego. "I wouldn't say that statement is entirely accurate although, yes. The system has been rebooted and is running as expected." His eyes narrowed at her tone although he wasn't stupid enough to respond in kind. Not yet, anyway. If she wasn't mistaken there was still plenty of gamesmanship and maneuvering he intended to play out.

"Well, now that I have some time, why don't you explain to me how this meltdown happened?" His tone sounded threatening, as if he was trying to intimidate her. *Bwah!!!* What a fool.

Subtly dismissive, she turned her back on him and leaned forward to indicate something on the huge monitor for him to look at. "As you can see here," she pointed, "this screen shows all systems currently operating at one hundred percent." When she straightened and looked back at him she had the unmistakable impression that he'd been checking out her ass. *What. A. Pig.* Irritated, Tori folded her arms across her chest and gave up trying to manage her normally short fuse. "It took some time, but we were able to pinpoint the exact cause of the problem. Apparently, *your* people modified a key code and didn't let anyone know."

"Are you telling me this supposedly state of the art system was hacked?" The accusation of incompetence on the part of the agency remained unsaid but was heard by her, loud and clear. Tori's breath kicked up a notch as anger surged to life inside her.

"Your system wasn't hacked, Mr. Barnes. An authorized user modified it internally. Nobody from outside your organization had access at any time." She watched Barnes' hackles rise her statement. He needed to blame someone and if it wasn't going to be the agency, it would fall on someone else's poor shoulders to deal with his wrath. Not only would he not be able to point a finger at Justice, the whole mess had been instigated by one of his own people.

Fuming, he turned angry eyes her way. "My security chief…."

She finished the sentence for him. "Is a brilliant man. I'm tempted to try and lure him away. A man with his skills would be an asset to the agency. There was no way for him or anyone to have found the problem until it was too late." When he stepped back as if she'd slapped him, she knew the threat held weight. He might want to fuck with Justice, but he didn't want to lose his head of security.

From the corner of her eye she saw Draegyn moving their way, rather like a storm cloud growing larger the closer it got. A shiver of awareness built in a part of her she hadn't known existed before this morning. He was angry by the look of him and dammit if the thought didn't excite her. Unless she was mistaken, Tony Barnes was about to get bitch slapped. She couldn't help the sly smile that formed on her face.

He hadn't been able to get to her fast enough. Knowing that Barnes was touching her hand, even if only in greeting, had him seeing red. Or maybe it was green. Anger. Jealousy. Fuck it. Take your pick. When he caught the sleazy motherfucker checking out her ass, it was all he could do not to race into the room and tear him limb from limb.

Just as he came around the partition he heard his little spitfire giving the oily businessman a verbal dressing down. She didn't need him to fight her battles, something she'd made abundantly clear from the get go. He might have caught her at a particularly vulnerable time in her life but that didn't mean she was completely down for the count. That aside, he'd never felt the compulsion to protect or defend a woman he was involved with. After the events of this morning, he was most definitely involved with Victoria Bennett, and nothing and nobody was going to upset or hurt her if he had anything to say about it.

"Barnes," he barked, earning a startled jump from the man in his eyesight. Going swiftly to Victoria's side, he laid a hand reassuringly at her back. "I see you've met our agency genius." He wanted his choice of words to let Barnes and everyone else know how important she was to the agency. And to him.

Barnes sneered at his insinuation into the conversation, just as he knew he would. "St. John," he muttered with clear distaste. "I should have known you'd be lurking in the shadows."

The two eyed each other as old animosities flared to life. Drae snorted a brittle laugh, churning at the man's tone. "Yeah, I just bet you did." Absently running his hand up and down Victoria's back, he looked down at her where she stood silently by his side. "I wouldn't want to disappoint." She bit her lip as humor lit up her expression.

"I've just left your man. He's done an excellent job of developing a new protocol for your employees that will limit access to the security mainframe. I take it Miss Bennett has informed you that the problem in your system was *internal*? The call literally came from inside the house, Barnes. You better get a hold of that if you don't want the same thing to happen again."

Drae watched, satisfied that his words had hit their mark. Tony Barnes was sadly mistaken if he imagined that he or Alex was going to shrug off the incompetence of the other man's employees. Not at the cost of the agency's reputation. No fucking way. And as for Victoria, the fact that Drae had yet to remove his hand from her back spoke louder than words.

"Yes, well," Barnes growled, clearly not happy. "I will discuss this with my staff. In the meantime, let me extend an invitation to the both of you. There's a pre-awards event in the main ballroom this evening. You'll be my guests. I'll leave instructions to seat you at the main table. I think you'll enjoy the night. Half of Hollywood is here."

Drae gave him a menacing smile. "I think we may take you up on the invite. Sounds like an interesting evening doesn't it, Victoria?" Before she could answer, Barnes waved them off as if he'd wasted enough of his precious time on them and simply melted into the scenery.

"That man is a tool bag," she muttered at his retreating back. Her choice of words made Drae laugh. He liked how direct she was.

He also liked that she didn't have any problem snarling at him when he deserved it. Everything about this sexier version of Victoria turned him inside out. It excited him that she'd responded to his loss of control earlier with such passion.

Some time later after a final run through with the security team, they were standing near the elevator when she leaned against him briefly and elbowed him in the ribs. "Hey," she chuckled.

"Hey, right back at you. What's up?"

"Were you serious about attending the event tonight?"

He shrugged. "Sure. Why not? Might be tons of fun or boring as dry toast. Depends on who is in attendance."

Tori thought back to the early, early morning. Before she'd been naked and whimpering in his arms. "Speaking of which, I saw that blonde actress, Stacey Adams checking in. She's pretty much an A-lister. If Stacey is here in the hotel, so will other big name celebrities."

Draegyn smiled at her. "Do you want to meet her?" he asked.

"Who?"

"Stacey Adams, of course. I could introduce you."

Possessiveness roared through Tori's senses. "You *know* her?"

"Yeah, I do. She's quite a piece of work, that one."

She tried for casual but when Draegyn said her knew her, a scenario worthy of a movie plot burst into her mind starring the man at her side and a very naked actress. She'd curl up and die if the perfect starlet had been in his bed. This was every nightmare she'd ever had. "How exactly do you know her?"

Guiding her into the empty elevator, Draegyn looked at her with a knowing expression. *Shit.* She was never very good at hiding her feelings. His blue eyes shimmered with an expression that bordered on hungry as he raked his gaze slowly over her body. Eventually he made it back to her eyes.

"We supervised security at the last Broadway awards show. She was a presenter. I helped the studio bodyguards get her in and out of the fan crush outside the venue." His gaze pierced hers. She wondered if he could read her thoughts. "That's all it was, sweetheart. Just business."

He didn't strike her as the sort to use endearments of any kind. The straight-forward explanation, clearly intended to set her mind at ease, reminded Tori that they were improbably more than just business associates now.

Silence reigned after that as the elevator ascended smoothly to their floor. A surge of excitement skittered across her nerves as they stepped into the foyer outside their suite and Draegyn placed a proprietary hand on her back. He wasn't quite grabbing her ass, but it was close.

The minute they were through the door, Draegyn gathered Tori in his arms and settled her against him. She laid her hands on either side of his chest. He brought his hand to her mouth and ran his thumb across her full lower lip. "I want you," he growled.

"I know."

His mouth quirked into a half smile at her straightforward response. Brushing his lips along her jawline he told her, "I'm too old to pretend there hasn't ever been anyone else in my bed, but I can say that there isn't anyone out there who can lay claim to much more than the occasional fuck."

She shifted back to look him square in the eye. "Is that supposed to make me feel better? 'Cause it doesn't."

"Here's the thing, Victoria. I don't want to just fuck you, regardless of how this morning may have seemed," he added as he held her in place. He leaned forward until his mouth stopped scant inches from hers. "Next time, and there will be a next time, and a time after that and a time after that - I'm going to eat you alive. Slowly. Until you can't think, and all that's left is you begging me to come inside you."

She gasped at his audacity as a quiver of spine tingling awareness rocked her. One of his hands drifted over her bottom as his hips rocked gently against her belly. When his mouth claimed hers, the contact was so hot and fevered that Tori found herself gasping for breath. She folded like a house of cards in a windstorm. When his lips sucked and nipped their way down her neck she whimpered as the ache between her legs increased with each tug of his lips.

Everything about him was just as she knew it would be. Without even trying he completely dominated her to the point where she was reduced to a puddle of goo every time they touched.

"Draegyn," she murmured. His eyes narrowed as he allowed some space between their bodies. "I'm not that girl. The one who drops her panties for any good-looking guy."

"Are you saying I'm good-looking?" he interrupted with a rakish grin.

"No! I mean, yes, you devil. You are most definitely good-looking. It's me I'm talking about." She noticed her hands were grasping his lapels so she eased off and smoothed the jacket against his hard muscled chest. Looking up she underestimated the effect his glittering perusal would have on her attempt to explain. It would be so easy to just surrender to the reckless urgency driving her.

"Being with you, well - I've never done anything like this." She pursed her lips and frowned, remembering the beating she'd taken in the press as a gold-digging femme fatale. *As if*, she thought. "No matter what you may have read about me, I'm not what you would call experienced." There. She said it. He needed to understand that while she fell to pieces every time he touched her, nothing like that had ever happened to her before.

"Yeah. I know. And for the record, I don't believe anything those rags print." He cupped the side of her face and softly kissed her forehead. "Things are moving fast between us. Maybe too fast for you. I get it."

Oh damn, she thought. The last thing she wanted was for him to back off, but her clumsy attempt to point out she wasn't an easy lay was backfiring.

The quick change of subject that came next hit her like a bucket of cold water. She understood why he changed course, but she wasn't happy about it.

"Do you have something short and sexy in that bag of tricks? I hope you do, because I'd like very much to escort you to the award event tonight."

Ah, he was being a gentleman. How sweet and totally unnecessary. She rather liked the primitive man.

Laughing she pushed against his chest forcing him to release her. "Short and sexy? Hmmmm. I do believe I have something fitting that description."

He swatted her behind as she moved away making her stick her tongue out at him in turn.

"Don't tempt me, woman!" he chuckled.

"Could I?" she asked innocently. "Tempt you, I mean."

"Victoria," he groaned. "Every damn thing about you is temptation."

She beamed at his answer, did a quick curtsey, and then dashed off to her room. "How long do I have?" she asked over her shoulder.

"One hour, darlin'. You have one hour to get ready. After that, I kick your door down and take you in your birthday suit if I have to. Come to think of it," he grinned, "that doesn't sound like such a bad idea."

DRAE WAS CONVINCED HE was on cloud nine. The evening was going even better than he could have imagined. With Victoria by his side, dressed in a little black dress that showcased her trim, toned body, he felt like a million bucks and was enjoying every minute of a gathering he would have normally avoided.

Barnes had kept his promise to seat them at the main table where they'd eaten, drank a ton of champagne, and happily hob-nobbed with a superstar couple, the mayor of Los Angeles, two mega-powerful producers with arm candy dates, and a big time co-median just coming off a string of highly successful movies.

As the event wound down, he and Victoria found themselves at the bar with the comedian and his lady, a famous swimsuit model who turned out not to be anything like her professional persona. An unlikely pair, Garry and Shawn were well-matched once you got to know them. He, of course, was funny and clever in an intelligent way. Drae liked the man for not selling out to the Hollywood ma-chine. Shawn was the surprise though. Learning she'd been a Rhodes Scholar in college, before she was discovered by a top mod-eling agent, meant she and Victoria hit it off in record time.

When the other couple suggested they take the party to a fifties supper club, the fun really got started. First they'd rather drunkenly commandeered a cab that required each of the women to sit on a lap in the close confines of the car. Drae would have happily driven all the way to New York if it meant Victoria would stay put with her luscious bottom sitting on his never ending hard-on.

At the club, they'd flashed a bit of V.I.P. gravitas and gotten a corner table away from the noise and commotion on the dance floor. The champagne kept flowing as did the lively chatter. It hadn't taken much for Shawn and Victoria to run out on the dance floor when the band leader announced a ladies only set, while he and Garry sat back and watched their women literally dominate the room.

Victoria was one fucking surprise after another; a thought that warmed him considerably, not that any more heat was necessary. He was on fire with barely concealed arousal as it was. She was an accomplished dancer, moving with a grace and agility that pleased him very much. Now that she wasn't shrouded in boring brown, he'd discovered the woman underneath all that camouflage, finding her exquisitely feminine and unbelievably sexy.

There was no way he'd be able to keep his hands off her once they were alone. She incited feelings in him that were deeply exciting. If it weren't for the noisy, boisterous crowd around them he suspected he'd be throwing her on the chaise next to him and fucking her senseless. She did that to him. Made him imagine things that could not have been more out-of-character.

"Wow! That was great!" she laughed dropping down next to him. Crossing her long legs as the short black dress crept up her thighs until he saw the lace at the top of her sheer black stockings peeking out, Drae enjoyed the sight she made sitting there in the sexy outfit that gave her curves an audacious appeal and showcased her sweet backside. The black, platform heels that added inches to her petite frame made him think things that were going to get him in trouble.

He and Victoria drank even more champagne, laughed a lot, and watched bemused while fans fell over themselves to pose for selfies with the other couple. It was turning out to be a very good evening indeed.

"Are you going to ask me to dance?" she questioned breathlessly. "C'mon big guy. Best time to hit the dance floor is with a champagne buzz!" she giggled.

He shot her a lop-sided grin. Even though her excitement was infectious, he was in no condition to stand up at the moment. "Nope," he chuckled. "No can do, milady."

Clearly shocked by his refusal she grabbed the front of his suit jacket. "Why?" she cried. "Please, plea*ssss*e, Draegyn. Dance with me."

Drae reached for one of her hands, quickly brought it to his lips for a swift kiss, then lowered it into his lap where, beneath the table and out of anyone's sight, he pressed her palm along the powerful erection pushing against his zipper. "That's why."

Her mouth formed a perfect circle as an understanding, "*Ohhhhh,*" hit his ears.

"Yes. *Oh.*" Her fingers shook, making Drae's heart thump wildly. For seconds that were way too brief, she mapped his hardness through the fabric of his pants.

Eventually, she leaned forward, turning toward him and laid her elbow along the table so all he saw was Victoria in his line of sight. "Do you know what a binary system is?"

"What?"

"The binary system. Ever heard of it?" She looked absolutely serious and completely earnest as if they'd been discussing the elements of science all evening.

"Uh," he sputtered, searching for a grasp on the change in conversation. "I don't know. Maybe." He shrugged. "I've heard the word, but can't say that I know the actual definition."

"Well," she began in a tone that said she was explaining

something complex to a newbie. “It’s a mathematical thing for counting or measurement involving the power of two. Like zero and one, or yes and no, on and off.”

“Ohhhh-kay.”

“I did part of my master’s thesis on the subject. Drove the review master crazy, too. He said I was employing female logic that in his estimation was illogical to the end result. Pissed me off, big time,” she bit out with a hair flip that would have done any reality show celebrity proud. “I think that was the moment my inner nerd connected with my outer temper. He just made me so frickin’ mad! He almost messed up my average by being such a prick. Threatened to disqualify the paper and everything because he couldn’t grasp the logic. I didn’t think it was fair to penalize a student for being smarter than the professor.”

“I couldn’t agree more,” Drae agreed, nodding vehemently. “And I’m thinking you didn’t sit by quietly and let him shit all over your work, right?”

She smiled. A tiny quirk at first that blossomed into a wide grin that hinted at her wicked side. “No. No I did not.”

Victoria shifted her chair even closer, holding his amused gaze with hers. Using a top secret whisper she said, “A friend and I painted his office hot pink. Every wall. Put the whole office back exactly as he’d left it. The only thing different was the wall color. It was obnoxious!”

Drae threw back his head and laughed at her college antics while she giggled along. “Thanks for sharing!” he teased.

“Well. Did it work?”

“Did what work?” Drae glanced around the table looking for clues.

“Psychology 101. Thought redirect.”

He didn’t get it. *Huh?* He looked at her in confusion.

Loosing an exasperated sigh she threw her hands up in defeat. “Hello? Thought redirect? You know! The party in your pants?

How's that going? I'd check myself, but I think that would defeat the whole purpose."

The light bulb went on over his head. "Let me get this straight…that whole story was meant to divert my, uh, attention – from the pants party?"

"Did it work?" she laughed. "I hope so because I really want to dance."

A wolfish grin lit up his face. She was fucking priceless. "I think a dance or two is doable." He reached out and twirled a chestnut curl around his fingers enjoying the slinky softness whispering against his skin.

Rising to his feet, Drae tugged at his cuffs then extended his hand and asked her to dance. On the dance floor, he tucked her petite body close to his as they swayed to the songs of a slow set performed by the house band. In her sexy high heels she fit perfectly against him with her head curved into his neck. He held on to her like a dying man grabbing a life vest, with one hand low on her back just above the curve of her backside and the other clutching her dainty hand against his chest. He was in heaven. She tipped her head back and smiled at him. "Thank you, Draegyn."

"For what?" he murmured lost in the soft glow of her chocolate eyes.

She gave him one of those Mona Lisa smiles that implied much but said little, then went back to nuzzling her face in his neck. He'd take it however he could get it, gathering her even closer, bending his head to breathe in her scent. Swaying together through the entire set, the music ended long before he wanted it to, forcing them apart. Grasping her hand as they walked back to their table, he marveled at how powerful such a simple touch could be. He wasn't normally a hand holder but nothing seemed more natural, than the feel of her small hand clasped in his.

All hell had broken loose when they got back to their table as Garry and Shawn had apparently decided on the spur of the moment that a trip to the wedding chapel was in order. Drae wasn't sure if they were serious or if their decision was based on Dom Perignon 1996. It didn't really matter because the two were high on each other and their joy was infectious. Before Drae knew what was happening, they were once again in a cab with two excited, tipsy females sitting on their laps. Apparently nothing got women giddier than the idea of a wedding. Shawn looked radiant while Victoria beamed.

By the time they found a wedding venue that wasn't tacky as all hell, things started happening with speed. Garry's assistant materialized out of thin air along with a photographer to record the event. Shawn and Victoria disappeared briefly and when they returned, the bride was decked out in a floral headpiece and carrying a humongous bouquet of tropical flowers, courtesy of the on-site florist.

Victoria came and stood quietly by Drae's side while the famous comedian cracked a dozen jokes about marriage as his adoring bride stood by and laughed at each outrageous jest and one-liner. The chapel they chose reminded the radiant bride of a summer she'd spent with her parents in Greece, and was decorated with every imaginable Greek column and statue making the whole place look like the Temple of Apollo. The person officiating was a distinguished-looking older man with a heavy accent named Stavros, who resembled a stern Greek papa in every way.

Instead of a hurried Vegas wedding, Stavros went for the gusto as the assistant filmed away. He intoned a short Greek prayer then launched into an off-the-cuff sermon about the sanctity of the vows they were making. The seriousness of the impromptu nuptials had changed from bawdy jokes to sacred. Once the old Greek man started talking to the couple about their responsibilities in marriage, Garry had grown solemn and quiet while Shawn shed a few tears.

Victoria fed her small hand into his so he grabbed on and held tight. The emotion of the moment had him in its grips, and her hand provided the anchor he needed. Having nursed such strong feelings against the state of marriage courtesy of his parents' arranged union, he wasn't prepared for how poignant the vows they were witnessing would be. He glanced at Victoria, saw tears on her flushed cheeks, and wondered what she was thinking. Did she long for marriage or was she lost in the memory of her parents' short-lived happiness? A week ago he wouldn't have cared one way or the other. Today, all he could think about, or feel, was connected to the tiny female at his side.

As witnesses, he and Victoria had an unexpected part to play when Stavros invited them to share their feelings. Or he thought that was what the Greek man said. His thick accent made it hard to catch every word, but it seemed like he wanted them to help consecrate the new union, so when he instructed them all to join hands, Drae and Victoria did so without hesitation.

A long prayer followed but with all the champagne he'd had, Drae didn't really try to follow along. By then, all that mattered was how turned on he was from the simple act of keeping Victoria's hand clasped in his. When it was all said and done, there was a new Mister and Missus to congratulate and even more champagne to drink in celebration. The assistant melted away and after a bit, a stack of papers got signed. It was all kind of a blur.

Garry and Shawn bade a fond farewell to their new friends, with the two ladies whispering in a conspiratorial way for a long moment before the happy bride pulled Victoria into a bear hug that ended in a waterfall of happy tears. Drae was content to sling his arm about her shoulders as the newlyweds hopped in a car arranged by the invisible assistant, and waved them off with a shout of good cheer. It was impossible not to smile.

"Well, milady, what say we call a cab and stagger back to the hotel?"

Victoria turned and looked at him. Stepping close, she rose on her toes and grabbed him by the lapels. "Only if you promise to make love to me once we get there," she muttered before running her tongue along his shocked mouth. He kissed her like a madman, standing on a street corner in Las Vegas, while people walked on by and cars sped past them.

"Done," he said in answer to her request as he waved a cab over and hastily scooted her across the backseat. Watching her backside shimmy to make room for him, he knew if he made it to the hotel before losing his sanity, it would be a miracle.

Victoria was quite proud of how calmly she walked through the hotel lobby. She'd begged Draegyn to make love to her and although it may have been the champagne doing part of the talking, she meant every word. It had been the most wonderful evening. He'd been an attentive and charming companion and surprised her by also being a fabulous dancer. Remembering how wonderful it felt to be in his arms as they swayed to the music made her senses tingle.

From the moment they slid into the cab, he'd been in charge of her hand. She liked the way he grabbed hold and refused to let go. When they arrived back at the hotel and she'd been pulled from the backseat, he'd raised her hand to his lips and placed a wet kiss upon her knuckles. Gasping, she looked into his face and saw the smoky shadowed eyes of a man struggling to keep control of himself. She didn't pretend not to know what those looks meant.

They weren't talking. After what she'd asked of him, no further words were necessary. Or possible for that matter. Not until they were somewhere private at least. She wouldn't have been able to hold a conversation anyway, not while her heart thumped and her nipples scraped against the material of her dress. She had no idea what was coming next and the anticipation was making her crazy. Feigning an air of nonchalance as they stepped into the crowded elevator had been a Herculean task. When she felt his thumb moving back and forth across the palm of the hand, her knees nearly buckled.

No man had ever affected her this strongly. For all her smarts, Tori never truly believed that such primal, basic need was in any way real. Oh sure, it was what she fantasized about when reading her romance books but never expected to find a real hero who would make her senses go all muzzy. The way Draegyn did. She couldn't wait to be alone with him. To find out if what they'd shared this morning had been a one-off or a preview of more to come.

Come. Now there was a word that had new meaning. When he'd taunted her earlier with the bold declaration that not only had gotten her to come but scream at the same time, she'd found his choice of words titillating. There was something about the way he talked that got her blood pumping. She knew he'd be even more direct and demanding with her if he knew how much it turned her on. She hadn't been offended when he talked about fucking her. The way he'd reacted in the aftermath of the wild, rough sex that exploded between them this morning told her he didn't mean it in a vulgar way. He'd been well and truly horrified by his demanding actions. She still hadn't been able to make him see that she'd been with him at every step. He could call it fucking all he wanted. Two sides of the same coin, as far as she was concerned.

As the elevator made its stops along the ascent to their suite, Drae plotted out how he wanted to proceed. Victoria asking him to make love to her had opened floodgates of erotic potential in his mind. One thing he knew for sure was that after the frenzied wildness from earlier, he intended to employ a slow down plan this time. He wanted so much more from her than just sex. This was the part that surprised him the most. How much he wanted to be around her. Talk to her. Maybe, wind her up a little and then enjoy the fireworks. He wanted to watch her doing ordinary things, because he liked the way she frowned and pouted when something made her pause. Suddenly, climbing inside her head to discover what she liked, what her favorite color was, which sports teams she rooted for, all those unique details had meaning to him. For the first time, *ever*.

As the elevator stopped to let out another person, she crowded closer to give some room for the exit, laying her hand in the center of his chest. That small movement had an instant effect on his sex. For all the quiet, everyday things he wanted from her, there was also this. A blazing inferno of red-hot lust that turned his cock hard enough to cut diamonds. She did that to him with a simple touch, a shy smile.

Every thought he had was new emotional territory for him. His view of relationships had been deeply damaged once he understood how corrupt his parents' picture-perfect society union was. From that time on, he'd believed marriage was a sham, a social convention that was all for show. He doubted the faithfulness of nearly every couple he knew and thought romance was nothing more than posturing. Until a brown-eyed beauty reached into his heart. The way his thoughts wandered to Victoria every chance they got was turning a lifetime of cynicism to dust.

Watching the lights on the elevator panel flick upwards as they neared their floor, Drae felt uncharacteristically nervous. There was an honesty in the way they communicated. She lacked the artifice he'd found in many women and spoke what was on her mind, even if it was harsh or critical. He was discovering a freedom in that, a feeling that he didn't have to live up to a reputation or be someone he wasn't. She liked it honest, blunt, hard, and dirty. What more could he ask for?

He still held her hand as they stepped from the elevator. Drae was fascinated by the sound of her heels tapping along the floor, and the way she felt at his side. Even her footsteps sounded small, dainty, and feminine. The knowledge that he would protect this woman with his life turned his world upside down and scared the shit out of him.

The moment they entered the suite, he heard her gasp as the first thing they saw was a huge floral arrangement set in the middle of the living room next to a magnum of champagne chilling in an ornate silver bucket. As they drew closer she laughed and gestured to an enormous platter covered in chocolates, tropical fruits and gourmet pastries.

"Chocolate!" she giggled "Get out of my way, mister!" Drae laughed when she dove straight in, plucking a small chocolate truffle from the center and popping it in her mouth. ""Ehrmygawd", or something like that came out as she licked her lips. He picked up a small envelope nestled in the flowers and saw that the whole thing, the chocolate, flowers and champagne, was a thank you from the newlyweds.

"The bride and groom send their love and thanks."

"Awww, how sweet," she said in that soft, gentle voice she used when something really touched her.

The champagne fit into his plans perfectly, making Drae silently note to thank Garry at the first opportunity for the gesture. The timing couldn't have been more perfect. "Hey. How 'bout some champagne? Let's toast to the happy couple."

"Oh, I'd love some!" she laughed, going to stand by the expanse of windows that looked down the glittering strip. "It's so oddly beautiful, all the lights. Don't you think?"

He handed her a flute of champagne, gently tapped his glass to hers, and then turned to look at the view. "I've never really thought about it." He skimmed the sight before him, taking a sip or two, then turned his gaze on her. "You, standing here, with a million lights twinkling all around. Now that's beautiful."

She turned a bright mega-watt smile on him; made all the more gorgeous by the faint pink flush that spread across her perfectly sculpted cheekbones. He tried to swallow back the thickness in his throat. Something in her eyes let him know that she wanted him to kiss her. Yeah, he was going to kiss her and do a whole lot more

But right now, keeping her guessing and waiting was more fun. By the time they were naked in bed, and he rolled her underneath him, he wanted Victoria mindless and desperate with longing.

He followed her back into the living room enough paces behind to give him an awesome fucking view of her cute little derrière swaying as she walked away in those mind-melting high heels. As if her toned legs weren't temptation on their own, when the 'come fuck me' shoes were added, he had a hard time keeping his hands off her.

"M*mmm*, chocolate covered strawberries. Want one?" she asked, gripping one of the big berries by the stem and holding it out to him.

He grinned. "Ladies first."

She bent to place her flute on the table giving Drae another quick flash of her lace covered thighs. He wondered what color panties, if any, she had on. Laughing at him she shrugged. "Your loss, darlin'," she sang in delightful faux southern twang. "Once I get started, there may not be any left for you!" She put the lush red berry in her mouth and bit off the chocolate-covered tip, in what Drae would swear was slow motion. Watching her lips pucker open for the fruit was sensual torture. Closing her eyes in enjoyment, he nearly blacked out when her tongue swept along her lips gathering the juicy sweetness. Next, she repeated the pucker, only this time she sank her teeth into the juicy delicacy and neatly snapped off the stem. Once again he heard her murmur "Ehrmygawd," as she reached for a napkin to wipe her sticky fingers.

Another strawberry went the same way as the first while Drae watched, enthralled. He was a guy, so imagining that pucker and those lips opening for his hard cock was a no-brainer. He wouldn't be human if that wasn't the first thing he thought of. But after the second strawberry, with the excitement gathering in his groin, he started to imagine something else quite different for those strawberries.

TORI WAS HIGH. MAYBE literally. They'd both had enough champagne over the past few hours to qualify, but she knew her euphoria was also because of the gorgeous, sexy, exciting man that she'd propositioned. He was so damn handsome that it almost hurt to look at him, but look at him she did. The man wore a suit better than any runway model and she rather thought they looked kind of nice together this evening. She loved her dress mostly because of a peplum that gave her modest curves a saucy boost and the way the sheer overlay emphasized the seductive curve of the sweetheart bodice. It was short and sexy, but not too much.

Being the only daughter of an unabashed southern beauty queen who knew how to work the pageant circuit like nobody's business, Tori had learned the art of walking in high heels at a very young age. Being a tomboy never stopped her from the pleasures of playing dress up, especially in some of her mom's fancy gowns. Crossing her legs, she sighed at the shoes she had on. She liked footwear, who didn't? The impossibly high black suede heels were a decadent indulgence she'd purchased during a round of retail therapy after she'd returned to the states. This was the first time she'd worn them, and they hadn't disappointed.

Men might say they didn't notice such things but she'd caught the gleam in Draegyn's eyes when his gaze had lingered on her shoes and then taken the slow route up to her eyes. When he'd pulled her into his arms on the dance floor, the added inches helped them mold together in a perfect fit.

"How about a toast?" He pushed the refilled flute into her hand and cleared his throat. He joined her, putting an arm around the back of the sofa making her feel like she'd been caged in by his powerful presence. "To the newlyweds," he said as they clinked glasses.

Tori drank deep and then laughed. "Are you trying to get me drunk?"

"No!" he sniggered, "although I think that ship has sailed, don't you?"

"Pretty much," she agreed cheerfully. Heaving a sigh, she relaxed and enjoyed his fingers sweeping along her back. "Champagne makes everything better!"

"Is that the alcohol buzz talking?" he murmured.

She smiled into his blue eyes. "That and the chocolate."

Draegyn drained his glass and gave her a serious look. What in the world was on his mind?

"Mmmm. I just remembered something."

"What," she asked, frowning?

He settled back into the sofa, arm still slung across the back, and crossed a foot onto his knee. "I think we're at two strikes to nothing on the payback scoreboard."

The payback scoreboard? *Oh shit*, Tori thought. What was he up to?

"I think it's time to collect."

She snickered and threw him a grinning pout. "Oh really? And just how do you propose to do that?"

"Stand up." He commanded, taking the champagne flute from her hands and putting it on the table. Tori's thighs clutched at the authority in his voice. It was pretty clear he wanted to play with her. She hadn't ever imagined responding to being told what to do, but dammit, it turned her on when he did it. Big time.

She stood up. Slowly. Smoothed her dress, and put her hands on her hips. "Now what?"

Drae sat there enjoying the sight she made with her hands slapped on her hips like a stern nanny facing an exasperating child. He wasn't surprised she did as he asked. Victoria didn't want hearts and flowers. Not really. She might not normally take anyone's shit, but when it came to intimacy, she wanted a strong man. Sometime to take the reins and be in charge. She wanted to flirt with being dominated, if only just a little. Lowering his leg to the floor, he pointed at his lap and said, "Bottoms up."

He had to give her credit. She got his intention in a heartbeat. "What?" she cried. "Are you kidding?"

He leered at her for good measure. "No Victoria," he growled. "Not even a little bit. Over my knee on your own steam, or I'll do it for you."

"Draegyn! Come on!" she wailed. "Don't be ridiculous. There's no way I'm going to let you spank me."

His smirk told her he wasn't going to let it go. Patting his thigh, he said, "I'm waiting."

She tried glaring at him, but he could see her mind working overtime deciding what to do. Shock turned to interest on her face, and he warmed knowing she was going to capitulate. Huffing in exasperation she waved her hands in the air and snapped, "Okay. Let's just get this over with. Jeez!" He patted his thigh again and waited.

Mumbling something under her breath about men, she lowered onto his thighs with all the grace and poise of a prima ballerina. Drae wasn't positive, but he was mostly certain nothing had ever been more tempting or looked more fucking awesome than her pert backside lying in his lap. He spread his legs a bit and thoroughly enjoyed the way she shimmied into position. It wouldn't have been a hardship to stare at her ass all night. It was that delectable.

Drae lifted the dress, revealing her sexy thigh high stockings and the flesh of her backside in a pair of satin panties that shimmered in the dim light of the room. He caught her startled gasp and smiled. *Good.* He wanted her to be shocked. Shocked at how much she wanted what he was doing. Peeling back a side of her panties he exposed one perfect, pale cheek making sure to palm the mouth-watering globe with slow, firm strokes.

"You have a beautiful backside," he muttered in a hoarse rasp. She wiggled on his thighs and sighed. She liked that. Liked him touching her. He smacked her on the bottom with enough force to make her jump. "That's for having a smart mouth."

He palmed her cheek again, grabbing a handful of flesh and squeezing. Smack! She jumped a second time as his big hand connected. "That's for making me hard every time I see or think about you." She moaned. He slapped her ass again, even harder. Smack! "That's for calling me a bully." Now she was wriggling in earnest. He caressed the red flesh on her backside, letting his fingers dance under the elastic of her panties where it dipped between her legs. That got both a moan and a gasp. Before the sound had fully left her mouth, he roughly slapped her flesh one last time. "And that's for hiding in that hideous brown wardrobe. Don't ever do that again, Victoria. Don't hide from me."

She scrambled awkwardly off his lap, standing on wobbly legs, hurriedly trying to yank her dress into place. "Ow," she muttered with a dark pout while she rubbed her backside. "That hurt."

"Good," he replied. "Little reminder of who's in charge."

"Don't growl at me like that!"

He could watch her pout all night. Those lips should be illegal. For the thousandth time Drae fantasized what her mouth on his flesh would feel like.

"And for the record, that bit of performance art was a one-off. Don't count on it happening again," she snapped.

He considered not just what she was saying but how she was saying it. Her body language and the way her eyes glittered told him a hell of a lot. “I heard a moan, not a cry.” *Yep.* He liked getting her going. Watching her get ready to tear into him was exciting.

“Honestly! You’re such an ass. This is what’s wrong with men,” she bit out, waving her hands in exasperation.

Ah. Such a wild temper this little lady had. Taming it had appeal but stoking the fire seemed so much more enjoyable. The idea that the passion she was running on at the moment would make it to the bedroom made his cock twitch.

“L-Look,” she stuttered, and then changed her mind about what she was going to say. Her pout returned. He smiled slowly and watched her eyes focus on his mouth. “Okay. You won this round,” she muttered.

Note to self – spanking wasn’t off the agenda.

“So,” Drae purred as he ran a hand up her thigh, under the hem of her dress to toy with the lace of her stockings. “What I’m hearing is a little spanking is okay, but you’d rather I kissed your ass?” She gasped at his statement and then laughed.

“You are a devil, sir,” she mocked. “But yes, I suppose that’s a better way of putting it!”

Relaxing into a casual sprawl, he fixed her with a knowing look, saying, “I would have guessed black.”

“Black? I don’t understand.”

“Your panties. They’re purple. I guessed either black or none at all.”

“Oh.” That shut her up although she continued to soothe the butt cheek he’d left red and smarting.

Nodding at her bottom he smirked apologetically and said, “Should I kiss that and make it better?”

Just like that, a naughty gleam turned her milk chocolate eyes a deep, dark brown flecked with gold. Down but not out, he mused. “Let me get back to you on that,” she murmured. This was what made her perfection.

She needed time to process what just happened so Tori padded in bare feet closer to the fireplace and watched while Draegyn stood and took their empty flutes to the champagne bucket. This time he poured half of what he had previously into their glasses and set them aside. With the push of a button on the remote control, small flames appeared in the gas fireplace at her back.

Removing his suit jacket, he flung it carelessly over a chair, loosened his tie, and flicked open the top two buttons on his crisp, white shirt. Watching him was a guilty pleasure, she thought. The way he moved, nothing was extra. No fidgeting, no extraneous motions. As he walked toward her she couldn't help the way her eyes automatically drifted south. Biting her lip she measured the tremendous bulge tenting his slacks and remembered the moment at the supper club when he had placed her palm upon his hardness.

It didn't take much to recall in vivid detail what it felt like to absorb his huge staff deep into her body. She was surprised they fit, he was so big and solid, and she so small and soft. When her eyes met his, she knew from his smug expression that he was reading her thoughts. In this instance his male arrogance was well-deserved.

"Like what you see?"

Accepting the champagne flute, she blushed and looked away. "You know I do."

"That's all you, honey. Every hard, throbbing inch." All she could do was blush even more. He came at her quickly with a question. "Tell me what you like. Tell me what you want, Victoria."

Tori clutched the delicate glass in her hand, sipping some more of the sweet bubbly liquid, peering at him over the rim of her glass. Hesitation punctuated her answer. "Honestly, I don't know how to answer that. I'm not all that experienced, and you already know that this morning was kind of a first for me."

His eyes shone at the mention of their earlier escapade. "Now, when you say, *not experienced*, what exactly does that mean? Don't be shy," he urged. "Honesty, remember? You can tell me anything."

"I know." She nodded, trying like hell not to start biting her lip. "First of all, I never slept with Wallace. It wasn't the way the tabloids described it. And that's all I have to say about him."

"Glad to hear it. The man was an asshole. Moving on." His words hung expectantly in the air.

"Don't laugh, okay?" she murmured with a worried frown. When he nodded she blurted out what he wanted to know in a rush of jumbled words.

"Okay. Here it is - college boyfriend. We lived together on campus for two years. Actually, it was more like playing house. He was in my major and yes, before you ask, he was part of the geek squad." Shrugging, after a moment she added, "We were more friends than lovers and too young and inexperienced all around. It was all sort of, *meh*. So there you have it. Until this morning anyway, a college boyfriend was the full extent of my sexual experience. When you ask what I want, honestly, I have no idea what the possibilities even are."

"Hmmm." He took a short swallow of the bubbly while he considered what she told him. "So, what you're saying is my only competition is a college dweeb. And your hand, of course." She wished his wicked grin didn't get her lady parts all tingly and warm but it did. "Here's what's going to happen, Victoria." He took the glass away and pulled her close. "You asked me to make love to you, and I intend to do just that."

Before he could say another word she breathed a sigh of relief. "Oh, thank God. The suspense was killing me. Will you kiss me now," she purred.

He ran his thumb over her lower lip, leaned in, and bit her softly before straightening. "No. No kissing for now. We seem to lose control rather quickly once the kissing starts and if you'd let me finish before jumping in all demanding, you'd learn that we're going to do things my way. Do you trust me?" She nodded but sighed disappointed, staring at the curve of his lips knowing she'd have to wait longer to feel them on her own again.

"I want you naked," he demanded in a voice thickened with unmistakable desire. "Don't think. Just do it. I know you want to."

She liked the way he growled his commands. The sound he made went straight to where heat and moisture was gathering in her core. Truth was, she more than liked giving up control to him. The arrogance she once despised in his character had been replaced with an appreciation of his alpha swagger that rocked her sensibilities. That didn't mean though that she was going to blindly obey without interjecting a little of herself into the process. Playing the coquette card, she peered up at him through lowered eyelashes. "I can't," she answered. "Take off my dress, I mean."

"Why the hell not?"

She almost smiled at his gruff tone. Poor him. He had no idea how badly she wanted to be naked for him and how determined she was to get him in the buff as well. That man's body would tempt a saint, and if he was going to get an eyeful of her bare ass, she damn well intended to get the same from him. Pirouetting slowly until her back was to him, she looked over her shoulder and pointed to the neckline of her dress. "Because I can't get at the button or the zipper."

Drae was enjoying this. Her willingness to play along was wracking his body with greedy wants and needs that he'd never experienced before. It was exhilarating, nerve wracking, awesome.

Enjoying the slide of her silky hair through his fingers, he pushed the tumbling locks over her shoulders revealing a tiny jeweled button above the zipper. Holy God, even from behind she stopped his breath. He was definitely going to enjoy peeling the little black dress from her body.

Nimble fingers made quick work of the fastening, making sure to slide across the skin along her nape. He was standing so close and was so in tune to every breath she took that he saw her skin prickle.

Pressing apart the sides of the sheer top, Drae gently ran his knuckle across her shoulder causing fine tremors to shimmer along her petite frame.

A taste. He needed a quick taste to satisfy the beast roaring to life inside him. Fastening his lips to the skin at the base of her neck, he pressed a wet kiss followed by a slow, sensuous lick from his tongue. Fuck, he was a dead man. Even that tiny stretch of flesh tasted like sin.

Moving on to the zipper, his trembling fingers were less dexterous than before but managed to get the job done while the tightening in his balls taunted him to just rip the dress from her. Restraint won as one of his hands palmed slow, smooth strokes over her hip while the other pulled the long zip down as his fingertips dragged against her skin. In the silence he heard the quiet rasp of the zipper and what could only be described as a hushed whimper. She was incredibly responsive to his touch.

Looking over her shoulder, the warmth of her breath hit him as she asked, "What's taking so long? Do you need my help?" He heard the wicked inflection of flirtation in her voice and smiled while his inner caveman let him set the pace.

"Hush that sassy mouth. I was enjoying the scenery," he teased, spreading wide both sides of the dress to completely expose her back to his view. She wasn't wearing a bra. Seeing the long line of her back with her pale skin made luminescent by the flickering firelight made his cock throb.

Knowing she wasn't like the other nameless, faceless females who had cavorted through his sex life with their practiced wiles and experienced ways made her response all the sweeter. When she stepped away from him and gracefully twirled around, he was struck by how utterly enchanting this little creature with the big brown eyes really was. She might be challenged in the experience department but that didn't mean this wasn't the hottest, most erotically charged moment of his life. What the hell had he done to deserve such a treasure?

Tori was running on emotion and sheer instinct when she turned to face Draegyn after teasing him into undoing the back of her dress. She instantly noted the way his cheekbones stuck out on his face, highlighted by slashes of color and the tense, hard line of his mouth. The muscle working overtime in his jaw mirrored the clenched fists hanging by his sides. Holding out her arm, she indicated the tiny, jeweled button at her wrist. "Please," she whispered, wetting her lips. When his breathing hitched and nostrils flared at the provocation, she silently whispered, *Gotcha*. She didn't want to be the only one whose heartbeat was thumping off the charts.

When he bent his head to concentrate on the tiny fastenings at each wrist, Tori leaned closer and breathed him in. God, he was like a banquet of primal delights. Earthy and basic. He made her senses swim. It frightened her a little.

Once the sleeves were open, she shimmied around and pulled one arm free of the sheer fabric, holding the unzipped bodice to her chest. Never having done an actual striptease before, Tori was running on imagination and a good dose of romance heroine panache when she coyly extended the arm still trapped in its sleeve and said, "Pull," as her fingers wiggled at him.

His expression, which started as a sly smile, grew to a wicked grin. He took her hand, flipped it over and pressed a kiss on the sensitive skin at her wrist. She shivered from head to toe. When he tugged on the sleeve so her arm could slide free, she made sure to hold the material close so none of her flesh was exposed. If she was going to do this, she was going to do it right and enjoy it at the same time.

Going to stand in front of the windows, with the twinkling lights shimmering at her back, Tori struck an innocent pose as his eyes singed her with their heat. *Well*, she thought, *it's now or never*. She wished her hands weren't shaking. The dress slid down her front as she swung her hips and pushed until it fell to the floor, leaving her in a pair of purple satin panties, lace top stockings, the 'come fuck me' shoes and nothing else. His grunt of appreciation as he devoured her nakedness with his gaze was her reward.

Drae was sure he'd never seen anything so beautiful in his whole life. As Victoria shucked off her dress her chestnut hair fell softly across her shoulders, spilling close to breasts that were all hers and not some plastic surgeon's work. They were the perfect size. He remembered that they fit his mouth perfectly and a yearning to suckle on her lusciousness beat at his sense of control. Damn. He was having a hard time playing it cool when that was the last thing he felt. She was driving him insane with need from a game he had started.

Remembering what he had planned helped get his rampaging desires under control. He'd never wanted such intimacy with a woman, preferring instead to simply satisfy his powerful sexual needs and move on. Discovering deeper wants, more powerful needs than any he'd imagined possible made this situation and this woman unique. Reaching out his hand, he murmured in a voice choked with desire, "You're incredibly beautiful, Victoria." He watched her eyes smolder at his praise. "Come here," he commanded, motioning with his outstretched fingers for her to come to him. *Now.*

Drae drank in the sight as she walked toward him without hurry, her trim hips rocking slowly with each step. Slender and graceful, her movements were beautiful to watch. He very much liked the sexy hosiery and shoes and the rich, jewel tone hue of the panties against her skin and the way her hair's luster picked up the twinkling lights. Fuck. He liked the whole package. A lot.

When her hand slotted into his, he pulled her into the living room as though walking around half naked was an everyday occurrence. He rather enjoyed the expression on her face, which swung between shock and enjoyment. *Just you wait, little one*, he thought. *What I have in mind for you will do more than shock.* He let go of her hand to grab a strawberry as she leaned her hips against the back of the sofa and watched him.

"You have too many clothes on," she muttered when he came to stand directly in front of her. "Not fair."

He laughed. She was cheeky and so damn adorable. "This is true," he murmured, staring intently at the strawberry and then at her mouth. "But you know what they say. All is fair in love and war." She inhaled sharply at his words.

Completely changing the subject, leaving her sputtering, confused, and still half naked he adopted an innocent air, asking, "Now what's the proper technique with these berries? First you eat the bottom," he whispered suggestively as his lips opened and the chocolate covered tip sank into his mouth. She was staring at him, wide-eyed and unblinking. Letting the sweet fruit roll around his tongue for a moment he grunted, "Mmmm,"and smacked his lips deliberately. Holding up the half-nibbled berry he continued, "Now what?"

Watching her nipples peak and breasts shudder as she sucked in a huge breath, Drae forced himself to remain calm. "Um…" Her voice sounded harsh and sultry. She had to clear her throat to continue. "You take that last piece and bite into it just under the stem and snap it off."

"Really?" he shrugged. "Shame to waste it all in one bite." Some things should be savored, don't you think?"

With that he took the ripe half-eaten strawberry and holding it by the stem, used the juicy pulp to highlight one of Victoria's turgid nipples, circling around the tip with the luscious fruit and finally rubbing against the pebbled nub. While the shocked, "Oh!" that rushed from her mouth still hung in the air, he zeroed in on the strawberry covered delight with his mouth, licking the juice from her flesh, nibbling deftly at her enflamed nipple and eventually sucking the perfect breast deep into his hungry mouth.

Drae wasn't sure if this was about her or him as he lost himself in the feel and taste of her. Cupping the mound in his big hand, he squeezed her flesh and molded her fantastic tit with restless fingers.

It wasn't enough. He slowly repeated the action on her other breast, rubbing the juices into her skin and then licking and sucking her clean. He noticed her legs were shaking as the sounds of him greedily feasting on her body filled the air.

Whatever he'd planned to happen next faded to insignificance; he felt her hands suddenly on his chest, clawing at his shirt in her insistence to get at his skin. Releasing the taut nipple he'd been rolling his tongue around with a resounding pop, he enjoyed, as only a man could, the sight of her flesh jiggling from the force of the sudden suck and release. *That's what tits should do*, he thought with satisfaction. They should bounce and jiggle not just stand at perpetual attention. He considered drawing the other nipple back into his mouth until her desperate attack on his shirt diverted his attention. He wasn't sure the buttons could survive her determination.

Covering her trembling fingers to calm her movements, he asked, "Need help?" but she shook him off with an unladylike curse that didn't require interpretation.

"No! *FUCK!* I do not need help," she huffed. "What I need is this damn shirt in a pile on the floor." His tie went flying a second later. One by one she managed to slip each button through its hole, yanking the tails of his shirt from his pants with rather a lot of impatience. He smiled knowingly.

WITH A COMPLETE LACK of decorum, Tori practically destroyed Draegyn's shirt in her frantic haste to uncover his body. When she'd dropped her dress on the floor, she half-expected him to rip off his clothes and tumble her to the carpet right then and there. There was no mistaking the electricity arcing between them or what the end result of that powerful current would be.

She should have known it wouldn't happen the way she imagined. He seemed hell bent on dragging out their foreplay, wringing every possible pleasure and feeling from each moment. That was why he wouldn't kiss her. Until now they'd proceeded with far too much feverish intensity. This time was all about the journey, not the destination. Hell. They both already knew how it would end. The shuddering orgasms from this morning were only the beginning, not the end.

She'd reached a point, during the ravishment he'd subjected her breasts to, where her nakedness and his clothing didn't mesh. Indulging him by prancing about in high heels and a tiny pair of panties was one thing. Denying herself the pleasure of putting her hands all over him was another. Tori pulled his shirttails out and hurriedly tore the unbuttoned shirt down his arms. She'd had quite enough, thank you. There hadn't been time to explore his body this morning, something she'd had time to regret all day. She'd enjoyed being held in his powerful arms on the dance floor and taken every opportunity to press against him. Now she wanted to know him with her hands and fingers and especially with her mouth.

Jesus God, but he had the most spectacular chest. Draegyn St. John was like a walking bulletin board for hard muscled abs with a sexy, well-defined mouth tingling V that disappeared into his pants. His fair coloring gave the hair on his body a softness that belied the power and strength underneath. She ran her hands appreciatively over his pecs, marveling at the softness of his skin. It wouldn't take much for Tori to get completely lost exploring his naked torso, but the thrilling bulge in his pants was calling her name. If she was going to stand there in her panties, then turn-about was fair play.

Trying like mad to concentrate, she was aware that he was watching her every move, groaning roughly when she stroked his nipples and sucking in his stomach as she unbuckled his belt. When her fingers found the snap on his pants, she slowed to a crawl, deliberately drawing out every slight tug on the zip as she pulled it down over an impressive erection. Enjoying the view, she measured him with her eyes feeling a purely feminine thrill at the evidence of his virility. Pushing her hands into his pants she shoved them forcefully down his legs, stopping to reach behind and firmly stroke her palms across his rock hard ass. *Holy shit.*

"Thank you… I think," he murmured letting Tori know her last thought had been uttered aloud. Stepping out of the pants, Draegyn kicked away everything but the black briefs he had on which were losing the battle of covering his manhood. She was fascinated by how the cotton stretched across his bulging sex, gaping slightly beneath his belly button from the tented material.

Meeting his eyes she let the amazement she felt show in her expression. "Wow. Your body is so beautiful, Draegyn." She ran her hand straight down the center of his chest until she hit the waistband of his briefs. Tucking her fingers into the elastic she used it to yank him forward. "Is there a kiss going to happen anytime soon?" she breathed into his open mouth.

Expecting him to give her what she wanted Tori jerked, shocked when he ran a finger over her lips then slid it into her mouth. Didn't take her but a second to recover though, sucking on the invading finger the way she would his body when she finally got the chance. He was fucking killing her with this slow, deliberate seduction.

Pulling his hand away, he reached between her legs, cupping her aching mound, making her acutely aware of the dampness her panties could barely conceal. "I think we're both going to enjoy what comes next."

Her response, the only thing she was capable of doing at that moment, came out in a low, rumbling moan as he pressed the heel of his hand firmly against her most sensitive spot and ground it in slow, circles. She wasn't going to be able to keep standing if he kept that up. "Draegyn," she implored shakily as her trembling hands flailed about until she gripped his forearms. "Kiss me, please."

Victoria's soft plea broke through Drae's determination to go slow. She wanted him so badly. Her breathless sighs and quiet moans were testing his control in a very big way. *Enough*, he thought as he swept her into his arms, cradling her perfect, petite body close, quickly making his way to the master bedroom. Once she was seated in his embrace she turned her mouth onto his flesh, leaving tiny, wet kisses along his collarbone as her hand gripped the back of his neck.

At the big, wide bed he lowered her carefully to her feet, caging her between his arms and the mattress. The effect her small, feminine body had on his made him feel big, powerful, and protective. "Open your mouth for me, honey." Pretty much all hell broke loose with his words. She flung herself at him, rubbing her gorgeous breasts against his chest, and dove onto his mouth. Flames shot along his nerve endings as dueling tongues swirled.

Each kiss with Victoria was like a world unto itself. It staggered him to think what that really meant. Totally unable or unwilling to hide her response from him, she held nothing back. Her lips clung to his, eager for each new sensation. The beast inside him was awake and prowling. Drae wrapped a section of her hair around his fist and yanked her head back. She pitched forward trying to get back at his mouth, but he growled and yanked her hair harder. Sultry chocolate eyes blinked up at him. "This will be over in minutes if you keep that up." He almost lost his resolve when she pursed her kiss-swollen lips and swiped them with her tongue.

Turning her around he swatted her behind and told her to get on the bed. It was a measure of how far gone she was that his demand wasn't met with a comeback of any sort. Instead, she complied by kicking off her shoes and lifting first one knee and then the other onto the high mattress. Grabbing her around the hips when he caught sight of her backside right in front of his face, he leaned in and placed a gentle kiss on the side of her ass that he'd turned red with a spanking. "There," he husked as she turned to stare at him. "That's for earlier. All better now?"

She dropped onto her side and rolled onto a bank of pillows with an air of innocent excitement that put warmth in his chest. With hair tumbling over one shoulder, she sat propped on one hip, feet crossed demurely at the ankles. The purple scrap of satin, black stockings and the briefs he still wore were all that remained of the slow down plan.

"Hold that thought," he said opening his travel bag and tossing a box of condoms on the nightstand. He saw her eyes widen and almost laughed. Jesus, she was one contradiction after another. She might know how to program the world's most sophisticated computer but a box of condoms stopped her dead in her tracks.

When she held her arms open in invitation he went head first without hesitation. In seconds they were entwined, rolling around the tremendous bed, clutching at each other and kissing like maniacs. It was hotter than the gateway to hell as they proceeded to set the bed on fire with their explosive passion.

A desperate need to taste her gripped his senses sending his lips and tongue on a slow journey under her chin and down the side of her neck. She writhed in his arm as her fingernails dug into his skin. He licked her with the flat of his tongue and found a spot that made her squirm. Turning all his attention to the sensitive area where her shoulder joined her neck, Drae left biting nips and wet kisses then settled into an open mouth suckle that was sure to leave her marked.

The temperature went up even higher when she pressed her hand on his head encouraging the erotic caress while her legs moved restlessly against his. She moaned and angled her head better to give him more access. He was happy to oblige. With hands gently caressing her breast, he feasted on the skin of her neck until a greater need sent his hungry mouth toward her puckered nipples.

Holding her breasts in his hands, he squeezed and molded the mounds until each had a perfect nipple, swollen with need, waiting for his lips. He warned her only once. "I'm going to devour every inch of your body until you cannot take any more pleasure. Then, I'm going to make love to you, Victoria," he groaned. "Sink deep inside and fuck you till you beg me to let you come. Is that what you want, baby? I need to hear you say it."

"Oh my God, yes. Yes!" she cried. Her hands were everywhere, desperate, rough. She grasped his forearms, ran her fingers down his back, clutched at his ass. "I need you so bad it hurts," she cried, rolling her hips against his. He knew the agony she referred to. His cock had been rock hard for so long he was afraid he was doing himself harm. It wouldn't be long now. By the time he sank into her she would be so wet and hot that the wait would have been well worth it.

He flicked a rosy, pebbled nipple with the tip of his tongue as her back arched, and he was treated to the sight of her tits quivering under his caresses. Keeping up the flicking torture until she sobbed for more, Drae savored her response. Each time she cried out, his balls tightened. The grip she had on his senses was tremendous.

Her breasts tasted heavenly as he sucked on each nipple. She had a particularly sensitive spot underneath her breasts that reacted to his stroking fingers with a full body shudder. "I think you like that, hmmm?"

Wrapping a leg around his hip, she shimmied against his hard-on to show him how much. "I love your hands touching me. And your mouth. Your mouth is so sexy, Draegyn," she murmured. He enjoyed the way she said his name and nothing sounded hotter than when she groaned it. Reminded him how every little thing about her turned him inside out and upside down, Drae moved to take her the rest of the way to the sensual paradise they'd been heading toward. At that precise moment, nothing was more urgent or had more importance to him than giving the woman in his arms the ultimate pleasure.

Rising to his haunches, Drae reached for the purple panties, peeling the damp fabric from between her legs, easing them free and tossing them aside. There was something decadent and sensual about ever-so-slowly rolling each stocking down her legs while she watched with those sexy chocolate brown eyes. Adjusting her position with his knees and hands, he spread her wide, draping each leg over his hips until he had access to her center. Fluffy soft brown curls flecked with moisture greeted him. When her legs opened, the position made her outer lips unfurl, giving him a perfect view. It was the most erotic thing he'd ever seen.

Drae kept his hands moving, traveling up and down her legs from knee to thigh, as he bent over her body, licking, kissing and sucking his way down her center from her breasts to her navel. She kept the fingers of one hand clenched at the back of his head while the other was fisted in the sheets.

When he'd finished licking all the skin his mouth could find, he zeroed in on the center of her sex, desperate to taste her and lap at the arousal flooding her shaking body. Her scent invaded his senses, making him even harder. The beast inside was turned on by the overpowering carnality of her response - from the way her skin prickled to the sounds she made. With each panting reminder of her arousal, an erotic drumbeat pounded in his brain directing him to suck on her sensitized flesh.

She was writhing in the most deliciously sensual way, her hand caressing the nape of his neck. He had to look, had to watch her response so he could burn the memory into his senses. Somewhere in all this a need to overwhelm her and make her uniquely his had begun driving him. Levering back slightly his eyes met with a sight beyond compare. Rosy shadows across the skin of her belly hinted at the oral enjoyment he'd been indulging in, a thought that gave him enormous pleasure. Slim hips quivered in his grasp as he dug his hands under ass, canting her hips so the mound of fluffy brown curls came into sharp relief against the backdrop of her pale skin. His mind went blank when need like he'd never known before gripped his senses. If he didn't taste her immediately, didn't suck her moist, tender flesh into his mouth, he might go mad with wanting.

The minute his head bent to press a hungry kiss against her inner thigh, she sensed his intent and started to close herself off as best she could considering the provocative way he'd positioned her. Luckily, he had enough brain cells still functioning to recognize her distress.

She was groaning his name. "Draegyn, wait. No! I just don't…I can't…"

He looked at her between spread open thighs, the scent of her arousal shredding his control. “Shhh, honey. It’s alright,” he soothed. “Has no one ever pleasured you like this before?”

“Oh, no. No. Never. Please, I…uh. Oh my God Draegyn. I can’t. I’m afraid.” Now, more than ever, he knew he’d better not fuck this up. Knowing just what to do, Drae waited till she’d surrendered her eyes to his, then without breaking contact, lowered his head planting a wet kiss on the skin just above her mound. She responded as he’d hoped, by shivering all over as she arched her neck and moaned.

“You don’t have to do anything sweetheart except feel. Feel my tongue licking and sucking your clit. I want to taste you, Victoria. Want to drown in your response.” Then he did just as he said he would, he licked her from front to back over and over in a series of languid tongue strokes that brought heat and desire swelling into her exposed sex. It was clear from the way her hips rolled and bucked that she wasn’t going to be able to take very much this first time. It was fucking exhilarating to know he was the only man to see her like this, spread open with his mouth pressed against her sensitive female flesh. Making her come wasn’t going to be a problem. Holding onto his sanity while his dick throbbed and pulsed right along with her, however, was going to be the challenge.

Everything about her was so damn perfect. He loved that he could hold her bottom in one hand while the fingers of his other hand deftly spread her swollen labia so his greedy tongue could get at the bundle of nerves that crowned her weeping slit. The nub of her engorged clitoris fit perfectly against his tongue and lips allowing him to suckle rhythmically on the succulent flesh. The sheer carnality of it made his inner beast grunt with satisfaction as she ground her sweet pussy against his marauding mouth.

Drae would have happily gorged on her luscious sex all day and be none the happier for having indulged in such a rare delight, but Victoria was shaking uncontrollably, her fists clenched tightly in the bed linens. One good flick of his tongue against her ripe, swollen clit would send her over, but he wanted her to shatter completely, not just fall headlong into an orgasm.

He found a dribble of arousal leaking from her center, which he slowly teased until it covered his finger. Bringing the sensual delight to his mouth he licked the creamy wetness off his finger while she panted, whimpering, watching through half-shuttered eyes what he was doing. More than anything he wanted her to understand how much he desired her and how much he enjoyed making love to her with his whole body not just his cock.

But she'd had enough. He could tell by the sound of her breathing and the desperate groans rumbling from her chest. For his own pleasure, he placed a greedy kiss in her center, to satisfy the primal desires of that other part of him. In his mind, that kiss marked her as his. The way it sounded in his brain wasn't quite so reasonable. The beast inside was howling *this pussy is mine*, a far cry from the civilized man he was pretending to be.

Drae eased his middle finger past the tender lips of her open sex and thrust into her wet passage. Victoria's hips jerked, and her thighs fell open further as he explored her with relentless precision, fingering her deep before drawing all the way out to coat her swollen clit with proof of her arousal. He was the one panting now.

In seconds he detected the first flutters of an approaching orgasm when her insides clenched at his invading finger. He could have continued on like that until she fell apart, but he was going for more and knew how to get her there. Licking her clitoris, he drew the throbbing nub between his lips as he thrust two fingers inside her. He massaged the tender walls of her pussy until he found a spot that made her passage flood with superheated arousal as her clit pulsed against his tongue.

She shattered, just as he planned, crying out his name as she convulsed and shook while an orgasm wracked her small body in deep shuddering waves. He had to fight the urge to fuck her into oblivion when her inner muscles frantically clutched at his fingers.

Only the driving desire to feel those same orgasmic convulsions clutching at his cock held him in place.

It took a while for her to calm. At first he gently licked at her sensitive flesh, making his way back up her quivering body. With her needs sated for the time being he was having a hard time with his own. Just when he thought he'd have to abandon his slow down plan, he felt her dainty hand reach between where he was pressed against her belly and shyly touch the tip of his cock.

He held his breath while she took her time examining his hardened flesh. Pulling his hips back, Drae fell on his back with his throbbing erection bobbing in the air, giving her more room to explore. Curling around his side with a leg thrown over his thigh, Victoria slid her fingers, hesitantly at first, and then with increasing vigor all along his dick, even massaging the twin spheres underneath in an untutored yet surprisingly erotic way that had him bucking under her questing touch while deep groans ripped through the silence. She was fucking killing him.

He'd reached his limit. Jack-knifing upward in haste, Drae pushed her back and got on his knees between her open thighs. With his cock standing straight so she could see what he was doing, he ripped open a condom and quickly spread it over the plump head of his dick while she watched, devouring him with glittering eyes, as he sheathed himself.

Guiding his pulsing cock to her swollen pussy, Drae felt the walls of her sex close around him as he went slowly at first, then thrust deeper when she moaned, until nothing separated them. *This is as close to heaven as I'll ever get*, he thought. Her hot, wet passage was unbelievably tight. He could feel each throb of his cock as it pulsed against her swollen depths. When she tightened around him on that first thrust he almost died.

"Oh my God, Draegyn," she cried, squirming uncontrollably under his bulk. "That feels so….I mean, you're so big!" She punctuated those words with a wicked rocking of her hips that sucked him deeper inside her. Her legs gripped him powerfully around the waist. She was so good for his ego, not that it needed any help. There was something powerful about the sense of wonder she displayed as he entered her, stretching her aroused body to accommodate his superior size. Made him feel more like a man than he thought possible.

"I don't want to hurt you, baby," he groaned as he flexed his hips, surging forward and then easing back slightly. He wanted to pound the fucking crap out of her but not hurting her as he'd done in fevered haste this morning was driving him hard. What he hadn't counted on was the way her body welcomed his or the greedy way her hips ground against him each time he pressed forward. The deeper he surged, the more she moaned and clutched at him with her incredible inner muscles.

Clasping her arms around his neck she pulled him in for a frenzied kiss. Tongues swirling, he began thrusting inside her with increasing vigor. She met him stroke for stroke, canting her hips and wiggling against him to increase the delicious friction as he fucked her deeply. Ending the kiss she pressed her mouth to his ear and groaned, "More. Need more, *Draegyn*. Oh, God."

He agreed. Levering onto his forearms, he spread his thighs wide, opening her even further while he built a thundering rhythm that shocked him with its ferocity. He took it all in, how her body felt as he hammered into her, the deliciously hot creaminess that made each deep plunge sound exquisitely carnal. The way their labored breathing hung in the air, the scent of her arousal wrapping their heaving bodies in a cloak of sensuality. His deep grunts punctuating each thrust and her answering whimper.

Framing her face with his hands, Drae wanted to see for himself the whirlwind he felt ripping through her senses. Her eyes reflected the absolute wonder and soul-clenching eroticism that was present in him as well. When her hands fell to her sides and she clenched the sheets, hoarsely grunting, "Oh fuck," Drae nearly whooped in satisfaction. Yes. *Yes.* She undulated against him, her feet digging into his backside. He decided then and there that nothing in this world quite matched the glory and beauty of the woman in his arms as an orgasm came to life inside her.

"Yeah, that's it, baby," he groaned. Grunting with each thrust as he sank deep over and over he fastened his teeth against the skin on her neck and bit down, hard. She moaned and writhed. It was all so animalistic and primal.

Holding deep inside her he whispered next to her ear, "You're going to come again. I can feel it building. Right here," he grunted as his cock pressed deep. "Ah, God. You feel like heaven. Wet and so fucking tight."

Victoria increased her grip on his waist, reaching down to grab his clenching ass with shaking hands. Her pussy started clutching and releasing in rapidly growing pulsations that squeezed his cock unmercifully. "Take it, baby. Take what's yours," he moaned as she rotated on his plunging cock. She was crying out, pleading with him to go deeper, harder. Begging him to fuck her. He was undone.

When the crest of her orgasm hit, he nearly blacked out at the strength of her inner muscles as they relentlessly milked his aching cock while he slammed into her over and over. Someone was screaming and someone was grunting like an animal. Finally, when he couldn't take it another second and keep his sanity, his balls tightened as his cock swelled and exploded in wave after wave of shuddering pleasure. He was surprised she hadn't been split in two by the force of his thundering thrusts.

When it was finally over and the shuddering convulsions fading, he'd rolled them until she was sprawled on top of him. He quickly dealt with the condom before drawing her tight against him. She feathered an endless succession of soft kisses across his chest and neck, as he smoothed his big hands up and down her back and across her backside.

Time passed in silence. Drae yanked the coverlet over them as they cocooned in its warmth, neither willing to let the other go.

Eventually calm returned and each of them drifted into deep sleep.

***OH JESUS*, TORI THOUGHT** when her eyes cracked open and the blinding rays of the sun through the uncovered windows hit her. Why the hell did her head feel like a marching band was in residence? Groaning, she turned on her side, jolting when her eyes met the sleeping hulk of a man at her side. Draegyn.

The fog of sleep started to recede but met resistance, an after effect no doubt, of the epic amount of very expensive champagne she'd imbibed the previous night. What was it she'd said? Everything was better with champagne? She'd have to amend that because this hangover was anything but fun.

She'd be needing a double dose of coffee, and soon if she was going to survive the thumping in her head. Trying to roll to the far side of the bed away from the sleeping giant, she was instantly awake when evidence of their sexy nocturnal activities made her wince in discomfort. Realizing what the ache signaled, Tori's mind filled with vivid memories of their intense lovemaking and how she'd really and truly begged him to fuck her.

Scooting back against the headboard, she must have made a sound because he was wide-awake and staring her down a second later. Barely having enough time to clutch the sheet against her naked breasts, she tried to seem unphased by what they'd obviously done although the way her body began thrumming when she met his eyes made those efforts a bold lie.

"Morning," she whispered, not all that surprised to hear how raw her voice sounded. What did surprise her was how Draegyn calmly reached over and tugged the sheet away from her body, exposing her bare breasts to his view.

"Now it's a good morning." His sleepy smile rattled her cage. Turning, he leaned his head on a raised hand and contemplated her.

Trying to pull tangled tresses away from her shoulders and neck, Tori managed a weak smile in return. "I must look like hell."

She watched as his eyes narrowed. "You look like a woman who had a screaming orgasm in my arms." He sounded smug, and she wanted to jab him in the ribs for the arrogance she heard in his voice, but the truth was she had screamed. He deserved to feel arrogant.

Tori was stumped. What was the protocol in these situations? Did she thank him? Something along the lines of, 'Gee, thanks for the wild fuck and the amazing orgasms'? Or perhaps, 'I hope it was as good for you as it was for me'? Was she supposed to clear out of his space now that daylight had returned? She hoped she wasn't expected to move from the bed fully naked, as she doubted her ability to walk at the moment.

She wondered what was he thinking when he kept his silence. Glancing at him from the corner of her eye she saw his jaw flex as his gaze swept over her nakedness. A quick drop of her eyes showed her what he saw, breasts still swollen from their lovemaking and the unmistakable signs left behind from his possession of her body.

He had the natural grace of a jungle cat, rising up from the bed while lifting her into his arms at the same time. In a replay of yesterday morning's events, he strode with her firmly in his arms only this time instead of taking her to the elaborate shower, he sat her on the side of the huge soaking tub. Adjusting the controls, warm water poured into the tub as he grabbed some nearby towels. *The man doesn't miss much*, she thought when he looked her over from head to toe and hurried away only to return seconds later with a hair-tie and a bottle of water for each of them.

"Drink that," he ordered, ripping off the cap on his and chugging half of it in one gulp. "May only have been champagne, but considering how much we drank, dehydration is a concern."

By the time she slid into the warmth of the deep tub, Tori felt some life returning to her body. When he dropped into the warm water and pulled her between his thighs, she went without pause. What good would it have done to pretend she wasn't sore and achy after what they'd done to each other? Letting him wash her was admitting the truth. He was big. Like, really big. And she had asked, no begged, for him to take her harder and deeper. The gentleness he displayed now, taking care of her, tugged at her emotions.

His hand dipped into the water and slid between her thighs. She couldn't stop the pained hiss that ripped from her throat when he touched tender skin. He froze at the sound of her distress. For some reason, his hesitation wrapped around her heart and squeezed. He might not want to admit it, but he was feeling a riot of emotions that like she, he didn't know what to do with.

Tori reached for his hand under the water and rather than grab his wrist to pull his fingers away from her tender flesh, she pressed his hand against her thigh. "Before you say anything, I want you to know that you didn't hurt me. Just, um….go easy. I'm a little tender down there."

"Don't bullshit me Victoria. You nearly jumped out of your skin when I just touched you."

"Well, yeah," she muttered. "Maybe a little, but honestly Draegyn, being sore isn't stopping me from wanting your hands to make it better." She didn't know who was more shocked.

He grew solemn and serious, refusing to meet her eyes as he

went about washing her intimately, as if his life depended on doing it right. She leaned back against his solid chest and felt her limbs floating, weightless in the water. The warm water, his gentle touch, sheer bliss. Tori sighed and contemplated some more amorous activities she wanted to try out in the big tub. If she wasn't such a wuss, she might have indulged in some touchy feely caresses of her own. The brief touches she'd gotten to enjoy last night had not been enough to satisfy her craving for his body.

But, there was no way, with all his concerned seriousness, that he would permit a repeat she realized. Not right now anyway, this was probably just as well. In short order she'd been properly bathed, dried, and left to dress while he did the same. Before turning away from her, he mumbled something about breakfast and taking her time. No hurry, he had told her. They could leave when she was ready, whenever that may be. He'd call and alert the hangar that he'd need the plane readied for their return to Sedona, but she shouldn't feel rushed in any way. *Ah, the uncomplicated life of a wealthy man*, she mused. She could get used to this.

In the end she opted for ease and comfort choosing skinny jeans with a pair of lace up ankle boots. Pulling an oversized t-shirt on she smiled at the agency logo discreetly monogrammed above her left breast, before adding a long, straight jacket with sleeves she could push back for a comfortable, casual look. Two minutes with the flat iron helped smooth out any tangles leftover from the previous evening's activities. Satisfied with her appearance, she stuffed whatever was laying around into her bag and was ready to face Draegyn again. She hoped he'd been smart enough to ready some coffee for her.

Drae was fit to be tied. All of his legendary cool had deserted him permanently as, all thumbs, he struggled with the coffeemaker like it was his first time dealing with a machine of any kind. What the fuck was wrong with him? He almost laughed. No, wait. He did laugh. What was wrong? Victoria Bennett was all that was wrong with him. Woman had him wrapped up in knots. The minute his eyes opened, and he'd seen her sitting there trying so damn hard not to wake him, he wanted her. Wanted her desperately. Under him. Over him. Didn't matter as long as the end result was his greedy sex buried inside her again. And again.

He'd tried to take it easy on her last night, unlike their first coupling that had been hurried and primal. There was no way she wasn't ripe and ready for him, had not complained at the time, even urging him on. The insatiable fire she lit inside him made common sense fly right out the damned window. Instead of getting off on how the incredible tightness of her sheath had felt squeezing his cock, he should have held back and taken it slower. Slower? He snorted in disbelief. Who the goddamn fuck was he trying to kid? There was no such thing as slower with Victoria.

"Will coffee be made available to me or do I have to kill you?" The teasing sound behind him startled Drae. Grateful for the lightness he heard in her voice, he shot her a mocking grin.

"While I have no doubt you could do me bodily harm," he husked letting the double edged meaning to his words sink in, "this morning, I aim to please. One half-caf hazelnut coffee coming to you in just a minute." The coffee machine dinged to let him know her cup had been brewed, but he found himself completely lost, taking in the crazy, sexy way she walked in the heeled ankle boots and the jeans that clung like a second skin. *Get the coffee*, his brain wheezed after lust sucked the breath right out of him. God! He had to snap out of it. "Have a seat and I'll bring it to you. Feel any better?"

"Oh, yes, loads better, thanks." She smiled at him and then made that perfect little moue with her lips that drove him wild. "Do you even know how much champagne we inhaled? My head is telling me it was a lot."

Handing her the steaming mug that he'd added a heavy hand of creamer to along with a good pile of sugar, Drae couldn't help but laugh, shaking his head in agreement. "Probably more than was wise, but as they say, *YOLO*!"

She burst out giggling. "YOLO? Really? That's what you have to say about last night …you only live once?"

"Fuck, yeah," he chuckled. "Damn straight. YOLO!"

"I wonder if the newlyweds feel like my head does right now. Who knew there was such a thing as too much bubbly?"

Remembering the couple who shared their epic night, Drae went to find his suit jacket. "Speaking of the happy bride and groom, Stavros gave me a stack of papers after they sped off. Probably their license and certificate. I remember stuffing them in my jacket pocket."

"Mmmm," she chimed in, "that reminds me, where's my cell phone? I've got a bunch of pictures saved. There's definitely a shot of Shawn mugging with the statue of a very nude, very male Greek god that she might not want anyone to see." Taking a hearty sip of the sweetened coffee, she put down the mug and slid off the high counter stool, going in search of her bag. "I love technology just as much as the next person but honestly, it's almost too easy to record for all time the randomly stupid things we do."

"I hear that," Drae snickered. "Last year we did security for a teen heartthrob during his European tour. The fucking kid needed to have his head examined. He took snapshots of every inappropriate thing he could think of and posted that shit online. It was exhausting, staying one step ahead of the shit-storm those pictures created." He reached into his jacket pocket, found the sheaf of papers and withdrew them, adding as an aside, "Although I wouldn't mind catching a glimpse of the unseemly behavior you two ladies visited on a piece of nude, male marble!"

Victoria howled with laughter. "It was all her, I swear!" Finding her cell phone she quickly scrolled through the photos, squealing with embarrassment. "Oh my God! It's so much worse than I remembered," she giggled. "Yikes!" she laughed slapping her hand across her eyes. "Each picture is worse than the previous, although I think in all fairness I should admit to egging her on."

When she held up on particularly salacious shot of the newlywed bride on her knees wagging her tongue suggestively at a nude statue, Drae bellowed with hearty laughter. "Is that what you women do when the men aren't looking?" he teased good-naturedly.

She blushed and shrugged. "Maybe." Sighing, she nodded at the papers he held. "Is there anything important in there? I have Garry's assistant in my contact list. We could text him if there's any need."

"Mmm-hmm. Good idea." Unfolding the papers, Drae eased onto the sofa and started ruffling through the pages. "Looks like the license and a bunch of legal stuff about filing for name changes." He was about to put everything in his laptop case when something caught his eye. "What the fuck?" he yelled, jumping to his feet. An angry red mist flooded his brain.

Victoria nearly choked on her coffee, he startled her so bad with his outburst. Suddenly, a headache began pounding in his skull, and his eye began twitching. Anxiety grabbed him by the throat.

"What's the matter?"

Drae shook his head repeatedly, as if that would make the words swimming on the paper in front of him change. His heart was pounding and a trickle of sweat started making its way between tensed shoulder blades. This had better be some elaborate punk'd scenario.

When he felt Victoria's hand upon his arm he reacted as if she'd burned him, snatching his body from her closeness and moving away at the speed of light. "Draegyn, what's the matter? You're scaring me."

He didn't know what to say. Words were frozen in his throat while his mind careened in panicked haste, trying to make sense of what was happening. Waving the paper at her, he ran his hand through his hair and gritted his teeth. "Do you know what this is?" he shouted.

"No. Why? Oh my God, what's wrong?"

He snorted dismissively at her. "What's wrong?" His voice had the distinct tenor of someone in free-falling panic. "I'll tell you what the fuck is wrong. According to this…" He bristled while still waving the paper crumpled in his fist. "It seems we are married." Somehow he managed to make the word *married* sound like a vulgar curse and a sentence of death all in the same breath.

"What?' she wheezed, as she gulped in air. "Married? Who's married? Garry and Shawn you mean?" When he didn't answer, just stood numb and frozen glaring at her, she paled before his eyes. "This is a prank, right?"

Something inside Drae detonated like a bomb. Married! Married. No, it just couldn't be. Marriage was not on the agenda. Ever. Didn't matter who it was. He'd learned that lesson early in life. Marriage was for chumps, and he didn't ever intend to be counted in that category.

"Here," he snarled, pushing the papers in her shocked hands. "See for yourself." Jabbing a finger accusingly at the sheet he pointed to her signature. "Look, see? You signed this. What the fuck were you thinking?"

"What was *I* thinking?" she screamed back. "Convenient of you to ignore your signature right next to mine." She looked as frantic as he felt.

He felt sick. If these papers were correct, not only had he and Victoria somehow gotten married, they'd very conveniently consummated the arrangement. *Motherfucker*. He was screwed.

Tori was horrified at what she held in her hands. Draegyn was right. They had gotten married. Searching her champagne infused memories for any clues to how this happened was useless. Most of the evening was a blur. They'd had way too much to drink over many hours making some moments crystal clear while others, well….blurry didn't do them justice. She looked at him over the offending document, taken aback by the fury she saw in his expression. This angry man wasn't the person she'd come to know. Something else was going on but right now all she could deal with was the current situation.

"Okay, let's calm down and figure this out," she offered. "I think that…"

Cutting her off in mid-breath, Draegyn erupted, sending her a scathingly dismissive glance. "I *cannot* be married," he bit out in terse, no nonsense language that spoke volumes. "Marriage is not in my wheelhouse."

Was he kidding? Disregarding the blazing rage evident in his face, she felt her ire go up at the anger she felt was directed solely at her. So much for any post-coital afterglow. Hurt and confused by his overreaction to their predicament Tori blurted out the first stupid thing that came to mind. "Oh, so…what? This is all about *you*? Marriage puts a crimp in your style, then? No more find, feel, fuck and forget for Draegyn St. John? Poor baby."

He winced at her pithy use of the expression he knew people used to describe him. It sounded so wrong coming out of her mouth but he was fucked-up in the head at the moment and wasn't thinking straight. "I do *not* want to be married," he yelled for no good reason.

"Fuck you, St. John," was her tart response. "Sorry to disappoint that infernal ego of yours, but you're not my idea of husband material. I want an annulment. Now!"

He snapped and started yelling like a madman, "Who are you fucking kidding? An annulment?" Sneering derisively he spit angry, hurtful words at her. "I think you're a couple orgasms short of meeting that goal. Last time I checked, we fucked each other pretty thoroughly last night. And there's still the issue of the unprotected sex yesterday morning. Scratch an annulment."

Drae was gripped by anger. A cold, dark fury exploded inside.

When his rage connected with her fierce indignation she became a hellcat, spitting and hissing at him. What was she so mad about? This wasn't about her. This was about him, dammit. What a mess. In twenty-four hours he had made himself a husband and a potential baby daddy. The corner of his eye twitched harder. "Get ready to leave. I need to get out of this place and think."

His turbulent emotions overrode any awareness of her stricken expression when he'd thrown down the orgasm taunt or the ugly fact that he'd fucked her with no protection. Drae knew he was callously riding roughshod over her part in all this, but the realization didn't stop long-held beliefs from taking control of his mind.

Keeping his voice hard and gruff, he laid out how he expected things to proceed with the absolute conviction that she would simply do as she was told. After all, he was the one calling the shots. "I will find out what has to be done to fix this - mistake." She flinched at his delivery. A feeling somewhere between cringing and disgust when he referred to fixing something he'd done, pushed him half a bubble off plumb. Awareness roared in his ears, momentarily blinding him to the presence of the other person in the room.

Draegyn was lucky she had the presence of mind to hold herself back. Why, that arrogant, son-of-a-bitch just called her a mistake! Outrage flooded her mind. And the way he was talking down to her, as if she was a piece of dirt on his shoe! Without thinking, Tori went into fighting pose, legs spread and unyielding, ready to kick some serious ass. Hands planted firmly at her waist, fingers twitching as if readying to slap a certain someone's conceited face.

The cause for this irrational display of anger was still a mystery, but his ugly words were not. His loathsome putdowns referencing her orgasms, and the very real likelihood that she could be pregnant, hung in the air like the aftermath of artillery fire. Oh, so this was somehow all *her* doing. She'd stolen his precious semen with her Jezebel ways and plotted to marry his unwilling ass, apparently all just to fuck with him. What. A. *Dick.*

"No one is to know about this," she hissed tersely. "I mean that. Absolutely no one. There cannot be even the slightest chance that some enterprising paparazzi might stumble upon this information and use it to build a salacious story. More importantly, I expect you to do as you've said. Fix this *mistake*, as quickly and silently as possible." She made absolutely sure to insinuate a wealth of meaning into her use of *his* description. "And stop with the icy blue-eyed stare. It doesn't scare me," she bit out, waving her hands dramatically in imitation of being frightened. "Save it for someone who gives a shit."

Dismissing him with a final look seething with distaste, Tori retreated to her room to gather her belongings. Needing to say one final thing to put a stamp of finality on something that had started out so exciting that was now crashing and burning in spectacular fashion, she snarled in his general direction. "Don't speak to me again, Mr. St. John. We have nothing further to say to each other. Understood? Unless it has to do with business, I don't want to hear from you. Ever."

THE SUPER-CHARGED EMOTIONAL SILENCE between them made the noiseless conditions in the main cabin of the jet deafening. Drae had been boiling over with raw, undignified emotions since the moment their confrontation ended. When she'd railed at him, calling him 'mister', he'd wanted to drag her back into the room by the hair and make her take back her words. Don't talk to her ever again? No one told him what he could or couldn't do. *The bitch.*

That was how he'd felt ever since. Angry. Raw. Out of control. He seriously wanted to hit something and had even measured up the damage he'd cause by slamming his fist into a wall before they'd made their silent, angry retreat from the hotel. Drae wasn't a fool. His rational mind was keeping up a running commentary while his irrational one drove his thoughts and actions. He knew that finding a marriage certificate with his name on it had detonated a psychological time bomb that had been silently ticking inside him for a very long time. It was one thing to have his normal Mr. Cool ways completely obliterated by a brown-haired pixie with a smart mouth and a sexy pout. Yet another altogether to find himself embroiled in the one thing that was sure to blow his world to smithereens.

Married. The word made his stomach lurch. He didn't do married. Didn't do relationships. Never wanted to either. Drae knew deep in his heart that he was far too emotionally scarred by his parents' bullshit to ever contemplate tying himself to another human being. He wasn't built that way. Didn't matter who the woman was.

He didn't so much as glance in her direction. Didn't need to. He knew what she was doing without having to look. If ignoring him were an Olympic sport, she'd be scoring straight tens in every category. Reluctantly acknowledging the psychology at work inside him that made him grind his teeth, Drae carefully checked the sigh he felt before it hit the air.

When the pilot announced descent for landing, she fidgeted with her seatbelt, turning sunglass-shielded eyes toward the window. He could have run through the cabin naked with his hair on fire and know with certainty that Victoria wouldn't have reacted at all. He should be glad, or relieved at the very least. But he wasn't, and didn't know why.

The ride from the Sedona hangar out to the Villa also played out in total silence, with the arctic chill wafting from her side of the car neutralizing the red-hot rage he was struggling to contain. When Ben cheerfully met them as they disembarked from the plane, nothing about her pleasant greeting or interactions with the gregarious man gave any indication of the shit-storm they were embroiled in. It was just him that she pointedly ignored. Well, one cold shoulder deserved another so he spent the wordless drive texting his lawyer with a plea for complete discretion regarding a confidential matter he needed handled. Trusting his long-time legal counsel wasn't a problem, but Drae felt it necessary to indicate from the outset the confidentiality he expected. The last thing he needed was for even the slightest hint of this mess reaching his parents' ears.

It was a relief when they made the turn down the long private drive to the main portion of the Villa. He needed out of the car and away from the woman next to him who was barely hiding her contempt at his presence. Not wanting to be married wasn't the same thing as wanting Victoria to be pissed off, making him grimly admit his handling of their situation so far effectively meant that ship had sailed. Pissed didn't even come close to the vibe she was putting off. Maybe he should have grown a set before throwing that tantrum, remembering that she was just as much a victim of circumstance as he was.

As was always the case, there was activity all over the compound. Dogs were barking, he saw a small group gathered around the horse yard, and several ATVs went zipping by as they drew up to the back parking area. He could have sworn she was out of the car and at the trunk before Ben put the vehicle in park. Drae struggled with the headache thumping behind his twitching eyes. Keeping their messy predicament a secret was going to be difficult if they openly treated each other with hostility.

Alighting from the vehicle, Drae stopped to speak with Ben, keeping an eye on Victoria as she struggled with her bags. He needed to say something although he had no idea what that might be. Getting control of his anger and approaching the problem with a calm mind was still a stretch too far. "Victoria," he growled at the same moment she turned away from the car, gripping her rolling bag as she stomped along. Nothing. *Dammit.* She didn't even slow down. "Victoria!"

This time his bark got the surprised attention of Ben who had been securing Drae's luggage in the trunk for the quick trip down the lane to his home. *Shit.* Catching the man's raised brows from the corner of his eye, he stood there stunned by her blatant disregard of his command. To his credit, Ben never indicated anything untoward had just happened, but that didn't mean Drae couldn't feel the man's brain working overtime trying to figure out what was going on.

The urge to hit something overtook him again as he watched Victoria's angry retreat in silent dismay. He wasn't handling this very well. Before he did or said something to make things worse, as if that was even possible, Drae needed to submerge himself in the distraction that could only be found in his woodshop. He'd run home, get changed, and hunker down with a project while he waited to hear from his attorney and set the legal balls in motion to *fix* the mess he'd made. This time he didn't try to block the cringe he felt at the word. It was like having his shrill, manipulative mother laughing in his face, smugly rubbing in the irony. The chilling notion that he was, after all, the woman's only son unleashed a wave of contempt that disrupted his ability to think rationally. After having vowed never to be like her, never to let cynicism and conceit inform his life, he'd turned cold and unreachable anyway. In his determination to avoid emotional attachment, he'd lost his ability to feel. The thought scared him more than it should.

Ben nattered on during the short jaunt to Drae's house, filling in the empty, silent spaces. It was a guy thing. Having just been pointedly dissed by a furious Victoria, they were hardly going to talk about what had just gone on. The older man, bless his heart, was acting like Drae hadn't just been shot down in blazing fashion. Once at the house, they chatted about nothing, pulling luggage from the trunk, pretending like pros. He couldn't ditch the business suit and hide out in the woodshop fast enough.

Tori was running on adrenaline, anger, and something else that felt wretched and gloomy. Taming her temper had always been a struggle, especially when something truly hit a nerve. That blasted egomaniac had shown his true colors, landing one direct hit after another. Whatever happy, shining contentment she'd briefly glimpsed was in flames on the ground.

Relieved to be away from him, she'd practically hurled her heavy suitcase as if it weighed nothing through the apartment door and then slammed it with an angry thud for good measure. It had taken every ounce of strength she possessed to remain silent and still during the car rides and plane trip, when what she really wanted to do was leap on the son-of-a-bitch and tear him limb from limb. Draegyn, *I'm-so-perfect*, St. John had behaved horribly in her eyes. His expression and tone upon discovering their shocking little secret had been offensive at best.

Flinging herself onto an oversized wing chair with enough force to shove it back a few feet, she loosed a sound from deep inside that started off a groan and ended as an angry growl. *Men! Self-centered narcissists, all of 'em.*

Why the hell was it always about the guy? Watching in stunned disbelief as he'd gone through the steps of an epic meltdown while totally disregarding her involvement had taken Tori back to another time when she'd ended up as nothing more than collateral damage. Well, she snorted, that was not going to happen this time. No effing way. As quickly as her temper flared, so did it sputter out when too-bright images of their physical intimacy knocked on her consciousness demanding equal time. *Not helpful*, she sighed, tucking a wayward curl behind her ear. Now that he'd shown his true colors and behaved like a jerk, it was easier to pretend that getting naked with him, twice in one day, had been an aberration at best. Sexual curiosity. Yeah, that sounded good.

At first, her response to the blond-haired Adonis had been suspicion and distaste. After all, he wore his arrogance and conceit like a second skin. But, little by little, he wore her down without even trying.

Something between them had shifted, changed when they'd declared their verbal truce. Once they'd stopped hissing, snarling, and taunting each other at every turn, she'd quickly succumbed to his wolfish charms. And it wasn't just because he had the sexiest ass she'd ever seen.

Oh dear God. Was she falling for him? Was that why she defaulted to fire and brimstone the moment he'd morphed into angry, alpha male? *Damn.* This wasn't good. She shivered and felt her nipples quickly peak against the sheer lace of her bra. Though she was upset and furious with Draegyn, the notion that she had developed real feelings for him scared the crap out of her.

Groaning, Tori turned her face into the upholstered chair and squeezed her eyes shut. *No, no, no*, she chanted. How stupid could she be? High profile, sophisticated men like Draegyn St. John didn't go for her type. Plain, half tomboy girls like Tori always ended up in the scrap heap in these situations. Allowing her body to override common sense had been a dumb move. And now look where she was. Married by mistake and realizing she had some serious feelings for her unhappy husband. Well, whatever. She had no choice but to put her big girl panties on and deal with the whole stinking mess.

Her cell phone going off startled Tori, bringing her upright in the big chair, silently searching with each ringtone until she found it. *Ah, damn*. It was Alex. She really didn't want to answer but knew if she didn't it would more than likely result in him banging on her door next. Another powerful man, another attitude.

"Hello?"

"Hey Tori. I know you just got in but could you come over her after you unpack? I want to run something past you."

Dammit. She didn't want to face her boss just yet, not with the secret she carried. Her feet felt like lead blocks as she stood with the phone pressed to her ear, suddenly fretting that Draegyn might actually tell his friend about their predicament. Sure, the fact that there was a marriage certificate between them was a big deal but at the moment, she was struggling to deal with the very real feelings she was harboring. A light bulb went on over her head. "Um, well Alex - to tell you the truth, I'm going to relax here if you don't mind. Maybe take a pain reliever and put my feet up."

"Why? What's wrong?" he demanded.

Trying to sound very matter-of-fact she answered in a way that would have any man backing off in a hurry. "Oh, nothing. Really. Y'know – female things. NBD."

"Oh!" A few seconds passed while he processed the information, then said, "I understand. This can wait." She didn't feed words into the silence. Just let him end the call on his own so he wouldn't wonder or ask questions. "Can I get you anything?"

"No, no. I'm good but thanks for asking." Tori shrugged and chuckled. "You know how it is. Nothing a gal can't handle given a handful of cramp meds and a heating pad. I'll catch up with you in the morning, okay?"

"Yeah. That's fine." She thought he might be about to hang up when she heard him ask, "Is Drae with you? He's not answering his phone."

Mentally counting to ten before answering, Tori kept her voice neutral, belying the hysteria churning in her gut. "Nah. Ben drove him down the lane. Guess he'll surface when he's ready." That sounded benign, right? Lord, she hoped so.

Call concluded, Tori put the phone on silent and tossed it on the coffee table. Putting Alex off until tomorrow meant she bought herself a little time to wrap her head around everything that happened in the last forty-eight hours. She'd have to talk to Draegyn at some point. Work out the legal details of the mess they were in but for right now she needed to be left alone. Needed time to figure out what she did next.

Alex was not a happy camper. Something was going on between his assistant and Drae. Their behavior was sounding alarm bells in his head that were hard to disregard. Not that he could ignore the fact that three days had passed and his old comrade-in-arms and current business partner had been off the radar the whole time or that Tori seemed unusually distracted.

When she'd turned up in the tech cave the morning following her return from Vegas, she seemed different somehow. The same yes, but also giving off a very subtle vibe that suggested something had changed. She looked the same but something wasn't quite right. He couldn't put his finger on it but he knew enough to conclude there was most definitely a disturbance in the force.

Whatever it was, he'd had enough. He'd known Drae long enough that the signs of unusual behavior he was displaying stood out like red flags against a snowy background. They'd done stuff and been through plenty of shit together over the years but this silent, hiding in plain sight nonsense was different. At first, he answered the phone when Alex called but shrugged off any suggestion of meeting face to face. He was, *busy*. Last night, the calls started going straight to voicemail.

The one and only time he dared to mention Drae by name in front of Tori, she had zipped so tight at just the mention that Alex had felt like a huge prick. He couldn't ever remember a subject being changed so fast in his life. There wasn't a lot he could do after that except wait them out. See what happened next. After all, if it weren't for the fact that Tori was his assistant, he would never consider sticking his nose into Drae's personal business. But the voicemail bullshit had annoyed the crap out of him. After all they'd been through together, it seemed a bit – bizarre. And not like his friend at all. That was why he was on his way to Drae's lumberjack heaven. So he could find out for himself what was up.

Stopping his quad in front of the unusual wood structure, Alex admired the massive custom-designed house with the wraparound decking and impressive windows that gave every room in the house a breathtaking view of the desert vistas surrounding them. *Drae is a genius for this kind of stuff*, he thought. Sidestepping the main entrance, he headed for the rear of the house and the large woodworking shop where he was sure Drae would be found. The closer he got, sounds of a buzz saw could be heard along with blaring music. Alex heaved a tremendous sigh. All the signs were there, now he just had to figure out what to do next. There was nothing to do but beard the lion in its own den and hope he got out in one piece.

Pushing through the massive wood barn door that opened into Drae's wood shop, Alex immediately pinpointed his friend with his back to the door across the wide room. With AC/DC cranking at full volume on the sound system and the noise generated by the serious looking table saw, there was no way to announce himself without shouting so he waited for the song to end before making his presence known. Removing his sunglasses, Alex cleared his throat and keeping his voice calm said, "Yo. Dude."

Clearly surprised by his visitor, Drae whipped around with a dark scowl, ready to bite the head off of whoever had been foolish enough to invade his sanctuary. Alex pinned him to the spot with one raised eyebrow and his very best smirk. "You're a royal pain in my ass, St. John," he drawled.

Drae switched off the noisy saw and removed the heavy work gloves he'd been wearing, tossing them carelessly on the workbench. Alex noted every movement along with the shuttered expression and prepared himself for the face-off he knew was coming. When his friend reached for a remote control and lowered the music, he felt the antagonism level back off, but only slightly.

"Takes one to know one," Drae snarled. "What are you doing here, Alex?"

Alex wandered lazily around the workshop, picking up scraps of wood and then tossing them aside. "You're fucking kidding, right? Going off radar for a couple of days and not answering your phone is what got my ass down here."

"I'm busy, and you're interrupting me," Drae grunted, wiping sweat from his forehead with the bottom of his grimy t-shirt. He was uncomfortable with the knowing way Alex was watching him. Actually, it kind of freaked him out. The man had a way of seeing shit and knowing things that the most observant people often missed. The last thing he needed was the third-degree, but he knew his odd behavior had brought about this confrontation so he had little choice but to deal with it.

"Well, I see that pleasant conversation won't be on the agenda today so let's just cut to the chase." The tone of Alex's voice suggested he was two clicks removed from ripping Drae's fucking head off. "You forced this on yourself dude, so fuck you and the shitty attitude. I'm not stupid. Something has your shorts in a knot. And why you'd think for even a second that I wouldn't notice something was up is a joke. It's been three goddamn days since you got back from Las Vegas and as far as I can tell, you haven't left this shop in all that time."

"You want a soda?" Drae asked, going to the refrigerator in the corner of the shop, grabbing two cold ones and tossing one Alex's way before he answered. Motioning with his head to a spot where they could sit, he flopped onto a wood crate and tore open the tab on the soda.

Alex was one of those guys who could drive a man insane with the deliberate, cool-headed way he approached everything. Drae knew him so well. Alex was always taking mental notes. Essentially, he was waiting him out, and he had to admit it was a smart strategic move on his part.

"Spit it out, would you? C'mon Drae. This isn't like you at all."

The notion of spilling his guts to someone he could trust was tempting but something held him back. Maybe it was because the knot in his shorts, as Alex put it, involved someone else and even after three days he still hadn't come to terms with what that meant. *Whatever*, he tipped his head back and drained the soda, crushing the can in one hand and flinging it into a recycling barrel nearby.

Alex watched him, sighed and then let it rip. "Y'know, we spent a lifetime watching each other's back in the war. Your reluctance to let me in doesn't make sense, dude. If we were women, I'd let you have it for hurting my feelings with your stubbornness, but as it is, I'll settle for reminding you that whatever messes with you, messes with me."

Drae winced at his choice of words. He was right, of course. "Fuck, Alex. You're making me feel like shit here. Ease off, okay?"

"No, I will not. And stop being a whinny bitch. This," he said while waving a hand at Drae, "whatever *this* is, involves my assistant, doesn't it?"

"No. Yes! *Fuck.*" He got up and started pacing as nervous energy shot along his nerve endings.

"Okay. What the fuck did you do?" Alex growled.

"Why the hell do you automatically assume that I did something?" *Fucker.*

"I know you St. John and I've never seen you so much as look over your shoulder as an endless parade of fuck buddies made the walk of shame from your bed. You're an asshole and you know it. Everyone knows it. Thinking you did something incredibly crass or mean-spirited to Tori isn't exactly a stretch of the imagination."

"Why? Has she said something?" Drae asked a bit wildly as his stomach dropped at the mention of Victoria.

Alex smirked. "Wow, that didn't take much."

Drae shifted back and forth on his feet, annoyed that he gave so much away with one question. Borrowing one of Alex's signature moves, he raked his hand across his scalp and grimaced. This whole thing was making him mental. He didn't know himself anymore, that was how far out of his comfort zone he was.

Alex watched him through narrowed eyes, slowly sipping the soda while nodding his head. "You're a fucking mess, brother. You look like death warmed over. Smell like it too. Have you even left this room because, *seriously dude*, you need a shower. And some clothes that don't look like they came from the ragbag. This is so not you, Drae."

Motherfucker. Some part of him wanted to blurt out the worst of it but he knew doing so would unleash an avalanche of questions he wasn't ready to answer.

"Alright, look - this is getting us nowhere. While I don't understand why you can't tell me what's wrong, I'm going to respect your privacy since you obviously have strong reasons for clamming up. But I will say this. Do *not* fucking mess with Tori Bennett. This is not the first time I've warned you, but it will be the last thing you remember before I knock the piss out of you if I find out you've been a dick. She's good people and you - well, seriously. You're my brother in every way that counts and I would lay down my life for you so understand that I fully recognize I have no business commenting on your personal life, but I have to say this. You're making a huge mistake involving Tori in your relationship-phobic life. If that's what's going on, I mean."

While Alex rattled off the terse lecture, Drae glared at him, his face a tense mask of churning emotions. The man was probably right, but he didn't want to hear it. "Understood."

"That said," Alex rose and walked toward him, tossing the soda can as he did. Swatting him on the back he continued, "The fact that you're such a butt ugly mess suggests this isn't your normal, run of the mill dalliance." He snorted, laughing sarcastically at his own words. "Jesus. I just used *dalliance* in a sentence. I better get outta here before we start doing our nails!"

"Alex," Drae mumbled. "Thanks."

The man shrugged while making a pained grin. "Whatever this is, you have to fix it. I'm here for you. Don't forget it. Okay?"

Bile rose in Drae's throat hearing Alex tell him to fix it. This was what his life had come to. *Fuck*.

"SO, WHAT DO YOU think of this, Tori?" Alex asked, tossing a big brown envelope of reading materials on her desk. "I'm off next month to Washington for a think-tank symposium. Range of topics – nothing that tickles my taint…oh, right. Sorry." He shrugged. "Sometimes I forget to watch my language around the ladies. Anyway, I'm interested in the holographic data seminar and was wondering what you think. Read that shit over and get back to me."

Pushing her chair back, Tori grabbed the envelope and shuffled to the coffee maker for a java jolt. God. She'd been sitting way too long this morning and her butt actually hurt. With her personal life in chaos, she'd been burning the midnight oil staying busy with work stuff so she didn't have to think about Draegyn. Or the mess they were in. Or the way her nose stung each time she thought of him as she fought back tears. As a result she hadn't been eating properly and had more or less been hunched over a keyboard or staring at a digital display for way too many hours each day.

Speaking over her shoulder to Alex as he moved around her workspace, she ignored the flat sound to her voice and concentrated on the new task he'd literally thrown at her. "No problem, boss. Are you presenting or just sitting in?"

He groaned at her question. "Fuck no! Not presenting this time. Sometimes these things are undercover attempts by the military guys to pick everyone's brains," he snorted. "Semper Fi and all but these days, I'm not inclined to share."

Tori considered that little nugget of inside information as she juggled the heavy envelope; shoving it under her arm while carrying a monster mug of black sludge with both hands back to her desk. The coffee was blazing hot and downright awful. Bitter didn't do it justice. Alex, for all his high-tech ways, eschewed having a modern coffee system in the office, opting for an ancient drip brewer that you just keep filling and using over and over.

Sipping, careful not to scorch her mouth on the disgusting beverage, she angled her arm just so, letting the envelope fall on her desk before settling back in a comfy swivel chair. Spinning to look at her boss, she expected him to be puttering so she was slightly unnerved to find that he was studying her like a bug under a microscope. The serious expression on his face made her completely forget what she'd been about to say.

Raising an eyebrow she asked, "Did I grow a set of horns or something, Alex?" She thought he looked a bit uncomfortable around her. Oh great. Just what she needed. Even though they'd only been working together for a few months, Tori had come to really like the man who signed her paycheck. He was incredibly smart and had an easy manner that didn't push any of her buttons. A born leader, Alex rarely wielded an imperious hand, preferring to get things done through teamwork and encouraging everyone around him to challenge themselves and seek solutions rather than more problems. Unlike his arrogant, conceited partner. *Squash that thought*, she reminded herself. All reminders of Draegyn St. John were off limits.

The way he was studying her though made a chill race up Tori's spine. Had she done something wrong or stepped over a line? It wasn't like him to be so obvious. A heavy knot formed in her stomach when she remembered that she had indeed stepped over the line by sleeping with Draegyn. Not that she thought Alex knew though. Embarrassment and anxiety intersected in her conscience at the notion that Draegyn might have told his friend what had gone down in Vegas. Oh Lord. She silently prayed that was not the case.

Alex glanced away and made busy with a pile of junk before he answered her. "No horns. Just lost in thought."

Mmmm hmmm, she mused. Nice try. Dammit. Something was definitely up. Swiveling around in her chair, Tori chose the low road and let the moment slide without further comment, but she could still feel his eyes on her.

Some time later, she wasn't sure how long because watching the clock was counter-productive, she sensed a shift in the air. When the hair on the back of her neck prickled she closed her eyes and tried to ignore the pulse of awareness intruding on her attempts at avoidance. *Shit and fuck.* The flicker of recognition that had her body sitting up and taking notice could be none other than the man she was trying to block out.

She didn't have to turn around to know he was in the room. How the hell had that happened? It was almost as if he was inside her, and while that thought started in wonder at how deeply imbedded he was in her thoughts, it quickly transformed into a Technicolor memory of how it felt to take him inside her body. Tori sucked back the earthy groan threatening to undermine her composure.

Okay. She could do this. She could slap a bland, indifferent expression on her face and keep things business as usual. There really wasn't any other choice. Not with Alex in the room. Gathering some courage, she peeked sideways without moving to see if she could ascertain what was happening behind her back. She saw shadows in the smoked glass windows of the two men standing side-by-side and heard the faint murmurs of conversation.

Relief coursed through Tori. He was here to see Alex. She'd

been on pins and needles the last four days, waiting for him to make an appearance and confront her about their stupid predicament. Surely he would have heard from his lawyer by now. Maybe she should have attempted to get legal advice instead of letting him take the lead, she considered with regret, but the realization that she might have taken more responsibility for finding a solution came too late. He was already in the driver's seat. The thought didn't bring her much comfort.

Her nerves exploded as Tori silently chanted, *oh please don't come over here, please don't come over here,* but she doubted he would get caught ignoring her in front of Alex. The silent pep talk turned to assuring herself that she could handle him, although she knew that was bullshit.

She'd been so damn angry with him when they parted, stomping off in a fit of pique as he'd called after her. Not much had changed over the last few days except the uncomfortable acknowledgment that try as she might to compartmentalize what had happened between them and maintain that it had all just been raging hormones, alcohol, and normal everyday desire, it was a whole lot more.

Somewhere along the line she'd started to fall for the panty-chasing playboy and reluctantly admitted that he wasn't quite the upper class snot she'd painted him as. The thought made her sigh. After everything she'd been through the past year and the way the press had hyped a shit-ton of presumptions into a character analysis that made her seem like something she wasn't, it pained her to realize she had done the same to him. To say she felt like a hypocrite was an understatement. Still, there was no denying he'd been a class A jerk. Snarling at him to never speak to her *ever* again was partly due to his shitty attitude, and also because she was having a hard time wrapping her mind around pretty much everything that happened between them.

Someone behind her cleared his throat. Really? Oh, for God's sake, *someone*? That was the best she could do? She rolled her eyes at her own foolishness. Tori knew exactly who was trying to get her attention.

"Victoria," he rumbled. The sound of his voice flowed over her senses like a soft shower of warm water. *Dammit. Well*, she thought, *there's nothing to do now except turn around and deal with him.* Throwing down her pen while shuffling a stack of notecards, Tori stood but took her damn sweet time responding to his presence.

The minute she faced him, she knew she was in over her head. There wasn't enough anger or hurt in the known universe to distract from how handsome he looked. Even with several days' growth on his face and a wardrobe choice that wrecked her thought process completely, no one had the right to look so gorgeous, or so dangerous. Dressed in head to toe black, he wore a t-shirt stretched taut across the spectacular abs she knew lurked underneath and a pair of black jeans that molded to his thighs like a second skin. She wasn't sure if he was wearing the pants or if they were wearing him.

All that black highlighted his fair coloring and made the tattoo on one of his biceps stick out like a sore thumb. It also matched the dark scowl on his face, something she had but seconds to ponder before he leapt at her like a beast stalking its prey. Snatching the glasses from her face so quickly she flinched, he glared at her like she'd just committed the ultimate sin. Jabbing his finger at her he barked, "You said you wouldn't do this anymore!" Two seconds later he snapped the frames in half and tossed the pieces on the floor.

Defensively crossing her arms across her chest she fixed him with a withering glare. The memory of him spanking her and demanding she never hide behind her clothes again played out in her mind. "I don't know what you're talking about." Oh my God, was she insane for saying that? His ice blue eyes turned dark and stormy, pinning her to the spot.

"You know exactly what I'm referring to." With each precise word he spit out, his expression turned more and more dangerous. He took a step toward her and if it weren't for the desk right behind her, Tori would have retreated in haste. Whatever bravado she'd hoped to portray deserted her in a flash.

"Whoa, dude. What the fuck?" she heard Alex mutter darkly.

Draegyn's head snapped around to his friend. "Stay out of this Alex."

"Uh – yeah. I don't think so. Tori are you okay?" Alex asked with obvious concern.

She felt like she was being held in a tractor beam with Draegyn's dark gaze boring into hers. A devilish imp in her subconscious was urging her to keep on provoking him but common sense and her boss's worried presence helped hold her tongue. Tearing her eyes away from Draegyn, she looked at Alex and feigned a calm smile. "It's fine. Really." She probably should have stopped at that but she didn't. "Mr. St. John has a problem with how I dress...."

"What?" Alex boomed, turning an angry glower on Draegyn. "Please tell me you didn't actually say that. Goddammit Drae." The tension swirling around them went off the scale right then and there.

Snarling like a wounded animal, Draegyn suddenly grabbed her arm, forcefully pulling her toward him as if he intended to march her out of the room. "Leave it Alex. This is between Victoria and me."

Tori struggled to free herself from his grasp although she knew it was a losing battle. Aware that Alex was moving to get in between them, she yelped, pretending distress, as if Draegyn's grip was hurting her. Just as she knew he would, her outburst made him quickly drop her arm.

She glared at him and rubbed at her arm. "Um, sorry but, there is nothing between you and me." Oddly, she didn't feel much satisfaction at the harsh, sarcastic jibe.

"Drae," Alex warned. "Back off."

"No!" Turning dark eyes on her he hissed, "We're going to settle this right now."

"There's nothing to settle, Mr. St. John."

"Stop with the mister shit Victoria. You know damn well we have to talk. Now!" He made two mistakes right then. Trying to order her around and looking her up and down with an expression of disgust. "I mean, look at you! What the fuck are you wearing?" he swore.

Tori quietly considered the plain blue slacks and oversize sweater she had on and couldn't hide from the accusation he'd hurled at her. She'd returned to type after their return from Vegas, dressing down and basically schlepping about like a fashion casualty. It had been too much for her to start dressing differently especially since the only reason she'd bothered in the first place was to shock the man shouting at her. Tears burned in her eyes. *Dammit.* She couldn't afford to cry right now. With her emotions spiraling out of control from several days of no sleep and little food, it was all she could do to not kick him in his shins. Everything went to hell in the next heartbeat.

Alex stepped up and put his hand on Draegyn's shoulder, muttering under his breath, earning a stern glare from his friend. When Draegyn went to snatch his arm away, Tori was standing close enough to get hit by the backlash as his elbow slammed into her chest, knocking her back a step. Then the yelling started as the two men went after each other, with Alex angrily chastising Draegyn's actions, and Draegyn barking at him to mind his own fucking business.

She didn't know why she did, but Tori took the excuse of the two men hollering angrily at one another to burst into tears and run frantically from the room, knocking over a chair in her urgent retreat. Somewhere in the commotion she'd also managed to squeak out an "I hate you!" *Shit.* This was turning into a banner day.

"What in the goddamn fuck is wrong with you?" Alex yelled.

Drae's equilibrium was quickly unraveling. When he'd approached Victoria he wasn't sure what would happen next, but at Alex's urging he knew he had to try and diffuse their antagonistic situation. Other people were beginning to notice and comment on their odd behavior.

Whatever he'd planned to say flew out the window when she'd turned to face him and he got a good look at her. Fury blazed to life as he took in the ugly glasses and dowdy wardrobe. In *his* mind she'd promised not to dress like some spinster librarian anymore and finding her doing just that had enraged him. That and the unavoidable fact that he'd been longing to see her again. Be around her. Listen to her voice and drown in those chocolate eyes once more. Finding her in little brown mouse mode struck him as a *fuck you*, directed at him and him alone.

"I'll tell you what the goddamn fuck is wrong with me! Those glasses," he yelled pointing at the broken pieces on the floor, "are a joke! Did you know they were fake? She doesn't even need them." He was pacing back and forth like a caged animal looking for a victim or escape. Either would do. "And those clothes! Jesus Christ, Alex. You know that's all bullshit, right?"

Alex was clearly furious with him and shouted, "So? What fucking difference does it make to you? Where do you get off acting like that, Drae? Shit. It's not like you to make somebody cry."

"I'll tell you what difference it makes to me," he bellowed. "She's my goddamn….."

Alex cut him off before he could finish the sentence. "Watch it buddy. You are stepping pretty far over the line."

Drae raked his hand repeatedly back and forth across his head feeling like it was going to explode any minute. In the angry silence that followed he could feel Alex's mind working over-time.

"Wait a goddamn minute," Alex snarled with bared teeth. Two seconds passed then, "Oh my God!" he yelled at the top of his lungs.

"She's your goddamn *what*, Drae? Holy fuckballs! What did you do?"

"Shit."

"I'm waiting, Lieutenant," his former commanding officer bit out. The reminder was meant to put him in his place, which it did quite effectively. Some habits die hard.

The two battlefield brothers stood silently, eyeing each other. Alex with his burly physique, barely containing his disapproval, ready to knock his fucking lights out and Drae, all restless, edgy energy and a guilty conscience as he fought for control before he made things worse. Throwing his hands up in surrender, Drae groaned, "Wife. She's my wife."

Alex's jaw almost hit the floor. It would have been funny under different circumstances. He even blinked a few times and shook his head as he absorbed what Drae had just admitted. "Uh…"

"Yeah, exactly," Drae muttered, shocked at how easily the word *wife* rolled off his tongue.

"You and Tori are *married*? When?" The dawning realization of when hit him before the question was fully out of his mouth. "Vegas?" At Drae's shaky head nod, Alex blanched.

"In all honesty, we didn't so much get married as we had a moment that many hours later revealed itself to have been a wedding ceremony."

"Jesus Drae. I hope you never get called to testify for anything because that explanation sucked a bag of dicks. Want to try that again?"

"Look, it's a long story and since it obviously involves Victoria, I don't want to say any more. It's partially her story to tell so let's leave it at that."

"Well, this explains a lot." Alex glanced at the doorway that a crying Victoria had just exited from. "Does anyone else know?"

"Fuck no! Well, one person knows, I suppose. I called Ted Collins and asked him to look into the legalities and see about how to clean this mess up."

"An annulment?"

Drae couldn't believe the heated flush that worked its way from his feet to his face. When he winced and muttered an inelegant, "Uh", Alex looked like he was going to throttle him.

"*Ah fuck.* You didn't! Did you? Goddammit Drae."

His world had become overrun with a series of firsts and an unending parade of uncharacteristic behavior since the moment Victoria had wandered into his life. Even so, he was surprised when all he could do was hang his head, not so much from mortification at what he'd done but because the truth was much deeper than that. He'd made love to Victoria. A couple of times and had not been able to diminish the impact of that or the way it made him feel, no matter how angry he'd been at what happened later. "I'm handling this, Alex," he tried to explain.

"Really? From where I'm standing, it looks like you've pretty much lost your damn mind. If by handling it you mean holing up for days off the radar and then coming here and in five short minutes managing to assault an employee and make her cry, then yeah. You're fucking handling it." For good measure, Alex pointedly kicked at the broken glasses on the floor.

Drae honestly didn't know what to say or do. Everything he'd ever thought about himself was suddenly no longer valid. With his legendary cool in tatters there didn't seem to be much he could cling to as normal. Yelling at Victoria as she stood there with her chin in the air, daring him to mess with her, had not been one of his finer moments.

"One of us has to go and check on Tori. Make sure she's not packing her stuff, or worse, plotting your murder."

At the mention that she might up and run away from him, Drae tensed. He didn't want her to leave, an admission that gave him uncharacteristic butterflies in his gut. *Fuck.* The woman was scarier than a whole team of bad guys. From his days on the battlefield to some of his agency assignments, he was used to feeling off the chart adrenaline. Kept him on his toes. This feeling however was wholly different. And he didn't know how to deal with it.

"I'll go find her."

"Are you sure, man? Don't want to get into your business Drae but maybe it would be better to let things settle down. She seemed pretty pissed off."

What a mess. "Yeah, I know."

"Alright. I'll stay out of it for now, but know this," his friend glowered at him. "I like Tori. Don't fuck this up, Drae."

TORI WAS A MESS. She'd been so shocked at her cry-baby reaction to what happened that she hadn't been able to turn off the waterworks. Luckily she hadn't encountered anyone else after she fled Alex's office making her way swiftly to the privacy of her apartment. Half a box of tissues later, she almost started bawling like a baby again when she caught sight of herself in the bathroom mirror. Red, unhappy looking eyes above a nose rubbed raw, her hair in shambles, she looked like someone who had weathered a terrible emotional storm. Her full lips were hideously swollen and puffy after chewing on them trying to get control of herself. In short – she looked like bloody hell.

Seeing Draegyn again had unleashed a metric fuck-ton of emotions, good and bad. His imperious tone and attitude when he'd accused her of breaking a promise she hadn't actually made pushed every one of her buttons. It was he who demanded she never dress like a bag lady again. She hadn't promised him anything but the simple fact that she'd been ass up on his lap as he smacked her backside while he issued that particular demand probably constituted her agreement.

She'd gotten snarky with him out of habit and also because she wanted to protect herself from the growing realization that she was, quite impossibly, falling in love with him. The admission sat in her belly like a lump of burning coal, making her emotionally fragile in a way she'd never experienced.

Tori always imagined that if or when she truly fell in love, it would be all hearts and flowers and involve someone much like herself, a tad on the nerd side and fairly down-to-earth. Never in her wildest dreams had she ever fancied being attracted to a man like Draegyn St. John. Someone sophisticated and drop-dead sexy, worldly with enough notches on his bedpost to be considered a legend. That sort of scenario only happened in the romance books she read. It didn't actually happen in real life to simple girls like her. Knowing he didn't feel the same wasn't helping things. When he'd accidentally jostled her as he and Alex started growling at each other, it had been the last straw. Running from the room like a hysterical teenager as the tears broke free, knocking furniture over in her rush to get away from the situation, made her feel like an idiot.

Was that her phone buzzing? She seriously hoped it wasn't her mother calling because she doubted her ability to keep it together through a conversation. Her mom would know within seconds that she was upset – parents were like that, but she wasn't ready to share what was going on with anyone.

Making a beeline for the table by the front door where she'd tossed the phone, she saw immediately that it wasn't a phone call coming through at all. No, it was a text. A text from Draegyn. *We need to talk.*

Worrying her swollen bottom lip with her teeth, Tori hesitated and then tapped out a short reply. *You've said enough, thanks.*

Several minutes ticked by in heavy silence. She supposed he was considering what to say next. Glancing up quickly, she made sure she'd put the latch on the door, suddenly fearful that he might actually show up to start round two.

Your choice Victoria. Either you come here or I'm coming to your place. This isn't negotiable. My door is open. If you're not here in the next half hour expect me to come knocking and if you don't open up I'll simply break the door down.

She let a good, long minute creep by before answering. *You made me cry. Nobody makes me cry. Why would I want to ever speak to you again?*

He instantly replied. *I'm sorry. Please. We really need to talk.*

Wow. Sorry? That couldn't have been easy for him. *Okay. I'll be there within the hour.*

Thank you.

A flight of butterflies opened up inside her. Remembering how god-awful she looked Tori made for the bathroom to try and repair the damage before she faced him. It was foolish to avoid talking to him, after all they had some pretty serious issues to discuss, but she'd be damned before appearing on his doorstep looking like hell.

Drae was pacing in the foyer of his home. More than half an hour had passed since their last text message, and he knew she'd be arriving on his doorstep at any moment. At least he hoped she would. Nervous, he kept checking the phone clutched in his hand to keep track of time and assure himself that she hadn't changed her mind and texted him a *fuck you* message.

After their ugly confrontation, he'd video chatted with his lawyer before texting her. It wouldn't do much good to talk without all the necessary information. He wondered how she'd react to what he was about to tell her. Not only was an annulment out of the question, he'd found out that details of their union had been officially filed and were available for prying eyes. Any resourceful reporter would have no problem finding out they were married with very little digging.

He wasn't quite sure how he felt about that. Besides the fact that being married wasn't on his life-agenda, wanting to protect Victoria from gossip and innuendo was also a factor. It took Ted reminding him that his parents would freak the fuck out if they heard about it to bring the situation into focus. Frankly, he didn't want them and their plastic, fake caring anywhere near him. He much preferred things just as they were with them and their society-fueled meddling ways far away from his life. It was better for everyone involved.

His sister on the other hand was another matter entirely. He adored Desirée and didn't want her to find out something so private and personal about him from the wrong source. There was also Victoria's mother. Alex considered the widowed Stephanie Bennett to be a friend. Not only that, Victoria was her only child. He wasn't a complete ass, he only acted like one where his wife was concerned, and he didn't want to inadvertently cause the woman any distress over her daughter's well-being. Not after the European fiasco. There certainly was a lot to consider.

Practicalities aside, Drae stumbled as he paced when the nagging reality of the intense desire he felt for Victoria shredded his nerves. He might not want to be married but he was and the truth of the matter was that he hadn't had his fill of the delicate waif. Not by a long shot. Her sassy mouth, and the way she flew at him when he acted like a dick, only made him want her more.

And then there was the unprotected sex issue. It didn't help to wonder what the fuck he'd been thinking because he hadn't been. Thinking, that was. Not with the head on his shoulders, anyway. Definitely with his other head though. As long as he lived he'd never forget the sight she made that morning in the tiny crop top and the workout pants that molded to her like skin. He couldn't get inside her fast enough. The way she'd responded set them on a course neither had intended.

A motion-sensor light flickered on at the end of the drive alerting him to Victoria's imminent arrival. No longer needing the phone, he chucked it aside and headed for the door as his heart thumped heavily in his chest. Drae stepped out onto the wide deck and watched her as she slowly came to him. *Oh my dear sweet God*, he thought. How was he going to keep his hands off her when she looked the way she did?

Dusk was at hand and in the dimming light she looked ethereal and almost dream-like as she approached. Wearing a simple white t-shirt and a pair of jeans that hugged her modest curves, she'd left her hair loose and falling against her shoulders. He never considered himself much of a blue jeans kind of a guy, but there was something about the way her slim hips swayed in the tight denim that made his mouth go dry. Stopping at the foot of the front steps, she shoved her hands into her back pockets, making the t-shirt stretch and highlighting the shape of her breasts. He tried to swallow but there wasn't enough saliva in his mouth to lick a stamp.

"Hey," she said.

Clearing his throat as best he could, he muttered a hoarse, "Hi". For a long moment they just stood there and eyed each other; she warily, and Drae with a hunger that wiped rational thought and the real purpose for this visit from his brain.

An uncomfortable surge of emotion cleared his vision fast when she glanced over her shoulder as if reconsidering being there. Turning back toward him, he noticed the tension bracketing her mouth and dark shadows under her eyes. Drae suddenly felt like a swine, ogling her tiny figure like a ravenous beast on the prey while she showed obvious signs of not having had an easy time of it the last few days.

"Why didn't you grab a cart and drive down here?" He growled, thinking of her making her way in the setting sun the quarter of a mile down the lane behind the villa in a groin-tightening pair of strappy sandals. Dammit. She could have stumbled or fallen, and he wouldn't have known she needed help. Good grief. When had he become some kind of frustrated hero, grinding away with concern for a woman's safety?

She lifted her shoulders in a half shrug that said more than words could. "I didn't want everyone and their brother to know where I was going," she sighed. The pained look that swept across her features reminded Drae how unusual their situation really was.

Holding out his hand to her he said, "C'mon inside. Have you eaten dinner? If you're hungry there's a humongous pot of chili in the oven that Ria sent over. I thought we'd sit out back and relax." He was babbling like a fucking teenage boy on his first date.

She worried her bottom lip but didn't move to take his hand. For a second he thought she might bolt but she finally came toward him and hesitantly reached out. When her small hand clasped his, he relaxed for the first time in days. There was no conversation as she let him lead her inside and while her silence scared the hell out of him, she didn't shy away from his touch. At least he hadn't destroyed that with his irrational behavior and stupid words. Why that should matter to him was something he'd have to examine later.

Once inside, he shut the front door and looked closely at her face. She was motionless, her eyes darting everywhere, taking in the house he'd built from his own design. The huge, contemporary home featured a heavy-timbered ceiling in an open concept with walls of windows that captured the changing light throughout the day. The second floor featured a distinctive walkway that looked down into the main living area. Everywhere you looked there was wood and handcrafted elements that brought a very cool wow factor.

He couldn't help but smile and feel pride at the approval he saw in her gaze. He wanted to take her on a tour and talk her ear off about every nail and cross-beam, and he especially wanted to show her his master bedroom with its custom designed platform bed underneath a soaring wood canopy that reminded him of a tree house he once saw in his travels. But all that had to wait. Right now he needed to stay focused on the matter at hand.

"Your home is, well- it's magnificent Draegyn. Truly. Did you design this yourself?" The astonishment and praise in her voice warmed a spot in his chest that seemed suspiciously centered around his heart. When she squeezed his hand, he smiled down into her up-turned face.

"Yeah," he shrugged like it was no big deal. Now that the ice had more or less been broken, some of the tension eased from his body.

"Here, c'mon," he said, pulling her along. "Let me show you the back deck. We can relax out there and talk, okay?"

Leading her through the main living space and the ginormous gourmet kitchen, he felt like the king of the fucking world. What was it about someone else's approval that made such a difference? Was it the actual expression of delight or the person giving it? In this case it was both. Drae was proud of his home, how it had been built and the attention to detail that showed in the exquisite crafts-manship. Seeing it anew through her astonished eyes was a powerful thing.

"Mmmm. That chili smells delicious," she murmured at the exact same moment her stomach growled. Taking that as a cue he reluctantly released her hand and motioned to the wide, open doorway that led to the deck.

"Grab a seat outside, and I'll bring us some. I'm a beer man when a bowl of chili is on the menu, but I have wine cooling if you'd prefer that."

She smiled and chuckled softly. "Wine? With Ria's chili? I think not. Sounds a little like sacrilege! Beer is fine for me, thanks."

They sat quietly after that, under a huge umbrella strung with tiny white lights over a long wood table, cradling stoneware bowls filled with steaming homemade chili. She was being cautious, he understood that, but he couldn't help but think that sitting with her just felt so right. Maybe they actually could salvage the budding friendship that had been developing before the shit hit the fan. Out of nowhere he looked at her and said, "I'm thinking about getting a dog. Alex has Zeus and Brody's been after me for the last year to take one of his Labs."

"Really? A dog would fit you nicely, I think. Is Brody the guy who trains the agency's dogs? I've heard his name mentioned but haven't met him yet."

"*Mmm hmm.* He's a Veteran, like most everyone who works for the agency. He goes back east for a couple of months every year. That's where he is now. He's got another life away from here. Usually, he turns up in early summer and sticks around till the winter holidays." He laughed and grinned at her. "Wait till you get a load of the animals he works with. Hope you don't mind barking!"

She smiled and tilted her bottle of beer at him. "Barking dogs, growling men. What's the difference, really?"

He threw back his head and laughed at her comment. She was right. "Do you like dogs, Victoria?"

"Absolutely! I love having Zeus underfoot at work, and my mom and I had a puppy for a while. I loved her to death in that way only a child could."

"Had?"

She frowned and sighed heavily. "Yeah. Had. She was wonderful but we lost her when she was only five years old. Some dog illness I think. Mom was crushed. Another loss of someone we both loved. It was hard."

"I'm sorry to hear that. Maybe you can help me pick out a puppy when Brody gets here." She didn't answer, and he wondered what she was thinking.

Night had come to the desert. With lights from the house illuminating the deck, this was Drae's favorite time of day. Everything was so still and quiet. Getting up, he walked to a covered control panel and flipped a couple of switches that lit up ground level lights marking the edge of the outdoor space. With another click flames appeared in a gas fire pit on the corner of the decking. "C'mon. Let's sit by the fire," he said with an outstretched hand. He was pretty sure she could walk the fifty feet without assistance, but he wanted to touch her again. "Want another beer?"

"Sure," she answered after accepting his hand.

He led her to a grouping of cushioned chaise loungers gathered near the fire pit and then hurried away to clear their chili bowls and grab the cold brews. Nervousness ticked inside him again. Now that they'd eaten and indulged in some small talk, they'd have to get into more serious matters.

Tori kicked off her sandals and settled on a doublewide chaise, leaned her head back on the soft cushion, staring blankly at the first sight of twinkling stars in the darkening sky. This was something she liked about life in the Arizona desert. There was something magical about the quiet wilderness at night that spoke to her soul. Right now she needed some of that calming power to do more than just fill her head with romantic fantasies. Though she was working overtime trying to appear relaxed, truth was, she was almost jumping put of her skin. Draegyn did that to her. One look from his startling blue eyes, and she was up the proverbial creek without a paddle.

The only thing keeping her from going off on a hysterical tirade was knowing they had serious things to discuss. It wouldn't help the already surreal situation for her to be unglued. Experience had taught her that. When her world shattered and the paparazzi hounded her every move, Tori clung to the lessons learned from watching her mother's pageant protégée's as they struggled to appear unfazed under glaring lights while judges picked apart each word and motion. Right this moment she might appear untroubled, but the truth was a far different story.

At Draegyn's approach, she sat up straighter and schooled her expression into something she hoped looked composed and reasonable. She suspected he was doing something similar. It was only the occasional eye tic and the way his mouth sometimes compressed into a grim line that let Tori know he had any emotions at all. The man was a sphinx of cool-headedness. She suspected it was second nature to someone in his line of work to keep his emotions and thoughts in check.

Her eyes, which had been marking his movement in her direction, dropped to the bottle he held out and landed on his zipper, which conveniently struck her at eye level. The wicked imp in her subconscious that was urging less restraint was cackling with glee at the sight. Damn her hormones.

Motioning to her, Tori politely clinked the long-necked glass bottle with his as he murmured, "Truce part two?" She hiccupped a startled laugh at his choice of words, pursing her lips in a lame attempt to stop from dissolving into a fit of giggles. Truce? Really? That had worked out so well for them the first time.

"This seems more like a negotiated cease-fire than a truce, don't you think?"

"Perhaps," he allowed with a tiny smirk. "I seem to recall your only term being never to speak to you again. At least we aren't yelling at one another, so yes. A suspension of hostilities in the hope of a truce." She had a retort ready for that comment but swallowed it along with a hearty slug of the cold brew. Sometimes it was better to say nothing and wait to see where things were going.

Drae lowered himself onto the lounger next to hers and gathered the thoughts that scattered when Victoria eyed the hard-on he knew was pushing against the front of his jeans. The woman was nothing but temptation and try as he might to reign in his response, he was failing miserably. Her shoes lay on the flagstone tiles and with one dainty foot tucked under the other, he saw that her toes were painted a pale raspberry color that triggered restless thoughts of those same feet digging into his haunches as he pounded into her. Taking a long pull from his beer, Drae tried to focus on the present but it was impossible to ignore those memories when she sat close enough to catch a whiff of her soft perfume.

Silence wrapped around them as he let his thoughts off their closely held tether, imagining tugging those damn jeans down her thighs and chucking them aside until all she had on was the white t-shirt and nothing else. If they weren't at war with each other he would sink to his knees between her legs and simply feast on her naked sex. Making love to her under the stars seemed like a viable option until he remembered why they were there. She looked sharply in his direction when a ragged sigh escaped his throat.

"Stop looking at me like that, Draegyn"

"I wish I could," he answered with a shake of his head. Shifting, Drae turned toward her with legs spread and forearms resting on his thighs as he fiddled with the beer bottle for no good reason. Words deserted while a frustrated grimace froze on his face. "Okay. Let's do this, then." Taking a deep breath he let the information he needed to share with her pour out in a rush.

"There's good news and not so good news. I've had my lawyer look in to our uh, predicament." Instantly wishing he could rephrase that or at least take back the biting way he'd said it, Drae continued. "Besides the obvious reason why an annulment won't work." He watched her squirm at the reminder and plowed ahead with all the finesse of a bull in a china closet. "The other consideration is much more straightforward. According to Ted, enterprising paps keep an eye on marriage filings and annulment requests that crop up soon after. Apparently, that sequence of events happens a lot. He suggests keeping a low profile for now so as not to arouse the attention of the media who are constantly on the look-out for a good story."

In a tone that sounded less than friendly she asked, "Is that supposed to be the good or the bad news?"

"That's for you to decide, I suppose. Ted seemed to think that for now anyway, the press hasn't picked up on our situation. Garry and Shawn's surprise Vegas nuptials hit the gossip mongers almost right away. So far, no one has looked beyond that particularly juicy story."

Putting her beer on the ground, Victoria slid from the chaise and turned away from him, going to stand near the edge of the tile patio. From behind, her body language suggested she was wrapped rather tightly at the moment. "Continue," she bit out while keeping her back to him.

"Keeping this under wraps is going to be the best bet moving forward. He suggests not letting the cat out of the bag, so to speak. Eventually, he'll file for a dissolution based on mutual accord. Should be simple and better all around this way. I can't have my family finding out."

Tori considered killing him just then, the arrogant, son of a bitch. True to form, it was all about him. What *his* lawyer thought. *His* family couldn't know. And better all around for whom, exactly? *Him*? Jesus.

Clearing his throat, he kept talking as if they were discussing the weather. "Buying some time is best, don't you think? After all, if you turn up pregnant…."

Turn up pregnant? Was he kidding? He made it sound like she'd made all this happen by herself. She didn't wait for him to finish the thought. "Yeah. I'm not."

"What," he quickly asked. "Do you know that for sure, Victoria?"

Fuck him, she thought. Would serve him right if she just stormed out of there without another word and let him stew in his own conceited juices. Unfortunately, behaving like a twit wasn't going to help so she reluctantly responded as she turned his way. "Well, no. Not exactly," she answered in a hurry. "But really, it was only one time. What are the odds?"

The look on his face suggested he thought the odds were not in their favor. Remembering the desperate, primitive way he'd taken her that first time, Tori shuddered at the notion that nature had been calling the shots.

With both of them reliving that fateful moment when sense had flown out the window and they'd fallen on each other with all the finesse of animals in heat, the temperature on the patio started to soar. He'd been horrified afterward at the way he'd treated her but Tori hadn't regretted any of it. Her female core twitched remembering desperate moans and the way he'd plunged inside her, over and over until she'd been shuddering and crying. When he'd come, she'd been beyond turned on as her orgasm finished him off with powerful contractions that had milked every drop from his body.

Suddenly, the desert air was infused with raw carnality. She was breathing a bit too rapidly with arms clutched across her chest as if to shield her puckering nipples from his view. She saw his hands clench at his sides where he stood just feet from her with a look on his face that let her know he was fighting his own battle for control.

"Shit. Victoria," he groaned. "I can't…" And just like that they were on each other. Tori didn't know who moved first, and it really didn't matter because the explosion that went off when their mouths connected made her mind go blank. Greedy sounds of want and need ripped from her throat as voracious tongues dueled and swirled. With a hand tangled in her hair, he pressed against her head so she couldn't pull away as Draegyn devoured her mouth. Where a minute ago she'd been ready to tear him a new one, now she was writhing desperately against him, clutching at his shoulders as he held on to her tight.

Collapsing onto the double chaise, Tori sprawled inelegantly on top of him as he thrust a muscled thigh between her legs while their needy groans split the quiet, nighttime air. He kept one hand on the back of her head as their kiss deepened, while the other hand cupped her jeans clad bottom, pressing her ever more intimately against him.

He is the devil, she thought, only to have that thought evaporate under the sensual onslaught of his wild kisses. Rocking her hips against his thigh, she whimpered into his mouth as a need so powerful and big that she couldn't contain it burst to flaming life inside her. With his hand controlling the fevered grinding of her hips, she felt a sensation in her center that was so hot, she was sure he could feel it through their clothes.

DRAE WAS LOST. *This is what she did to me*, he thought. No matter how hard he tried to remain in control around her, one touch, and he was a goner. He hadn't meant to kiss her but the reminder of that first time when she'd been so responsive in his arms had destroyed his carefully thought out plan to just talk to her and nothing else.

Yeah, right. So much for letting cooler heads prevail. With her grinding against his thigh and their tongues swirling in a sensuous dance that made him think of another, more intimate dance, he was on sensory overload. They shouldn't be doing this but they were.

How long they lay there with her draped over his body, he couldn't tell. All he knew for sure was he had a raging hard-on that was painfully surging against the snug fit of his jeans where it pressed into her belly as she gripped his thigh with her own. At their point of contact he experienced a fiery heat that fed the wild lust raging through him. She was writhing and moaning, her hands touching every part of him they could reach.

Shock and undiluted satisfaction surged through him when she shuddered on top of him as the frenzied grinding triggered a climax that he felt rip through her in waves. He wanted to slide his hand into her jeans and search out the wet heat he knew would greet his fingers. The need to taste her overwhelmed his senses, momentarily blinding him to what happened next.

Completely engulfed by her sweet response it took a minute for Drae to realize she had wrenched her mouth free of his. Having yanked his shirt from the waistband of his pants, she'd shoved it high on his chest so she could press wet, fevered kisses across his upper body. His neck arched and his head felt like it weighed a ton as he closed his eyes and absorbed the tongue-lashing she was subjecting him to. When she licked his nipple and nipped at the beaded flesh it felt like he was falling into a desire so greedy he could only groan and hang on for dear life.

As her small hands roamed his torso, he felt her fingernails digging into his flesh while her insatiable mouth wrecked him completely. She licked, bit, kissed, and suckled every inch of skin she'd uncovered while scoring him with her nails in an animalistic offensive that went beyond just sex. It seemed so primitive, so very basic, as if she wanted to devour him in her need.

Drae considered stopping her with the last, half formed thought of sense left in his brain when he felt her hands struggling with the snap of his jeans. She overrode his thoughts with greedy desperation, quickly unzipping him and tugging his pants down with determined hands. He felt the cool nighttime air on his wildly surging cock as she freed him from the confines of his clothing a second before her fingers wrapped possessively around him. "Oh my God," he groaned, his heart thundering in his ears when she settled between his thighs and pushed his legs open wide.

Tori couldn't believe what she was doing but that didn't stop her from finishing what she'd started. Her panties flooded with moisture from the orgasm she'd stolen from him and all she could focus on at the moment was the primal instinct that had her in its grip. She desperately needed to taste him. Fill up her senses and her mouth with his beautiful body, experience his essence in a way even more intimate than taking him inside her. She had no idea what she was doing, never having dared anything like this before, but that didn't stop or slow her down in any way. Through eyes that felt hot with desire she studied his erection, marveling at the surprising beauty of his maleness. Wrapping both hands around his impressive length, Tori slowly stroked every inch in an intimate inspection that stopped at nothing.

Lifting his hardened cock away from his body she touched the twin spheres below, noting his groaning response. He liked that. So did she. Using the fingers of one hand to cup his balls, she massaged them gently while her other hand continued its firm grip on his staff, sliding from root to tip, marveling at the smooth skin encasing the throbbing hardness. He was a looker from any position but from this intimate angle, he was nothing short of magnificent.

He ground out her name, "Victoria," in a strangled voice that let her know she was on the right track. More grateful than surprised, Tori learned the strokes and pressure that he liked when Draegyn reached one trembling hand to cover hers. She supposed it was a measure of her inexperience that she was so shaken by the strength of the grip he demonstrated. Who knew that a hard cock reacted so favorably to such tight pressure? Well, she hadn't before but she certainly did now, making her double down on the firm strokes that made him quiver and moan.

Rather liking the view, Tori was transfixed by the appearance of a clear bead of fluid that appeared on the plump head of his sex. *Ooohh, I like that.* Had she said that out loud? She didn't care. It was the truth although in his current state, she doubted Draegyn would make much sense of anything that came out of her mouth.

Using a single finger she scraped it across the tip of his cock, capturing the liquid proof of his arousal. Keeping a firm grip on him she lifted the finger to her mouth as her gaze lifted to his face. He was watching through half-closed eyes that burned her with icy intensity. Licking her finger clean with a moan, she bent her head toward his straining flesh and placed an open mouth kiss where her finger had just swiped. Before she could draw away, he tangled a hand in her hair. Opening her mouth, she lowered it over the bulbous head and let her tongue lap at the underside of his cock. When Draegyn nearly jack-knifed off the chaise she sucked on the weeping tip like a lollipop while he groaned and shook, still gripping her head.

"Oh God, babe. Have to stop. You don't know what you're doing to me." His words didn't match the pressure he was exerting on the placement and movement of her head. His hips started to shimmy, searching for the perfect angle as she squeezed tight and continued sucking on his staff. It was slightly shocking to realize the pleasure was not all his. Tori discovered she rather liked the way he felt in her hands and against her lips. Daring to go further she lowered her head, taking more and more of his cock into her mouth. Pretty soon his groans were punctuated with ravenous, greedy moans rumbling up from deep in her core. With one hand gripping the arm of the chaise until his knuckles turned white while the other continued to encourage the movement of her head as she gobbled eagerly at his sex, Tori never missed a beat, just kept sucking him deep only to occasionally stop to swirl her tongue around the swollen head.

"Victoria," he groaned. "Stop." His legs quivered and his hips started to buck up into her mouth. She understood biology. Knew she was driving him to the edge and briefly considered backing off before she ended up taking him the whole way to orgasm when she wasn't sure what to do in such an eventuality. But in the end, whatever primitive longing she'd been satisfying belonged to both of them, making this so much more than a simple blow job. No. She wanted all of it. Wanted to devour him in every way she could.

Her fingers found their way back to the rounded balls that felt firm and swollen to her inexperienced touch. Fondling them while she stroked his huge cock with her other hand in tandem with the rise and fall of her mouth, she felt saliva escape her lips, as murmurs of earthy delight mixed with the sound of her slurping at his sex.

Is this really happening, she wondered? Did she actually have Draegyn St. John's hard dick literally stuffed in her mouth? She shivered at the thought. Her lips felt stretched and swollen as they moved again and again along his shaft. Occasionally, eagerness made her gag when she went too far but even that seemed exciting and rather than cause her to back off, she'd make that '*mmmm*' noise that signified how awesome he felt in her mouth and just keep going. The feel of him sliding against her tongue was almost indescribable and more pleasurable than she thought possible.

When the fingers teasing his balls touched a spot that made him groan louder, she experimented with lowering her head, squeezing the base of his cock and pressing against his tender flesh until he started bucking his hips while pressing on her head forcing her to take the full measure of him whether she gagged or not. It was wild and unbridled, with her sucking on him like his cock would be the last thing she ever tasted and him thrashing about while she milked a climax from him with no shame.

She knew the moment he lost control, when nothing could have prompted him to ease his hardness from her plundering mouth. Feeling his dick pulse along her tongue was a revelation of sorts. It was so sexy, so perfect, as he surged up over and over with a loud growl erupting in the silence. She even liked the way his hand grabbed her hair and held her mouth on his exploding staff.

Hot streams of fluid hit the back of her throat as she sucked him dry. It was more thrilling than she ever imagined and she'd imagined quite a lot where Draegyn was concerned. Nothing about what just happened was a turn-off. Quite the contrary. Tori had been gripped with rapturous delight. Continuing to softly stroke him in the aftermath, she licked his softening cock, well-pleased with her efforts.

Drae was stunned. She'd dealt him a knock-out blow with her

wicked mouth and questing fingers. No stranger to a well-performed blow job, he'd never, *ever* experienced anything as exciting as her mouth, shy at first and then bolder and bolder, sucking him to a thundering orgasm that left him helplessly emptying his balls into her insatiable mouth.

Being a gentleman meant he at least tried to halt her oral offensive but in the end, she managed to fire him up to such an extent that any attempt to stop the inevitable had been pathetic at best. He'd been fantasizing about those lips of hers wrapped around his hard dick from practically the moment they met but nothing in his vast experience had prepared him for the reality of her perfect pout stretching around his hardness. The last time they'd fucked, he thought he'd never known such an explosive orgasm. He was wrong. The way she'd so perfectly sucked him off was the single most enjoyable and deeply satisfying climax he'd experienced. *Ever*.

He couldn't move in the aftermath, not a single muscle. It didn't help things that she'd barely backed off once he exploded in her mouth, continuing to stroke his shaft, leaving soft, wet kisses along his length and across his stomach. There was something powerfully satisfying about her face nuzzling the hair of his groin. Drae couldn't recall a time when a thought such as that had ever occurred to him. Being with Victoria was like opening Pandora's Box. Her innocent ravishment of his much more experienced body was like wandering into a new world, one with far-reaching consequences that were scaring the holy shit out of him.

Her hand still possessively wrapped around his cock as if she was loath to release him, she lifted onto the chaise and stretched alongside him. "Are you mad at me?" she whispered in a voice stretched thin with uncertainty.

"God. No," he growled, as he finally found the strength to move enough to wrap an arm around her waist so he could hug her close. "Why would you think that?"

"You're not saying anything. Did I do it wrong, Draegyn?

Please tell me," she stuttered.

He almost laughed. There they were, she fully dressed and him with his pants down around his ankles with her gripping his dick like it was a lifeline, and she wanted to know if she did it wrong. Jesus Christ. How could he possibly explain to her how fucking right she'd been from start to finish?

Reaching for her hand, he gently pried it away from his half-swollen flesh and brought her trembling fingers to his mouth. Pressing a kiss to the center of her palm, he laid her exquisitely delicate hand upon his chest, where he hoped she could detect the way his heart still hammered. "You'd never done anything like that before, am I right?"

She turned her face into his neck and shook her head. "It's not something I ever wanted to do. I," she hesitated, "I, um, couldn't help myself." He enjoyed the way she murmured against his skin almost as much as he delighted in what the words meant. A sudden overpowering sense of possessiveness grabbed hold of him at the mere thought of her mouth ever touching another man the way she had him.

"There was nothing, absolutely nothing, wrong about what you did, honey. Nothing. If I'm being quiet it's because I just wish I'd shown a bit more restraint and not let things get so out of hand. Coming in your mouth was not my intention, I swear."

Her head popped up at his words and searched his face with a confused frown. "But I wanted you to. Was that wrong? I thought you'd like that and, well…to be honest, I liked it too. Maybe too much?" That she made her last statement into a question tore at his emotions. She was so open with him. So honest. It wasn't what he was used to. He couldn't ever remember a woman telling him she liked giving oral sex. Not unless there was something in it for her. Victoria admitting that she liked having him in her mouth was almost too much for him to handle.

"C'mon," he said, rising them both to sitting position. "Let's take this conversation inside." She scrambled off the chaise to give him room to yank up his jeans and tug his shirt back into place. Taking her hand, he pulled her alongside him and ushered her silently into the house.

Drae was acutely aware that they were in way over their heads. One minute they'd been talking about how to pull the plug on their unusual union and the next they'd been frantically pawing each other. She also hadn't been all that happy with him if her body language and tone were anything to go by. To make matters worse, the thundering orgasm he'd just experienced, far from having satisfied the almost unbearable desire he felt for her, was only making him want more. More of her shy amazement at the explosive way their bodies reacted to each other.

Forcing his mind to turn away from the impulse to strip her naked and drop her to the floor where she stood so he could lose himself in her deliciously tight, wet, heat was an almost impossible task. How the hell could he talk reasonably to her about divorce when his libido was feverishly working overtime to get into her panties?

The word divorce had the same effect on his senses as an iceberg. He might want to fuck her senseless but the little matter of an unforeseen marriage was complicating things. He couldn't continue to avail himself of her body while making plans to distance himself from her legally. Damn. This was such a God-awful mess.

The only thing to do was be direct and stop behaving like a teenager unable to control himself around a beautiful, desirable woman. It wasn't fair to Victoria, no matter how conflicted his feelings were at the moment. Having her warm and willing in his bed was one thing. Being married to her was another thing entirely. Although it made him feel like a dick, he had to stop this thing in its tracks before any more damage was done.

"Victoria," he murmured. She turned hopeful brown eyes his way as she fumbled with putting her sandals back on. Her face was highlighted with a disarming rosy blush that reminded him how wrong their present circumstance was. She simply wasn't the type to have a sexual relationship without the promise of deeper emotions coming into play. Not with him and from what she'd told him about her romantic past, not with anybody.

Drae sighed deeply, boldly blurting out a ramble of words that seemed wholly out of place considering what had just past between them. "We can't keep doing this. It's not right. You're a wonderful girl, and you deserve somebody who can be more than I ever could."

Tori snatched her hand away from his grasp when the words he'd just thrown at her sank in. *Oh my God*, she thought. He was rejecting her, after everything they'd done, he was telling her it meant nothing to him. How could she be so stupid? With his illustrious sexual history suddenly hanging over every word and action, he was letting her know she was nothing but one face out of hundreds. Maybe thousands. She thought she might get sick. Ten minutes ago she'd been on her knees with his dick poking at the back of her throat. Hearing him say they couldn't keep doing this turned her inside out. *This?* What they were doing was just a form of *this*? Covering her mouth with her hand she could only keep silently repeating, *Oh my God, Oh my God*. She had to get out of there, and she had to get as far away from him as she could.

Finding the courage and nerve to turn the tables on his egotistical ass was no small feat but a lifetime of standing up for herself in the face of cruel taunts came to good use. She might be short, and she might not be a sex goddess, but she was nobody's fool. He was about to find that out.

"You're right, of course," she sniped with no attempt to hide the hurt she felt. "This whole thing has been an epic disaster." Without so much as missing a beat, Tori made her way back to his front door before he had a chance to react.

"Let's just chalk this up to your *er*...impressive history combined with my foolish inexperience. It's not every day that a girl gets a chance to bang a bona fide sex machine, Draegyn," she sneered.

Her hand on the doorknob, she blindly continued, oblivious to the expression on his face or the tears gathering behind her eyes. "It's best that we avoid each other after this stunning loss of decorum, don't you think? You do whatever you think is right about ending this farce. I don't care one way or the other."

Yanking the door open with more force than necessary, she flinched when it slammed against the wall. "And don't worry about the pregnancy thing. I'm sure it's not going to be a problem and even if it is, I wouldn't bother you with the details, or want you involved in any way, come to think of it. After all, you have a reputation to protect. I hear your *I can't be married* bullshit loud and clear."

Stepping out onto the porch she let loose one final withering comment. "You're so fucking full of yourself Draegyn St. John. Maybe it would do you good to remember that this situation was a two-way street and not a one-lane path. As much as you don't want to be married, I don't want to be tied to a man with the emotional depth of a thimble."

For parting shots, that was the best one she could muster. Just like when she'd marched away from him after the car ride from the airport, so too did she again as he barked after her. "Victoria! You can't walk half a mile in the dark"

Dammit. He was right. Hiking from the main compound down the winding road to his house had been one thing in the daylight. It was an act of folly to wander the desert, even along a roadway, in the pitch dark. With head held high, Tori turned and stomped back up onto the porch. "Give me your keys," she snarled.

"I'll drive you."

"Oh no," she ground out. "I'm through being taken for a ride by you. Give me. Your. Keys. Now!" The hand she held out wanted so badly to slap him across the face.

Draegyn stared at her, his eyes dark slits above a mouth drawn in a thin line. She didn't miss the way his jaw tensed as he considered the hand demanding he surrender his keys. The look she gave in return dared him to say another word at his own peril.

Reaching into his pocket, he pulled out a key ring and dropped it without another word into the palm of her hand. Tori quickly glanced at the insignia on the ring, noted that he'd given her the key to his SUV, turned and skipped down the steps walking briskly to the big, black beast of a vehicle and climbed in. Seconds later she drove into the darkness and away from the insufferable man who she'd been foolish enough to fall for as he stood on his front porch and watched her disappear into the darkness.

DRAE COULDN'T PACK HIS bags and get the hell away from the Villa fast enough. After Victoria marched off into the darkness in high dungeon the previous night, he'd polished off most of a bottle of really expensive whiskey trying to erase their ugly confrontation from his mind. It hadn't worked, of course.

Whether the memory of her indignation at his clumsy attempt to cool things down or the vivid scene etched forever in his brain of her licking and stroking his dick, both had the power to reduce him to a tangled mess of conflicting emotions.

She'd landed quite a few direct hits to his ego and his sense of self. She was right on one thing. He hadn't really considered anyone but himself. It didn't require a map to figure out that had been the fatal flaw in how he'd handled everything. Victoria was a power unto herself. Unique and without guile, she wasn't anything like the hoards of women he'd been consorting with his whole life. Women like his cold, calculating mother. By limiting his involvement to an endless parade of experienced females, all possessing a keen eye for the prize, he'd been able to cling to his belief that relationships were a sham and something best left to others.

When she'd told him in no uncertain terms that he wasn't man enough to be privy to whether he'd gotten her pregnant or not, his heart seized up and hadn't relaxed since. Seemed like something of a low blow but considering his reputation, he couldn't blame her for feeling that way. That didn't mean he wasn't gutted by the knowledge that she'd vanish into thin air if she was carrying his child and would probably head for the hills even if she wasn't.

Despite a raging hangover, an unexpected early morning call with a request to provide personal security for a visiting foreign dignitary could not have come at a better time. Even though it wasn't like him, he was eager to run as far as he could get. Put a bit of distance between him and Victoria. And Alex of course. With his old friend knowing the truth about his and Victoria's messy situation, he hadn't a snowball's chance in hell of pretending everything was fine. It seemed like the best thing all around for him to get out of the line of fire until things calmed down or he found a way to handle the mess without making things worse.

Since the call had come early even by East coast time, Drae had left a text message on Alex's office computer explaining what was up and leaving him all the details of the assignment. He'd decided to drive himself to the airport, he could leave his car for Ben to pick up later, and booked a last minute seat on an eastbound plane.

Maybe a few weeks in New York City would bring a measure of perspective back into his life. Hiding away in his woodshop hadn't helped. Nor had trying to work things out with the feisty female at the heart of the matter. With his life turned upside down and nearly everything he'd ever felt about himself and his place in the universe turned on its head, he didn't know what else to do.

By the time Tori stumbled into Alex's workspace, after a restless night that left her feeling fuzzy headed from lack of sleep, she still hadn't decided what she was going to do. She'd made a mess of things, having quite stupidly fallen in love with a man who made a career out of never getting involved with the women he slept with. The signs had been there all along. Even when they were verbally sparring with one another, she'd been gradually warming to him, conceited arrogance and all. She'd briefly considered running home to Mommy but dashed that idea because there was no way she'd give him the satisfaction of knowing he'd rattled her cage that thoroughly. No, she was going to stay put for now.

After checking the calendar fifty times she noted that she'd be getting her period soon. She wasn't ignoring the fact that their unprotected lovemaking had happened during the one time in her cycle that could really mess with her in a big way. Instead, she simply refused to consider that one foolish moment could have such a potentially life-changing effect on her life. Not even she could be that unlucky. Right?

Letting herself into the heavily air-conditioned tech cave, Tori shivered when the chilly atmosphere cut right through the light shirt she'd worn. After Draegyn's hissy fit over her wardrobe, she'd vowed never to hide behind that particular masquerade again. She hadn't actually fooled anybody after all. It wouldn't take a genius to figure out after the tabloid hell she'd been through that schlepping about like the nerd she professed to be was nothing more than a self-defense mechanism while she dug her way out of the mud she'd been dragged through.

Today, she'd opted for a figure hugging, v-neck tunic with a belt slung low on her hips over a pair of black leggings that fit easily inside her favorite boots. Her outfit was simple yet decidedly feminine. In some ways, what she chose to wear this morning was a subtle *fuck off* directed at Draegyn. The cold temperature, a necessity with so much technical gear running, was a bit much so grabbing a baggy sweater off the hook in her cubicle she wrapped herself in its warmth and went to find her boss.

Alex looked up from the phone call he was on when she entered the room and waved a polite hello in her direction. She heard him rattling off numbers to whoever was on the other end and deciding she didn't need to get involved in whatever he was doing, grabbed a mug of coffee from the brewer and headed back to her area. It wasn't until lunchtime when she and Alex actually had a conversation that went beyond a couple of quick questions.

Hey," she called out to him. "I'm going to run out to the kitchen and grab something to eat. You interested?"

"Nah. But thanks for asking, Tori. I'm about finished for now. Was thinking about heading off to the workout room. Too much time perched on that damn stool and every muscle in my body feels like it's locked."

"Sounds good, Alex but you really should eat something too. We've been working for hours, and you haven't even stopped for a drink."

"Okay, Mom!" he chuckled.

Tori whipped off the sweater she'd donned for warmth and tossed it on a chair, earning a wolf whistle from her boss. "Nice boots, lady," he teased. "No wonder Drae got his shorts in a twist. Shame on you Tori for hiding behind those God-awful clothes you've been sporting."

At the mention of Draegyn's name, Tori felt a heavy weight thud in her stomach. Out of sheer reflex she snarled at Alex letting him know in precise terms what his friend could do with his opinion.

"I don't give a good goddamn what that man thinks." With specific hand motions, she used sign language short hand to let him know how she really felt.

"Whoa. What's that mean?" Alex's expression swung between 'yikes' and 'uh oh' as he waited for her reply.

"I basically said that he could eat shit and die."

"Oh my. That bad, huh? What's he done now?"

"Nothing. Nothing, really," she murmured, feeling guilty for reacting like a bitch. "I shouldn't have said anything. Let it go, Alex."

"Yeah, I don't think so. Look Tori, maybe it's none of my business but you should know that Drae told me a little of what's going on."

"What?" she screeched. Her head felt like it was going to explode.

"Calm down," he pleaded, moving quickly to her side and drawing her with him to sit on a wide bench nearby.

"I can't believe this!" she cried. "What did he tell you Alex? Oh my God, I'm going to kill that man and his big mouth."

"Well, judging by your reaction I think you know exactly what he told me."

Tori dropped her head into her hands and groaned. "This can't be happening," she cried. "We agreed not to tell anyone."

Jumping to her feet she clenched her hands into angry fists and started for the door. "Goddammit. He lied to me. That's it," she growled. "I'm going to rip his face off for this!"

"Uh, Tori. Better hang on there. He's not here at the moment. Left early this morning."

She stumbled over her own feet and barely got it together before falling flat on her ass. Feeling the dark scowl that ended up on her face start deep in the pit of her stomach, she turned in slow motion. "Where is he?"

Checking his watch, Alex frowned. The tension in the air was so thick you could scoop it up. He seemed to weigh his response for a brief moment. "He'll be landing in New York City in the next hour." Lifting a shoulder in a half shrug he added, "I figured he would have told you."

Tori was flabbergasted. *Why, the dog turned tail and ran*, she thought as anger that he lied and confusion over his having left so abruptly threw her emotions into disarray.

"I thought you two were together last night." At her look of pure shock he quickly added, "C'mon. Nothing happens around here without my knowing." Pointing to the screens flickering with surveillance views depicting every angle of the main compound, Alex motioned impatiently. "Don't sweat the details, Tori. I simply happened to glance at the monitor at the exact moment that you headed off down the lane. What happened after that is between you and Drae."

Tori hoped a sinkhole would open up under her at that moment so the embarrassment she felt would go unnoticed. Vivid snapshots lit up her mind with a tableau of images from what happened on Draegyn's patio. This whole thing was getting worse by the moment.

"I'm not sure that *together* quite describes last night. Yes, we had a conversation," God, she prayed the rush of color into her cheeks didn't give too much away. "But it uh," she tensed. "Well, it didn't exactly clear the air."

Alex watched her with an expression that suggested he was more than capable of filling in the blanks. It was worse than the withering frown her mother used on her as a child when she'd behaved badly. Crooking his finger, he patted the empty space next to him and waited for her to sit back down.

Sit wasn't quite what she did. Instead, she flung herself like a ragdoll onto the bench as every muscle in her body turned to jelly. Throwing her head back she made a sound somewhere between an angry growl and a defeated whimper.

Alex let her have a moment then silently reached for her hands, forcing her to turn teary eyes his way. "I'm sorry, boss," she murmured. The urge to run, just like she had before when her world crumbled, made its way into her mind. "Maybe it would be best for everyone…you, the agency, even Draegyn, if I just left. This is his home," Tori whined as the reality of his having left to get away from her settled into the pit of her stomach.

Alex let her hands go, patting them solemnly where they lay limp in her lap. Putting his arm around her shoulders, he drew her against his hulking body like a parent consoling a crying child. "No rash decisions, Tori. I grant you that Drae's actions seem a bit off." He paused and gave her shoulder a little squeeze. "But maybe there's something you should know about the St. John family. He'll probably freak out on me for telling you this, but I think it may help you understand him."

"I don't know, Alex. Maybe me understanding what motivates him is just useless information. Especially if he hasn't shared it with me himself. That's not, well - that's not the type of relationship we have. Talking isn't exactly our strong suit."

"Perhaps you're right, I don't know. That's for both of you to decide but you should know that his parents fucked him up pretty good, a long time ago. Haven't you ever wondered why he went into the military? Trust fund kids like the St. John's lived a life most people can only imagine. Spending a decade slogging through dead bodies, sucking in misery through the air we breathed, was hardly what anyone expected of him. If you think about it, the life he chose tells you more about who he is than the life he was born to." Tori fell silent, considering Alex's words. She *had* wondered but in truth, she was so fixated on his conceited arrogance that there wasn't much oxygen left after that.

"Don't put much stock in whatever turns up on Google. Most of what's written about him is salacious gossip." She snorted in derision remembering the endless pictures and tabloid hits depicting him as a conceited man-whore. "I know what you're thinking, believe me. But consider this – in all the years I've known Drae, he's never thought twice about any of the women he's gotten involved with. This is the first time I've seen him at loose ends. Only you two know what's really going on but he hasn't been behaving like himself for awhile now and I can't help but think it's because of you."

"He lied to me, Alex. He swore no one would know." She sat

up and shook her head. "I don't know what he told you but it's so much worse than you could imagine. I'm not sure knowing that he came from a dysfunctional family makes much difference in the long run. Really. Despite everything else, I assumed he could be trusted."

Alex nodded fractionally and asked, "Tori, if your mother were here, would you tell her that you and Drae had gotten married?"

"Yes, of course."

"The Justice Brothers, we're more than family to each other. We share a bond that goes deeper than blood. Drae didn't lie to you, Tori. Not really. His confiding in me is no different that you reaching out to your mom." Tori stood up and walked away from the sofa, organizing this new information in her mind. "He didn't run," he insisted until she glared over her shoulder at him in disbelief. "Okay, maybe that was part of it, but his leaving really was because of business."

She'd had enough. Her head was pounding, the black sludge disguised as coffee she'd drank earlier was burning a hole in her stomach and her whole body felt hollow and empty. There was nothing she could do about Draegyn and their situation while he was in New York and she was in Arizona. What she needed right now was something…but she couldn't quite put her finger on what that was. "I'm going to grab a sandwich before my stomach eats itself."

Alex's face tightened at her obvious pivot away from the subject at hand. "It was business, Tori." He insisted a second time. "Don't do anything rash, okay?" She nodded but didn't meet his eyes. *Don't do anything rash?* You mean like forgetting about little things like birth control? Anything that came after that was hardly going to seem rash.

Damn him. Jetting off to the East coast, especially after what happened the night before felt like Draegyn getting the last word. Allowing him to dominate her in the bedroom wasn't the same as letting him always have control, although he certainly hadn't been the one calling all the shots last night.

Murmuring a lackluster, “Understood,” Tori hurried away from the tech cave without looking back. She heard Alex sigh as he watched her escape but didn’t slow her roll at all. He admitted knowing they were married and probably figured out that they’d gotten naked and sweaty more than a few times but he didn’t, *couldn’t*, know how complicated it all really was. What a friggin’ mess, she thought for the thousandth time as she headed for the kitchen and an opportunity to be alone with her thoughts.

THE POUNDING BEAT OF music that was so loud it made thinking impossible, thrummed in the air as flashing lights illuminated the dance floor of the club where Drae had gone to lose himself in yet another bottle of whiskey. Somehow, the crush of bodies bouncing and gyrating along with the mind-melting music seemed more conducive to his mood than something sedate, less manic.

The moment his work assignment had ended, this had been how he spent his time. While he'd been managing the security for a high-profile foreign dignitary, Drae had punished his body with daily workouts at a gym he found on Tenth Street that specialized in the mixed martial arts he excelled at. Kicking ass and occasionally getting pounded in return kept him focused on the important work he'd been hired to perform.

Unfortunately, the moment the assignment wound up and he was free to return home, his thoughts about what awaited him in Arizona unraveled his carefully composed façade of cool, control. The solution? Whiskey and women. Always worked in the past, only this time around just the whiskey made a difference. While every female with a pulse that came anywhere near him tried to entice him with promises of a different kind of pounding, Drae hadn't been able to muster enough interest to follow through. Not even the potential of some hot, naked, balls to the wall sex got a rise out of him. *Literally.*

Tossing back the last of the drink he'd been nursing where he sat hunched over at the end of a bar littered with fake-tittied women and the men trying to pick them up, he motioned to the bartender for a refill and tried to reign in his wandering thoughts. Fuck it if the alcohol wasn't doing its intended job. He was headed for a royal hangover but didn't care. Not even that could keep his mind free of memories that were wrecking his sanity. Memories of Victoria, verbally sparring with him in that feisty way she had, made him want to tame a little bit of her fire. Memories of sinking into her body, again and again, chasing an orgasm that threatened to blow his world apart. And then of course, the movie playing on a constant loop in his brain of his surprise wife on her knees, sucking him off with untutored skill that had turned him on so much, he'd lost his fucking sense and exploded in her mouth.

Feeling like shit, he knew that refusing to ask about her during the couple of phone calls he'd had with Alex had been petty and childish, but that was exactly what he'd done. He heard the censure in his friend's voice and ignored it because, well – he didn't know why. Maybe if Alex had indicated she wanted to talk to him, he would have backed down. But no such message was revealed and he'd simply doubled-down on the miserable attitude he was wallowing in.

Damn women, he groused silently, slugging back yet another mouthful of amber liquid. *Oh wait, amend that*, he thought grimly. Damn *woman*, was more like it. *Just the one*. Just Victoria and her mesmerizing eyes and those sinfully decadent lips.

"Oh, well look who we have here," a familiar voice trilled close enough for him to hear. "If it isn't the golden cock himself!"

Drae looked up and blinked a couple of times until the blurry face in front of him came into view. *Ah fuck.* Jessamyn. And judging by the expression on her face, she was all too happy to have stumbled upon him in his half-inebriated state.

"Drinking alone, darling?" she purred. "That's not like you Drae." He didn't invite her to sit down but that was just what she did with as much flourish as possible, whipping off her wrap and facing him so her crossed legs touched his. True to form he watched her push the skirt up enough that he got a good look at her long legs and bare thighs.

"Jess. Long time." She smirked at his slurred response, eyes sparkling in a way that made him uneasy. The last thing he needed right now was an old lover coming upon him while he wasn't exactly at his best. "What brings you here?" he asked. The way she laughed at his question suggested the words hadn't been quite so clear or concise as his imagination thought.

It all pretty much went downhill from there. Before he knew what happened, they were ensconced in a private booth with the remnants of several rounds of drinks littering the table while she clung to him like a damn rash. Maybe it was because he was drunk or maybe because he'd never really looked all that closely at her when she'd been performing in his bed, but Drae found himself studying her through whiskey-fueled eyes and didn't care much for what he saw.

She was an actress after all, a high profile paparazzi target, out for a night on the town and completely dressed for the part. The long, flowing blond locks that her fans adored were actually a mass of hair extensions and careful styling that were a definite no-no in the touch department. The bright violet eyes watching his every move were as fake as her hair, made possible by colored lenses. In fact, there wasn't much about her that wasn't plastic, manufactured, sculpted or tweaked from her Botox injected lips – that frankly, gave him the creeps – to her massive boobs that were smooshed into too-tight lingerie making them overflow the cups of her bra in a very deliberate way.

What the fuck had he been doing with her in the first place? Oh yeah. He'd been screwing her every chance he got until she'd started making those tedious relationship noises. Had she been any good in bed? Strangely, his dick didn't seem to care at the moment. Everything about her was rendering his sex limp as an overcooked noodle.

"Why don't we check out of this place, baby, and go someplace more private?" she cooed. Drae wasn't sure what turned his stomach more. The blatant invitation or the way her hand traced the inside of his thigh. He choked back a laugh when the crazy bitch palmed his sex because he knew damn well her assault on his trousers was coming up empty-handed. No amount of alcohol or attempts on her part to get him hard was going to change the fact that he'd rather throw up on her right now than stick his tongue down her throat.

"S'not gonna happen Jizz, uh, Jas, I mean, Jess," he ground out in a drunken slur as he shook his head with each wrong pronunciation of her name. The look she gave him suggested she didn't care what he said. Drunk or not, the randy actress intended to get her way. Drae knew she'd stop at nothing to get him naked and on his back where she could ride him like the bitch in heat she was. The thought made him shudder.

Searching for his wallet with hands made clumsy by drink, Drae finally located it in his suit jacket not a second too soon for Jessamyn was attracting the attention of the club-goers who were always on the look-out for a celebrity sighting. Watching her fake and phony posturing left him cold. She had this way of waving her fingers – she called it twinkling – that made her look like a spastic twelve-year-old trying to get the attention of whatever guy happened by.

Tossing a bunch of bills on the table, he motioned to the waitress to let her know he'd left her a hefty tip and that the bar should close out his tab. Getting away from the noise and the smell of Jess's perfume were priority one. The minute she caught on that he was leaving, she all but jumped on top of him. Drae stood on unsteady feet, tugging on his cuffs and straightening his tie while his brain tried to get in gear with his body. A couple of deep breathes later; he squinted through the flashing lights, marked the exit and then made for the door in haste. Unfortunately, he hadn't counted on his unwanted companion wrapping around him like a fucking clinging vine.

Once he'd maneuvered through the mass of gyrating dancers and stepped into the club's reception area, he knew that getting rid of the actress was not going to be easy. Especially not in the rough condition he was in.

"Look, Jess," he said while disengaging her arm from his in as gentlemanly way as possible. "I've gotta go. Good seeing you," he added at the exact moment she shoved him out the door onto the pavement outside. Suddenly she was all over him, twining her arms through his, pressing those fake lipstick covered lips along his jaw as a flurry of lights flashed.

Drae was instantly furious, all evidence of having drunk a large quantity chased from his system by the presence of a pack of tabloid cameras clicking furiously as at least a dozen paps jockeyed for position. Jess for her part was putting on quite a show, hanging all over him, leaving no doubt in the mind of those watching that she would gladly drop her panties for him at the slightest provocation.

"Hey Jess!" one of the paparazzi hollered. "Who's your date, sexy lady?"

"Wouldn't you like to know!" she giggled as she twinkled those damn fingers of hers and blew kisses to the waiting cameras. He wanted to kill the fucking bitch. She knew he hated the press. For her to deliberately use him as bait for a goddamn photo op made his blood boil.

The doorman whistled for a cab that materialized out of thin air. Drae pushed his way through the gang with the flashing lights and dove for the door with Jess hot on his heels. When the cab door closed she instructed the driver to take them to her hotel while Drae sat silently, glaring at her with malice in his eyes. Fuck if she wasn't so completely wrapped up in herself that she barely noticed, prattling on about how shocked and surprised she was by the frenzied pap attack. Yeah, right. Everything she did was calculated for maximum exposure. Amazingly enough, she seemed to be under the impression that he was going to blindly follow her lead and actually return to her hotel where she promised him the blowjob of his life. Maybe tossing his cookies up into her lap wasn't such a bad idea after all.

At her hotel, the driver jumped out of the car and opened her door as yet again, flashes from the reporters that hung out at the five star hotels lit up the night. Ever the actress, she rather deliberately shimmied from the backseat in such a way that triggered a thousand camera clicks and more shouts of her name as she stopped and preened for their photos.

When he didn't slid out right behind her she looked back and froze when she caught sight of his face. There was no mistaking the anger in him. She leaned into the car saying, "Sorry about the press, darling. But you know how it is. Let's go up to my room, and I'll make you forget all about them." She used her tongue to make a suggestive motion that was probably meant to fire him up but instead made him physically sick.

"No thanks. That mouth of yours is played out as far as I'm concerned. If you need a dick to suck, I suggest you ask one of your adoring fans or any of that rowdy crew taking your picture." He shut the door on her shocked expression and barked at the driver to pull away.

Fuck, fuck, fuck was all he could think on the short drive to his hotel just a few blocks away. Maybe New York was past its expiration date. For the first time in days, all he wanted was to go home.

The commotion at the Villa when Lacey and Cam returned from their honeymoon gave Tori plenty of much-needed duck and cover. The longer Draegyn stayed on the other side of the country, the more Alex fretted. Everyone, it turned out, was shaking their heads behind her back.

This morning, her boss was down at Cameron's cabin, enjoying a bit of family time with the blissfully happy newlyweds, leaving her to putter aimlessly around the office. She'd gathered a huge can of paper to recycle and even sharpened every pencil she could find in an effort to keep busy. Truth was, she was one unhappy camper. In the three weeks that Draegyn had been gone, she'd put on a good show of pretending that all was happy and pleasant in her world while she silently crumbled, bit by agonizing bit.

He'd talked with Alex a couple of times but never asked about her or sent a greeting in all that time. She knew this because after every phone call, email or text, her boss got quieter and quieter. She felt awful about him being caught in the middle.

Looking for something to occupy her time, Tori decided to take on the task of cleaning Alex's ancient coffeemaker. Maybe freshening it up would make the coffee taste a little better. She had to remember to bring one of her oversized insulated travel mugs with her from home each day so she wouldn't have to drink the crap her boss thought passed for coffee.

It took at least ten minutes to shift equipment around enough so she could crawl under a table to unplug the brewer but finally, she'd pulled the right plug and freed it up so she could carry the whole thing to the kitchenette sink for a thorough cleaning. For a good minute she considered accidently dropping the unit in the hopes that it would smash into a hundred pieces but quickly dashed that idea. Knowing Alex and his penchant for tinkering with anything electronic, he could probably put it back together with a roll of duct tape and not much else. No, cleaning the brewer was her only hope of getting some decent coffee out of it.

The minute she yanked the brew basket out to empty it, the smell of burnt coffee grounds made her gag and shudder. “Ew, yuck,” she muttered aloud, quickly banging the basket into the trashcan to dispose of the offending mess. Unfortunately, the trash now smelled awful, filling the room with the nauseating odor. Sweat began beading along Tori’s hairline as she fought back the urge to vomit, making her drop like a stone into a nearby chair. She tried fanning herself with a magazine but the roiling in her stomach refused to back off. *Oh man, this isn’t good*, she thought, leaning forward to drop her spinning head between her legs.

It took a good minute or two for the nausea to ease off giving Tori the opportunity to study her shoes, the tile under her feet, and the couple of pieces of trash that had been tossed at the can but ended up on the floor instead. Somewhere in the midst of that distracting reverie, came a thought that lit up in her skull like the fireworks on the fourth of July. What was the date?

Scrambling to her feet hadn’t been such a swell idea as her head started spinning like a top but she had to find a calendar, *stat*. Cautiously picking her way across the room using the furniture as aides, she found her phone and brought up the month at-a-glance and started counting. After the third time, panic fed into her senses accompanied by a shortness of breath that wasn’t helping matters.

“No!” Tori squalled as the dawning realization that she had missed her period caught up with her. Shaking her head vehemently she kept on saying, “No, no,” as if the words would change things. Soon the “No” changed to “Oh my God, oh my God,” as her emotions ran the gamut from denial to possibility to inevitability.

Just like that her stomach heaved sideways and her eyes began watering as she made a frantic dash to the restroom seconds before she emptied her guts into the toilet. Did it actually happen this fast she wondered? Did everyone experience the feeling that everything was dandy one minute and then changed forever in the next as wave after wave of unimaginable nausea swept you away?

Thankful that Alex wasn't around to witness what just happened, Tori waited for the spinning and churning to back off, then washed her face and hands as calmly as she could. After swishing water through her mouth, she straightened with a wet paper towel pressed against her forehead and caught sight of her reflection in the mirror.

She looked like death warmed over. Dark smudges under her eyes gave them an owlish look as she blinked over and over trying not to give in to the tears. Her face was pasty white making her cheekbones stick out. Suddenly, everything made sense. She was moody and cross one minute, sad and melancholy the next with occasional bouts of giddiness that came out of nowhere. In short, she was fucked. Big time, if what she suspected was true.

She'd have to get right on ordering a pregnancy test online. The idea of going into town and picking one up at the local drugstore made the whole thing seem way too real. It would be easier to stock up on toiletries and hide one in her order so she could continue pretending this wasn't happening. Feeling like the weight of the world was crushing down on her, Tori grabbed her keys and purse, stuffed her cell phone into a pocket, and headed back to her apartment and her laptop. Strings of pithy, colorful swear words rang in her head the whole way.

She hadn't made it very far when Tori came upon Carmen and Ria, their heads together as they whispered back and forth while looking at something spread out before them. Coming from behind, she saw that they were reading one of the trashy gossip rags that made Tori tense up. There was never going to come a time when even the smallest reminder of the hell she'd been through was going to let her look kindly on that tabloid garbage.

"Men! Such idiots." She heard Carmen mutter. "You think anyone else has seen this?" she asked Ria as the older woman shook her head in the negative.

"I don't think so. Not yet anyway. My granddaughter left this in the car when Ben took her home."

"Hey, whatcha' got there?" Tori asked, curious about whatever they were discussing. "Brad and Angie have a fight or something?" The two women reacted to her unexpected presence like they'd been shot. Carmen slammed the paper shut and rolled it into a tube while Ria rushed toward her with concern etched on her face.

"Miss Tori. I didn't hear you coming," she muttered as she and Carmen exchanged anxious frowns. "Where are you off to?"

"Well, I was going to run home for a bit. There's uh....um, there's something I have to do." Tori motioned to the newspaper Carmen was clutching in her hand. "What's going on ladies?"

A heavy silence descended upon the room. Tori's curiosity was definitely piqued by the odd way the two women were behaving. Something was clearly going on. "What's wrong Carmen?" she asked sharply, thinking she was more likely to get a direct answer from her than from Ria. "Don't try and bullshit a bullshitter," she muttered while the cook and housekeeper engaged in silent communication that made Tori's skin prickle. Something wasn't right.

"Show her," Ria finally said. "She's going to find out anyway."

Carmen didn't look happy about it but she handed Tori the gossip magazine anyway. "Open to page four" was all she said.

There was a déjà vu quality to whatever was happening making Tori hold her breath in apprehension. Was there another one of those blasted articles about her? She couldn't imagine why there would be. It had been months since the financial scandal had quieted down and while she didn't know the exact details, she knew Wallace had plea-bargained his way into a shortened sentence that would keep him locked up until next year. Dropping her purse on the counter she cautiously opened to the page Carmen indicated as if the paper contained a booby-trap. What she found staring back at her was pretty much the last thing she ever expected.

Award-winning actress out on the town with Sexy Playboy, screamed the bold-faced headline. Underneath were a series of pictures that instantly tattooed themselves on Tori's brain. Shots of Draegyn with Jessamyn Winters partying together in New York City. One of the photos showed the glamorous superstar draped around him like a fur coat on a cold evening. Another, one of those hideous up skirt angles, clearly announced the actress had gone commando as a sickening shot of her flashing a neatly manicured landing strip was there for all to see. It was the photo though of the Winters woman kissing Draegyn, leaving a trail of lipstick along his jaw that made her physically sick.

That fucking pig. He'd left her without so much as a backward glance and jetted off to the Big Apple, *on business* Alex had insisted. But that hadn't stopped him from hooking up the first chance he got. For a brief moment the room started to spin as the cold reality of the situation slapped her upside the head. *Fuck him.*

Slapping the paper on the counter, Tori forced her spine to stiffen a second before she loosed a somewhat hysterical laugh that set the women staring anxiously at her back a step. "Boys will be boys, right?" she bit out. Snatching up her bag once again, she laughed some more and put on a rather convincing show of not giving a shit what the high and mighty Draegyn St. John had been getting into in the big city.

Winking mischievously at Carmen, Tori lowered her voice to a whisper, "Find, feel, fuck, and forget. Some things never change." And with that she calmly walked out of the kitchen like nothing unusual at all had just happened. By the time she reached the door of her apartment, her heart was well and truly shattered. Stepping inside her comfy hideaway she quietly shut out the world and sank slowly to the floor, tremendous sobs bursting from her chest as an unending torrent of pain and loss ripped apart her soul.

TO: Draegyn St. John
FROM: Ted Collins
RE:Legal Advice

Drae,
I've put together some information for you and your wife to look at. As I explained in our last conversation, the most prudent way forward will be not to make any changes to the status quo for a minimum of six months so we can establish the hard facts necessary to move for a divorce based on irreconcilable differences. During this period it is imperative that two separate households be maintained and neither of the parties involved make any effort to solidify the union in question.

Should you have any questions, please feel free to contact me. If anything changes, please inform me immediately.

Ted

Humph. So much for checking email when you're in a lousy mood, Drae griped. He'd been home for less than an hour, after a God awful plane flight and had managed in that time to neatly avoid seeing or talking to anyone. The message from his lawyer was the icing on his cake of annoyance.

He considered heading over to the cabin to welcome the newlyweds home and see how they liked the theater room he'd designed but something about facing the happy couple left him cold. Right now, he had no interest in seeing his old friend basking in some sappy romantic glow. Not while he was all tied up in knots.

The only visit he knew should be on his agenda was to Victoria. And not because he had news from his lawyer. It had taken him awhile to get there but eventually he'd been forced to admit that he missed his little spitfire and the messy havoc her appearance in his life had caused. Behaving badly wasn't something he was comfortable with, especially not when he had in fact behaved like a king-size dick.

Maybe it was the chat he'd had with his sister last night that helped clear his head. Desirée grew up in the same cold, loveless environment he had. She knew the bitter truth about their parents' marriage and how it had more or less been a business deal with payment for each healthy offspring. But she hadn't let any of that steal her ability to develop into a beautiful, accomplished woman who found not just love but a life that was fulfilling, with a husband and children she adored.

She said something that kept repeating in his head; that instead of letting their parents damage her life beyond repair, she'd felt challenged to prove them wrong. By not giving in to the forces of money, greed, power, and social standing, she had gone out and fought tooth and nail for a different life. Even after a day when the kids had been off the wall and her husband a boob, she still looked around and gave thanks for her sometimes-messy life. If she'd wanted surface perfection, then she would have gone down the same path as their mother and father.

Hearing Desi say all that had made him feel like a coward. Instead of being brave and fearless as she had been, he'd let the twisted life of their family follow him like a tracking device. He was a thirty-five-year-old man who had never been in an actual relationship. Protecting his emotions at all cost had left him no real future to look forward to. Even the big house he built with its empty bedrooms was a constant reminder that he was alone and probably always would be.

Victoria had managed to squeak by all his defenses. She was the first woman who had ever stepped foot in his home. How fucking sad was that? While he could pretty much have any woman he desired, he hadn't counted on meeting a witch with a smart-ass mouth who was *so* not interested in falling at his feet. Served him right.

Maybe I should text her, Drae thought, reaching for his phone. *Coward*, whispered his overworked inner voice. *Fucking moron*, came the response of his conscience. The grimace that followed felt glued on his face.

Tearing off for weeks, even if it had been under cover of an assignment, without contacting her, wasn't something he could easily explain in a few hastily typed words. Hell, he could barely justify the behavior. No, this was one time when he was just going to have to take whatever happened on the chin and grow a set if he had any chance of making things right. Trouble was, for all his worldly experience, he hadn't a clue how to go about doing that. With a cold bottle of water in his hand, Drae headed outside to think only to quickly retreat back inside after an overload of sensory input from what had happened last time he'd been on the patio came screaming into his head. *Fuck.* At that moment he sincerely doubted he'd ever be able to erase from his brain the vivid image of Victoria and her provocative mouth taking him on an erotic no-holds barred journey to heaven and back.

Realizing all the time in the world to think wasn't going to give him any more clarity, he threw in the towel and decided to get on with it. He was pretty good at thinking on his feet. Hadn't survived being shot at by some very, very bad guys on luck alone. It was time to jump in headfirst and see which way the winds were blowing. He'd know what to do then.

"She's not here, man." Alex told him in a strained monotone that let Drae know he had some damage control to do on that front too. "Doubt she'll be back before nightfall. She and Carmen went to the mall. Something about a sale or whatever."

Wandering with no real direction, Drae strolled around the great room of Alex's Spanish Villa while his friend clicked through channels on the satellite TV system. Resting his hips against the back of a sofa, he searched for inspiration about what to say next. Alex beat him to the punch.

"What's with the 'man in black' wardrobe? You figuring to be Johnny Cash or something, dude?" Drae looked at his reflection in a nearby mirror and considered what he was wearing. Yeah, he'd probably taken the black thing too far. Maybe the color choice had more to do with his general mood than a fashion statement.

Black jeans, boots, and t-shirt under a well-worn black leather jacket made his fair coloring a dramatic counterpoint to all the darkness. That and his obvious need for a haircut gave him a scruffy appearance that could give Cameron a run for his money. Dressed as he was, Drae who normally came off like an Armani runway model, looked completely out-of-character.

Settling on a sporting event on the big screen TV, Alex smirked at him as if he was reading his thoughts. "That dark cloud hanging over your head is your own damn fault, you know."

Drae nodded, started to say something and then thought better of it. Alex was needling him in the way brothers did when a sibling was going off the rails. There weren't any words to make things right and he knew it. "Alright. Go ahead and say it. I'm a dick, right?"

"Your mouth to God's ear although I'd add fool to the laundry list." Throwing some serious side shade his way, Alex's look of disgust made him inwardly wince.

"How bad is it?" he asked in a cautious voice.

Shrugging, Alex turned his attention to the action on the TV. "That's for you to figure out but you should know that Tori thinks you lied to her."

"What?" he bellowed. Lied? He hadn't lied to her. *What the fuck.*

"She thinks by letting me in on the situation you deceived her about keeping the matter of your marriage a state secret."

Drae groaned out loud and hung his head. Anything else?

"Have you heard from your lawyer?"

Yeah, he'd heard from Ted all right but he was so damn conflicted and tied up in knots that he didn't really give a shit about the man's legal advice. "I need to see Victoria," was all he said.

Grunting a sarcastic laugh, Alex said, "Good luck with that."

Feeling like all the wind had been knocked out of his sails, Drae went and threw himself on the end of the sofa, earning a raised eyebrow from his friend. "Brother," he murmured, "I could really use your help right about now. Made a mess of things."

"Drae, I'll remind you yet again that I really like Tori. If you're just messing with her, well – there's a special place in hell for you."

"It's not like that. I'm…," he sighed. "Fuck. I don't know what I am."

"Okay, look. This one time and this one time only, I'm gonna stick my neck out and try to give you a hand." Drae lifted hopeful, grateful eyes to his friend. "I'll find a way to get Tori down to your place in the morning. That's the best I can do. What happens after that is on you, dude."

The morning. Great. That gave him a little more time to figure out what the hell to do. It wasn't much but knowing they'd have a chance to see each other face-to-face gave him a glimmer of hope.

It has been an awful day all around, Tori thought. She still didn't know if she was pregnant because the test she ordered hadn't been delivered. Regardless of that, she'd come to a huge decision after seeing irrefutable proof that Draegyn had not been lacking for female company while on the other side of the country. In her mind, it didn't really matter if the test came out positive or negative. Not now. Having shown his true colors she'd been forced to admit that there was no hope of a future between them.

Hitching a ride into town with Carmen under the pretense of doing a mall crawl, she'd met with a lawyer instead, while the other woman had lunch with friends. The attorney she'd found after an Internet search had listened to the implausible Vegas tale without much reaction. After Tori vehemently declared there wasn't a snowball's chance in hell of her wanting to stay married to the man and stating passionately that she also wasn't inclined to wait passively, trusting him to handle the arrangements to end their hasty union, the attorney had taken steps to initiate the dissolution without much fuss. Tori didn't know what was worse. The lawyers or the cut and dried way these things were handled. It kind of made her recoil at the idea that marriage had become something as easily discarded as the recycling.

Having arranged a late afternoon rendezvous with Carmen at a nice little bistro near the mall, she'd run pell-mell through one of the larger department stores after her visit to the lawyer, making blind purchases just so she'd have something to show for her supposed shopping trip. To her immense relief the conversation once they'd met up centered almost entirely on the other woman's recounting of her visit with friends, giving Tori an opportunity to dial back some of her tension. They'd grabbed something to nibble on and headed back to the Villa while all she could really focus on was the over-stuffed envelope in her bag with the paperwork the lawyer had given her.

Not knowing when or if Draegyn would ever return to Arizona she had come up with several options for presenting him with the documents. Plan A was the direct approach in which she imagined a civilized meeting where they would behave like adults and calmly agree to take the steps outlined in her divorce petition with a no harm, no foul outlook. Plan B took into account the very real possibility that they'd never see each other face-to-face whereby she'd be forced to employ a cut and dried approach through the mail or with intermediaries. Plan C was a messy slash and burn affair that made her endlessly queasy stomach percolate even more.

Carmen must have sensed that there was something on her mind because she eventually came right out and asked her what was up. "Are you okay, honey? You seem awfully quiet. "

The lonely road leading into the desert zoomed by as Tori sat quietly wondering just what to say. Carmen had been sweet to her from the moment she'd arrived on the scene. Fiercely protective of and devoted to the Justice Brothers and the colorful cast of characters who came and went from the Villa, Tori knew she could trust the woman completely. Carmen was the sort of person who didn't suffer fools gladly and was at the heart of it a true and loyal friend.

Turning a sincere smile on the woman who glanced over while driving the nearly deserted road, Tori felt a surge of emotion at the thought that one day, probably soon, she'd have to say good-bye to her. If she was expecting, there was no way she could remain at the agency and even if she wasn't, the situation between her and Draegyn had become untenable. In that cold, harsh light it became obvious what she'd have to do.

"Oh, I'm fine. Just tired, that's all." Remembering the packages she'd tossed in the backseat she added, "Too many dressing rooms and too much walking." Her answer seemed to satisfy Carmen and for the rest of the drive she made a real effort to cheerfully engage in their companionable chit-chat.

She was gathering her bags from the back seat of Carmen's car when Cameron and Lacey pulled in right behind them in one of the compound's electric carts. "Hola!" Lacey announced as she bounded from her side of the cart. "I'm glad we ran in to you two." She said smiling broadly as her new husband appeared quickly by her side with a similar smile brightening his dark, good looks.

"It's good to have you guys back," Tori told them in earnest. She hadn't known them for very long but even so it was hard not to be affected by the joy and happiness of the newlywed couple. Seeing their love reflected in each look and with every gesture made tears sting her eyes. *If only*, she thought wistfully.

"I still can't get over the fact that you two are married," Carmen told them as she hugged each one in turn.

Laughing, Cam grabbed his bride's hand and raised it to his lips for a quick kiss. "Well, when you hear our news, you'll be even happier that we're man and wife."

Carmen's face leapt with joy as she clapped her hands excitedly and gasped, "Oh my God! Is it what I think? Oh Lacey, honey! Is it true then?" Bemused, Tori smiled and waited, wondering what news could possibly elicit such a reaction.

"Yes!" Lacey cried gleefully. "We're pregnant!" Touching her belly gently she grinned, misty-eyed, into her husband's beaming face. "Almost four months."

Boom! The thud of Tori's heart dropping into her stomach almost had her doubled over and retching on the spot. Holy shit. What were the odds of such an ironic coincidence?

"Have you told everyone?" Carmen wanted to know.

"Yep," Cam said proudly. "We found out before the wedding

but wanted to wait until after the honeymoon to let the cat out of the bag." One of his big hands joined his wife's where it stayed pressed against her middle.

Putting a hand up to her mouth like she was telling a secret, Lacey made an adorably shy face saying, "I'm starting to show already so there was no use in delaying the announcement."

"Wow," Tori muttered through lips numbed by shock. "I'm so happy for you both. When are you due, Lacey?"

"September" came the reply as both parents-to-be answered in unison.

It was unavoidable that Tori would quickly do the math in her head and conclude that if she was pregnant, she was looking at a Christmas birth. It was all too much for her to take in. Gathering her many packages and bags, she hastily made her good-byes after congratulating the happy couple once again and ran quickly to the quiet and privacy of her apartment. Now her mind really was made up even if her heart resisted.

"**G'MORNING TORI.** How're ya' doing today?"

Alex's chipper mood got a wry smile out of her. She would need a vat of coffee and a super-size bearclaw covered in sticky sweetness to wring that much morning cheer out of her. "I'm good, boss. And apparently so are you. Why so upbeat this morning?"

"Oh God," he chuckled. "Is it so unusual for me to be pleasant in the morning? Better work on that, huh?"

Deciding now was as good a time as any to have the serious discussion with Alex she knew was necessary, Tori took a deep breath and crossed her fingers. "We need to talk."

"Sure, sure," he said. "Yeah, in a bit, okay? I have something I need you to do first."

"Oh," she said surprised. "What's up?"

"Let's sit down," he said, directing her to pull up a chair. "First of all, this is a don't shoot the messenger moment, okay?"

Tori shrugged. What else could she do? "Um, sure?"

"Drae's back." The rushing sound in her head felt suspiciously like the precursor to her fainting dead away. She wondered if the numbness in her hands and the heaviness in her legs was the result of all the blood in her body zooming south. Whatever it was, she didn't like the feeling. Unable to move, she lifted doleful eyes to Alex but said nothing. She wasn't sure of her ability to say anything coherent making silence her new best friend.

"Are you okay? You seem a little pale."

She shook her head ever so slightly, first to indicate yes and then a shaky no. Things just kept going from bad to worse. The concern etched on Alex's face eked into her awareness. "I'm fine," she bit out. "Sorry. You surprised me."

"No, don't apologize." He waited her out, his eyes never leaving her face. It took her a good minute or two to get herself together but once she did, Tori folded her hands neatly in her lap to disguise their shaking and looked back at him. "Better?" he asked. She nodded jerkily and schooled her expression to one of feigned indifference. She knew he could see right through her but pride dictated that she not crumble.

"Okay, good. Now," he said, "I want you to go talk to him." At her quick inhale and the way her body twitched he held up his hand to silence any further reply on her part. "Tori. Go talk to him. Don't pass go. Don't collect two hundred dollars. Just grab a cart and go to his house. He's expecting you."

Now *that* got a reaction from her. "Oh for God's sake Alex! Don't I get a say in this? Frankly, I don't give a shit that he's expecting me." She thought of plans A, B and C and knew she was being an unbelievable coward. This was what she wanted. To meet with Draegyn and let him know she had taken steps to fix their very messy, very unpleasant situation. She had to do this if for no other reason than to give herself a measure of peace. The last time her life had blown up in her face she'd lost everything through no fault of her own and eventually ran away, with her tail tucked between her legs. *Not his time*, she vowed. Another man had behaved like a swine and she'd be damned if she'd accept responsibility for the faults of another. Been there, done that. *Ouch.*

"If it helps any, he looks like crap and this can't go on Tori. I can't have you two warring with each other."

Fuck my life, she thought fighting back the tears. He was right. The agency and the bond that joined the Justice Brothers came before anything else. She was the outsider and if that meant she had to cut her losses and go away, so be it. There wasn't any way around it now that Alex had made it clear he'd had enough.

She stood on shaky legs. Looking anywhere but at her boss's face. "I'm so sorry Alex. You're right. Really, I am. Sorry, that is," she mumbled nonsensically.

"Tori," he scolded. "You have nothing to be sorry for. I just don't want to watch two people I care about tearing each other apart." He stood and pulled her into a brief hug. "You go talk to him. Keep an open mind, okay?"

What could she say? Keep an open mind? For heaven's sake, didn't he know about Draegyn's tabloid tryst with the Hollywood actress? She sighed as a single tear escaped and drifted slowly down her cheek. Impatiently wiping it away, she turned a hollow smile on her boss. "I'll go, Alex. Because you asked me to. But don't expect too much. Some things aren't easily fixed."

"You have spirit, Tori Bennett. I knew the first time I met you that you were a woman of rare integrity. Now's a good time to access some of that strength and put it to good use."

Once again, Drae was pacing impatiently, waiting for Victoria to come to him knowing full well that he was being hopeful at best. He doubted she'd willingly appear on his doorstep – not without some serious pressure on Alex's part. *Damn.* Why hadn't he considered that before? The thought didn't sit well with him.

He'd been up and prowling around his huge house for hours, shot full of restless energy after a sleepless night. Unable to relax enough to wind down and get some shut-eye, Drae had abandoned his bed well after two in the morning and dragged his jet-lagged ass to the living room where he lounged on the sofa, closing his eyes occasionally until snippets of his time with Victoria danced on his eyelids.

The clock ticked in a sort of slow-motion hell as he waited. How long he paced and watched for her appearance in the lane he didn't know. Time had ceased to be relative. Drae was considering going and fetching her when he heard the approach of a cart, it's low whirring sound growing louder and more distinct the closer it came. He put a hand over his heart to calm its suddenly erratic beating.

She'd come. He'd been figuratively holding his breath, fearful that no amount of coercion would force her to this meeting. His cage was being rattled, big time. One of them was fearless – and it wasn't him. He had planned on greeting her on the porch but nerves kept him motionless for long moments as he struggled to find his equilibrium, giving her enough time to mount the stairs and tap softly on the front door. *Showtime St. John,* he thought. Don't fuck this up.

Tori took her good, sweet time making her way to Draegyn's house. After Alex's direct request that she go and talk to the man, she'd gone back to her apartment to grab the legal documents. Instead of simply fetching the envelope she took a shower, styled her hair, and ripped apart her closet in search of something to wear.

Good Lord. For someone who imagined herself a nerdy tomboy, she certainly wasn't acting like one. Maybe it was his harsh taunt about her ragbag wardrobe that made her take extra pains with her appearance, but probably not. No. In this instance it was a defense mechanism. One of those female impulses driven by jealousy and fear. The memory of Jessamyn Winters in all her stylish glory, clinging to Draegyn like a vine, shredded her confidence.

It was an unusually warm spring day as she climbed the wide wooden steps leading to Draegyn's front door. It was like that in the desert. One moment it was mild and pleasant. And then there were times like today, when a sudden blast of heat reminded everyone where they were. Tapping lightly, three rapid beats against the hand-tooled wood, Tori pressed a trembling hand to her heart. She hoped she could keep it together long enough to get in and out with as little drama as possible. Clutching her big designer bag close, she took a few deep breaths and waited.

Nothing prepared Tori for what she saw when Draegyn finally opened the door. What a sight he made. She found it disquieting that he looked so *raw*. That was the only way to describe what she was seeing. It must have been several days since a razor touched his face, and his blonde hair was unkempt and much longer than she was used to, giving him a rugged air that had her nipples pebbling with alarming speed. Shit. Even looking like hell, he was still incredibly sexy.

Frown lines showed between eyes that bored into hers with an icy blue intensity that forced her to swallow the lump in her throat. For a second she glimpsed a fierce hunger in his gaze that quickly vanished as he shielded his expression with a slight dip of his head. "Thank you for coming," he murmured solemnly.

The corner of her mouth quirked upward. "I wasn't given much choice." When he didn't move or say anything else, she shifted uncomfortably and started fidgeting with the strap of her bag. "Are you going to ask me in or am I to wilt out here on the porch?"

Draegyn's eyes snapped to hers as a warm riot of color washed across his features. "Oh, sorry. My bad," he said, pushing the door open wide allowing her to pass by. Her senses prickled when she picked up the scent of minty toothpaste and the subtle hint of spicy bodywash as she skimmed close to his body. *So much for calming my heartbeat*, she thought darkly.

"Living room?" he asked, signaling with his hand to the large open space at the bottom of a three-stair descent from the foyer. Tori grasped the handrail making her way on legs turned to jelly, wearing the very same strappy sandals she'd worn the last time she was here. *Perhaps that wasn't such a good idea*, she thought as a riot of images reminded her what had passed between them flooded her brain.

She was tossing her bag on the enormous sectional sofa, taking in the breathtaking views visible through the two-story wall of windows offering an unparalleled panorama of the desert landscape when he asked if she'd like something to drink. After a clumsy shake of her head in the negative, Tori reconsidered and asked for some water. She'd need something to head off the dry mouth attacking her senses.

Handing her a glass filled with water and chunks of ice, he gestured for her to sit. *Ah, so polite*, she thought. It was as if they both needed this veneer of composed civility in order to deal with each other. One part of her wanted to jump on him and tear his lying, cheating ass to pieces. The other part still wanted to jump on him, but for entirely different reasons.

Tori took a large sip of the icy water and cleared her throat. "How was New York?"

Drae watched as the sip she took slid down her throat. It was all he could do to remain seated and not lunge at her like a dying man in need of one final desperate connection. His mind had gone blank when he opened the door and found her standing there in a white sundress edged in black with thin straps that showed off her arms and shoulders. Her dress was simple and enticing, gathered beneath her breasts, ending above her knees with an embroidered handkerchief hem that made her legs look fantastic. Sitting as she was, with one leg draped over the other, smoothing the material covering her thighs, she looked angelic and damn desirable. The urge to lean in close and press his lips against her delicate collarbone had Drae reaching for his drink to cool the sudden thirst he felt.

Get your shit together, man. Lusting after his wife wasn't going to help matters. There it was again. That word. *Wife.* A couple of weeks ago the term seemed like a loathsome curse. It has been rolling off his tongue rather easily in recent days.

"New York was business," he shrugged. "Nothing too strenuous, but talking about an assignment isn't why I asked you here."

She seemed to be weighing what he said with an undercurrent that made him feel uneasy. Quickly assessing her body language for clues he noted the rigid tension in her torso and how she was sitting ramrod straight on the edge of the sofa, her back no where near the soft cushion behind her. *Fuck.* Not good signs.

"Business, mmm hmmm." she murmured. He detected a hint of sarcasm. Also, not good. Maybe a quick apology for leaving so quickly and never once contacting her would take some of the wind out of her sails.

"A day late and a dollar short, I know, but I really did intend to stay in touch with you, Victoria. Things just got," he looked away with a grave expression, "complicated." Oh Jesus. The way her eyes smoldered at his choice of words didn't bode well for this conversation or their relationship.

"Complicated, you say?" The arctic blast coming from her unsettled him.

Attempting to change the dynamic, Drae tried to shrug off further mention of the time he'd spent on the east coast hiding from not just her but his whole life. "Yeah, yeah. You know. Business. Nothing to write home about."

She sat straighter, if that was even possible, untangled her legs and then re-crossed them. "I see," she answered bitingly. "That's it? Complicated business?"

So much for changing the subject. Apparently she wasn't going to let this go. Apprehension gathered in his stomach. He thought she might say something else, maybe ask a question, but she surprised him with a display of reserve that did nothing to settle his nerves.

"Go on."

Thinking a quick conversational pivot might help level the playing field, he blurted out the first thing that came to mind. "You look very pretty. I like the dress." He knew it was the wrong thing to say when her expression froze.

"Alright. Cut the crap St. John. You had Alex practically cattle-prod me down here for reasons that remain a mystery." *Shit.* This wasn't going as he'd hoped. Not by a long shot. "New York was business. It was complicated and you like my dress. Is that what you wanted to see me for? A fashion critique and some lame explanation for your time away?"

Her fire seeped into his senses making reason and whatever he planned on saying vaporize in the heat. The chocolate eyes he dreamed about were shooting flames of red and gold his way, practically burning him alive.

"No," he answered quietly, his voice turning to a low growl as frustration and desire clashed inside him. Something snapped, as it always did when she got in his face, and he knew in that instant he was in over his head. "Seeing you had nothing to do with explaining away where I've been and everything to do with wanting to taste you coming on my tongue."

Victoria's shocked gasp filled the air a second before her hand shot out and soundly slapped him across the face. Appalled by his own lack of finesse, Drae thought he'd reel in his crude words until he caught the glimmer of sexual tension light up her expression.

"You're a pig!" she screamed. "A lying, cheating pig, and I ….."

He cut her off, leaning sharply into her body space, his face inches from hers. "Oh yeah? And you're a bitch, lady. A tart-tongued hellcat!" She never failed to surprise him, predictably throwing him off with a taunt or gesture that fed the excitement arcing between them. To his astonishment, she stuck her tongue out at him, grunting aggressively as she raised her hands in the space separating their bodies and tried to shove him back. The second her small hands pressed against his muscled chest, he was a goner.

It wasn't a case of who reacted first because they each launched at the other, Drae grabbing fistfuls of her hair as he yanked her head closer while Victoria flattened herself against him, their mouths crashing together as the simmering passion surrounding them burst to life. Fueled by intoxicating desire and emotions tinged with anger and frustration, they kissed like fucking maniacs. She whimpered, he growled, and it got hotter and more frenzied by the second. This was what they did. First some fireworks and then they lost their clothes with unbelievable speed.

She wrenched kiss-swollen lips away from his, gasping. "We can't do this." He remembered saying something similar the last time they were together. Bloody hell.

"Yes we can," he snarled, sucking her pouting lower lip into his voracious mouth. "You *want* me to fuck you. I can feel it, taste your desire. Don't lie to me Victoria."

TORI WAS VISIBLY TREMBLING in his arms as he took the stairs two at a time, in a Rhett Butler-ish display of masculinity that scattered her thoughts and banished whatever resolve she'd imagined would keep this very thing from happening.

She didn't know this woman, the one wiggling desperately in an attempt to crawl inside his skin, but she was beginning to understand there was something about the energy they created whenever they came together that brought her to life. Pretending couldn't change that nor could any of the thousand safeguards she hoped would protect her heart and body from wanting him as desperately as she did.

"Dammit Draegyn," she groaned, sinking her teeth into the flesh on his neck. His fingers gripped her more forcefully as she worked her tongue against his skin, sucking wildly while he hurried them into his bedroom. Tori let out a startled cry when she felt herself gliding weightless through the air as he threw her aggressively into the middle of his enormous bed. Somewhere along the way her sandals had slipped off, and having been tossed unceremoniously onto the plush mattress, she landed with a thud, legs askew with her dress hitched up around her hips.

She had about a second to consider the dangerous wolfish expression on his face before he fell on her, thrusting a knee between her thighs as his mouth mimicked the onslaught on her neck and shoulders that she'd just subjected him to. He was like a glorious beast, undone by primal instincts, feasting on her flesh as wild, grunting sounds tore from his throat. This was what it must feel like to be eaten alive, devoured. *Oh God. Please don't let it ever end*, she thought.

She wrapped a leg around his thigh, grinding sinuously against the hard muscle encased in soft denim as her dress shifted out of the way leaving only delicate white panties covering her body. Clutching at his shoulders, she curved an arm about his head, crying out each time his teeth sank into her neck. There was something basic and exciting about his bearded mouth scraping along her skin that made her quiver uncontrollably. She liked the dapper secret agent look very much but nothing quite compared to this rough, savage side of him. Panting, her hips rocking against his thigh, Tori whimpered raggedly close to his ear.

Draegyn pulled back from his ravishment of her neck and searched her eyes. "You *will* come on my tongue and when you can't take the pleasure any more," he growled, stopping only to run his tongue along the seam of her mouth, "I'm going to make you beg, Victoria. Beg me to come inside you." She gasped at the rawness of his words, trembling and shaking as a flood of moisture drenched her panties. The scent of her arousal filled the air around them leaving little doubt how badly she wanted him.

With a sudden whoosh, he reached down, grabbing the hem of her dress and yanked it over her head. Tori was aware of the rapid rise and fall of her chest as she struggled to find air. With each deep lungful of oxygen, breasts swollen with need, inched closer to his mouth as he lowered his head in agonizing slow motion. Hovering so close that her nipples reacted to the warmth of his breath, he touched the tip of his tongue to one of the aching nubs and growled, "Tell me. Tell me what you want."

Her leg gripped his thigh as she shimmied against him. "Oh," she moaned. "Please, Draegyn. Put your mouth on me." His hand cupped her breast, bringing it to his waiting mouth, while his tongue flicked her swollen nipple as she cried out in an agony of wanting. When his lips sucked her breast forcefully until most of it was throbbing in his mouth, she nearly came apart as the pulse from his suckling matched the one deep inside her. She couldn't stop her hips from bucking, as liquid heat poured from her body.

Incapable of anything but feeling, Tori writhed and moaned as he repeated the same actions on her other breast while his hand pinched the nipple he'd teased, rolling it deftly between his fingers, stopping to massage the plumped mound as her excitement rose off the charts. He kept both hands cupped around her breasts as his wicked mouth placed damp, open mouth kisses between her mounds, slowly leaving a wet trail of desire down the center of her body. Tori's hands had ceased to function, flung wide, clutching loosely at the bedding beneath her.

At a spot just below her navel, he licked her with the flat of his tongue then turned his face and bit her sharply at the waist. She was shaking uncontrollably, her legs moving restlessly, searching for relief from the agony of pleasure he was wringing from her. Was it wrong that she thrilled as his trembling hands ripped her delicate panties to shred in his haste to uncover her? She didn't care. There was something beyond exciting about his untamed forcefulness.

"Mmmm," he groaned, leaning in to inhale the tangy aroma of her desire. "So sexy." She couldn't help but think he owned her response. Every sweet, throbbing pulse and the moisture she felt spreading across her inner thighs. It was all his. Lost in a wave of sensation, Tori canted her hips in invitation as he laughed, pressing a hand against her abdomen. "What are you trying to tell me, honey?" A single finger drifted softly along the length of her unfurling slit.

She hissed at the teasing touch, her head rolling from side to side. “Is this where you want my tongue?” he asked hoarsely as his fingers spread the liquid pouring from her until the lips of her sex quivered beneath his caress. She tried to tell him but no words came, only a low strangled groan. “I’ll take that as a yes,” he said, shifting their positions until she was spread before him as he pressed her thighs open wide. Pushing both hands under her bottom, Draegyn lifted her into his waiting mouth, making Tori come completely undone as his tongue licked her once, from bottom to top, stopping to swirl around the swollen nub of her desire before suckling hungrily on her tender flesh.

Her hips jerked as her back arched off the bed. Overcome by agonized desire, she cried out, placing her hand at the back of his head urging him on. This time her voice worked just fine. “More,” she pleaded. “Oh my God. More.”

He seemed all too eager to comply, stabbing his tongue deep inside her slit and sucking hungrily on her sensitized flesh. “You like that,” he growled, flattening his tongue against her pulsating clit, making tiny explosions go off inside her.

With one hand clutched on his skull, the other grasping the bedcovers, Tori raised her knees, opening herself up even more, as she ground against his marauding mouth. A fire was climbing up her nervous system, making her gasp and writhe under his touch.

“This is the part where you come on my tongue,” he told her as he slid a finger past her opening, deep inside the passage flooded with desire. A low, strangled groan rumbled up from her core as he withdrew his hand and waited.

“Draegyn,” she moaned, overcome by the sensations he was wringing from her body.

He bit her inner thigh and thrust his finger inside her. “Say it again. Say my name again Victoria.”

“Draegyn, oh, oh….” She cried as her insides tightened and

throbbed.

"Are you ready, honey? Should I make you come now?" No answer was necessary as her back arched again and again, and she writhed frantically while a climax built to near painful heights inside her. Adding a second finger, Draegyn pumped them rhythmically in and out and then lowered his mouth once more, flicking his tongue in time to his thrusting fingers. "That's it," he groaned. "Fuck my fingers. Harder!"

Her hips ground feverishly, a strangled cry lodged in her throat and then he sucked her clit into his mouth. His tongue surging again and again against the swollen, aching nub caused bright lights to detonate on her closed eyelids a second before she screamed as a powerful orgasm wracked her body. Unending waves of sensation tore through her, as he made greedy sucking noises between her legs, ramming his fingers deep and massaging the inner walls of her sex.

Instead of backing off, the tightness in her core increased with each spasm of release making her desperate for something more. Draegyn jerked upward, hauling his t-shirt over his head and reached for the zipper of his pants. She didn't need to beg him with words; her body was doing that for her.

Shoving his jeans down, he grasped his swollen cock and grimaced while his eyes never left her weeping, pulsating center. Something wild and unfulfilled broke loose inside Tori as he moved into position. Surprising both herself and him, she swiftly rose up and pushed at him until he lay flat on his back, his huge erection, standing proud. Swinging her legs astride his, Tori reached between their bodies holding him in a firm grip as she guided his throbbing cock while she impaled herself with agonizing slowness, inch by inch, onto him. It took a bit of effort because in this position his size was a challenge but finally the outer lips of her pussy ground against his groin as she took him, balls deep inside her. He groaned, closed his eyes, and muttered a hoarse, "Oh fuck." She couldn't have agreed more.

Putting her hands aside his head, Tori began a torturously deliberate and very slow up and down motion. On each downward surge his hard length sank into her wet passage drawing grunts and groans from each of them. Grabbing her hips, Draegyn began guiding her movements, helping her on the upward motion then pulling her down hard, making her breasts sway and bob each time. He pressed a hand against her back, encouraging her lower so he could catch the plumped mounds with his mouth.

It was wild, raw pleasure at its very best. Nothing was wasted in her drive for the *more* she'd begged for. Each movement flooded her with sweet pleasure. Every sound a symphony of carnal indulgence that set her nervous system aflame. Even her eyesight was on sensory overload as she absorbed the sight of his achingly beautiful body as he bucked up into her. Pleasure like this couldn't last. Eventually the drumbeat inside would send her into a shuddering release but Tori wasn't quite ready to give in. Not yet. Framing his face with her hands, she kissed him, swirling her tongue around his and absorbing his grunts when she started slamming her body down on his.

He broke away first, rigid tension evident in the straining of his neck. Seeing him starting to come undone as she impaled herself over and over on his swelling cock while feeling him press deep against her womb, threw her senses into disarray.

"Ahhh," he groaned. "Fuck me. C'mon baby, take it all." Grunting, he thundered his hips on each downward stroke, pounding into her with such force, her knees lifted off the bed.

She was losing control, gyrating on his enormous cock in an age-old dance that could only end one way. Her inner muscles tightened unbearably around him, fisting his hardness in ever-intensifying spasms. "Draegyn," she moaned helplessly. He wrapped her in his arms, pulling her flat against his surging body as the first tremors broke free. Never stopping, he continued thrusting as her pussy throbbed and pulsed, finally exploding with a rush of super-heated moisture that bathed them both with physical proof of the unimaginable ecstasy ripping through her. She cried out, sobbing and gasping while her insides desperately milked his cock.

Before her orgasm had cleared the peak, he flipped them over, guided her legs high on his back and hammered into her shaking body for all he was worth. He grunted, "Fuck, fuck, fuck," with each powerful stroke, pounding into her relentlessly. The furious way he stroked deep and then pulled all the way back, only to lunge forward again and again, sent her soaring once more. The weight of his body pressed her into the mattress with each flex of his hips. She shuddered and flew apart, splintering into a million pieces, crying out to him as his cock swelled and twitched inside her. Tori knew he was there when his rhythm faltered. Wrapping him in her arms she urged him on, moaning, "Come for me," and then lost her grip on reality when he did just that, surging deep while he groaned and emptied his balls inside her.

It took a long time to come back to earth, each of them shuddering and twitching in the aftermath of what had just happened. Not caring that he was heavy and big, she used her legs and arms to hold on tight, relishing the feeling of his cock still buried deep within her. She felt the wet evidence of what they'd done leaking out of her body, sliding down the crack of her ass. She shuddered in exquisite awareness, relishing the blatant carnality.

Long moments later, Draegyn shifted his hips and gently withdrew from her body, causing her to wince in disappointment that they couldn't just stay joined forever. He pulled a soft throw blanket around them snuggling close with her back to his chest and one very possessive feeling arm wrapped around her waist. It just didn't get any better than this she thought a heartbeat before she fell into an exhausted sleep.

Drae struggled with what had just happened as he felt her relax and drift off. Pressing a soft kiss to her shoulder he tried to relax as well but his body wasn't going to allow that. Not when he'd just been subjected to the most thorough, satisfying fuck of his life.

Victoria might be small in stature but she was an amazing dynamo in bed. The way she'd climbed on him and taken him deep left him speechless. And wanting more.

No matter how many times he recoiled from the thought of being married, he couldn't deny that this woman did things to him he hadn't known were possible. With her, the feelings ran deeper and he wasn't just referring to the strength of an orgasm. She tasted sweeter too and the moment that she'd come on his tongue, just as he told her she would, he'd been filled with such bliss that it nearly stole his sanity. Nothing seemed to matter more than losing himself inside her. Somehow, Victoria Bennett had become his salvation from a life lived without texture, empty of anything more than superficial awareness. He grimly suspected that he needed her more than she needed him, a fact that stabbed at his soul.

Nothing had been solved by making love to her and maybe the simple fact that it had taken him this long to recognize that lovemaking was exactly what they'd been doing was at the heart of their problems.

He wasn't a fool. She wasn't going to wake up, confess her undying love for him, and ignore the past. He wasn't that lucky. There was still the piper to be paid for his contemptible behavior and that little issue of the marriage license. He wondered if she knew by now whether or not their rash behavior in Vegas had resulted in a pregnancy then cringed at the realization that it didn't matter anyway. Once again, he'd gotten carried away, making love to her without any thought of protection.

Drae didn't make those kinds of blunders, always having been scrupulous to the details anytime he'd taken a woman to bed. Victoria was a first on that score. Hers was the only body he'd felt without a barrier wrapped around his dick. Coming inside her was like nothing he'd known. The way her body spasmed along his length, forcing his fluid to erupt, shook him to the core.

Where did they go from here? He didn't know and could only

hope that she didn't light him on fire once she realized what they'd done. She'd called him a lying cheat, those words coming back to haunt him now. What had she meant by that? Alex warned him she felt he'd deceived her when he insisted that no one knew about their marriage so he was ready to defend on that score, but cheat? Where had that come from?

The sleeping woman in his arms wiggled against him making Drae tighten his hold around her waist. When he heard her whisper his name, his heart swelled to bursting knowing she called out to him even in her dreams. That was the last thought he had before exhaustion overtook him, and he fell into his first deep sleep in days.

THE RUMBLING IN HER tummy brought Tori awake with a start. *Oh no.* Scrambling desperately she fought against whatever it was that was holding her in place only to freeze in shock when she remembered where she was and whose arm was wrapped so snugly around her waist. *Fuck.*

Without a moment to lose she pried his grip off her body and ran frantically toward what she prayed was the en suite to his bedroom. Didn't matter whether it was the bathroom, a closet, or a public auditorium because she was going to hurl up her guts regardless. Making it to the toilet just in time, she sank to her knees as the violent spasms erupted. Without much in the way of food to fuel the vomiting, she wretched painfully again and again as her empty stomach reacted.

"Oh my God," she cried. "Stop. *Ugh.*" Weak and trembling, all she could do was hold on until the waves of hideous nausea subsided. She felt her hair being swept back off her face moments before a cool, damp cloth was laid across the back of her neck.

Speaking to her in soothing tones, she heard Draegyn saying, "Shhh. Easy, honey. Just relax. It'll be over in a minute." All she could do was hang onto the cold porcelain and moan. What could be more embarrassing than collapsing naked on a bathroom floor while hugging a toilet? Nothing.

As the horrible wrenching spasms eased off, she felt him wrap a plush robe around her shaking body. Helping her to her feet, Draegyn was ready with a glass of water that she gratefully accepted so she could rinse the foul taste from her mouth. With barely enough strength left to spit out the water, she was forced to hunch over the sink with her jaw slack as the liquid dripped. Afraid to look up lest she catch sight of what she knew would be her ghastly reflection in the bathroom mirror, Tori closed her eyes as he gently wiped the cool cloth across her face, then scooped her up as she clutched at the robe and carried her swiftly back to the bed.

Laying her gently against the pillows, he helped put her arms into the sleeves of the big robe and wrapped her in the blanket. She rested against the headboard and waited for the room to stop spinning. Finally opening her eyes she was immensely relived to see that he had pulled his clothes on. She wasn't so sure she could face a naked Draegyn at the moment.

His face seemed almost as pale as she felt. *Dammit.* She knew what was going to happen next. He was going to ask the *are you pregnant* question. Despite the fact that she hadn't done the test yet, all signs pointed to the obvious.

Tori was struggling, big time. Struggling to comprehend why she couldn't control herself around a man who put up so many emotional roadblocks that she couldn't keep track. She grappled with the sickening fact that she'd just had sex with someone she knew to be little better than a man-whore while trying to figure out where her self-respect had vanished to. How did a girl go from being a *don't fuck with me* badass to a….well, she didn't know what.

Drae stood silently by the side of the bed with his hands jammed into the pockets of his jeans, rocking on feet that felt a bit numb, searching the air for what to do. The scene that just played out in his bathroom hit him square in the solar plexus. Unless he was an idiot, the little woman swamped inside his big robe, the same woman who was carefully avoiding his eyes, was pregnant. Unbelievable.

Jesus, was the air conditioning on, he wondered? It suddenly seemed awfully hot as sweat broke out along his brow. Victoria shifted on the bed, drawing the robe that was way too big around her dainty body. Funny. She didn't seem hot although he certainly felt like the bedroom had turned into a fucking sauna. No, she actually looked pale as a ghost. Even her sweet lips were devoid of color and as his eyes lasered in for a detailed inspection, he noticed for the first time a hollowing of her cheeks and what appeared to be dark rings under her eyes. His body temperature rose even higher as a walloping dose of fear and apprehension grabbed him by the throat.

"Feeling better?" he asked as gently as his nerves would allow. The last thing he wanted to do was add to her unease but in all honesty, it was taking all his strength not to fall to his knees. Keeping her eyes downcast, Victoria nodded jerkily but didn't utter so much as a squeak.

"Is there something you want to tell me?" To his astonishment, her lips, the very ones he'd been devouring not all that long ago, began to quiver. He swallowed the lump lodged in his throat and didn't move for fear he would lose his ability to function if he did.

"Would you hand me my dress?" she asked in a hushed, trembling voice. Drae walked around the end of the huge bed and gathered her pretty little sundress, noting the torn panties he'd ripped off laying nearby on the floor. Feeling sick, he thought he might be following her act in the bathroom with one of his own.

He wondered what a guy did in this sort of situation. Was there a right or wrong thing to say? She hadn't answered his question, and he wasn't sure if he should press her for a response. He had a right to know, didn't he? Remembering her bitter words about his manhood and how she wouldn't want him involved if she was, increased the sweat trickling down his back.

She murmured a quick, "Thanks," when he handed over her dress, taking it from him with hands that were clearly shaking.

"Victoria, talk to me," he pleaded. "What's going on?"

She threw off the blanket and swung her legs down the side of the bed, tugging the sundress hurriedly over her head as she shucked off the robe and smoothly stood as the dress neatly fell into place. Under normal circumstances he would have been impressed with how little skin she showed during this maneuver but at the moment the only thing he was feeling was a bad case of nerves. Crossing her arms under her breasts, she looked so small and fragile–adding to his increasing anxiety. He had to hand it to her though, even in this odd situation, she was doing everything she could to give off the appearance that she was in complete control. Shame that her pallor and shaking hands told a much different story.

When she finally looked at him he took a step back as hunted eyes shadowed with something that looked like pain landed on his face. "I know what you're asking," she whispered. Gesturing toward the bathroom she continued. "But despite what just happened here, I don't know how to answer."

How the hell was he supposed to react to such an obvious non-answer?

"I'm going to head home now," she murmured, making for the sitting area in the open walkway on the second floor.

"No. I don't think so. We need to talk about this."

Pushing past him she turned as she reached the long walkway with an incredulous look on her face. "Talk? Are you joking, Draegyn? Good Lord! Every time we try, well," she said in a voice that was rising in intensity and tone. "We end up naked, and I'm thinking that's how we got in to this mess in the first place."

He couldn't believe she was trying to leave when his whole world was crashing at his feet. Raking a hand through his hair, Drae scrubbed at his face and then at the hair on his jaw.

"Jesus Christ, Victoria. Do you really imagine that you can

show up here, fuck my brains out, then heave your guts up in the toilet and simply turn around and walk away?" He hadn't meant to shout but it was too late to turn back now. She looked like she'd been slapped, making him instantly regret the *fuck my brains out* comment. That hadn't been fair. Not by a long shot.

"Oh, nice!" she hollered back. "Once again, just like in Vegas, this is all my doing, right?"

Nerves, panic, and fear, hers and his, fueled the raging argument that broke out. He demanded answers. She told him angrily to fuck off. Somewhere in the midst of the yelling she'd called him a lying cheat again and he reacted with offended indignity.

"I did not deceive you and most certainly have not cheated! And besides, how exactly do you cheat on someone who is constantly screaming in your face about what an asshole they are? From where I'm standing, you wouldn't care one way or the other!" he bellowed.

A noise below them made each turn to see where it was coming from. Cameron's shocked and embarrassed face looked up at them, having clearly witnessed them screaming and hissing at each other. "Sorry to interrupt," he said quickly as he motioned to the driveway. "I just stopped by to drop off that shipment of Koa wood I had sent from Hawaii."

Victoria looked away from the man standing below and fixed Drae with a scathing look. "You couldn't be more wrong," she hissed. "Only your smug arrogance supersedes your unbelievable stupidity."

With that she flounced down the steps, picking up one of her discarded sandals along the way as Cameron remained motionless in the doorway, slack-jawed and plainly shocked by the ugly scene he walked in on.

Flying past his flabbergasted friend, she descended another set of stairs into the living room where their encounter had begun and snatched up her purse. Arriving back on the landing, Drae watched her struggle to pull something from the big bag. Stomping over to

Cameron, she slapped a brown envelope and what looked like a folded up newspaper against the man's chest, and told him, "That's for Mr. Double-Oh-Jerkoff. Make sure he gets it."

Practically running from the house she whipped around at the last second, clutching her bag and one lone shoe, zeroing in on his face with neat precision. "Consider yourself served!" she bit out, then flew out the door like a fire had been lit under her ass.

"Fuck!" Drae raged as she slammed the heavy wood door for maximum emphasis, climbed into the cart she'd arrived in and sped up the driveway.

"Dude," Cam uttered, shaking his head in amazement. "What the hell was that?"

Drae thundered down the steps scowling darkly. "Shut up," he bit out at Cam, just because he knew he could. Snatching what Victoria left from his friend's hands, he continued down the long hallway on the first floor to his study and just like the angry female that had run screaming from him, slammed the door for good measure.

Several glasses of whiskey later, he sat with head in hands, going over the ghastly row and wondered where it had all gone so wrong. It was a very long time after that before he left the study. Passing the table where he'd thrown the envelope Victoria left, Drae absently picked it up, watched the folded newspaper fall and reached for it. Opening the glossy tabloid his eyes blurred as his gaze connected with the single page spread showing a series of pictures featuring him and the glamorous Jessamyn taken during their recent unexpected meeting in New York.

Anger swept through him as he read the salacious story underneath the provocative headline. That fucking bitch. She'd even given a quote to the tabloid insinuating they were friends with benefits. An arctic blast of worry replaced the anger feeding into his system drip by icy drip. Drae was so undone by what he was reading that the brown envelope slipped from his thoughts. He'd realize how unfortunate that was later.

Tori didn't know how she made it back to her apartment in one piece. After their ugly confrontation, she'd been shaking so bad it was a miracle she'd been able to handle the electric cart. Supremely conscious of the fact that she was sans panties under her white sundress, she'd hurried up the stairs clutching her one shoe, unlocking her front door with trembling hands.

Leaning against the closed door, she flicked on the switch that filled her tiny home with light, dropped her bag on the floor, and pressed her hand against her quivering tummy. *Now was not the time to be sick again*, she thought. Not when she had so much to do.

Of course, the first thing her eyes lit on after she'd taken a few deep breaths was the package that arrived earlier that morning, containing the random toiletries and makeup refills she'd ordered along with that damnable pregnancy test.

"Great timing," she muttered aloud as she tore the package open and read the directions. At this point she didn't really need the verification, all the damn signs were there plus some, but sticking her head in the sand wasn't going to help. If she was pregnant, there was another consideration she had to deal with. Healthy babies didn't happen by chance, and she would need to start taking steps to ensure her well-being and that of her child.

Twenty minutes later, Tori sat on the edge of the toilet, clutching the little plastic stick in her hands with the two lines indicating she was carrying Draegyn St. John's baby. It was a long time before she could move. When she finally did, she went to her bag, searched for her cell phone and punched in the numbers that would call her mother.

First things first, and talking to her mom was at the very top of the list, followed by a hurried packing of her things and lastly the resignation letter and expression of thanks she was going to leave behind for Alex.

She'd loved living in the desert and getting to know everyone at the Justice Agency. This place had been a lifeline during a difficult time and she'd come to feel a part of the family. But those days were gone and now, nothing was more important than the baby she was carrying. Nothing.

Tori didn't consider what she was doing as running. Maybe there could have been a chance for them to find some kind of middle ground, despite his relationship phobia, but his little escapade in New York pretty much squashed that. Trust was a big deal to her. Giving him her body she was going to chalk up to hormones and good, old-fashioned lust. He was, after all, sex on two legs. But trusting him with her heart was another thing altogether, and when it came to a baby – well, she wasn't a mother yet but suddenly she understood how that five letter word could come between two people.

THE NEXT MORNING DRAE was standing in his kitchen when he heard the front door slam followed by quickly approaching footsteps. Curious who was stomping like a madman in his direction, he rounded the corner and ran face first into a fist smashing into his jaw. The jolt sent him flying backwards onto the floor with a painful thud. Jumping to his feet, he immediately assumed a defensive posture ready to kick the shit out of whoever had just cold-cocked him only to find himself staring into Alex's rage-filled eyes.

"I'm gonna annihilate your fucking ass, Drae! You were warned, man!" Alex shouted.

"What the fuck, Alex?" Drae yelled back, letting his hands go from clenched fists to a gesture of surrender. "Can the condemned man hear the charges before getting jumped with no warning?"

"Oh, that's how you're gonna play this? Don't act like you don't know exactly what you did." The rage emanating off his friend's body made an impression on him. He'd seen Alex mad before, plenty of times, but this was different. He actually looked and sounded like he really did want to murder him.

"Back off, bro. You know damn well that one good kick to your leg and you'll be out of commission for a week."

"Well," Alex bellowed, "Suppose I should expect a low blow like that from you. This time you've gone too far!" he yelled as every vein in his neck stood out in stark relief from his skin.

"C'mon man, you're scaring the shit out of me here. I've never seen you like this. What in the hell is going on?"

Alex glared at him with a venomous look made all the more dangerous by his brawny physique which was practically bursting with pumped up aggression – directed solely at him. "Y'know Drae, you're my brother and all that but you really are a miserable human being. Care to tell me what you did to her?"

"Uh, did to who?"

"Tori, of course! What in fucking fuck – did you – DO?" Alex's voice was so loud it could probably be heard from the fucking Space Station.

Was it possible to know you were giving off a deer caught in the headlights look, because that was precisely how Drae felt. Had news of the screaming match he and Victoria had yesterday made it to Alex's ears? "What did Cam tell you?"

"What? Oh, holy shit. Cam's involved in this too? Mother-fucker…"

"Alright, settle down and let's get on the same page, okay? Cam isn't involved in anything but clearly I am."

"Damn right you are! She left, as in, she took one of the trucks early this morning and drove into town. I just got an email from her telling me where to pick up the vehicle."

"What?" It was Drae's turn to start bellowing.

"You heard me. Tori has left. No warning, no explanation, nothing - so I'll ask again, what the fuck did you do to her?"

An instant replay of everything that happened yesterday unraveled in his mind. Victoria coming to talk to him, the crazy explosion that led to their wild lovemaking, the ugly argument that followed her throwing up in his bathroom and the God-awful gossip rag pictures that had fueled her anger. He knew she was hurt, mad, maybe even a tad jealous – none of those things made him feel very good about how he'd been behaving but he thought after a night to cool off, he'd have a chance to make things right between them. Apparently he was wrong.

Why would she leave, he wondered? It didn't make sense. The hellcat he'd come to love wasn't afraid of anything as far as he could tell. She'd stand her ground no matter what, even if just to be perverse. Then it hit him. She was carrying his child but didn't think him man enough to accept the responsibility and especially didn't understand yet how much he loved her. It had taken a long time to get there but he had. Only she didn't know that. *Fuck me*, he thought.

"Let's go," Drae barked, grabbing the keys to his truck and sprinting past Alex for the door.

"Where exactly are we going?"

"Light a fire under Cam and have him meet us at her apartment. We do surveillance for Christ's sake – hopefully she left some sort of clue," he murmured, his thoughts careening all over the place.

Once in the truck, Drae floored it out of the drive and drove like a madman up to the main house while Alex tapped a text out to Cam. When he was finished he grumbled, "You gonna let me in on what's going on?"

"Eventually."

Less than two minutes later he brought the vehicle to a screeching halt outside the building where Victoria had been staying. Leaping from the cab, he took the steps two at a time after leaving the driver's side door open with Alex still exiting the truck.

He didn't bother to try knocking. She was already gone and had left the door unlocked so he simply shoved it open and dashed in. His heart sank as he took in the scene before him. Two large suitcases sat in the middle of the room with a garment bag draped over top. Next to that were three big boxes, neatly addressed and ready to be shipped along with two envelopes. One addressed to Alex and another for him. Ripping open his envelope, he found a single sheet of paper on which she'd scribbled,

Draegyn,

By now you've read the papers I left you. *Shit, he'd forgotten about them after reading that damn tabloid article.*

I'm sorry to have messed up your perfect life. *Oh my fucking god.*

Will be in touch once I've made some decisions. *This can't be happening.*

Some truces don't always work out. *Is this what a heart attack feels like?*

He dropped onto the sofa as the sheet of paper slipped from fingers too numb to feel anything. "I'd consider hitting you again," Alex bit out, "But from your look, it seems like Tori landed a knock-out punch."

He looked up into Alex's scowling face but words didn't find their way out of his mouth. Shaking his head in censure, Alex reached for the paper Drae had dropped and read the four short lines.

"What papers and what kind of decisions?"

Feeling vacant and hollow, Drae struggled to answer. "I forgot about the papers." At Alex's renewed scowl he let the rest pour out as Cam came pounding up the steps and into the apartment. "She came by to talk yesterday and we, uh….we got sidetracked." He ignored the dark look of fury directed at him. "An argument broke out and we said some stupid shit."

Cam added, "That was one seriously pissed off lady."

"Yeah, well – she had good reason. Somehow she got hold of a gossip magazine that ran a story about me and Jessamyn Winters. All lies by the way," he added quickly with a malevolent scowl of his own. "Anyway, the story did more than insinuate we were friends with benefits and, unfortunately, there were a few paparazzi shots that made it worse."

Cam whistled and did a bit of tut-tutting while Alex dialed his rage back a notch and asked, "These papers. Are they about a divorce?"

"A *what*?" Cam wheezed, caught completely off-guard by what he was hearing.

"Probably," Drae groaned, hanging his head in his hands. "Fuck."

Alex took it from there. "For those of us just tuning in, Mr. I-Don't-Ever-Want-to-Get-Married St. John and Miss I'll-Kick-Your-Arrogant-Ass Bennett had themselves a drunken wedding ceremony while on a work assignment in Las Vegas."

Cam whistled again as his eyebrows shot to the ceiling in surprise. "Explains the angry, pissed off thing."

"Exactly," Alex bit out.

Still trying to get up to speed, Cam asked Alex, "How do we go from drunken Vegas wedding to naughty actress and the paparazzi?"

"Well now, there's the million dollar question but I suspect the two intersect in New York while he was doing a protection detail. Am I right?" Drae could only nod. Cameron chuckled, not that Drae could blame him. When he heard someone else explain it out loud, it did sound like the plot to a bad chick flick.

"Wow. I go away for a few weeks and all hell breaks loose. Whatsamatter Drae, you jealous of me and Lacey getting hitched?" he smirked. "Went about things the wrong way."

"Bite me," Drae snapped.

"So – let me guess," Cam continued as he fixed Drae with a pitying look. "You freaked out, acted like a dick, said all the wrong things and basically made the lady feel like shit. Am I anywhere near the truth?" he asked looking back and forth between Drae and Alex.

"I'd say you hit the nail on the head," Alex replied drily.

Gesturing with his head at the other envelope in Alex's hand, Cam asked, "What's that say?"

"Uh, well let's see. It's your basic thanks for everything resignation letter along with a bunch of please don't be mad at me thrown in for good measure. She loved working for the agency, blah-blah-blah but this is also Drae's home and she couldn't stay with the way things are. Ship her stuff to her mother and give Carmen and Ria a hug good-bye. Reading between the lines there's a shit-ton of hurt mixed with regret. Good going there, bro."

Two pair of disappointed eyes turned on him. Drae stood, murmuring, "I gotta hit the head," and staggered off to the bathroom. He didn't really, but the way his chest tightened each time he realized she was gone, made him need a moment. It in no way helped his frame of mind when he shut the bathroom door only to be assailed by Victoria's scent. It clung to everything in the small space. Perfume mixed with shampoo and bodywash made his senses reel. He leaned on the edge of the sink and held on fast, trying to calm his nerves.

That was when he saw it. A small white stick tossed in the trashcan and the remnants of a box looking like it had been hastily torn open and just as quickly discarded. He reached for the stick with badly trembling hands. There was no mistaking what he held – the two lines on the end of the stick labeled PREGNANT, stared back at him. All the oxygen got sucked out of his lungs, making his head spin uncomfortably.

Stumbling like a toddler just learning to walk, he lurched out of the bathroom and into living room, the pregnancy test still clutched in his hand. Alex and Cam both stopped talking and looked at him. He didn't doubt for a second he was pale as a ghost. It was Alex, in his role as big daddy, who reacted to the sight of his pallor and the damning stick he held in his hand. This time when he punched him, Drae didn't even try to defend himself from the hit. In his mind he deserved that and more.

Cam stepped in, being the biggest physically of the three, and managed to restrain Alex from beating him to a bloody pulp. There was a lot of yelling and swearing, none of it coming from Drae, followed by an angry sounding Alex leaving a message on the voicemail of Victoria's mother asking her to call him back ASAP.

Drae never realized how shock could slow down the thought process until this moment. It was like trying to think in a thick, dense cloud that made everything feel like a slow-motion slog. He was going to be a father. *Jesus.* He and Victoria had made a baby together. *Keep breathing, just keep breathing.*

Suddenly, his thoughts became crystal clear when he remembered her delicate body shaking uncontrollably as she heaved up her guts into the toilet. Thoughts of her paleness, the hollows he noticed in her cheeks, and the way she screamed at him afterwards kicked him harder in his conscience than any punch Alex could have thrown. The dots continued to connect in less than flattering ways for him. The childish way he'd reacted to their marriage, him running off to New York without a word, that damn tabloid story, and the way he couldn't keep his hands off her, all without any words of feeling or commitment on his part attacked not just his already smarting conscience, but his heart as well. What the fuck had he done?

Cam finally broke through the fog. "Where do you want to start?" Leave it to the surveillance expert to get them back on track.

Alex answered first. "She left the truck at the market off the interstate. We should check that out first. Hopefully her mother will call me back, and maybe she'll know more." Looking at Drae who was walking in circles, he shook his head and scraped his hand back and forth through his hair. "Get the zombie an ice pack for his face."

Alex stayed at the Villa while Cam drove Drae to where Victoria had left the truck. The ride was one of the most uncomfortable half hours of his life.

They didn't have any trouble locating the vehicle. With the extra keys Cam remembered to grab, they checked the interior of the cab for clues but found nothing out of the ordinary. Frustrated, Drae was pacing and checking his phone praying that Victoria would reach out to him when he heard Cam shout, "Bingo!"

"What'd ya' find?"

"Nothing yet buddy but take a look down the street." Cam said pointing over Drae's shoulder. Whipping around to follow Cam's pointing he saw in an instant what his friend was referring to. A car rental place. Bingo, indeed.

The manager at the rental place was all kinds of understanding but there was only so much he could tell them. Yes, a Victoria Bennett had rented a car but beyond that the details got murky. She paid up front for a thirty-day period, unlimited mileage, add-on insurance. He would not however give up the credit card details and just before Drae reached over the counter to grab the guy by the neck and force the information from him, Cam stepped in and stopped him with a look.

Back in the parking lot, Cam reminded Drae in blunt and specific terms that finding people was what he did best, earning his friend a sheepish look and a grumpily muttered, "Understood."

"You okay to drive?" Cam asked.

"Yeah, yeah," he answered. "I'll meet you back at the Villa."

"What are you going to do, Drae? Don't go off half-cocked. It won't help." Drae paused and looked at the sky shaking his head with hands pressed on his waist. He'd made so damn many mistakes. Luckily for him he had brothers, true brothers – not just the kind that come with matching DNA – who had his back.

"You don't have to worry. I won't do anything without you, but I want to stop at home and grab the papers she left. More clues, y'know?"

"Good thinking, buddy," Cam replied. "Look Drae, if it helps any, I kinda know how you feel right now. I'm happy to pass my

Ass-Clown of the Year trophy off to you. My lovely wife had to damn near rearrange my brain before the light made it through years of dark. Know what I mean?"

Drae snorted a laugh and gave him a *not surprised to hear it* look. "Shit. Men really are dumb as dirt where women are concerned, huh?"

Laughing heartily, Cam slapped him good-naturedly on the back. "Now *there's* an understatement!" Drae climbed in the truck and thanked his good friend for being there.

Cam grinned. "I didn't get to know your lady very well before the wedding, but she's one smart cookie. And unless you ran over her dog and drove away laughing, I'm pretty damn sure you can fix this."

Tori had been behind the wheel for way too long. It would take about eight hours to make it to the coast, and she'd had enough for one day. She had stopped for a pretend lunch that stayed in her stomach for less than an hour before reappearing in her latest bathroom drama. Was there anything worse than getting sick in a roadside rest stop? She didn't think so.

There was something about driving in silence that made her mind wander all over the place. Had she done the right thing by leaving? She didn't know. Her mom had been duly horrified when Tori immediately burst into tears at the start of their call. The best advice she could give her was to slow down. She didn't know Draegyn but she did know Alex and dear old Mom refused to believe that he would be close to or trust anyone who didn't have at least some integrity.

The tears had gotten worse when her mother suggested

pregnancy hormones were shading her judgment. Did she think she didn't know that? Of course she did – it was something she considered when she'd jumped on Draegyn and went off like a sex-starved wanton. But the paparazzi pictures had carved out a hole in her heart that she couldn't ignore. Even if nothing intimate had happened with that awful woman, he'd still been with her. Who did shit like that? The man she was in love with, that was who.

Each time she said those words, her soul felt like it weighed a ton. Why didn't he love her back or at least like her back? Sex wasn't enough. Maybe for guys it was but not for her.

She needed to pull over and get a room for the night. By tomorrow afternoon she'd be in Los Angeles. Why she chose L.A. she didn't really know except that it was away from Arizona and big enough that she could disappear for a while and get her shit together. Right now though the priority was a decent hotel, a shower, and something, anything, to calm her stomach. Tomorrow would have to take care of itself.

A WEEK HAD GONE by and Drae still didn't know where Victoria was. Not for sure, anyway. He'd acted like a complete lunatic with her lawyer after reading the papers she'd left. The female attorney was a definite shark, and he had no doubt she could probably eat Ted Collins for lunch. His legal people were all top notch but this lady had a *nail his balls to the courthouse door* shtick going on that earned her a demon reputation as a divorce lawyer.

Divorce. The word made him shudder. For someone who never wanted to get married he suddenly found the idea of divorce even more odious. He understood why Tori had done what she did. The dates on the paperwork were after she'd seen the tabloid story, a fact that made remorse churn in his gut. He couldn't imagine anything that could have hurt her more than to see photographic proof that he'd been cavorting with a glamorous actress. When he finally caught up with her he vowed to make it very clear that the plastic starlet was nothing compared to how beautiful he thought she was.

Alex had finally connected with Victoria's mother and aside from passing on that she thought Drae was a jerk, she hadn't been much help. She did offer some hope though by pointing out that if was her; she'd high tail it into a big city where she could remain anonymous.

Phoenix was out, it was too close so that pretty much left Los Angeles. Cam had been working every angle and managed to pin down one of her credit cards. She'd withdrawn a hefty sum right before she left Arizona – obviously trying to fly off the radar. What she hadn't considered though was that she could be tracked through her cell phone. Even with the GPS locate switched off, the minute she connected with social media, checked her email or enabled a mapping program, they'd know exactly where she was. It was just a matter of time.

For his part, Drae had let their attorneys know that there would be no divorce. *Period.* Telling them both that Victoria was pregnant had changed the entire dynamic. Beyond that, he was pretty much useless. He'd tried going into the woodshop thinking a project would help distract him but that hadn't been such a good idea. Not if he wanted to keep all his fingers. That left rattling around his big empty house as his only alternative.

Somewhere in the midst of his anxiety he'd begun sketching plans for a nursery. The house already had a handful of extra bedrooms, but he wanted something special for their baby so he set about re-designing a large space next to his bedroom into a baby's suite with a comfortable sitting area, a small kitchenette and a custom bathroom with all the bells and whistles.

He could imagine his sweet Victoria, cuddling with their son or daughter by the French doors opening onto a private deck connecting to the master suite. It would be a special space that she could decorate, someplace where their child would begin their life. It was the only thing that gave him any sense of peace – planning for a future that remained uncertain.

On day nine, Cam woke him up with a flurry of texts that had him bolting from his bed and into the shower faster than he could ever remember moving. She had used a credit card in Malibu of all places – at an executive stay apartment. One of those places that rented by the month and catered to visitors. Alex had already called for the company jet to be readied and the minute he was packed, the three of them were heading to California.

All of them going might have seemed like overkill, but having his brothers with him gave Drae some calm. So had telling Desi what was going on. Letting his sister know she was going to be an Aunt had made the whole thing seem real for the first time. She'd cried and laughed and given him a raft of shit when he'd admitted that he had fucked things up royally but in the end, she just loved him and let Drae know how proud she was of him for finally pulling his head out of his ass.

He'd had a small bag packed for days, ready to leave at a moment's notice and just before Cam and Alex came to pick him up, he threw the notebook with the nursery plans into the bag.

Putting on his big boy undies, he'd also taken it on the chin and called Victoria's mom himself. Stephanie Bennett was one of those genteel southern ladies who had a way of making you feel like a giant ass without really trying. He let her know how desperate he was to make things right and assured her that the welfare and safety of her daughter was his highest priority. She was relieved to learn that Victoria had been located but wasn't all that happy when she heard where she was.

"That's no place for my daughter," she'd told him, and he couldn't have agreed more, promising to have Victoria call her the first chance she got. Before the brief call ended she told him, "Remember who you're dealing with young man." He knew what she was referring to, that Victoria had already been dragged through the mud once and also that she didn't quite feel that she measured up in the beauty sweepstakes. Vehemently informing Stephanie that her daughter was the loveliest creature on the planet and that he'd happily smack the shit out of anyone insisting different had earned him a softening in her tone.

Now all he had to do was figure out what he was going to say and how effectively he could grovel in order to convince his feisty beauty that her future and the future of their baby was with him. Yeah, that sounded easy – *not*!

Their flight into Los Angeles yesterday had been a test of Drae's cool. He could barely sit still and no amount of jovial banter – an attempt by the guys to displace some of his anxiety – helped for more than a few minutes. It had been like this that first year after Alex had finally been released from the hospital and rehab center where the medical folks had served up a series of miracles, saving his leg and giving him back his life. The physical therapy was grueling so he and Cam had adopted a Three Stooges way of dealing with the situation. The atmosphere during their flight reminded him of those days. Jokes, slapstick, ribald commentary – typical guy stuff. He hadn't really stopped to think how important his brothers were in his world until now. They were the glue that held everything together. "So, tell me guys – did you come along to help me find Victoria or are you here for damage control?"

They both busted up laughing. "Both you asshole!" Cam taunted. "Considering what a bang up job you've done so far, you should be thanking us for holding your hand."

"Yeah. What Cam said." Alex chuckled. "I figure with your less than stellar track record with the fairer sex, it won't take long for you to open mouth and insert foot. Somebody has to referee if you have any hope of convincing Tori you aren't an A-1 douche nozzle."

Drae winced. "Nice choice of words."

"Hey. I call 'em as I see 'em." His friend chuckled.

Cam laughed too and then turned serious. "Lacey made me

come, not that I wouldn't have anyway," he added hastily.

"Wow. Pussy whipped already, dude?" Alex mocked.

"Fuck off, Major. Your day will come," Cam snickered. "And for the record, a bit of wifely needling is a whole lot more fun than being the lonely guy."

"Oh fuck," Drae groaned. "Hadn't really thought about what having a bunch of women around would mean. Jesus. Female solidarity makes me nervous!"

"Yeah, that's true," Cam said, "but in this case Lacey's interest is more personal." Drae and Alex shot quizzical glances his way so he continued. "I didn't have any family growing up which is how I ended up saddled with you two losers. Neither did she. I figured, or rather my wife pointed out, that with Tori being pregnant too, our kid would come into the world with a growing family already in place."

Alex nodded in silence with a serious expression on his face while Drae struggled to swallow the tremendous lump of unexpected emotion that lodged in his throat. The seriousness of the situation hit him between the eyes. It wasn't just him and Victoria anymore. It was everyone. They were all involved in one way or another. "Remind me to kiss your wife when we get back," he muttered. "This isn't the first time she's been the voice of reason."

Cam laughed. Drae still had trouble getting used to this happier, smiling, lighter version of the brooding loner. "No smooching for you Mister Double-Oh-Jerkoff! Lacey really likes Tori. She was a huge help before the wedding. Even with a growing belly, my wife will gladly kick your smarmy ass if you don't make things right."

"Understood and duly noted," Drae offered in all seriousness.

They'd landed in Los Angeles and checked in to an exclusive hotel after which it took the other two men all but sitting on Drae to keep him from running off to find Victoria the moment he'd dropped his bags on the floor.

Cam was working the phone and his laptop, gathering

information about her movements and habits while Alex babysat him. After a serious talking to, Drae reluctantly gave in and let the pieces fall into place. They were right. He couldn't just bust in and make demands. It was going to take a whole lot more than a display of arrogance. No, this situation called for real finesse, plus he had to get his act together and be ready to lay down the hard truth that underlied everything. He loved her. Plain and simple. She belonged to him, even if she didn't know it yet. Tomorrow would be here soon enough and then he'd go and get his spitfire.

From the living room window, Tori could see the Pacific Ocean over the rooftops and palm tress below her short-term apartment. She was tired of being in a hotel and just wanted to find someplace where she could relax. After a horrible week and a half that was mostly tears and regrets, she'd come to no conclusions, only a bone-weary ache for the man haunting her dreams. It was a little galling to recognize that a sky high IQ did not give her special skills in dealing with the emotional side of life. Nope, she was wracked with insecurities and doubt, and no amount of rationalization seemed to make a bit of difference.

She'd almost broken down and called Draegyn once she'd found a place to settle until she remembered that doing so would blow her attempt to stay low. On an impulse, Tori had rented this apartment under an alias, although not much of one. If he was trying to find her, and she wasn't altogether sure he would be, using her real last name would lead him straight to her door. And right there, she'd hit on the crux of the matter. Was he trying to find her or had he figured good riddance to someone that had been a thorn in his side? Would knowing the answer to that question make a difference?

Blaming the pregnancy for her emotional scatter seemed kinda lame but, there you have it. She was also becoming quite adept at the heavy sigh, each bleak murmur reminding her the shambles her world was in. Was it the same for him? Dammit. That was the problem right there. With every thought and feeling assailing her brain, she'd stop and consider Draegyn's reaction.

Maybe she'd been a coward by leaving like a thief in the night. After all, she couldn't stay furious at him for having done almost the same thing. And just like the silence that hovered over them while he was doing whatever the hell he'd been up to in New York, she was doing the same. That thought didn't sit well.

Well, she thought, gathering her purse and the keys to her rental car, too much introspection wasn't helping her general outlook. She had something or rather someone else to consider now and sitting around in a grey funk couldn't be good for her or the baby. No, she had to get some air, maybe walk around a bit and find something to eat that didn't provoke the nausea that was her new constant companion. She certainly couldn't live forever on carbonated soda and water crackers even though that particularly disgusting combination seemed to go easy on her stomach.

Deciding to walk through the country mart and grab some supplies, she'd stop at a small café and take it easy – maybe do some people watching for shits 'n giggles. That was one thing she'd already learned about Malibu. There was always a celebrity or two to be found. Well, at least she'd found an amusing distraction.

Later on she admitted it had been a good morning. Her walk through the outdoor shopping mart had been relaxing and even a bit productive. She'd eaten some outrageously beautiful organic pastries and browsed through a high-end children's store, indulging in the purchase of a tiny set of pale green booties that she thought would suit either a girl or a boy.

At lunchtime she found a spot at the outdoor café where she sat quietly and watched the world go by. Tori felt better than she had in some time. She'd even managed to eat half a sandwich and though it wasn't her favorite, she'd ordered a small glass of milk to wash it down with. She didn't really know if drinking milk was something she should do, making her tap a note into her phone about picking up some books about pregnancy.

She'd been sitting there for a while when the bubbly waitress stopped by her table with a big smile and something else. Putting a large container in front of her, Tori frowned and let her know she hadn't ordered anything else. The waitress grinned and said, "Hazelnut decaf, four sugars, and an extra dollop of creamer for table seven." This *is* table seven she added. Tori was confused.

"There's been some sort of mix-up," she murmured as the aroma of her favorite beverage wrapped around her senses.

"Nope," the friendly waitress replied. "You have that gentleman over there to thank," she said while pointing toward the cash register area. Lowering her voice in a conspiratorial whisper she added, "Lucky you. That's one seriously hot guy!"

Tori's head whipped around so fast, it almost fell off her neck. Draegyn. *Oh my fucking god*, she moaned. It was impossible to see his eyes behind the dark sunglasses he had on but she'd know that proud bearing in the crowd of a thousand. His presence at the café scattered her thoughts. Ignoring the sudden uptick in her heart rate or the way relief washed through her along with a very telling flutter of awareness, was nearly impossible.

She wasn't ready to face him. Not yet, so she grabbed her stuff and made a mad dash for the rear exit just steps from where she'd been sitting. Luckily she'd dressed simply in jeans with sneakers on her feet so making speed was no problem but he had beaten her to the lot, where he was casually leaning against a high class but very suburban family-looking sedan with an expression she couldn't read. As she stepped from the pathway he opened the side door of the car and waved her on as if he were a chauffer. Dammit. This wasn't how she envisioned seeing him again and just to make matters worse, she was fighting back an awful urge to throw herself on him and cry.

"Let me help you with your packages," he murmured softly, reaching to take her purse and carry-all bag from hands gone numb in shock.

She needed to find her voice she realized, struggling to wrap her mind around the fact that he was very much here and very much trying to take control yet again. Some things never change. "What are you doing here, Draegyn?"

"I think that would be obvious," he answered while placing her things on the backseat.

"Maybe to you, but not to me," Tori answered defensively. Did he really think it would be that easy? That he could just show up out of nowhere and command her to do as he asked? Her itchy conscience reminded her that she'd absolutely fallen for this act before, sometimes with gleeful abandon.

Drae was having a hard time remaining calm. When he'd found her at last, sitting all by herself at the outdoor café, it was all he could do not to rush in, toss her unwilling butt over his shoulder, and steal her away to his private lair. She looked all sorts of adorable in her faded Fleetwood Mac t-shirt and a pair of worn jeans that didn't exactly cling to her curves. She looked thinner, if that was possible, with an exhausted air about her that squeezed his heart. Seeing her so vulnerable with that edge of fragility helped soften his approach. She was backing up, taking small steps away from him but that didn't stop Drae from reaching out and placing a hand in the small of her back to ease her toward the car. "Get in, Victoria."

"No."

He had to smile at the petulant frown she was making. "We can do this the hard way if you'd prefer. Believe me honey, I have no problem stalking your cute little ass until you're worn down from trying to get away from me. Or…you can hush that gorgeous mouth, get in the car, and listen to what I have to say. Your choice."

It didn't help his composure when her bottom lip, the one he so badly wanted to suck into his mouth, started to quiver. She stomped her foot and tried glaring at him and then let out an anguished wail.

"I can't do this now, Draegyn. Please. Just let me go."

It was his turn to say, "No."

She continued to hem and haw, looking for any means of escape. Finally, Drae sighed and gently placed an arm around her shoulder for a brief hug. "Everything's going to be alright sweetheart, but first you have to get in the car."

She turned watery eyes his way but lowered her lashes when his dark glasses got in the way. Quickly removing them so she could see for herself the sincerity of his words he tried again. "Please," he begged.

Forgetting about the remnants of the black eye Alex had given him, he was caught off guard when she gasped and reached up to touch the fading bruise. Before she could say anything he quirked a smile her way and simply said, "Big Daddy."

After that she slid silently into the passenger seat. Reaching across her torso, he clicked the seatbelt into place and shut her door, rounding the back of the car to get in the driver's seat where he quickly started the car and got the air conditioning running. It wasn't hot, but the way her cheeks were flushing, he didn't want to take any chances.

Her voice was quiet, little more than a whisper. "Why do we have to go anywhere? Can't we just talk here?"

"C'mon Victoria. You know this isn't going to be a five minute chat." She looked away and stared out the side window of the car as he eased it out of the parking area and headed for the coast highway. The silence was deafening so he tried asking a simple question, trying to break the ice. "How are you feeling?"

"Peachy," she sniped. Then more silence.

Okay. *That went well*, he thought. Maybe it was best to go with a direct approach. He had to cough slightly to clear his voice, as emotions clogged his throat. "Have you seen a doctor yet?"

She fidgeted in her seat and sighed. "No."

"Why not?" Yeah. That did it. She turned on him with that all-too-familiar flash of bitchiness that he knew so well.

"I've been a bit busy, you know. And why exactly do you care, may I ask?"

He had something to say, had a lot to say in fact, but maybe the car wasn't the place to start such an important conversation so he neatly changed the subject. "We're staying in a penthouse suite at the Beverly Wilshire."

"Who's we?" she asked tartly.

His mouth quirked up at the corners. Damn, she was something else. "We. As in me and my wife."

She stared at him with mouth agape. "I'm not your wife!"

"Is that so?" he asked silkily. "Then care to explain why you rented an apartment as Victoria St. John?"

Yeah, that shut her up he thought as her mouth snapped and the pout appeared. He though he heard a softly muttered, "Shit," come from her side of the car.

"Sit back and enjoy the scenery. I always liked this drive along the coast. We'll talk at the hotel when we've had a chance to relax. The last couple of days have been hard on both of us."

Tori wondered what he meant by that but said nothing. Sitting close enough to him that she could pick up on the scent of his cologne was making her crazy. He was dressed in a pair of trousers that made her hands twitch with wanting to run them along his muscled thighs and a simple button-down white shirt, having already lost the sport coat to the backseat. He looked as he always did. Dangerous and unbelievably sexy. At a stoplight, he'd undone his cuffs and folded up the sleeves of the shirt, revealing the pale blonde hair on his arms that she found so appealing.

The scruffy beard was gone, but his need for a haircut was not. He seemed different somehow. Like all his hard edges had been smoothed over. She stared at his hands where they gripped the steering wheel and willed her libido into hibernation when thoughts of those very hands cupping her breasts as he held one and then the other up to his marauding mouth. So much for remaining calm.

It is always like this with him, she thought. Put them together in a confined space and the sparks started. Soft at first until a full on bonfire erupted. It was so very primitive and quite obviously nothing that either of them had control over.

She wished she could read his thoughts. Was he feeling it too? That slow burn spreading in waves along the senses. Tori thought she'd die of embarrassment if all this was one-sided on her part until her eyes caught the distinctive ridge in the area of his lap that let her know the fire was mutual.

THE SUITE WAS INCREDIBLE. Opulent, beautifully decorated, and first class the whole way. So much so that she felt like an idiot schlepping through the magnificent lobby with its glittering chandelier and marble floors in her jeans and sneakers. Draegyn never missed a beat, guiding her into the elevator, sweeping her along to their room as if he didn't have a care in the world. In fact, he looked mighty pleased with himself.

"Are you tired? You look a bit pale. What can I get you?" She started at his rapid-fire questions and comments, struggling to find her way in this bizarre situation. Tori *was* tired. More tired than she could ever remember being and she didn't doubt she looked pale. Being unexpectedly pregnant and overwhelmed by their circumstances had her struggling.

Dropping onto the sofa like a lead weight, she asked for some soda, if he had any, which got Draegyn running to the mini-bar like his life depended on it. It would have been funny in a different context. When he returned to her side, handing off the glass filled with ice and cola, she had to turn her eyes away from the prominent bulge staring her in the face.

"Did you understand the papers I left behind?" She figured it best to start this conversation where she wanted and not wait for him.

He sat down next to her and leaned back, putting a foot on the opposite knee in a laid back posture that only made her nerves flutter more. "Yep. Got 'em. Read 'em. Called your lady shark lawyer and let her know what I thought about the whole thing." The look he gave her contained a bit of mischief that surprised her greatly.

"This isn't funny, y'know."

"I didn't say it was." He leveled his eyes to hers and let the moment speak for itself.

She was getting twitchy. The impulse to rail at him was steadily growing, but with heated moisture dampening her panties, and the way she kept licking her lips each time he spoke, she was losing her shit alarmingly fast. She underestimated him because he didn't beat around the bush at all – just jumped in and addressed what was at the heart of the matters at hand. "Those pictures you saw were not what they seemed."

"Oh really?" Her tart-tongued response took even her by surprise. "How do you figure that?"

He sat forward then and rested his forearms on his thighs, staring for a long moment at the floor. "Alright," he sighed heavily. "Yes, I was photographed in the company of a certain actress who shall remain nameless. She's a royal pain in the ass, and I'd just as soon not give her any further thought."

Tori sipped her soda, willing her percolating stomach to back off.

"For the record, I was by myself tying on an epic drunk when she appeared out of nowhere. Yes – she propositioned me, and yes, we have a brief history but nothing I'd care to revisit." Tori felt what color she had drop into her feet. Why was he bothering to explain? Those damn pictures spoke loud and clear.

"Hey," he choked out, running a finger down the side of her

face. "Don't look so upset. She's nothing to me Victoria. Fuck, she's less than nothing. I didn't go looking for a companion that night or any of the nights for that matter since the moment you darted into my life."

"I can't trust you," she answered solemnly.

He took the glass from her and put it down, gathering her cold, trembling hands into his. "Yes you can."

She tried looking away but he pulled her closer, kissed her on the forehead, and kept on talking. "You're a handful, that's for damn sure but I'd rather be bickering with you than spend my time with some empty-headed Barbie doll."

"You see, Draegyn – that's just it! All we do is argue and yell, and…well, you know. One thing leads to another and before I know what's happening my panties are ripped in two and we're raging at each other in another way. I just can't live like that."

He laughed. She tried to look at him with a stern expression, but it melted under the heat of his gaze. "I've given this plenty of thought, Victoria. All that yelling," he teased, "it's not what it seems. I think it's how we make love to each other."

"That's not what you called it the other day."

"And I was a pig for saying those things. Look, honey, I'm not perfect. I've never been in a serious relationship, *ever*. Every single step we take is uncharted territory for me. You too, I think."

She nodded and inched closer to him. There was something infinitely comforting about his solid presence. "Going from zero to flaming bitch in two point five seconds is because I'm a little afraid of you. It would help if I understood where you're coming from. Alex tried to tell me something about your background – your parents I think – but I didn't understand."

Drae had to remember to thank Alex for sticking his two cents into the middle of this. By asking she opened the floodgates, and he hoped he didn't scare her off with the explanation. She was resisting his presence less with each minute that passed so he took a chance and relaxed against the sofa, pulling her against him so she could rest her head upon his shoulder while he talked.

"My parents are seriously flawed people and frankly, I don't like them very much. Theirs was an arranged marriage – a business deal. My entire childhood was phony. Perfect on the outside but rotting and decayed on the inside." She reached a hand up and laid it over his heart. She had no idea how much that simple gesture meant to him.

"When I was old enough to understand, I vowed never to get close enough to anyone in case one day I woke up and found myself shackled to someone like my mother. Cold, calculating, evil." The shrug he threw in at the end spoke volumes. "You know, guys don't pick shit apart like you women do. For me, it was black and white. There was never any grey. What my family started, the military finished."

He could feel her nodding under his chin and working at the button in the middle of his chest. When she got it undone, he had to fight the urge to pin her to the couch when he felt two fingers slide into the opening and press against his skin. *Wow.* Where was he?

"I'm sorry for the way I reacted in Vegas. That was not one of my better moments. And I'm more sorry than you could ever know for running off to New York without saying anything."

"Me too," he heard her murmur.

"You're sorry I ran off?"

"No. I mean I'm sorry for doing the same thing." She looked up at him with those soulful brown eyes, and he felt himself drowning in the emotions he saw shining there. Time to lay all his cards on the table.

He covered the hand on his chest with his and hugged her tight. "Victoria, I love you more than there are words to describe. I'm sorry that it took me so long to say it."

"Wait," she whispered, her voice catching on a quickly indrawn breath. "What?"

He tilted her chin with his finger and looked into her eyes. "I. Love. You." To his astonishment, tears welled in her beautiful eyes.

"Don't say it if you don't mean it Draegyn. Is it because of the baby because if it is…"

"I mean it you little hell cat and no, not because of the baby." Tears erupted making silent tracks down her cheeks. He thought it was the most wonderful thing he'd ever seen. "Can you forgive me, honey? Can we make a new start, because I really want to?"

She hid her face against his chest as hot tears leaked from her eyes. "I thought it was all me. That you didn't feel anything."

"Are you saying what I hope you are?" he asked, emotions clawing at his throat.

"I love you, you impossibly arrogant man. How could you not know it?" He didn't bother to answer, just swooped in and captured her pouting lips with his for a kiss that was all emotion. Probably the most real kiss they'd ever shared. No, not probably. Make that definitely.

Many minutes later he drew back and kissed the tip of her pert little nose. "Victoria St. John. I like the way that sounds."

She grinned and looked up at him in a very sexy way. "Don't you have something you'd like to ask me?"

Drae threw back his head and barked out a laugh. "Women!" he chuckled. "So the words aren't enough, huh?"

"Be nice. I'm pregnant," she pouted prettily.

He smiled the biggest smile he could ever remember making. "And so you are." Laying his hand solemnly against her belly, he raised one of her dainty hands to his lips and pressed a kiss into the center of her palm, then folded her fingers meaningfully over the spot. "Victoria Bennett St. John. I give you my heart. It's yours forever. Will you do me the exquisite honor of being my wife and having my babies?"

To say she beamed at him would be the understatement of all times. "Yes, Mister Double-Oh-Trouble. I will marry you and give you all the babies you want!"

He kissed her soundly, then jumped to his feet saying, "I think this calls for champagne – the non-alcoholic kind!"

She laughed and shot him an embarrassed grin. "We did everything ass backwards."

"This is true," he agreed. "Will give us a great story to tell the grandkids!"

"Whoa, slow down there husband. Let's enjoy the here and now, okay?"

Drae ran to his bag and pulled out the notebook he'd remembered to bring from home. "Look. I've started sketching a suite for the baby," he told her, proudly describing each detail as he envisioned them.

When he realized she wasn't saying anything he searched her face. What he saw reflected in her adoring gaze would stay with him forever. "I love you," she whispered.

"And I love you too. Now let's celebrate!" Whipping out his cellphone he tapped on some keys and then looked at her with a sly grin. "Get ready wife. The brothers are about to descend!"

"Oh my goodness! Both of them are here?" She laughed and rubbed her belly. "Well baby, here comes the whole Justice family. Speaking of which, I should call my mom."

Drae beamed with love for the woman who had done more than fix his fucked-up life. With her by his side, he really would feel like the king of the damn world. "Not necessary, my love. I've already spoken to Stephanie and let her know I'd be bringing you home where you belong. As soon as we're settled back in Arizona, Alex is sending the jet to bring her out for a good long visit. I have a mother-in-law to charm! And while we're speaking of family, my little sister Desirée is chomping at the bit to meet you to. She's ecstatic that she's going to be an aunt.

"Wow," Victoria muttered. "From only child to expectant mother, sister-in-law and best of all, wife."

A great pounding sounded at the door to their suite heralding the arrival of Alex and Cam who came bursting in carrying balloons and a tremendous bouquet of flowers.

"Here's to the bride and groom!" Alex chuckled. "May all your days be less stressful than the last week and filled with as much love and laughter as two people could survive!"

It really didn't get any better than this.

Three extraordinary men and the women who love them…

THE JUSTICE BROTHERS

BROKEN JUSTICE

FIXING JUSTICE

REDEEMING JUSTICE

Two Justice Brothers down, one to go!

REDEEMING JUSTICE

The third book in the JUSTICE BROTHERS series
Alex and Meghan's story…..

If war were about memory and learning to live with the aftermath, he'd have the rest of his life to deal with his remorse and guilt. She's collateral damage, having lost her the man she was going to marry under his watch. When fate throws them together, the past collides in the present and makes the future an uncertain emotional minefield.

Alexander Valleja-Marquez. *The Major*. Born to lead, he'd been recruited by Special Forces in the aftermath 911. A decade later, the victim of a devastating suicide bombing, he'd escaped the war but not the emotional fallout. They'd pieced his body back together but his conscience would never again be whole. Not even a successful business nor the love and support of his family could change the nightmares he lived with.

Meghan O'Brien. She knew all about service and survivor guilt. The only girl in a family of cops and firemen, she lost her best friend and fiancé in the suicide bombing. Years later she knocks on the Major's door to thank him for the condolence letter he'd written. That simple note had helped get her through some dark times and forged a connection to a man she'd never met.

He wasn't what she expected any more than she fit the picture he held in his mind of a young woman he'd never met but always remembered.

Life has a way of throwing curveballs when we least expect them. When their surprising attraction lights a bonfire of lust and desire, things get serious fast. Maybe too fast. Until he remembers that she's off-limits and why he doesn't deserve to be loved.

As the saying goes – life is what happens when we're busy making plans.

Excerpt from **REDEEMING JUSTICE** by Suzanne Halliday

There was no doubt about it. Meghan O'Brien loved sunshine. When the story of her life was written, surely there would be a notation about her love hate affair with the sun. Being a fair complexioned Irish beauty meant she'd learned to be clever about protecting her skin. Tilting her head skyward, Meghan felt the mass of auburn curl tumble down her back the same second the blazing sun lit up her face. Both sensations were delicious and made her sigh with delight. As she stood there absorbing the invigorating energy, she closed her eyes and concentrated on her other senses.

Pressed up against the side of an SUV, her butt was warmed from the heat of the desert southwest radiating off the vehicle. It was an oddly pleasant feeling that helped alleviate some of the tension in her back from long hours spent behind the wheel.

There were muffled voices from the people in the roadside rest area where she'd stopped for a break. Kids laughing. Parents yelling. *The usual*, she chuckled. There was even the low bark of a big dog, and the dull rumble of an idling motorcycle.

She clutched a very cold bottle of water in one hand, while the other rested on the door handle. Her inner teacher's voice fed fast facts into her thoughts making Meghan grin. *Vitamin D is primarily synthesized in skin exposure to UV light and is essential to healthy skin.* The grin became a laugh. Some things won't ever change.

Where a year ago she'd known exactly what she wanted to do and how she wanted to live her life, today she was in a curious limbo. Recently having turned twenty-eight, her resume was perfection. Bachelor's Degree in Education followed by a Master's in Kinesiology. Every job known to mankind in those two fields; camp counselor, fitness trainer, motivational coach, gym teacher, licensed massage therapist, she was a respected member of the Belmont Circle School District Faculty where she was assistant athletic director. Not bad for being a girl in a man's field.

She was also loud and proud, a true Irish Daughter of Boston and was more than capable of taking care of herself. Having three brothers taught Meghan how to navigate the world of men. She was competitive by nature and didn't cry when she lost. With a straightforward, take no shit attitude, her students liked her, and the parents and her fellow faculty members respected her. Life had been damn good. She had no complaints and while the idea of finding a guy she could put her faith in, someone she could trust, was a shining ideal, she was content living alone as a successful professional.

And then it happened. One day, one very *ordinary* day, she'd been nesting at home, cartons of takeout food on the table as she hunkered down with her Kindle to catch up on some reading when the phone rang and her entire life changed.

Meghan, along with five colleagues from her school, had pooled their money and purchased a lottery ticket that had incredibly won them a mega jackpot. That phone call had done more than change the direction of her life. With the staggering amount of money she suddenly had, the mortgages on her parents' and brothers' homes got paid off and a sizeable trust fund established for her nieces and nephews ensuring that each of them would have money for college when that time came.

With the job market being such a tough place for educators, Meghan reluctantly stepped down from her position so someone else could have the chance to chase their dreams as she had. She didn't want to stop working but others immediately started showing signs of jealousy and disdain for her and her fellow jackpot winners. Hanging onto a job when she didn't need the income was only inviting judgment.

The midday heat starting to make her clothes feel heavy and uncomfortable got Meghan moving into the driver's seat of her shiny, new SUV on a reluctant sigh. As much as she enjoyed basking for a few minutes in the relentless southwest sun, it didn't take long for her to throw in the towel once the heat took over. Starting the engine she flipped the AC to low and took a long, slow pull off the bottle of chilled water, settling comfortably into the plush seat. The car had been her first big purchase. She'd felt giddy at the freedom of having unlimited options and went a little crazy when it came to all the bells and whistles.

All that stuff, from the navigation system to the satellite radio and heated seats, had come in handy though. On a whim, she'd packed up her apartment, put everything she owned in storage, and headed off on a cross-country road trip. *Because she could.* That was three months ago.

In that time she'd traveled from Boston to Seattle then down the California coast, stopping at every giant wind chime or world's largest whatever along the way. Putting her teacher skills to creative good use, she'd been taking thousands of pictures either with her phone or the fancy 35mm digital camera she loved; then designing digital scrapbooks with a running commentary of her adventures.

While in California, her mother had flown to join Meghan for a weeklong spa retreat and a sweet mother daughter bonding experience. Maggie O'Brien was everything Meghan hoped she'd one day be; smart, loving, fiercely devoted to her family, and possessing a wicked streak a mile wide. They knocked back a couple of bottles of Jameson Irish Whiskey during their ten days together laughing like schoolgirls, and at night she would sit at her mother's knee like she had as a child, listening to her mom's calming voice as she smoothed Meghan's curls.

After California, it was time to get back on the road, which is what brought her to this rest stop along old Route 66. This portion of her American adventure had been the most fun she'd had. The rich history turned her on. The desert southwest was so incredibly beautiful that she pulled over to take pictures constantly.

Tonight she'd be in Flagstaff where she planned to stay for a few days. After that it was a slight detour south toward Sedona and a visit she'd been thinking about for a very long time. More than five years in the making, she would at long last be meeting face to face with a man she barely knew who had been uncommonly kind to her during a dark time. Knowing that his kindness came during a difficult period in his life, she'd always hoped to share her enormous gratitude in person. Now that the opportunity was upon her, Meghan was excited and a bit apprehensive too.

It had felt so forward and pushy to tap out an email that basically said - *Hey, I'm in town and inviting myself over to your place for a visit* – but that's what she'd done. *Well*, she thought as her SUV pulled onto the highway, *the deed was done.* Now the stage set for whatever came of her impulsive desire to settle an emotional debt that only meant something to her.

Alexander Valleja-Marquez was fit to be tied. Depending on which hat he was wearing at any given time, whether Spanish Don of inherited nobility or retired Special Forces Commander or senior partner in a prestigious security agency, or friend, he was a handful at the best of times. When he had an itch up his butt though, he was a fucking nightmare to deal with. And he knew it. But frankly, knowing didn't slow his roll for a second.

The agency's summer calendar was fully booked for the season making the Marquez Villa and surrounding Justice Agency compound a bustling mini-town of activity. It was their busiest time of year and with both his partners slightly distracted by personal matters, Alex had assumed a bigger role in overseeing day-to-day agency operations.

As out of sorts as he was, that didn't stop Alex from a moment of happiness recalling the unexpected chain of events that found two of the three Justice Brothers married and with babies on the way. As if Cameron's life changing romance with his ponytailed wife wasn't mind-boggling enough, the approaching birth of their first child had blown everyone's mind. And then there was Draegyn who was also a married man with a baby on the way. Never in a million years had he thought any of them would be the happily ever after sort.

Snorting in disbelief for the thousandth time, Alex left the dimly lit tech cave where he spent the majority of his time and made his way to the tiled walk leading to the pool. Zeus, his constant companion and the only female to speak of in his life, trotted along amiably at his feet. At least the dog seemed to like him.

He was heading for the pool to work off an excess of nervous energy that was tying him up knots. With the non-stop agency activity to keep him busy you'd think he wouldn't have time for wandering thoughts, but pretty much the only thing he could think about for the past couple of days had been an email from someone he'd known briefly during his special ops days. Back when he ordered people into danger, then was the one to tell families about their son or daughter's brave sacrifice.

That last awful day of his command not only ended his military career, it was when the families of more than a dozen soldiers and civilians he was responsible for had gotten bad or devastating news. Even though Alex had been one of the severely wounded, he hadn't shirked his responsibility as the commanding office in charge to write personally to each family. Was the least he could do and while it did nothing to ease the black mark left on his soul from that day, it did serve as a reminder of his own humanity, something that came perilously close to being lost in the months before and for a long time afterward.

One of those he wrote to was the fiancée of a young soldier who hadn't stood a chance when the bomb went off. He'd been surprised when she replied, sending a long heartfelt letter about her fiancé and how much he loved every minute of his time in the service and respected his C.O. At the time, Alex was struggling through months of endless surgeries, physical therapy plus mental and physical anguish that were stripping his soul. Her letters had been the start of a brief pen pal exchange. By the following year when he was stateside again and starting to build a life outside the military, they'd remained Christmas card pals but nothing else. Until she emailed him out of the blue and said she'd be in the Sedona area soon and could she come by for a visit.

Could she come by for a visit? Alex had been flabbergasted. It wasn't everyday that a ghost from the past came a knocking. Even though they'd never met, she was still a reminder of an awful time. Then he remembered how friendly and sweet she'd been during his long convalescence – sending long chatty letters full of everyday details that helped take his mind off the pain and his weary spirit.

She'd intrigued him with her straightforward outlook, refusing to wallow in self-pity for her loss. He liked that. She wasn't a cry-baby. For reasons he didn't want to mull over, he sent her a holiday card every year that she always reciprocated. It was an unusual friendship without detail or substance.

And that was part of the problem. The idea of finally meeting her was rattling his cage. What did you say to someone whose future was destroyed by his decisions and actions?

Reefing his t-shirt over his head in one smooth motion, Alex dropped it on the deck and dove smoothly into the deep end of an enormous lap pool. A dozen slow, measured laps later he felt a little better.

Coming to the decision it was no big deal to entertain someone from the past, he tried to calm his nerves by concentrating on what the visit should entail. He'd talk to his housekeeper, Carmen, and tell her to expect company. He wouldn't have to do much more than that. Carmen would take care of everything – it's what she did best.

Alex relaxed and let the water take him away. They agreed she'd text once in Sedona so he could give her detailed directions to the Villa. There wasn't anything else to do now except wait for her to contact him. The slow burn of excitement in his groin unsettled Alex more than it should. It was just a visit. This was a courtesy call, nothing more. Why did he feel so anxious?

Look for Alex and Meghan's story

Summer 2014

About the Author

Suzanne Halliday writes what she knows and what she loves – sexy adult contemporary romance with strong men and spirited women. Her love of creating short stories for friends and family has developed into a passion for writing romantic fiction with a sensual edge. She finds the world of digital, self-publishing to be the perfect platform for sharing her stories and also for what she enjoys most of all – reading. When she's not on a deadline you'll find her loading up on books to devour.

Currently a wanderer, she and her family divide their time between the east and west coast, somehow always managing to get the seasons mixed up. When not digging out from snow or trying to stay cool in the desert, you can find her in the kitchen, 80's hair band music playing in the background, kids running in and out, laptop on with way too many screens open, something awesome in the oven, and a mug of hot tea clutched in one hand.

Visit her at:

Facebook https://www.facebook.com/SuzanneHallidayAuthor

Twitter @suzannehalliday

Blog http://suzannehallidayauthor.blogspot.com

Check out the Pinterest Boards for my stories
I love getting feedback from readers!
http://www.pinterest.com/halliday0383/

Printed in Great Britain
by Amazon